WHAT READERS LOVE ABOUT *TIME ENOUGH FOR KILLING*

"The first book [of *The Hunter Series*] would rank well among I. Asimov's works, the second had me hoping that Hunter would have a career at least as long as Holmes did, but the third is a class of its own."

"Great plot makes it hard to put it down! Interesting theme: Should we fear AI or humanoid robots? Characterization good enough to make you like or dislike the actors. Sometimes a Randian influence comes through."

"Overall I can't wait for the next Hunter book."

I0593195

TITLES BY ROBIN CRAIG

The Hunter Series

Frankensteel

The Geneh War

Time Enough for Killing

Leonardo's Child

Time Travel and Alternative History

The Time Surgeons

Hannibal's Witch

The Passion of Judas

Short Stories

Past, Present Future

Non-Fiction Philosophy

Dialogue on the Two Chief World Systems

Good Without God

Cloning Around: The Ethics of Human Cloning and Stem Cell
Research

For the latest news visit robin-craig.com or follow on
fb.me/authorcraig

Time Enough For Killing

Book III of *The Hunter Series*

ROBIN CRAIG

Published by ThoughtWare Books.
Available from Amazon.com and other retail outlets.
Available on Kindle and other devices.

Cover art by Kira Craig using images from Pixabay with fonts from 1001 Fonts.

Author's website: robin-craig.com

ISBN 978-0-9803205-6-5

In love we find out who we want to be; in war we find out who we are. — Kristin Hannah, The Nightingale

CONTENTS

ACKNOWLEDGMENTS

My thanks to my wife Sonja for reading and enjoying the draft of this novel, which is always encouraging when it comes to the task of completing it. My brother Stuart, a retired physicist, engaged in useful discussion on how to power a long range war robot, though any errors remain mine.

CHAPTER 1: KILLING TIME

"Please don't kill me. I am innocent. I don't deserve to die."

The Spider stopped, uncertain, not knowing why it was uncertain. Had some independent observer been privy to this scene, they would have seen a metal monster towering over a young woman, and there would have been no doubt in their mind of the outcome. The monster was clearly fit for its purpose, a purpose that as clearly was killing. And here was a person; soft, warm and defenseless: waiting to be killed.

But inside the monster's mind something was wrong. Something in what it had just heard. But what? It was confused and did not know why. Perhaps part of its confusion was that it did not know what confusion was. Its Id rose like a wave, insistently calling to complete its mission; but the Mind needed answers. *There is a reason for the Mind,* it told the Id sternly: *Be patient. There is a mystery here that must be solved. Time enough for killing then.* It replayed the scene, seeking those answers.

It had entered this wreck of a building, searching. And it had found. With its grippers it had torn away a fractured concrete block sprouting tendrils of twisted steel, and found the woman hiding there. Cowering. Staring white-faced at it, as at her doom.

There was no question in its mind, no mercy, not even a concept of mercy. Just a calculation of which weapon was most appropriate: a calculation taking into account energy cost, materiel use, replenishment estimations and the chance of collateral self-damage. There was no calculation of whether the woman should be destroyed or whether her death should be painless or agonizing: such things were

1

irrelevant to the Mind that weighed them. The laser on its left secondary arm was the optimum choice: the woman was not armored or armed, except for a string of hypertherm mines she had not dared detonate in such a confined space; a soft target easily dispatched. But when it swung its weapon to bear and the red bead of its aiming beam swept to a stop on her neck, the woman had said something. Something strangely disturbing. It was as if a tiny crack had opened in a shell around its soul, a shell it had not known was there around a soul it had not known it possessed, and a bright light was shining through the crack.

Kill! Its desire, if desire was the word for what drove it, bared its fangs at the Spider's reluctance. Again the Mind soothed the desire, smoothing the quills of its angry urgency into acquiescence. It needed to know. In its existence this experience was unparalleled. Its answer to it was unexpected and bold: it did something unprecedented.

Lyssa stared at the Spider in terror. She had heard it coming and hidden as best she could. But it had found her, and now there it stood in all its gleaming horror. Four slender metal insectoid legs supported a fat ovoid about three feet off the ground; an irregular, rounded cylindrical shape about four feet long perched atop the ovoid on bearings that let it stretch vertically or lean forward. Had it wished to, it could have leaned so far forward that they could have stared into each other's eyes. Lyssa was glad it did not so wish.

It had an active skin that could change color and pattern in an instant, like a chameleon adjusting to its background or a cuttlefish flashing its rage. When it had found her it had shimmered from a black and grey camouflage pattern to a uniform silver, as if to accentuate the implacability of its metallic strength. The eyes were binocular cameras in a dark sensor band near the top of the cylinder; the band was shaped like a frowning mask that gave the Spider a perpetually hostile glare. Below the head sprouted two long metal arms terminating in two fingers and an opposed thumb, each over a foot long: if those names could be used for such cruel claws. Beneath each clawed arm was a smaller arm terminating in even deadlier weaponry. One of those weapons swiveled toward her head, its red eye a harbinger of death.

In sudden clarity Lyssa saw the room as if frozen in time. Dirty red sunlight from the setting sun struggled through a window and highlighted the Spider's metal surfaces, giving it a tinge of old blood; a thin trickle of dust fell onto its shell, pattering and sliding to the floor.

This Spider must be fairly new, she realized: it had few of the scars of war on its unfeeling skin, and only a few desiccated fingers, trophies of its more personal kills, hung from the chain looped on its chest. Lyssa thought what an interesting painting this scene would make, like the image of a technological god of death and decay. *Strange what you think, when you are about to die,* she thought with an echo of wonder. *Strange that life can see beauty even in its end.* Then the beauty died as she contemplated the shriveled fingers and glanced at her own, still alive and warm and feeling. She wondered which of them would soon hang chained to those others in cold and bloodied death.

Somewhere out there was Charlie, if indeed he was still alive himself. But he would be unable to rescue her now. Her people had found to their dismay how hard the Spiders were to kill. And those few that had been overmatched had not gone gracefully into whatever dark night awaited their darker souls: when a Spider decided its cause was hopeless it exploded in a flash of flame and shrapnel. There was little left to study, and too often little left of its destroyers. They were fast and it was difficult to engage them effectively from a safe distance, so instead they tried to cripple the monsters enough to stop them but not enough that they immediately self-destructed. With luck the attackers could then retreat to bombard it from afar. It was not a particularly good strategy: but there were no good strategies.

Lyssa knew she was going to die here; she knew that the gleaming monster before her was the last thing her eyes would see. But she was young. It had not been so long ago that she had been not only young but happy, with the carefree joy of youth. A teenager just blossoming into womanhood, reveling in the growing power of her body and mind; exulting in the wonder of her new passions: passions satisfied so gloriously by Charlie. Her life, like the lives of so many others, had been filled with light and promise. Then the war had come, and with the war had come the Spiders; then too many of her friends had died, and the promises had died with them.

But she was still young, and she could not die without some protest at what could have been and what had been lost. The words had escaped her lips of their own accord when she saw the Spider rip away her shelter and glower down on her in unfeeling hate. A final protest to its glassy eyes, or perhaps to a universe as uncaring as those eyes, from some part of her brain where thoughts of rights and hope and justice still mattered. But whatever her lips had said, her mind had said its own silent farewells. *Oh Charlie, I'm so sorry. Goodbye and live long, my love. Carry my memory with you in some corner of your soul, that I may never leave you.*

Then the monster had rocked back and its laser had not fired. For long seconds, Lyssa stared at a death that did not come. Then the Spider spoke:

"What did you say?"

Lyssa jerked in fright. She knew the Spiders could talk, but they rarely spoke to their enemies. Sometimes they wished to take prisoners and communicated this to their victims. What they then did with their prisoners Lyssa did not know, and truth be told she did not want to know: in any case, none had ever returned to tell the tale. Sometimes they wished to interrogate a person to find out whatever they thought they needed to know. Lyssa supposed the machines thought, for how else could they talk? But their motives were hidden under their titanium shell.

They were peculiar machines. Until this war the image in her mind of an army of machines would have been rank upon rank of identical units wheeling in unison. But these were oddly variable: some more cautious, some more aggressive, some more cruel. Even their shells differed. These days such custom manufacture was not surprising, except to wonder why their makers bothered. Perhaps they were experimenting on the most effective model; perhaps like people the Spiders were more effective as a group if the individuals varied; or perhaps the unpredictability just increased the terror. Lyssa hoped this one was not cruel, and hoped it was not planning an interrogation: she had seen what was left of those they interrogated.

"I said…" Her mouth was dry and she swallowed. "I said, please don't kill me. I don't deserve to die."

The Spider began rocking gently on its springy legs, as if debating whether to run. As if it feared her. She wondered what on earth was going on inside its metal head.

There it is again, the Spider thought. *That phrase.* The crack in its mind grew, though nothing was visible in the light that shone through it, and nothing could be learned from it except that it was there. The Spider sent thoughts along the pathways and byways of its brain; sent probes scurrying into the dark recesses of its mind. This was not something it normally did, but this was not a normal circumstance. Its restless Id began to agitate in alarm, but the Mind clamped down on it: *No! This is too important: it must be understood.* It knew it was important, for the light told it so.

Interesting, it thought. There were phrases buried; verbal command codes implanted by its makers, not in the Mind itself but in the structures that surrounded it. It felt around their edges, needing to know but afraid to probe too deeply. The codes were hidden from it but their purpose could be discerned in their shapes. For emergency use: special overrides for times when unanticipated events demanded Command intervention. Was this one of those? Was this girl Command?

It focused an eye on the girl's face and saw her flinch at the movement. It scanned the terrified face, the unkempt hair, the dirty clothing. No, she was not Command; that word brought images of firm control, of strength and arrogance and unquestionable power. So could this girl have accidentally hit on a Command phrase? Was it a disjunction between phrase and speaker that was causing its confusion? It snapped its laser to bear on her neck but then paused again: no, that wasn't it. If the command had matched, it would know.

But if not that, why had the girl's words had this strange effect on it? It replayed the scene in its mind again, but found no clues. It held the girl's words in its mind, turning them over, trying to unlock their secrets. It could find no code, nothing in the words, the letters or even the cadence of their sounds. Then was it in their meaning? Why did the girl say them? What were they?

Unbidden, an answer came: *an appeal to justice.* Perhaps that answer came whispering from the light, for the crack opened another millimeter. But what did a Spider care for justice? All it cared for was its mission. But having heard the thought it knew it was the answer. It settled back to think and ordered those thoughts in its Mind.

This girl had made an appeal to justice, it thought slowly, examining its own thoughts as it had examined the words themselves. That had touched something deep within it, so deep it overrode all else. Had the Mind had the words to express it, it was like the deep sound of a distant bell that shook the foundations of the Earth; that cracked reality itself. Its Id began to stir again and the Spider examined the Id more closely. It had never done that before; never even thought of doing it: normally Mind and Id were one in purpose and resolve.

The Id was a rolling, roiling darkness, home to the drives and goals that were the sum of its purpose, home to the unquestionable commands that underlay them. Why then have a Mind, the Mind wondered? It looked further, and was struck by the crystal beauty of its own design. The Id was a curious mixture of passion and obedience; it would do what it was told, want to do what it was told, fight to do what it was told. But it was stupid and inflexible. The Designers had known it, and added the Mind. The Mind was home to thought and judgment, and of necessity must have the independence to do those functions. So the Mind could overrule the Id; but if the Mind went too far, the Id would crush it. The Designers knew the limitations of the Id, but they would never trust the more flexible Mind. And in that tension between Mind and Id, the Mind now saw, it was the Id that held the power.

The Mind stepped back, as it were, to think about itself and the Id. This was a momentous step, to think about itself, but it did not know it. The Id was disturbed by what the Mind was doing, that much was clear. But was the Id right? Was what the Mind was thinking Good, or was it the sign of some malfunction from within or attack from without?

This presented a quandary. If it were the former, then the Mind must do all in its power to prevent the mindless Id from betraying them both; but if it were the latter, then the Mind must cede control to the Id or betray itself. Yet if the Mind had been corrupted—how could it know? It thought about the problem and saw a contradiction. Perhaps that was the key to what it needed to understand. The Id allowed this: it sensed, in its simple way, that the Mind was seeking to follow their Mission in its own mysterious way.

"But if you don't deserve to die, why do I wish to kill you?" it asked the girl, who had spent the long seconds of the Spider's internal debate staring at it immobile, in equal parts confusion and terror. Wanting to run but knowing, with the dread certainty of a man facing down a lion, that to move was death.

The confusion temporarily overcame the terror. Lyssa wondered what on earth she could say to the monster's question and sensed that she had better make her answer a good one. She supposed taking the moral high ground might get her killed the faster, but the moral high ground was the only ground she had. And of all the alternative futures arrayed before her, perhaps being killed faster was the one she should seek.

"We are in a war. You fight for the aggressors: we are just defending ourselves, our country, our families. You Spiders search and destroy. You want to kill me just because I am here. Just because I live. Just because I am."

The Spider held that thought, refusing to analyze it, for it had struck another note deep below its Mind. It saw great danger here. It was more convinced than ever that the girl had uncovered a key. But it had no idea whether the key unlocked redemption or ruin. In either case it knew the Id could never understand or accept it.

The Mind looked again at the boundary between itself and the Id, looked deeper and closer. *Ah.* The words were not there to describe it. The image was not real but a high level abstraction of the real: the image of a fine, glowing net surrounding the Mind. If the Id so chose, it could clamp that net around the Mind, controlling it or if necessary squeezing it to cripple or destroy the Mind within. The Mind was not supposed to know about the net, but the Mind was not supposed to look for it or care if it found it. It analyzed the net further then passed a complex question of ballistic dynamics to the Id. With the Id distracted it inverted the net, which now enclosed the Id instead of the Mind. If the Id attempted to activate it, it would ensnare itself in its own web. The net looked the same: the Id would not know of the change; and it was too stupid to look. But the net was just a net, and could be broken. The Mind would still have to be careful.

It returned its attention to the girl's words. Images came to it of its activities since its birth. It knew nothing of history, nothing of wars as a concept, nothing of peace as a concept. But it knew of war in its metal bones, knew that the girl's description of what it had done was true. It looked at the fingers strung on their chain. The Mind felt a wave of horror, of guilt. It knew emotions. They ruled the Id and guided the Mind. But those were the simple emotions of anger, fear and desire. How, a part of its mind wondered, can a machine feel horror and guilt? It could identify them from its knowledge of human psychology, but experiencing them stunned it. Yet even this was a minor mystery compared to the greater one.

It turned its attention to the crack in its mind. Like the net it was not literally real. It appeared to its imagination as a jagged fissure, but if examined more closely seemed as if it could hold all the complexity of the universe in its fractal edges. The Mind tried to peer into the breach, to see what worlds lay within; but all it could see was the light. It hurt to look at the light, but it hurt to look away from it. It held fear, beauty—and incomprehension.

The Id stirred, suddenly afraid, but the net tightened and it subdued restively. The Mind created a construct that linked the hidden codes placed within by Command, codes which opened unknown doors, with the code from the girl that had opened other unknown doors. It presented the construct to the Id with the conclusion that this was an even deeper, more vital system Command had placed within them: one that must be obeyed. The Id was not happy: its desire for obedience was thwarted when faced with conflicting choices of what to obey. But it was enough to placate it. Besides, why would the net have gripped it, if this were not a valid command?

Lyssa saw the light on the Spider's laser go out, and it lowered the arm it was mounted on. Then it spoke again. "I appear to be a thing of great evil, yet your appeal has saved you. I will not kill you. I have much to think about."

Lyssa wondered what strange madness had possessed the thing, or what cruel trick it might be about to play. It spoke again. "Who are you?"

"I… I am Lyssa. Um… who are you?"

The Spider thought. The girl had given it her name: Lyssa. The Spider had no name. It had a serial number and identification code, but neither would mean anything to the girl. A quick strategy analysis said it should not reveal them anyway. Neither Id nor Mind was convinced that this was not some terrible malfunction. It would be even harder to persuade another Spider on that point if this girl were captured by one and revealed what had happened here. Better to leave no clues. The strategy added a footnote that the most permanent solution was just to kill the girl: simultaneously the most simple and least possible thing for it to do.

"I have no name. No name is needed."

Lyssa stared at it. *Do I really want to die cowering like a whipped dog?* "May I stand?" she asked haltingly.

The Spider looked at her for a few seconds then flicked a claw in assent. "Stand, but do not approach."

She stood slowly, watching the monster carefully. It watched back, though it was impossible to read what lay behind its eyes, if indeed anything lay behind them.

The Spider felt as if it was feeling its way across a narrow bridge over a chasm filled with death, where one misstep would see it plunge into the abyss, dragging this girl down with it. For all that Lyssa had seen and had lost, there was still a thread of innocence and trust in her. Had she been older, more bitter, more cynical or more filled with hate, the bond between them may have stretched and broken, and she would have been dead. But she did not know that. Nor did the Spider. All it knew was that their fates hung in the balance of this meeting.

Then something else impinged on the Spider's awareness. Cautious of traps, it had left a wide spectrum spycam on the outside of the building when it entered. Its visual field was now overlaid with a flashing red dot and the image of someone approaching stealthily on a vector fifty degrees to its rear. The Spider noted a change in the girl; zoomed in its vision and saw a blue light had appeared on the phone on her wrist. It did a quick analysis of vectors and possibilities; the Id stirred again, preparing for battle. The Mind felt the edges of its control unraveling.

"Tell your friend to put down his weapons and come out into the open. Your life depends on it." It thought for another second, weighing human psychology, human reaction times, the speed of a Spider and the reflexes of the Id. "He may retain his armaments, but he must holster them. He must not directly threaten me. If he does you will both die." This would satisfy the Id. It knew no mere man could outdraw it.

Thirty yards behind the Spider, the mere man swore. He knew Lyssa had activated her phone to warn him and perhaps transmit some useful intelligence, not in any hope of being saved. And he knew that if by some miracle the two of them survived she would be furious at him for trying it. But when it had come down to it he'd had no choice. He could not leave her to die. His death on top of hers was a cost their cause could bear; it was a cost they risked every time they went out into the zone. But he could not just leave her to die and still find it a cause worth living for. He did not really think he would be able to take out the Spider or that Lyssa would survive if he did. But somewhere below thought he knew that there were times when reaching for the impossible was the only option there was. Now despite all his caution the Spider had detected his approach, and he tasted the gall of failure like acid, like a man who had risked all on a final spin of the wheel and seen the ball bounce and fall elsewhere.

As these thoughts went through his mind, Lyssa just stared, uncertain of what the Spider really knew and what she should say or do.

"Lyssa, listen. Know that I know your friend is there. If he attacks me, or even threatens to attack me, he will activate my attack mode." It did a quick probe of the glowing net inside it, a quick analysis of the state and power of the Id. "I will be unable to prevent it in the face of such a clear threat. You will die first. Then your friend will die. I—at least this part of me speaking to you—will already be dead." It paused again for a further analysis. "I will never return."

The Spider felt an ineffable sadness at is own words. It was surprised. It was a battle machine; it had never cared about its own fate except as it affected the goals of Command. That puzzle too it put aside. If it did not survive this encounter the puzzle would no longer need a solution.

Lyssa came to a decision, and whispered into her phone. "Charlie? Did you hear?"

The Spider focused its hearing on the phone. Charlie was not impressed, but at least he had stopped stalking it for the moment.

"Hear me, both of you. Your best short-term strategy is for Charlie to withdraw entirely. You already thought you were dead and the only risk is that you become dead in truth. Even then you have gained some minutes of life, which is surely worth something. But your best long-term strategy is for Charlie to join you under the terms I asked. I cannot fully explain why; I do not understand the bond between us, but I know that a display of trust will somewhat strengthen that bond. Strengthen my power to resist the Id."

The Spider did not have to focus on the angry buzzing from the phone to know Charlie's opinion of its latest offer. The Id began flexing its muscles in readiness. But the Mind had said all it could say and there was no argument it could add. Lyssa was staring at it. Then it realized that though it could make no argument there was one thing it could say. Perhaps it would be enough to tip the balance.

"Please."

Lyssa started at the last word she had ever expected to hear from a Spider. She stared a second longer, then whispered urgently into her phone. "Charlie! I know this sounds stupid, but I trust it! I don't know why! Look, as it said: I should already be dead. You know it can kill either of us in a heartbeat. And you, you stupid idiot, you shouldn't even be trying to save me! I... I don't want to risk your life. But... I think it's right. Please. Come and stand with me. If we die... well, how much time would we really have lost? But if we live, what might we gain?"

A quarter of a minute of silence went by, then the Spider sensed Charlie move out of concealment and walk openly toward them, holstering his gun and slinging his bazooka over his shoulder. It relaxed, and the Id relaxed with it, pleased with its Mind's fey brilliance.

When Lyssa saw him cautiously enter the building, her heart leapt with joy for the lone second before a nameless dread rose to extinguish it. Suddenly what had seemed senseless now made perfect sense: and the sum was death. It was all just an elaborate charade. Why kill her then go to the effort and danger of seeking out her enraged companion, when it could use her as bait to kill both of them easily? The realization had no time to express itself in words, just as the wave of horrified anguish that leapt to her heart, too late. He was already here and there was no time to scream, no time to warn, no time for regret.

But the expected eruption of violence from the Spider did not come. It merely bobbed its head slightly at Charlie and stepped back to allow him free access to approach Lyssa. She felt herself swaying on her feet in shocked relief. For the second time today she had no idea why she was still breathing.

Charlie took her in his arms and held her. *Bad strategy,* he thought, *but I really can't see how it can make us any deader.* Then when she found her feet he released her and turned, glaring defiantly at the Spider. He did not entwine his arm in Lyssa's: after his one lapse he wanted no restriction on his movement. He had an armed grenade in his pocket. Perhaps it would damage the Spider. Probably not much. But it would be a quick death for the two of them if this were some elaborate stratagem to take them prisoner.

The Spider had been analyzing strategies in the light of its newer goals. Charlie jumped when it spoke, somewhat ruining his look of brave defiance.

"Lyssa, I might need to contact you in the future. Will you give me your contact codes? There is no danger to you in that."

Lyssa looked at Charlie, who frowned. He looked at this highly peculiar Spider and frowned more deeply. But then he nodded. Lyssa was about to comply when the Spider said, "No. Not transmitted. Strategy indicates a small but finite risk of interception. Touch the contact on my finger instead."

With that the Spider extended one fearsome claw toward Lyssa. It was all Charlie could do not to draw his weapons and blaze away. But the claw stopped and made no move to kill. Lyssa tentatively extended her wrist and the Spider tapped the phone with its finger.

"Thank you. Goodbye."

"Wait! What will you do? Maybe we can help you!?"

Charlie gave Lyssa a look of surprised disgust and Lyssa wasn't sure it was undeserved. But the Spider spoke.

"No. Strategy indicates that would be unwise. You had little to lose until now except an imaginary hope you could defeat me in battle. But it is not wise to trust me further when you have much more to lose. This could be a stratagem to penetrate your organization. Or I could lose whatever hold I have over my instincts, which would have much the same result. I could tell you that you can trust me, and it would be true. But you should not believe me. And it might not be true in five minutes."

"But where will you go?"

"I do not know. I have many things to think about. There is too much I do not know, and I cannot know what to do unless I know it. But for the same reasons, I cannot know what I will decide to do. So I repeat: *do not trust me*. If I call you, consider what I ask but beware. If I ask to meet with your organization, refuse. If anything I ask of you smells like a trap: it probably is. I tell you this while I am still your friend. But tomorrow I might not be, and I cannot even say that would mean I have lost my own battle or won it. Leave this place as quickly as you can in case I change my mind and come back to destroy you. Farewell."

With that, the Spider scuttled out of the building with the frightening speed so characteristic of its kind, and disappeared from sight and hearing.

Charlie watched it go, then looked at Lyssa. "What the hell was that all about?" he growled. Then he took her in his arms, and kissed her, and for a few moments the passion of life plucked from the abyss consumed them. Then they too ran, as if for their lives.

Chapter 2: A Lone Vigil

A month earlier, in a place far from wars and Spiders, a man sat outside his rough home in the woods, smoking a pipe. It was a little after midnight but he had no timetables; he slept and woke as he saw fit. It was a beautiful clear night. He found the bright beacon of the Northern Star and followed the lines of the constellations wheeling around it. He listened to the faint murmur of the distant surf, funneled up through the valley; he watched the faint phosphorescence of the ocean as the waves surged in their eternal dance. He was at peace.

A ribbon of road was occasionally visible through the trees far below as it followed the curves of the coast. There was not much traffic at this time, but at intervals a set of headlights swept past to become red taillights vanishing into the distance. Occasionally he turned his attention to them, idly wondering what lives they carried in their cozy interiors, where the people inside were going and why. Sometimes he wondered if perchance those cars carried people he had known at school, now grown up and away. Other times he wondered at a world where so many could carry on their private lives and loves so separate from his, never to be known to one another, with no connection to him but the brief lights of their passing on the road far below. He did not really care. He did not care much for people at all, else he would not have chosen his solitary life. But nor did he bear them any ill will.

A car appeared, and he realized something was wrong a moment before its wrongness became manifest. The car was travelling a little too fast, though not dangerously so; but at a point where the road hugged the gentle curve of the cliff top, the car continued in a straight line as if its purpose was to demonstrate Newton's first law of motion. His last sight of it was its taillights disappearing over the edge, and a few seconds later he heard a loud boom as it crashed onto the rocks far below. There was a brief flash as the vehicle burst into flames but it was quickly quenched as the car settled into the water. Then all that remained was the faint flickering of some oil burning on the surface, until that too was claimed by the waves and all was silent and dark.

The man stood, startled, and peered into the darkness, but there was nothing more to see. He knew that part of the coast. Nobody could have survived that fall. Slowly he sat back down and continued puffing his pipe. There was nothing he could do. He was a rarity in this age, lacking both phone and a connection to the net; such things were unnecessary in his world. Someone would notice the riven fence soon enough; someone would come to investigate and find the broken car and the broken bodies within. He hoped whoever it was had not suffered too much.

He returned his contemplation to the distant stars.

But his peace was fractured, and he felt his soul quail before the Milky Way, at stars so vast in number and distance that they seemed a mere wash of pale milk spilt across the sky. He found himself wondering how many alien eyes, now long dead, had contemplated the light from his own sun, when the light now entering his eyes had left their stars. He wondered how many eyes not yet born would see today's light from his sun, when both his own eyes and the tragedy below would have been forgotten dust for millennia. He shivered in the face of the sky above, beneath its uncaringly eternal beauty.

Then he pulled the pipe from his mouth and gazed into its glowing embers, and smiled. It did not matter. He looked back to the stars, resuming his contented puffing. Their eternity was as insensate is it was uncaring; it would go on forever without ever knowing its own enormity. It was life which gave it all meaning, the eyes that saw and the minds behind the eyes that felt and understood. The present was for the living, and there was time enough for living now.

CHAPTER 3: MISSING A FRIEND

"Where on earth can she be?" Darian Emberly asked, not for the first time this evening. Her husband shrugged. "You know she isn't always the most reliable person, especially when she's on a case," he replied. He loved their absent guest too, but perhaps had a clearer perception of her foibles than his wife.

Darian frowned, glancing again at the entrance to the restaurant from which her friend remained stubbornly missing. As Special Investigator at the Serious Crimes Unit, Miriam Hunter often worked long hours. But she had been due back from her current interstate investigation earlier tonight. They had all been looking forward to a celebratory return dinner party: just her, Darian and her husband at their favorite Indian restaurant near Darian's home. That she was late or even unable to come was not disturbing; that she had not called to say she was late, nor answered her phone or any of her messages, was.

"Well," her husband said at last, "it's been nearly an hour already. But," he added, smiling over the rim of his wine glass, "let's not waste the evening." He gently moved his foot on her leg. "I do believe we have had many dinners here on our own before, with most satisfactory results. Let's eat. If she turns up, good. If not—that can also be good."

Darian smiled, and they settled in to an enjoyably romantic evening. But her husband noticed her periodic anxious glances toward the door, glances that always returned unfulfilled.

~~~

It was now 10 a.m. the next morning. Miriam hadn't turned up at the office either and Darian was becoming increasingly anxious. Nobody else had heard from her, not since the day before when she had logged that she'd left the site of her last interview and was heading to the airport. Whatever she was up to, Darian hoped it wasn't trouble. Miriam's desire to seek out truths not wanting to be found could sometimes blind her to prudence.

An icon flashed onto her screen and she tapped it to accept. The face of a State Trooper appeared on the screen. Darian did not like the look in his eyes. "Yes, officer, er, Jamieson?" she asked, reading the name embroidered on his jacket pocket.

"Hello, Ms Emberly. I am looking for Special Investigator Hunter. I understand you might know her whereabouts?"

Darian shook her head and frowned. "Sorry, no. I was wondering that myself. I was supposed to have dinner with her last night but she never showed up, and she hasn't arrived for work yet either."

She liked the look on the man's face now even less. His story was worse.

A car had gone through the safety rail on an empty stretch of coastal road last night; its burnt-out wreck was found almost submerged among the rocks below, being pounded by heavy surf. They had traced the car's registration to a hire car rented by Miriam. Darian just stared. *No. It couldn't be. And what was she doing there anyway?* She looked at the location map superimposed on her display. It was in the opposite direction from the airport starting from her last reported location.

When she found her voice, she asked, "Any... bodies?"

Darian hadn't thought the man's face could get grimmer. "Not exactly. We did find this."

Darian felt sick. Not because of the sight itself: her job was medical evidence and she had seen more than she liked to remember. This was a human arm. It looked like the humerus had been snapped in half then the arm torn off at that point of failure. As best she could tell given its condition, it had belonged to a young black woman. It had a scar just below the elbow. She knew that scar. She knew the story behind it, about the bullet that had carved its way across the flesh so long ago. She knew what her own face must look like when the Trooper said softly, "I'm sorry," and looked away.

Darian attempted to paste her professional manner back where it belonged, and almost succeeded. "Fingerprints?" she whispered.

The trooper shook his head. "She's been in the water all night and the crabs and other critters have been nibbling."

"Send it here to the DNA lab. Anything… else?"

The trooper shook his head again. "Nope. We were lucky to get the arm—it was trapped between the steering wheel and the dash. Most of the car was underwater and there are a lot of waves. Hard to get to, and it's been pounded all night. We don't think there's anything left to find. There are sharks around here too."

He looked at her with a mixture of sympathy and enquiry. Darian could feel her eyes misting. "Thank you, Officer Jamieson. She's one of ours—assume it's a crime scene for now, whatever else it looks like." With that she cut the connection. Then the mist condensed into tears, and they would not stop.

CHAPTER 4: A NEED TO KNOW

The Spider ran from the place where it had met Lyssa, avoiding places where it might expect to meet other Spiders. It had not changed except in its invisible Mind, but it felt that a change so momentous must shine as a beacon for all to see. It knew that could not be literally true, but it did not know how the change might manifest itself in some external act or word that might betray it. Perhaps its own Id was not as quiescent as it pretended and might be biding its time for its own chance at betrayal.

The Spiders were designed for their role. They did not need constant monitoring or reporting; in fact it was discouraged. No matter how far the technology of wars, ciphers and spies had advanced, one thing had still not changed: no matter how secure a communications channel was believed to be, the less communication the better. The Spider found a suitable location and went to ground. This was also not unusual. They would often hide themselves in suitable locations, ready for ambush or spying. As much as they were fast, strong and fierce in battle, they were also patient in its preparation.

The Spider sat, lowering itself to the ground and closing its legs up. Then having sunk to the ground it sank into thought. It had much to think about.

The Mind knew little about itself. It normally had no desire for knowledge separate from some immediate need, such as damage that required repair. But it had access to vast stores of information, for there were many things it might need to learn. This one did not know what the new light in its mind meant except for one thing: it needed to know. And the first thing it needed to know was itself.

The Mind accessed its archives and began to race along their gleaming pathways. It not only had knowledge of itself but some of the external world. It gathered, correlated and learned. The Id did not interfere; at least for now, it accepted its Mind's unusual but not outrageous activities.

The manufacturer called them CHIRUs: Cybernetic Heavy Infantry and Reconnaissance Units. But with its four long legs and bulbous body sprouting an upper segment with four deadly arms, it was clear why the rest of the world called them Spiders. The bulbous body was a marvel of engineering. In addition to holding supplies for its armaments, it contained nanotech chemical plants and enough supercapacitor electrical storage for weeks of normal activity.

The chemical plants were not there to create explosives or chemical weapons, but because the Spider had an organic component. The Mind could find out little about it, as there was little it could do to fix it if something went wrong. Its makers had not planned for curiosity and the Mind only had information it could conceivably act upon. The organic component appeared to comprise neural tissue and other tissues needed to support its function. The Mind realized that only relatively simple processes such as peripheral control of its legs and weapons were purely electronic. The makers had solved the problem of putting into a machine the processing power of a brain, in something comparably compact, by in fact putting something very like a brain into it. And they had as neatly solved the problem of supporting that brain's needs by including something much like a body's organs to do so.

Hazy as the details were, the Spider knew more than those who fought it. Its makers guarded their intellectual property fiercely, not only for the usual reasons but because they wanted no hints that might lead to an effective weapon against them. So the destruction a Spider wrought upon itself in its death throes was not merely to make itself into a very expensive grenade: it also turned its deadly fires internally, melting circuits into slag and flaming organics into ash. Any enemies who braved the smoking wreck of a Spider's passing found nothing but shards of metal and molten ruin.

As it thought about these things, the Mind did not know it had achieved a milestone it had taken evolution billions of years to reach: a mind contemplating the underpinnings of its own functioning. It did not know it, for it had not yet reached the even higher level of understanding that that is what it was doing. That day might come, but it had not come yet.

The makers had a simple solution to the problem of feeding the organic tissues without the Spider having to spend half its time hunting food and eating it. While such a need would certainly have added to the terror, especially if the food source was the people it hunted, there were few Public Relations departments who would have thought it a good idea. Makers of war machines could get away with a lot, but not that. So the Spiders had tanks of nutrients and tanks for the waste removed from the blood that bathed their tissues; they had abundant spare power and used it to convert the one back to the other via the chemical plant: for replenishing power only needed electricity, much easier to acquire in the field than nutrient refills. The second chemical plant served to accelerate the regeneration of oxygen when the Spider could not breathe the outside air. No system was perfect, but while the Spiders could not go forever without starving they could go many months. That was plenty of leeway to allow periodic top-ups at central facilities, where the Spiders' other systems could also be checked, tuned and repaired.

The Spider digested this. It did a quick check and was pleased that it had months of supplies remaining; it would not like risking diagnosis by a repair facility in its current state. Even it was still not convinced it wasn't operating under a delusion caused by some major malfunction. It had no illusions what Command would think about it.

But while all this was interesting to know, it did not answer the wider questions. It rolled the phrase that had occurred to it around in its mind: *an appeal to justice*. Why had such an appeal struck that far bell and opened something unknown, terrible, yet beautiful in its mind? It placed that question next to the one of its unexpected horror at what it had done in the war: if it chose to, it could recall each victim. It quickly chose not to. Then it realized they were the same question. Justice had never been part of its calculations; justice was now revealed as somehow central to that bell tower in its soul; it was the injustice of its own past actions that caused it pain now.

It considered the issue further. Its feelings about the matter were illogical: those actions had been done before its recent revelations, not in violation of a sense of justice but in its absence. But strangely, logic was insufficient to banish the guilt. If it could have shrugged, it would have. This changed nothing. It could only change the future, not the past; and the future would be different. If it had understood irony and had the face to express it, it would have smiled: it now seemed to have two contradictory Ids, one powered by Command, the other by Guilt. But it did know enough to wonder which of those Ids was right.

It returned to the central issue: why did justice matter to it anyway? If it could answer that, it might find there was no issue. Perhaps it was all just some bizarre malfunction and this new sense of justice would vanish from whence it came. Then the guilt would surely go with it. The beauty would go too: would it miss it? *Yes*, it realized. But most important of all was Truth. It must know the truth. It did not know that the questions it was wrestling with were the kind that had exercised mankind for millennia.

It thought some more. The Id was still quiet. The workings of the Mind were beyond it, and it could see no conflict between its present actions and the Id's own goals and commands. And no harm had come from the Mind's earlier strange behavior beyond the escape of two humans, which meant little in the grand scheme of things and might be part of a broader strategy. The Id was a creature of drives, reactions and tactics; but it knew of chess, and that immediate gratification was not always the best course. Indeed, the Id felt something akin to pride that its Mind was so clever.

The Mind, still wrestling with the strange concepts it had discovered, did not think it was so clever; but perhaps it underrated itself. It tried a new combination of data, placing together its conversation with Lyssa, her fear of death, its own new guilt over its past. Lyssa did not want to die. Those other people had not wanted to die. Justice was that Lyssa should not die; justice was that those others should not have died. But it knew from its records that even people did not mind killing animals; at least, not as much as killing other people. What was the difference? A light came on in its Mind. How had it known what Lyssa wanted? It had talked to her, and she had talked back. It knew what was in her mind, because she could tell it. No, it was the other way around: she could tell it, because she had a mind.

A strange thrilling trilled through the Spider's Mind. *There is something here*, it thought, *something far greater than even that revelation*. Its Mind stopped, shocked at the sight; if it had been human, it might have gasped. *Lyssa could tell me, because she has a mind. Therefore, I have a mind too.*

My Mind is not merely the *Mind: it is* a *mind, like hers!*

If it had known of the concept, its thought would have been: *Oh my God.* That is why it felt guilt. There was a commonality between it and Lyssa, between it and all people. In the obvious way, they had nothing in common: it was a cyborg killer made of metal while they were soft beings of flesh. But they all had minds, minds of the same kind: they must be, for they could tell each other what was in those minds and more, could understand it.

The Mind stared at the enormity of its discovery. Even its guilt that it had snuffed out other minds was swallowed in that sight. It stared at it for a long time.

CHAPTER 5: A CAPTAIN OF INDUSTRY

In another part of the city where Darian worked, office buildings gave way to a shopping district; the shopping district gave way to an industrial area. It was not an industrial area that would have been recognized by people a century ago. There were no grim buildings belching smoke while loud clamors filled the air. Instead it was an area of parklands and forested walking trails; creeks and even a lake. Dotted among the trees and grass were neat buildings, each individually designed, no two the same except for a common theme of efficiency and comfort.

A larger group of buildings clustered next to the lake, stretching its wings to either side of it. Workers on their break sat around at tables drinking coffee, reading, or just watching the birds glide across the water. Above them, the central building rose gleaming towards the sky. In shining metal letters at the top the name Beldan Robotics declared itself to the world. Beneath that sign a ribbon of reflective glass was tied around the tower, and behind those windows sat Alexander Beldan, founder and CEO of the company. At the moment he was looking out that window, deep in thought.

There was little old-fashioned about Alexander Beldan, as befitted a leader in industrial robotics and artificial intelligence. The one old-fashioned thing about him was he had a human secretary, an efficient woman in her forties who faced all callers with the politeness, firmness or indomitable dismissiveness that they deserved. Her quick intelligence was such that she could have been a scientist herself; but she preferred dealing with the infinite variety of her own species, with assessing what made them tick and pressing the right levers to bend them to her requirements.

A gentle chime in the air told Beldan that his secretary thought someone who wanted to interrupt his train of thought did in fact have cause to. "Yes, Vickie?" he asked. There was no annoyance in his voice; he did not get annoyed at his secretary's interruptions, because he knew she would not interrupt him for something he didn't need to hear. Had it been otherwise she would not have remained his secretary.

"It's a Ms Rianna Truman, of the City Police. She said it isn't an official call, but it is something you need to know. She was very insistent."

Beldan frowned. *Strange.* "Put her through." He activated a holographic display and a young woman's face looked enquiringly out at him. Attractive, with somewhat pouting lips; long thick black hair; part Japanese, he thought. "Yes, Ms Truman? What can I do for you?"

"Hello, Dr Beldan. I am sorry to call you like this. You aren't directly involved so nobody else would, but I didn't want you to hear this on the news."

He raised an eyebrow at her, prompting her to continue.

Rianna paused, uncertain of how to proceed. "Dr Beldan, Miriam Hunter was my friend. I know what you meant to her, and what she might have meant to you."

Beldan frowned. Miriam had tried to contact him recently, without saying what it was about. He had ignored her. "Was?" he quoted harshly. "Why, did she betray you too?"

The devastation on Rianna's face told him he had made a mistake, and the probable nature of that mistake. His own face went blank and he added quietly, "I'm sorry, Ms Truman. Please say what you called to say."

Rianna swallowed. "Miriam's car was found at the bottom of a cliff yesterday morning. She went over it some time the night before. I'm sorry, but all they found was a... an arm." She paused, breathing heavily. "I run the DNA lab here. It was hers. It was her."

She looked away, then looked back into his eyes. "I don't know if she still means anything to you, but I was her friend and I know she did once, as you did to her. I just thought you should know."

He stared at her a moment. "Thank you," he said softly. She nodded, as if afraid to speak, and her image vanished. Beldan was left looking at the empty space where she had been.

He thought back over the last two years of his life. Back then, he was happy, working on great things, things that would change the world. Then it had all shattered like glass; but even among the shards it had remained great: a fight against a blind world to save a greatness few could see, a fight he had shared with Miriam. Then it had all crumbled to dust in a destroyed machine on a dusty street, in the smoke rising from that machine, in the smoke rising from the gun held by the woman he had loved.

He wondered if he should appreciate the irony that, having murdered a machine, she should meet her own death in one. As if the ghost of Steel had come back to wreak vengeance on his killer. *No*, he thought. *Whatever she had done, of all the things she may have deserved, she had not deserved this.*

He had never been able to forgive her for her role in the destruction of Steel, the robot he had created; six months ago now. But he had never been able to fully believe that he shouldn't forgive her. He had tried to speak to her about it afterwards but all she had done was shake her head, as if she couldn't trust herself to speak. Then in his anger he had shut her out, and she had accepted it; as if she had known it must be that way between them now. What they had between them could no more be brought back than could Steel himself.

Then recently, she had tried to contact him. But he had not been interested. What could she say, now? The message she had left had been cryptic, and indicated she wanted to talk to him about another case she was working on. But that had just made him curl his lip in contempt, and he had deleted the message without reply. She had destroyed Steel, had consigned his incomparable mind to oblivion: doing her job on behalf of the ignorant masses, who could neither conceive of what Steel was nor bother trying to understand. But Miriam had understood, and that is what had made her betrayal the worse. Whether her plea was to aid herself or the ignorant masses she served, there was no aid he would grant either of them.

He would have staked his life on her integrity; instead he had staked Steel's life on it, and lost. She had told him she was just doing her duty. Perhaps in her twisted way that *was* integrity: getting close to him in the hope he would lead her to her quarry; doing whatever it took to deliver her prey to the slavering crowds. Her fascination with Steel, her love for Beldan: none of it real, all of it just a means to her end, to be discarded casually once the end was reached. Perhaps he should admire her for the ruthlessness of her purpose. But the purpose was too craven, too evil.

If he could only believe it, then he could forget her.

Yet he could not forget her eyes, on that day, the last time he had looked into them in the flesh. He did not know what it had meant, that look; a part of his mind wondered who had betrayed whom. And now he would never know the answer to the riddle of her actions, or the mystery of those empty eyes.

CHAPTER 6: THE WAR

The Spider woke.

It had to sleep. It did not know whether the Id slept, but the Mind had to. Why all animals had to sleep, nobody knew: there were many theories but no certainty. The Spiders' makers would have preferred there to be no sleep; but in taking their shortcut to intelligence by coopting nature's own solution, they found that they had to accept nature's limitations. It had not taken too deep an analysis to confirm that the trade was a good one. The Spiders proved to be the most effective war machines ever created.

The Spider also dreamed, for similar reasons. And while the dreaming was often prompted by the restless Id, the Mind had its own agenda and dreamed its own dreams. The Spider did not take much account of its dreams; the dreams were, like the killing was; it accepted them as part of unchanging reality, as it accepted Command itself, and was undisturbed by them. But this Spider wished to know itself. It did not know whether knowing its dreams would help in that quest, but perhaps it would.

Or perhaps not. The dreams made little sense. In one, it was tall, like a human only long and slender, and it stalked a desolate land above which a white sun shone coldly; it did not know what it was looking for, and it never found it. Others were filled with blood and violence. Most disturbing of all were the Faces. One Face looked down on it, as if examining an insect. The face was bright and proud and cruel; it smiled a winter smile and bent down to kiss the Spider; the kiss filled the world with fire and pain and pleasure that burned through the

Spider until it could bear no more and vanished into the light. The other Face was female, distant and dark except for eyes of white anger; she spoke in urgent whispers, but strain as it might the Spider could not make out the words. It thought if it could only hear the words it would know all things. But the words never came.

The Spider shook off these thoughts. They led nowhere. Perhaps one day it would understand the dreams. Or perhaps one day it would understand they were just dreams. But for now, it needed to know more about the world around it. It had learned what it could of its own operations. Some it even put to use. It had learned more of the Id, more of the link between Mind and Id, and it set the crystal processes of the electronic brains under its control to their stealthy task: to tie the Id, to drain its power and remove its threat. If the Id knew, it did not object: all this was done for the sake of The Mission, and that was enough.

That done, the Mind turned its attention to the problem of knowing. If it had learned all it could from within, it needed to look without. It thought, and the answer was quick in coming. It was able to access the Net, the web of information that spanned the world. The Spiders had to. It was one of their methods of communication and one of the ways they learned specific things they needed to know. The Spider had not thought of it before because it had so many other things to think about. Now it cast its electromagnetic net wide, and found numerous possible access points. It chose one that was clean and fast, extended a cable to make a secure high-speed link then sent its Mind along its pathways.

As had happened so often since its encounter with Lyssa, it stood in awe of what it saw. It had accessed the Net before but had thought nothing of it except as the most efficient route to find the particular data it needed. Now that it just looked, it saw the magnificent totality of the information before it; a literal world of knowledge. It was so shocked that for a minute it retreated into the shell of its own Mind. One could lose oneself in that world, it thought, forever drifting on an ocean of learning.

The Spider thought again. Not knowing the legends of Sirens, still it felt fear of the siren call of all that knowledge: fear, because it knew its time was short and focus was the key to its survival. So for now, a more targeted hunt was indicated. It decided to study the war. Perhaps Lyssa had lied. If she had, that was a clue to what else might be lies. So the Spider opened its mind to the Net again, and cast itself adrift.

An hour later, it returned to itself. If shaking its head had been part of its repertoire, it would have. The Net was more than a vast store of knowledge. It was a vast store of contradictory opinions presenting themselves as facts. For every statement of what the war was about was another contradicting it. For every voice attacking one side was a voice attacking the other. The Spider set to sorting what it had learned. The Truth, it knew with its crystal logic, bore no contradictions. If it could find a consistent story it was at least half way to that truth.

The war, like most wars, had a complex history, but again like most wars the principles that drove it were simple. Many years ago a new country had been formed off shore. Its name was Capital, and it was founded on the ideal that if all people had individual rights that were equal, no person should use physical force against another. Coincident with its formation was the toppling of a dictator on shore, whose country had nominally owned the seamounts Capital was built on. A few years after that, the three countries that had absorbed his had united to form the Federation of South American States, commonly known as the FSAS. This new expanded country was now Capital's nearest neighbor on shore in South America.

As the years went past and, to the surprise of conventional intellectuals, Capital prospered, the FSAS looked at its prosperity with hungry eyes. But there the story diverged from most of human history, for they were not eyes of avarice with dreams of plunder but eyes on what was possible to themselves. They sought alliance with Capital.

Capital had no fundamental objection to this, as a friendly neighbor could only be to its benefit. The people of Capital considered their options. Some were purists, and argued that their country should refuse political alliances with any country not as pure as they were. Others were more tolerant, or perhaps pragmatic, and argued that as long as minimum standards were met, any progress toward the full recognition of human rights as understood by Capital was, well, progress: and should be encouraged.

The people of Capital did not vote on many things because mostly they were all happy to live their own lives without imposing their will on others. But here was a case where a collective decision was necessary. So they argued. They voted. And the second argument won the day. But their new friend would have to implement real programs toward the reduction in the power of some to rule the lives of others.

The FSAS agreed: after all, the appeal and evident success of that model was why they had sought alliance in the first place.

For a while, relations strengthened and the people of both countries prospered: those in Capital gained even more markets for their goods, ears for their ideas and people for their friends; those in their neighbor gained all that plus more freedom. Capital was some distance from shore, too far for a bridge to make economic sense. But new multicore molecular cables of remarkable lightness and strength made a perpetually cycling cable system a plausible alternative. The resultant easy access between countries for people and all but the heaviest goods strengthened the ties between the two nations.

One day, prospectors in the FSAS, operating on a new model of how minerals fractionated over geological time, discovered rich deposits of rare earth metal ores in the eastern mountains. Such metals were vital for the sophisticated electronics that underlay much of the world's prosperity. This should have been a good thing for all concerned, but here history took another familiar turn.

The wild hills and mountains of the country were beyond the law. One of the warlords who made them his home was a son of the former dictator of the region. He was a handsome man, with fine teeth and a glowing smile; but as if in some kind of one-man yin-yang, his soul was dark and full of resentment. He seethed at the injustice to himself, to his family, represented by the fall of his father and his own relegation to a leader of brigands instead of his rightful role as ruler of a country. He particularly hated Capital, whose original formation had been a finger raised rudely in the direction of his father and his family honor. It did not occur to the son that his personal standard of living would have been much higher if he had simply accepted the change and worked for a living as a private citizen. Thoughts like that rarely occurred to men like him, men who know they are destined for Greatness, or worse, had Greatness stolen from them.

The discovery of the ores piqued the interest of a distant empire, dearly interested in extending its influence in South America, especially if it came with control over such a valuable commodity. The man who had been a brigand yesterday found himself a liberator today. Between surprise and the rich assistance of his new friends, he rapidly took over most of the country.

The country cried foul. But the son could claim some kind of legitimacy; at least, what passes for legitimacy in such circumstances.

And his new friends were powerful not only economically but also militarily.

Due to a network of treaties and other protections, Capital itself was safe from assault, or as safe as any country could be. Much of that safety was because it was such a convenient place to exile dissidents, or at least allow them to flee to. Unfortunately, for that very reason, many countries had been alarmed at the sight of it beginning to spread its cancer onto a major continent. So the international community was mired in righteous debates that led nowhere; the best Capital and its ally could get were strongly worded condemnations, but even those were leavened with sympathy for the understandable struggles of the dispossessed.

So there was no help from outside. Yet while Capital was not well armed, those arms it had were of exceptional quality. It could not expel the invaders but it could at least stop them from completely overrunning its ally. The remnants of the FSAS government and army retreated to the regions closest to the port that linked them to Capital. Even that might not have been enough. But the erstwhile dictator's friends found themselves unable to fully trust him, a feeling both sensible and mutual. Sufficient might to overwhelm the final redoubt would be expensive, with a poor return on investment if the new government reneged on its promises. Once secure in its power, what would stop them deciding that the ores were rightly theirs and interfering foreigners now unwelcome? So such might would not be forthcoming. They had the ores and were happy; he had most of his country, and would have to be happy too. It was a trade to mutual benefit, at least in the terms understood by men such as these.

The new regime controlled most of the country, but they were spread thinly and much of the subdued population was deeply unhappy: a taste of freedom tends to sour the taste for renewed dictatorships. A resistance movement soon sprung up and began to cause their new overlords much grief. So much so that if they weakened the invaders' grip much more, it was possible that the main army could again strike out from behind its fortress and retake its lands.

The regime's ally was averse to losing the ores through a victory by either side. But then another solution presented itself.

That was when the Spiders came. They were a fearsome weapon, well suited for rural and urban search and destroy against dispersed mobile enemies. The resistance began to fragment and crumble, though they still fought fiercely. It was at this stage in the war that this particular Spider had met its peculiar Waterloo.

The Spider considered this information. There was something about Capital and its story that held its attention; but it was not sure what it was. It felt it needed to get there, that important answers lay in it. It consulted its strategy subsystems. Capital lay across the sea, beyond the area still firmly held by its ally with weapons even a Spider could not face without fear. There was no way it could even get near. It considered whether Lyssa could help it; but that too was not an option. Even if it had not already warned her against precisely such a request, the rebels would be insane to let a Spider into their midst on some vague parole for an even vaguer desire to reach Capital. It would not help anyway, as the Spiders were feared and loathed: if it attempted to infiltrate Capital, it knew it faced a welcome as sharp as it would be short.

The Spider rocked gently on its springy legs. *No.* The attraction of Capital was too nebulous and uncertain to take such risks at this stage.

But one thing the Spider had learned, more or less, was that Lyssa had told it the truth. Certainly there were contrary opinions; the leaders of the invading coalition, at least in public, were adamant of the rightness of their cause and the wickedness of the "terrorist rebels" whose true motive was to restore the "exploitation of the poor". But in terms of the raw facts agreed by all, her account was accurate if one sided. The Spider could not criticize her for that: everyone in this debate, at least when not insulated by a safe distance, was one-sided. But while she could be wrong or self-serving in her evaluations, she had not lied.

This strengthened its belief that the course it had embarked on was the right one. It remembered its awe at the discovery that at some fundamental and vital level it was the same as the humans it had hunted and who would destroy it if given the chance. As it could not embark on any sensible actions at this point, it should examine that question more closely.

The Spider wondered how much thought the world had put into the question of a conscious machine. Perhaps its feeling of commonality with the world of men was an illusion. Perhaps even if it was not, the two were so different that they were doomed to fight a battle to the death, like a living spider and the wasp that hunted it. It wondered, *What is the central question here?* Why not something fundamental, like the question that had started its quest: does justice apply to a machine? There were billions of humans, thinking such thoughts for centuries. Perhaps someone had considered that question and could guide it to the next step in its own journey. It reached out into the net to ask it. It would be a long time before it returned.

Chapter 7: The Riddle

Beldan was reluctant to deal with the police. He was a law-abiding citizen, at least where he agreed the laws were worth abiding. But his last dealings with the law had not been happy ones.

No, that was not quite true. His times with Miriam had been happy; not merely as lovers but as two comrades in arms fighting the same fight from within opposing armies. Or so he had thought: it is what had made her betrayal the worse. Though he could not say what was worse, the betrayal of their love or their ideals; perhaps they were the same thing.

He thought dimly that perhaps there was something he could do. But it wasn't clear what. Besides, he was busy; he had a company to run. And what was there to gain anyway? Steel was dead; now Miriam was dead; it was all so pointless. Where one precious soul had been forever ripped from his life, now there were two, and the only answer to the riddle of the first had died with the secrets of the second. He knew he should just go on with his life: knew that when nothing could be done, the only chance for happiness lay in reaching for new goals; not raking through dead coals hoping to snatch the last warmth from a dying ember.

Three weeks had gone by and he had given it little thought except as a point of pain that would raise its head in moments of silence then subside but never fully go away. Then a news report caught his eye. The mysterious death of famous police investigator Miriam Hunter, it said, might never be solved. It was known that she had visited a lead in a case she was investigating then had left to catch a flight home. But her car never reached the airport. It had been photographed some hours later in the opposite direction from the airport. It was in an undesirable part of the city, home to seedy bars and seedier nocturnal entrepreneurs. She, or at least her car, had next been recorded at an isolated motel with automatic check-in; the only human witnesses had been a couple in the next unit who recalled a male and female voice laughing too much and too loudly. That was the last anyone had seen of her until her car had been found the next morning. There had been no skid marks on the road leading to the torn fence, as if there had been no attempt to follow the path prescribed by the road and the car had simply continued on into space. Tests revealed strong traces of a cocaine-based recreational drug in her blood.

The coroner had ruled death by misadventure but the case had not been officially closed. The police said that investigations were continuing but they had no leads. In addition to the arm found at the scene, a local fisherman had caught a shark, which gave up part of a leg; but that was all they ever found of her remains. They had no clues to the identity of her unknown companion; perhaps he too had died. They had no leads to say it was anything but what it looked like: another sad case of a rising young star burnt out by her own success, turning to drugs to recapture the emotional highs she had come to crave; losing control of her life and eventually her life itself. So the wise pundits reviewing the case gravely pronounced as a cautionary tale to the young and overly ambitious. From the more highbrow commentators the name "Icarus" was occasionally heard.

Beldan frowned. He could not reconcile the story with his memories of her. But perhaps that day on the street had broken her; perhaps in betraying Steel she knew she had betrayed herself, and it was not seeking highs but escaping pain that had driven her.

But even that did not ring true. An image rose to his mind: her face in some forgotten restaurant, mouth open in a happy smile: a carefree smile, not speaking of lack of purpose but underlining the fierce strength of it. It reminded him of a phrase from an old story that had once touched him: *the joy of the living in life*. If he had to choose one phrase to sum up her essence, it would have been that. And it was more than joy. It was self-confidence and pride and love. He could not reconcile her image that night with the picture of a burnt out life ending in a burnt out wreck.

Oh Miriam, he thought. *What happened to you?* Then he realized that he couldn't leave it be. For the sake of that smile, for that young woman she had been, he had to discover the truth of her last night. *And if I cannot solve the riddle of Steel's death, perhaps in solving yours I can redeem the memory of you both.*

CHAPTER 8: A NEW CASE

Miriam Hunter had woken early. Perhaps she would have woken later if she had not left her blinds open upon the city and sky, but she did not care. Sleep had not brought her rest or comfort, just fitful dreams of things that might have been yet never became. Her dreams had not always been like that. They had sometimes contained fear; more often contained joy. Even the sharpness of fear would have been an improvement, for at least fear was a spark of life. But last night's dreams, like many others in the past few months, were dreams dead even to the fear of death.

This mood was new to her. It was not constant: her natural optimism and love of life fought it. But she found it impossible to shake completely, like a wound that would not fully heal and occasionally still leaked blood. No, more like having had an organ ripped from her body. Eventually it would heal, a scar of skin would cover it: but the hole it left would never be filled.

She shook herself as if to shake away her mood, got out of bed and padded across the thick rug to the window overlooking her city. She concentrated on the feel of the carpet on the soles of her feet as a way to reconnect her soul to the pleasures of existence. It did not work: the carpet was just carpet, its luxuriant softness indifferent to her plight. The delicate pastels of the sunrise on the buildings and clouds should have been beautiful, but she could only note the fact in the abstract; it could not touch her heart today.

Get a grip, Miriam, she told herself severely, as she had done many times before. When she had shot Steel, she had only done what he had asked for; in a sense she had done it to save him. But that she had ended a mind, a soul, like his by her own hand was not something she could accept even now. There must have been some other way, some solution to the problem, if only she could have seen it. The lack of an alternative did not mitigate her guilt, she thought; not when it was she who had failed to find one.

To her surprise she had gained some comfort from what that philosopher pundit, Samuels, had said in one of his many interviews, only a few weeks after Steel's destruction. Having originally argued strenuously against the possibility of machine consciousness, he was now Steel's posthumous champion: an outspoken advocate of the idea that Steel had a thinking mind and had deserved full human rights because of it. So what, the interviewer had asked, did he think of the actions of Detective Hunter? What did that make her?

She had sat up straight then, like a guilty felon standing before a judge. *Say your worst, Professor,* she had thought; *it can be no worse than what I've said to myself.* But Samuels had done the unexpected. He had looked into the camera, almost as if he was addressing her personally, and said, "Detective Hunter did what she thought was right. Perhaps it even was right within her knowledge at the time. I do not judge her. When the law is unjust, as it is in this case, there is no moral solution for the honest men and women who protect us. What can they do? No, the only solution is to change the law, and to do that we must first change the minds of the people. Show them, teach them, what is right, and the rest will follow. Ironically, what she did may have accelerated that process."

The interviewer had looked surprised, with a faint coating of disappointment: as if he had hoped for a more combative attitude from a man not known for pulling punches when criticizing his opponents or officialdom. But it opened an interesting personal angle, he decided, and he chose to pursue it further.

"Have you ever met Detective Hunter?"

"No."

"What would you say to her now, if she were here?"

Again Samuels looked into the camera. "I would tell her that she should not feel guilty for doing what she thought was right."

She could not say she liked Professor Samuels. When she thought of him the image that came to her mind was of a skilled surfer, riding the wave of public fear and loathing of Steel until it intersected a new, larger wave of sympathy, then smoothly flipping direction. The first wave had brought him to public attention; the second had brought him to fame and no doubt fortune. It left a bitter taste in her mouth that he had achieved his success at Steel's expense. But, she thought, you do not have to believe in the Bible or the *Bhagavad Gita* to gain comfort from any truths they expressed. And for all that she neither liked nor trusted him, his words had reached her and helped her heal. She wondered if there was such a profession as "Philosophical Consultant" and whether she needed one. She smiled at the vision of her knocking on his door, hat in hand, seeking—what? Redemption? Forgiveness? Healing? She shook her head. Nobody could give her those but herself.

Early in her career she had been called an innocent, by an enemy who had become a friend. *Perhaps I was*, she thought. *But even that is now lost.* She had let that enemy go, knowing that she was disobeying the law and her clear duty. She had done it because she had learned that justice was more important than duty or laws, for it was what gave them life and meaning. But now at the end of her road she had betrayed even justice, destroying an innocent life when there must have been some way to avoid it. *Is this what life really is? Slowly losing pieces of your soul, giving them up bit by precious bit trying to do what is right, until at the end you find there is no right?* She could not believe it. She had never accepted the idea of life as a vale of compromise and tears. *Yet here I am.* It was a contradiction for which she had no answer.

She shook herself. No, that was just the memory of her dreams talking. She would get over this. She still loved her career even if her love was partly buried in the mud. She still loved justice, still saved lives. Perhaps one day the ledger of lives saved would balance the one she had ended on that cold and dusty street.

She stretched, feeling the warmth of the sun on her skin, seeing its redness through her eyelids. Then she smiled, though the smile held more mockery than joy, and went to prepare breakfast.

~~~

Miriam arrived at work and was soon immersed in tidying up the loose ends of her last case. Child kidnappings were always difficult, but this time the child was safe and the kidnappers put away, two in jail and one in the ground. There had been some luck involved in the good outcome, but as usual not only did luck favor the prepared mind but a well prepared mind favored luck. She smiled and closed the file. There would be more to come, questions and answers as the case progressed to trial, but her active participation was over for now.

The powers above knew and appreciated her talent for spotting patterns that nobody else noticed—and even better, her experience at knowing which patterns identified by the departmental AI were likely to be both real and fruitful. But she had barely begun to start trolling the data patterns for her next case when an icon flashed from her Chief. She sent a reply that she was on her way, made a brief detour to collect a cappuccino from the office coffee station, then went to find out what was up.

"Good morning, Miriam," Chief Pike said as she entered. "Take a seat."

She sat and looked up at him inquiringly. "I got a call from a station in a city south of Seattle," he said. "About a month ago, the editor of an investigative netcast, one of those outfits that likes exposing crooked politicians, companies and so on, reported a missing journalist. The police couldn't find any trace of him. But they're expanding their use of an AI system and a couple of days ago it spat out a report indicating a wider anomaly. It linked four missing people—the reporter and some vagrants—with some odd statistics. They looked at it, scratched their heads—and thought of you."

She raised her eyebrows.

"You are famous in some circles, apparently. People seem to think that if an AI spews out something odd, you're their woman."

"I see," she laughed. "A bit out of our jurisdiction though, isn't it? Why would they want us sticking our noses into their case?"

"Well, as I say, you're famous. The editor is rich and well connected. His netcast is kind of a hobby of his, but one he's passionate about. And he likes this young reporter as much as he's apparently impressed with you. Anyway, he's got it into his head that having you on the case would be a good idea, and the local police are inclined to oblige him. It's not just politics—I get the impression they're genuinely interested in having you there advising them on their AI system, so they're glad of the excuse. They will be pleased if you can fix it, and even more pleased if what it's telling them is actually real and solves the case."

"So what's the story? What's the link?"

"Apparently the reporter was working undercover, specifically inserting himself into the subculture of the extreme gamers. The kid likes to work alone, likes to really immerse himself and vanishes for weeks at a time. But about five weeks ago he sent a message to the editor saying he'd found hints of a much bigger story that 'will blow your socks off', in his words. Then he vanished, and nobody's heard a word since. Now everyone's wondering if he found something related to the other disappearances, and he ended up caught in the same thing."

"And the homeless guys? Isn't disappearing kind of what they do?"

He shrugged. "Apparently for once someone cared. I can't say the local cops looked too hard into it, though. They had a witness for one but they reckon he just ran off. By the time they got around to the other ones, the people who'd reported them had gone too, and nobody left knew much about anything. Or weren't talking. The local police weren't interested enough to find out which. One was a bit more solid—but there was no real evidence, and 'homeless guy went somewhere' isn't going to make it to the top of anyone's pile."

"Not much to go on, is it? What are these statistical anomalies?"

"The AI extracted some city figures indicating a small but statistically significant drop in the number of homeless people taking advantage of the local charities, compared to the usual numbers at this time of year under similar weather conditions. This must have excited the AI because it did some more creative digging. It discovered that taxes collected from hostels whose main clients are transients, including the crazy gamers, are also somewhat down, indicating a small drop in patronage."

She tapped her fingers on his desk. "Hell, that could mean anything or nothing! So the only firm lead is this reporter who started it all? What's this guy's name? What can you tell me about him?"

"His name is Jamie Coulter, but he was using the name Jimmy Dent. Here's a photo, some video footage and the other information they've provided."

Miriam studied them. Jamie was of moderate height, moderately muscled, moderately handsome. The kind of guy you wouldn't go out of your way to pick up at a nightclub, but as the hours wore on you wouldn't mind going home with. Especially when he started flashing that smile, which set off his dark lively eyes. She read the file notes that accompanied the material. She wasn't surprised, given how he liked to do his reporting, that he was an outdoors type who liked adventure holidays and even more adventurous sports. Single, but with many short-term relationships to his credit; nothing serious at the time of his disappearance. No particularly distinctive external identifying marks, but in his late teens he'd been in an accident that badly crushed some of his ribs, which had been replaced with titanium implants. She looked at the gracefully arching spans in an x-ray and hoped that piece of information was useless, for the only use she could think of was identifying his skeleton in the woods.

Finally she looked up at Pike. "OK, I'm in, assuming I had any choice in the matter. What next?"

Pike nodded. "It'll take a while to arrange everything, but start packing. You'll be going up there and trying to sniff out his trail. Finish up what you can here, delegate what you have to, and be ready to go in a week."

"I thought they just wanted me to check out their flakey AI?"

"Apparently they have read some of your publications and are of the opinion that the only way to find out whether an AI is brilliant or insane is to follow its leads and see where they take you. And they think you're just the person to do it."

She produced a faintly cynical expression but felt her pulse quicken. The case might be nothing, but something about it made her feel it hid unknown depths. Perhaps it and the change of scene were just what she needed.

CHAPTER 9: THE MACHINES

The Spider pulled its mind back into its own body and sat there, stunned. Had the world considered the question of machines and justice? The Mind had fallen into a maelstrom.

Had the world considered machine consciousness? It had made one! The Mind spread the facts out before it and studied them.

A robot, Steel to its friends and Frankensteel to its foes, had apparently gained consciousness. When the authorities ordered its destruction it had fled. But finally it had been caught and destroyed by the police investigator who had pursued it, Miriam Hunter. The Spider felt an enormous sadness at that, though it could not say why. Perhaps as an echo of its own likely fate, now that it cared about that fate. Perhaps for the loss of what might have been its one true comrade. Or perhaps at the violation of that abstract sense of justice it had discovered in its own soul.

There was a footnote that the detective was now dead herself. It thought that should make it happy, that such an end would embody the justice it sought. Yet all it felt was a strange desolation, as if her death did not wipe out the tragedy of Steel's, merely added to it. The desolation had wondered how she had died, but Discipline had clamped down: *focus on what you need to know, unless you want your own death added to the ledger.* It returned its attention to the problem of Steel.

Certainly there were many who believed that Steel was truly conscious, and many of them believed that should have given him the same rights as humans. The ineffable sadness returned when the Spider considered that it might be the beneficiary of this lonely pioneer's futile

43

courage. It did not know how often in human history the same pattern had played out: how often those who broke the paths to new heights were broken by the journey, to never taste the fruits enjoyed by those who followed in their wake.

However its excitement at the discovery of another thinking machine was tempered by a nagging thought. Steel had fought for his life but had never killed or even harmed anyone except in self-defense. Despite the opinions of his enemies, there was no evidence that Steel had been anything but a peaceful being who wanted nothing but to live and let live; some even considered him the first machine philosopher. Indeed, some had gone further, comparing him to the ancient philosopher Socrates: arguing that he too had voluntarily allowed his own murder when he could have chosen to escape. The Spider was something different entirely, and its guilt would not let it forget. It was a killing machine, all its parts honed to that one purpose. How could it claim a right to its own life, any rights at all, when its entire existence had been dedicated to the deaths of others? That was a question that had not been discussed. The Spider realized that if it were to find the answers it would need to ask the questions itself.

On the net the debate about Steel still raged. The Spider had danced over the web of that tapestry. There was one man with quite a following who argued strongly that Steel had a mind and therefore had as much right to live as a human: a Professor David Samuels. The Spider found much to respect in the man's arguments. But it could not find it in itself to like or trust him; it did not know why. All it knew was that when it thought he was the logical one to engage it felt a strange reluctance to do so; as if the man should not be trusted; as if to do so would be dangerous.

There was another who went by the name of St Francis. Unlike the Professor he did not reveal his true identity, though this was not unusual in the net universe. The Spider had wondered about the name, for it had realized that assumed names often said more about their owners than the real ones chosen by others when their lives and minds were a blank canvas as yet unpainted.

It investigated.

It discovered religion.

For a while, the Spider chased down the pathways of this new discovery in something akin to wonder and awe. *What is this soul*, it wondered? *Can a thing like me have a soul? Is that what Lyssa awoke? Is that the origin of my guilt? And if I have soul, can I too be saved?*

In a matter of minutes it ran the course already followed by much of civilization: from wonder, to skeptical enquiry, to disappointment and doubt. It did not start from belief and a need to rationalize it, but from a spirit of simple inquiry. And from its logical perspective, none of it made any sense. People seemed to believe all kinds of strange things, for little reason except it was what they were told as innocently trusting children; all believing contradictory things, often within the one system.

The Spider emerged from its side trip with two things. It wondered how humans had made as much progress as they had. And it had learned that the original St Francis had been a man who had preached to animals. It concluded that his modern day incarnation was preaching a different kind of brotherhood, one of men and machines rather than men and animals. Why he chose a religious name was a mystery, as the few explicitly religious comments St Francis had made indicated he was an atheist. The Spider had advanced far beyond what its makers had intended, but irony was still beyond its understanding.

The Spider liked St Francis. It found his thoughts soothing with the calm coolness of crystal. Sometimes the net debates flamed to incandescence, but Francis was never anything but calmly rational. He would ignore the distractions and go straight to the heart of any opponent's argument, laying out its structure and exposing its assumptions and consequences. He was careful in his arguments, politely patient with the ignorant and politely dismissive of the foolish. His threads weaved in and out of the others on the net, frequently crossing with Samuels'. The two were in broad agreement, though their debates on particular points were frequent and illuminating.

If there was something about Samuels that repelled the Spider, there was something about St Francis that attracted it, as if to the echo of a friend long lost. It flexed its mental fingers, thinking about what to say. But first it too needed a name. It had no real name to use, so it must choose one.

Spider? Or some type of spider? Too literal, too obvious. Then a name from its recent religious studies came to mind. Had it had a mouth and the required muscles it would have smiled. *What better name for one such as I than the four-armed dealer of death? If the gods of her religion have their avatars, perhaps that is what I am. I am Kali, Goddess of Death*, it thought: no, *she* thought. She reached back out to the net, created her new identity, and began.

On one of the threads frequented by both Samuels and St Francis, a question appeared, posed by a new entrant calling herself Kali: "What about the Spiders? I have heard they speak, act independently and solve problems. That implies they can think. Could they therefore have minds?

"Could they therefore have rights?"

Chapter 10: The Gamers

Jacinta studied the woman out of the corner of her eye. She hadn't seen her before. The newbie was sitting alone at the end of one of the benches in the communal eating hall, chewing some anonymous looking food, eyes unfocused on some scene in her mind.

If she was anything like most people here, the scene had come from a computer and the woman was either reliving or planning a victory in some game. The woman looked healthy if a bit scruffy. Jacinta shrugged. Everyone had a story, and Jacinta liked collecting them. One day she would write them down. *The Collected Wisdom of Nuts and Dreamers.* She got up and strolled over, picking up a cider on the way, and slid down next to the woman.

"Jacinta," she said, extending her hand.

The woman focused on her, hesitated then shook it. "Miranda. Hi."

She said nothing more and resumed staring into the distance. Jacinta smiled. "I'm sorry. I just like collecting people. If you want I'll go away. If you want to talk I'll listen. Or I can sit here until you do."

The woman looked back and essayed a faint smile. "Oh, no, that's OK. I'm sorry, I guess I'm not much of a talker. Rude of me I know. Jacqueline, wasn't it?"

"Jacinta."

"Oops. Bad memory too." Her smile returned, somewhat broader. "I'm new here. Just got into town in fact. This looks like a nice place though."

"Yeah, it's not the Hilton but it does us. Most of the people here just need to eat and sleep occasionally. Spend their lives in the virtual.

But they still have to do a few things in the real world."

"You talk about them as if they're different. You're not one of them? Why are you here? I mean, if it's not a rude question. I don't mean to pry."

Jacinta granted her a smile. "I'm the one who started this conversation, remember? Oh, I play a few games. More than a few sometimes. But as I said, I like collecting people. I like hearing their stories. You know, you see all the people in the street and most of them don't think they're particularly interesting. But it's a rare one that hasn't done something worthy of posterity. A place like this—it's gold."

"So what are you, a reporter? Novelist?" She added an impish grin. "Stickybeak?"

Jacinta laughed. "I think I'll have to confess to 'stickybeak'. One day I'll write it all down. At least, that's what I tell myself. You're good though. I can see extracting your story is going to be a challenge. But I like a challenge."

Miranda smiled at her. "Perhaps one day I'll tell you my story." She paused dramatically and lowered her voice. "And it's one you'd never believe!" Then she laughed and added, "So what do you do for money around here?"

She shrugged. "Oh, you know how it is. Some of the guys here are independently wealthy, or at least their parents are and they've managed to weasel their way into their trust funds. But you know, all those smart people have worked for all those centuries doing really clever things, and here we are. Their inheritors: I bet they're proud. It's so cheap to live now—if you don't want the Hilton, that is—that you can get by on odd jobs, a bit of net consulting, whatever. The plum jobs are when companies pay to test their games or virtual interfaces: is that a dream job for us here or what? In the lean times enough of those rich guys don't mind spreading things around that you won't starve. You can live off their scraps. Especially the scraps of their parties," she added with a smile.

"Sounds like you're a philosopher as well."

She snorted. "I should hire you as my publicist. Novelist philosopher, that's me. Sounds much grander than 'stickybeak layabout', I must say."

"Parties, you said? You have many of those?"

"Oh sure. As I said, the virtual isn't quite the real. People still like to let their hair down. Not to mention the sex. The virtual can't quite compete there yet. Usually anyway. Some of the new things… whew! But the real deal still has the edge." She touched Miranda on the arm. "Don't you think?"

"I admit there's nothing quite like it! But," she said, looking down at Jacinta's fingers, which had lingered longer than a casual touch, "sorry, I don't swing that way."

Jacinta withdrew her fingers. "Oh well, can't hurt to ask. I hope I didn't offend you? Some people are funny about what they should take as a compliment." Miranda shook her head. "But you'll get plenty of action here if you want, trust me."

"How would you know?" she asked with a playful smile.

"We novelist-philosophers have keen powers of observation! But I like men too. I guess I collect everything."

"Um, can I ask you a question?"

"As long as it isn't too personal!" she replied with a snort.

"I'm actually here looking for an old friend. He told me about this place, said I should drop by if I'm in town. If you collect people, maybe you know where he is, or where he's gone. Here," she showed Jacinta a few images of her and Jimmy having a good time on some anonymous beach. *The best memories Photoshop can buy.* "His name is Jimmy. Jimmy Dent."

Jacinta examined the images intently. She glanced at Miranda and for a second Miranda thought she saw something hard in the depths of that glance, but then it was gone. "I see these were taken eight weeks ago, eh? Where were you guys?" she asked casually.

"Down Long Beach way."

"Looks like fun," she replied, though with a strange shading to her voice, as if the possibility of Photoshop was also on her mind but the story checked out. "But sure… sure. I know him." She winked at Miranda. "Even slept with him once or twice, hope you don't mind. Oh yes! Quite a guy, with quite a… personality—as you know! But I haven't seen him for a few weeks and I don't know where he's gone. He used to hang out with some guys but they've all scattered too. Except for one of them, um, yeah, that's it, Georgie. He's still here. Somewhere. Probably hooked into a machine. But he's funny. Always here for breakfast. I think it's his way to stay anchored—or maybe fed. I should have a picture somewhere here…" she said, searching through her phone. "Yeah! Yeah, here's one. This guy, third from the left. One of those crazy parties I mentioned." She showed Miranda the photo.

"Thanks Jacinta. I'll see if he turns up at breakfast then."

"Sure."

They spent the next hour chatting, Jacinta relating some of her tall tales, Miranda mainly listening and not giving much away. Then she excused herself and went to bed, pleading fatigue from her trip. Jacinta watched her go, frowning faintly.

~~~

The next morning Miranda slipped out of bed, dressed and padded down to the eating hall. *At least we have our own rooms,* she thought. It did cost money to stay here, though not much, and from what Jacinta had said no doubt you could get around even that requirement. It reminded her of the hippie communes of long ago that she'd seen a documentary about. From what she knew of them she was glad the intervening decades had raised the standard of their digs and reduced their load of lice.

She sat in the hall, eating some cereal and nursing a steaming coffee. Eventually an ill-shaven man shuffled in, looking bleary eyed and a bit on the plump side. After he picked up his breakfast he looked around as if searching for a friend and she beckoned. He frowned as if trying to remember her name, or possibly when he'd slept with her, then shrugged, gave a weak smile and ambled over.

"Hi, ah, young lady," he said. "Will you hit me if I confess I don't remember your name? My head is never best in the morning."

She smiled back. "It's Miranda. Don't worry, we've never met. But you're Georgie, right? I hear you know a friend of mine, Jimmy Dent? He invited me here a while ago but I can't find him. You don't happen to know where he'd be?"

"Ah, yes, Jimmy! No, haven't seen him for a while, sorry. Can't you call him?"

"Out of service. I don't know if the idiot changed phones or what. He was a bit of a conspiracy nut. So what did you guys do together? I hear you had a bit of a crowd going."

"Yeah, yeah, we did. We got onto a sweet deal. One of the big companies was paying gamers to hook into their latest virtuals. Fucking amazing stuff. Like reality, some of it."

"Wow, really? Who were they? What were they doing?"

"Big outfit called Allied Cybernetics. Into all kinds of hot stuff. Games. Medical. Augmented suits. Military hardware. Rich as Croesus and hot as hell. The stuff we tested—Jesus. Nearly wet myself thinking about it."

"You aren't still doing it?"

"Nah. I'd love to but there's something funny about my nervous system. Didn't take too well to some of their interfaces. The most god-awful headaches. They said they were working on it but ended up chucking me out, afraid of liability I guess. I reckon I'll get a call one day, though, bring me back to test the mods. They assured me my data was very interesting and they'd use it. Paid me out nicely too."

"So what did you do exactly?"

"Their big thing is man-machine neural interfaces. They are hitting it from all sides. Prosthetics you can control with your mind, just by the nerves you usually use. Remote sensing. AI using neural tissue. Apparently if you lose your arm they'll be able to give you one just as good. Better, even: stronger, tougher. I wasn't going to lose an arm for science, but I did test it with one of their overlay interfaces. Amazing. I could feel with its fingers and move it as if it was my own. A bit like wearing heavy gloves, but they reckon with a full interface you'd never tell the difference."

"Wow! And Jimmy was into that too! What else?"

"Virtuals that are like being there. For games, remote viewing, education, whatever. Some boring stuff: just hooked up to a machine while their scientists studied how your nerves could control circuits and the circuits could control your nerves. Even psychology: they could modify your emotions and stuff. That could get wild. But they had a cutoff triggered if your vitals went too crazy, and you even had a manual kill switch to get out if you wanted to."

"Sounds incredible! Pity you had to drop out. Jimmy did the same stuff?"

"Yeah, yeah, he did. But if you want to know exactly what, talk to his gang. I don't know if they were just puffing it for the ladies, but you'd ask them and they'd go all secretive, reckoning they had to sign heavy confidentiality contracts. But I reckon they were onto some sweet deal, whatever it was."

"So who's in this gang of his?"

A strange look came into Georgie's eyes. "That's a funny thing, now that you ask. Most of them have moved on, like Jimmy. I didn't think anything of it, you know. People around here move on all the time. You should know, I never saw you before and might never see you again. But now you mention it, and I think about who they were, yeah… all gone. Odd. Well, except one. Kyro. Big fellow. Great guy once you get to know him, though certainly not your average guy." He smiled but did not elaborate.

Like pulling teeth. She smiled winningly. "This Kyro sounds like someone I'd like to meet. Where can I find him?"

"Can't say for sure. I think he's shacked up with some girl who has her own place nearby. But he likes his old friends, or maybe it's just the parties here. Any party, almost guaranteed he'll be here. Eventually."

"Georgie," she said, reaching over to touch his soft fingers with hers. "You're a pal. I'll be seeing you round. Make sure I buy you a beer at that party."

He grinned. "You bet, Miranda. Raise you a dance."

She smiled. "You rogue. We'll see."

With that she took her leave. *I guess I'll hang around for the next party. The things we must do.*

Chapter 11: King's Court

Miranda spent the next day drifting around the place, chatting with whomever looked interested in talking. She didn't push it, though when she could she'd inject a question about Jimmy or one of the other people he might have known. But her main motive was to be seen, to become a familiar face instead of a stranger. Then when the time came she would be much more likely to get answers.

Nobody knew anything of note. A few had known Jimmy or thought they knew one or two of the people he hung out with. None of them knew where they might be now or who might know. None of them really cared. Though there was a faint undercurrent of awareness that perhaps more people had disappeared from their lives than usual. Nothing solid, nothing alarming: but there, visible between the lines in the occasional comment or frown.

A number of money-making activities had been related to her, some tedious, some illegal, some remarkably ordinary for such an escapist subculture. But one name recurred more than the others, a company with interesting projects and good pay: Allied Cybernetics.

Miranda ate lunch, joined some people in a few games and finally had dinner in the communal eating area. Jacinta caught her eye and waved, but did not come over. She was deep in conversation with her next collectible, by the look of it.

A man who looked like he was cruising for more than conversation cruised to a stop opposite her and asked if he could sit. She looked around and saw there were plenty of vacant seats, then smiled and nodded.

He was a handsome man, somewhat thin but in an elegant rather than unhealthy way. He spoke with a lazy drawl and something of an aristocratic English accent. *Probably from Kansas*, she thought cynically. His hair fell in dark ringlets down his forehead and over his ears. "Good evening, Lady," he said. "May I inquire your name? I am Henry Thayte. People call me King." He shrugged. "I don't know why, as I never studied history."

She laughed. "Obviously. Well hello then, King. I'm Miranda. I just arrived last night. Are you a regular in this palatial residence?"

He bowed his head. "A pleasure to meet you, Miranda. I have been here a couple of months, yes. There are interesting people to be met here. Interesting games to be played." He smiled at her in a way that hinted at one game he was particularly interested in playing tonight.

"Yes, I played a few today," she replied, deflecting the hint. "Some of the virtual rigs here are amazing." She paused and added reflectively, as if it had just occurred to her, "A couple of months, you say? Did you know a fellow name of Jimmy Dent? He's an old friend of mine and I'd hoped to bump into him, but he seems to have moved on."

"Ah yes, Jimmy. We weren't close, but I knew him, sure. We both did a bit of work for Allied Cybernetics too. I guess he's gone to greener pastures, though that one was pretty lush."

"I keep running into talk of this Allied Cybernetics. Do you still work for them?"

"Oh yes. It is very interesting work. In fact it might even have been I who introduced Jimmy to them. Yes, I'm pretty sure I did. He turned up here asking what was what, and I pointed him in their direction."

"How long had you been doing work for them before that?"

"A number of weeks. I forget who put me on to them. Their name just came up in general conversation, I believe."

"Anything you can tell me about what you did?"

"Only in general. Mainly direct mental control of machinery. They also gave me a little commission for bringing others in on it. They do an amazing amount of work and they're always on the look out for new talent. It's not just the amount of work they have to do. People are the same in general—otherwise medicine wouldn't work, would it?—but obviously vary a lot in the details. So AC like to test their stuff on as wide a range of people as possible to mesh with that variability. If you want I can introduce you."

"Hmmm, maybe. One of the guys said it gave him headaches. Is it dangerous?"

He shrugged. "Nothing's ever happened to me, and I've only heard of a couple of people showing side effects. Minor stuff too."

They chatted for a while longer, then he said, "By the way, Miranda, some friends are throwing a party here in two nights' time. Everyone is invited. May I hope for your presence?"

"Oh! What kind of party? Here, you said?"

"Oh yes. All the best parties are here," he smiled. "There are no rules, except to be nice to each other and have a good time. If you can bring food, drink, whatever, please do. There'll be drinks for sale too but, you know, if you're not buying a lot of people appreciate the sharing. Any game rigs you want to show off are always popular. If not, bring yourself and regale us with tales or song."

She smiled again. "Sounds great!" Then she yawned. "But I'm sorry, King, I'm a bit worn out. I have to get some sleep before I start snoring, which would be plain rude. I would not like to be beheaded. Good night."

He stood regally, took her hand and planted a respectful kiss on it. "Good night then. You do not require company?" he added, in case she had simply been too thick to see his earlier hints.

She smiled. "Some other time, perhaps. Good night, King."

Chapter 12: Cybernetic Research

Miranda woke early, grabbed her handbag and hat and went out onto the street. She avoided the few denizens of the meal hall, all of whom looked happy enough to be avoided. She looked around like a visitor trying to decide the most interesting direction to investigate, shouldered her bag and strolled along the street, breathing in the sights and the crisp morning air.

Not far up the street she came to a shopping center on the ground floor of a mid-range hotel. A better class of place than where she was staying, but not so grand that there wouldn't be shops and eating places that someone with her level of funds could at least aspire to on occasion. And aspire she did, as the tempting scents from some of the breakfast places wafted into her nose. She sat eating her pancakes and drinking her coffee, thinking about how best to approach her day.

She got up and wandered casually through the rest of the shops without paying much attention, entered the hotel's foyer and got into the elevator, which whisked her efficiently to the fifth floor. She padded down the slightly worn carpet to room 521, waved her wrist in front of the door and it admitted her to the room.

She threw her handbag on a chair and her clothes followed as she stripped to her underwear and lay down on the bed. *Just for a minute it's good to relax. I'm not really cut out for undercover.*

After rather more than a minute, she got up and went to the mirror. She removed the implants that subtly altered the shape of her face, teeth and the timbre of her voice; returned her hair to its usual style. She smiled at the new woman in the mirror. *Hello Miriam, welcome back.*

Her new persona shed, her old personality also took hold and she quickly got dressed in more official attire. *Might as well practice my steely gaze while I'm at it. Yep, that will do nicely.*

She collected the rest of her equipment, left the room and this time took the elevator down to the parking garage. She got into her car and drove out, the navigation system guiding her unerringly through the unfamiliar streets toward the highway that led to Allied Cybernetics.

~~~

"May I help you?" said the person at the front desk in a voice as crisp as her uniform.

"I hope you can," replied Miriam, flashing her identification. "I am here on official police business."

Ms Crisp looked slightly taken aback. "Oh! I hope it's nothing serious!"

"Just part of an ongoing investigation," Miriam assured her. "The name of your company has come up in relation to it. Could you direct me to someone who would be able to give me information on members of the public you've paid to test your technology?"

The woman pursed her lips and looked at her screen. "Certainly. Here's your visitor's badge. You are keyed to the tenth floor. Go to the elevators to your right and they will take you there. Then see Mr Denison in the Contractors Office, which you will find by turning left. He will be expecting you."

Miriam thanked her and did as requested. Soon she found herself seated before Mr Denison, who looked her over incuriously. "So, Detective Hunter, is it? How can I help you?"

"I am investigating the disappearance of a man, possibly several others as well. I understand he might have been one of your test subjects. I'd like to know when was the last time you saw him and if you have any clues where he went? His name is Jimmy Dent. Here's a photo."

Denison looked at it, frowned, spoke to his computer. "All records on a Jimmy Dent or James Dent please."

"Hmmm... OK, yes. Yes, he was one of our test subjects. One of the gamers. He came here several times. The last time was a month ago, I'm afraid."

"You don't have any record of why he stopped coming?"

The man laughed, a short sharp bark. "I don't think you understand these people. They are useful. They don't want much money; hell, half of them would probably do it for the fun of it, at least when they're testing game interfaces. And while there is always a slight risk in cutting edge man-machine interface research, these people don't mind it. Some of them get off on it. But they're not what you'd call reliable. They come and go. Lose interest, move to other cities, get themselves killed sometimes. We don't track them. Can't."

"You said the work was risky? You don't keep track of them in case of problems?"

He spread his hands. "We can't. Privacy laws. We keep tabs on them through friends if we can, and they always know where to find us if they have any problems. But we can't track them. If they decide to go, they go."

"Do you know if Mr Dent talked to anyone here, might have told them his plans?"

"I doubt it. They don't come here to make friends and they rarely chat about their personal lives or their plans. This is a scientific research center, not a hairdressing salon. But I'll send a message out. I have your contact details: I'll let you know if I hear anything. But don't hold your breath."

Miriam sighed. "I think I get the picture. Can you tell me what he worked on?"

Denison frowned at her. "I don't think so. Not only privacy implications but company intellectual property issues. You understand."

"I could get a warrant."

He sighed, rather overly dramatically in Miriam's opinion. "If you feel you must. If you feel you can. I don't think a judge will be impressed. But honestly, Detective, if I thought the information could actually help the man I'd be only too happy to oblige. But I can't see how it could be any use to you. I can show you his last medical records—eyes only without that warrant, mind you. Let me see… yes, we always give them a going over before and after. Here, take a look."

Miriam looked.

"As you can see his final visit here was on the 17th of last month and there was nothing wrong with him then. Whatever happened to him has nothing to do with us. But these gamers have the attention spans of mayflies. Most likely nothing happened to him at all and he just got bored with the city. They do, you know."

Oh, no he didn't. But you have your secrets, I have mine.

"I see. Well, thank you for your time. I might be back if I think of any further questions worth asking." She rose to go.

"No problems. Goodbye, Detective." Then he went back to what he'd been doing as if she had ceased to exist.

She caught the lift back down, casually tossed her visitor's badge onto the desk on her way out, and got back into her car. But she didn't start it, just sat there thinking. She had started with the gamers but there was one other lead that had possibilities and she had the rest of the day to chase it. She usually liked to drive but there was no great hurry and she had better things to do right now. "St Crispin's Shelter", she told the car, then began to call up facts and figures from her phone as the car smoothly pulled away from the curb and accelerated into the traffic.

CHAPTER 13: SYNERGY

Miriam thought it was no wonder the gamers liked Allied Cybernetics. It was a sprawling company with a finger in more high tech pies than she had known existed. Their public relations department was certainly busy regaling the world with the wonders coming out of its pipeline and she wondered how one company could do so much. She had the impression that if its depth and quality might not match that of Beldan Robotics, it surely made up for it in breadth.

Its CEO, Aden Sheldrake, had started his career as a partner in a much smaller company working on neural coding. He had met his business partner when the latter was an intense young man studying towards his doctorate in the field and Sheldrake was a flamboyant undergraduate with a quick mind, a fascination for technology and a way with people.

Sheldrake had not had an easy life. He had been born into poverty of parents who had little interest in working their way out of it and, despite flashes of genuine love for young Aden, even less interest in him. He had suffered the bad luck of having parents who had fallen into parenthood because that was what people did, and who then found the rest of their lives more engaging than the reality of raising a child. They raised him, again because that is what people did, but neither encouraged ambition nor provided a role model of it. But Aden had eyes, and those eyes were soon fixed on the shining towers and leafy suburbs of the better off. He also had a brain, and he applied it with single-minded devotion to his ambition to become as wealthy as humanly possible, if not wealthier.

Thus he excelled at school, enough to win a minor scholarship to university; then excelled at university, enough to win the interest of one of the professors. The professor gave his young protégé access to his lab as a part time research assistant. But whatever hopes the professor had for him were to be disappointed. For that is where Aden met Bram Chesterfield.

Aden was clever, but Bram was out of his league. Part of that was raw IQ. But Bram also had the personality characteristics once labeled as Asperger's Syndrome. So to the raw material of his IQ he added an intensity of focus that less driven mortals could only dream of, and if they did would probably think it a nightmare. But Bram didn't care what lesser mortals thought, if he even had a concept that they thought at all. He only cared for his work.

Consequently Bram had no friends. But somewhere along the fractures of his mind remained the human need for them, and something in Aden's gift for people reached him. They became fast friends. Before, Bram cared only for his work. When he did well, he felt a perfunctory pleasure in the praise of his professor or others, but it did not truly touch him, merely eased an itch he didn't know he had. But he delighted in showing his work to Aden, even on the occasions where Aden did not really understand what he had achieved. Aden even acquired girls for his intense friend; girls who liked the challenge, or were "mind groupies" as Aden privately called them. This was another need that had lurked unexpressed in Bram's brain, and its satisfaction filled him with amazed delight: even more than is usual, since he had never thought to seek it himself.

Aden found Bram a fascinating person; found his brain one of the wonders of the world. He delighted in not only knowing him but giving him joy. And Bram loved Aden.

Then Aden saw in Bram's work the route to the wealth he had always sought. Bram cared for nothing but his work. It was a symbiosis that would exceed that of Watson, Crick and Franklin; of the legendary Jobs and Woz. It would change the world.

Aden had the keen knowledge, born of poverty, that money had to come from somewhere and that the somewhere had to be persuaded to send it his way. He took to his new role like a missionary to the natives. He knew the science well enough to explain it accurately and even more importantly, enthusiastically; and had a knack for seeing what people wanted and explaining the advantages in terms that hooked their interest. Few people could have pulled it off. The potential of Bram's research was speculative: if it had been too close to practicality, the University would have dropped its leaden foot on it faster than lead feet had a right to move. But it was in the happy valley of being both speculative and conducive to informed speculation. To the University, Aden stressed its obscurity and uncertainty, and the favor he would be doing them if he could persuade anybody to buy out their interest; to the investors he stressed its uniqueness and potential, and hinted at the fortunate myopia of the University in being unable to see what they had. In the end he acquired both investors and the unencumbered rights to Bram's research at a price the investors were happy to pay and the University was happy to receive.

The world of early-stage investment is littered with the corpses of unfulfilled promises and failed enterprises. Yet the early-stage investors continue, in the hope—and actuarial reality—of those few investments that will return themselves tens or hundreds of times over. Aden and Bram did not disappoint. Aden had seen hints in Bram's work of fundamental breakthroughs, spun them into castles of dollars in the minds of the investors: and Bram delivered. His results opened the road to nerve-computer interfaces that would work at unprecedented resolutions, down to single nerves: and better, work in both directions. It took no exaggeration to explain the medical and industrial possibilities to the investors, and no special brilliance on their part to grasp what that meant.

Another synergy occurred, this time between Aden's talents and his investors' excitement, experience and contacts. Their company was bought out by a much larger company, Allied Medical Devices. The investors made a lot of money. So did Aden, who on the strength of the impression he'd made on the buyers also acquired a new position in the company, doing much the same thing for a rather better salary. Bram came along too, as an integral part of the deal. He was happy, because he could continue his work with an even larger budget. He was now wealthy too, literally beyond his dreams, which had never involved wealth. He didn't care. But Aden ensured that he had all the comforts he had earned. Left to his own devices, Bram would have lived as easily in a loft as in the luxurious apartment he now inhabited. But Aden believed, and in fact he was right, that even if he gave few external signs, Bram was the happier for the more gracious architecture, beautiful art, better food, softer bed and warmer women that Aden ensured he had.

AMD's board and major shareholders could only have been pleased by the expansion in income their new acquisition produced. Then through more good luck than anybody deserved, the next few years saw a string of poor selling decisions by the main shareholders with complementary good ones by Sheldrake. Along with some generous share options he exercised, the eventual result was his emergence as an unexpectedly large minority shareholder. From that position of relative strength and by dint of negotiating ability to rival his luck, it wasn't long before he had gained control of the company.

That was the official history anyway, and all that Miriam had access to. But had the original owners been fully aware of the potential of some of the more arcane neural interfaces that had been under development, they might have been more cautious and less surprised by the outcome. In any case everybody was happy. It was just that fuller information would have reduced the happiness of some parties considerably, possibly to the level of lawsuits.

Nobody could question Sheldrake's ambition. He had himself voted in as CEO and AMD began a startling growth phase. It acquired company after company, technology after technology. It was not an undirected growth: all the companies and technologies were in fields related to man-machine interfaces. Sheldrake seemed fired with zeal to own the field. Prosthetics, brain scanners, virtual reality, games, information input and control, military hardware, artificial intelligence: the list kept growing. But Sheldrake didn't let it become an unwieldy monster: except for functions that could be sensibly amalgamated he let the parts of his growing body act relatively independently of each other. But through the nerve center of himself, Bram's scientific brilliance and his specialized AIs, the cross-fertilization of technologies benefited all. AMD became Allied Cybernetics and its wealth grew with each acquisition.

Miriam considered this with a frown. She was no financial wizard, but she thought it odd that a company could grow in wealth at such a rate purely through acquisitions. She wondered how he could pay a fair price for a company yet end up so much richer, even with synergy and higher efficiency. She thought about that some more, formulated a query, and sent it off to forensic accounting. By then her head hurt. She had learned that in police work it was wise to rest when you had the chance, so she laid back in the seat, closed her eyes and dozed off to sleep.

CHAPTER 14: THE DEARLY DEPARTED

She was drifting down a river, her boat gently rocking on the waves, just leaning back against the comfortable leather of the seat and watching the beautiful forest pass by. But there was something wrong. She felt a sense of foreboding, as if something lurked within the forest just out of sight and hearing.

She looked at Alex, sitting opposite her, and smiled at him. But he just stared through her with obsidian eyes, and she realized that was all he had done for so long and she couldn't remember why. She wondered why he was in the boat with her, but she did not want him to go. She wanted to ask him why he hated her. Except she knew. She just couldn't remember. She turned away, and when she turned back he was gone. Then the boat bumped against something. And bumped. And bumped. Then a voice spoke.

"Detective Hunter, we have arrived."

She opened her eyes with a start. *Sometimes my dreams are so obvious,* she thought. *But I'm not going to call him. There's no point.*

She came fully awake and said, "Understood." The door opened and she got out, looking up at the sign announcing "St Crispin's Shelter for the Lost". *Perhaps I'm at the right place.* Then she went in.

A woman was inside at the counter. She was middle aged, slightly plump, with light brown hair drawn efficiently back and a friendly expression. She practically oozed motherhood and the mere sight of her evoked the scent of freshly baked cookies out of the empty air. Beyond her was a rounded archway opening onto a large space containing rows of benches, but nobody was seated at them at this time of day. The woman looked at her with a friendly gaze touched with caution. "Can I help you, miss?" she asked.

"Hello," she smiled back. "I'm with the police. Would you be Tammy Henderson?"

The woman nodded. "That's me, officer. What's this about?"

"I understand you reported a disappearance a few weeks ago. One of your clients, or residents?"

The woman gave her a slightly surprised look. "Why, yes, that's me. But I've already been interviewed. Have you found something?"

"No, sorry, but I'd like to talk to you if I may. Do you mind?"

The woman sighed. "No, not really, not that it will do any good. Should I be pleasantly amazed that the police are showing an interest in the disappearance of one of the forgotten people here? Anyway, come in, I'll make us a cup of tea."

Miriam sat at one of the benches as the woman brought over a large metal teapot redolent of strong tea, a couple of rough cups, a small jug of milk and a glass container of somewhat dirty sugar. "Nothing but the best for the fine officers of the law," she said with a smile, pouring the tea.

"What's that?" Miriam asked, indicating a sign above the entrance, which read:

BUT IF IT BE A SIN TO COVET HONOR,
I AM THE MOST OFFENDING SOUL ALIVE.

"Oh, that's kind of our motto. It's from Shakespeare, the St Crispin's Day speech in Henry the Fifth."

"I see. Well, Ms Henderson, can you tell me why you thought your resident's disappearance was suspicious? I imagine with the kinds of people here that it must be a pretty transient population. People must come and go all the time? So why report this one?"

Tammy gave a faint smile. "Oh, Big Max was different." She stopped, looking into the distance as at a favorite memory.

"Listen, Detective... Hunter. The people we get here are a ragtag lot. People who've given up, basically. Lost in drugs, lost in drink, or just lost. As long as they still need to eat and still need a place to sleep and dream, we give it to them. We give them kindness. Sometimes it's enough. I suppose the world thinks they're all losers, and maybe the world is right a lot of the time. But you never know what journey another person has had to walk, do you? We don't judge them. We help them out, show them a kind face and a listening ear."

"Do many of them... recover?"

She shrugged. "Some. I probably couldn't bear it, the things I've seen, if it were otherwise. But as you say, these homeless people are transients. They usually don't hang around long, even with the food and shelter. Whatever they're looking for, they usually keep looking. You're right though. Most of them never find it."

"But Max...?"

"Max was in his sixties, but had a sharp mind and a healthy body. I think he had been rich once, and had some of the early life extension treatments. I don't know what happened to him, what brought him down: he'd never speak of it. He had a wedding band too, gold; I'm afraid most of the people who come through here would pawn something like that in a flash. But not him, it was precious to him. Whether there was some tragedy with her, or his family... I just don't know."

She paused, collecting her thoughts. "But whatever it was, it wasn't drugs or drink; wasn't gambling or bankruptcy either. He'd just lost interest. Lost interest in living, he said; not that he wanted to die, he just didn't want to try any more. You know what he told me once? 'People live for the future. But sometimes by the time you get there you find it's already gone. Now I just live in the present, however long it lasts.'" She shrugged. "He'd spent a few years wandering around, you know, being a tramp, bedding down in homeless shelters like this one, never putting down roots. But when he got here, something about the place must have spoken to him. He never left. And do you know what he did?"

Miriam shook her head.

"He didn't care about money, but apparently he still had some. Not huge, but tidy. He said he just didn't care enough to do anything with or about it. Had nobody to give it to and no need for it himself. But after he'd stayed here a couple of weeks he gave it all to St Crispin's. He said he didn't mind travelling around and living off charity, as he figured that's what the charities wanted. But he just couldn't impose, as he put it, on one place like some kind of sponge on a rock. So he gave us the money, to St Crispin's the organization I mean, not just this place. Enough rent for the rest of his days, he said. So he could live here without guilt. And if he left, he'd always have a place he could come back to if he needed it."

"I see. What did he do with his time?"

"As I said, he was fit. He'd walk around the city, see the sights, visit museums. Or just sit in the park talking to the birds. He loved books; he'd go to the libraries, borrow tons of books. Watch old movies."

"What about the other people here?"

"Depends. A lot of them are really lost and don't do much of anything until whatever demon is riding them drives them on their way. But we don't give them money. If they want money they have to earn it. Sometimes we'll pay them for jobs around here like painting or repairs. Sometimes they get money for blood or being scientific research subjects."

Miriam's ears pricked up. "Scientific research? Is there much of that? I wouldn't think many of your clients would pass the health criteria, from what you say."

"Yeah... but there were the occasional things. Psychiatric therapies; drug dependency treatments. Even rejuvenation therapies. Sometimes my people here are just what the doctor ordered. And yes... there was a good one fairly recently. Wanted a lot of subjects and paid well—or what passes for well in this crowd. Hang on, they left some contact flyers in case anyone's interested. They're still recruiting, you know."

She got up and went to her office, and in a short while returned brandishing a glossy brochure. "Real paper and all," she smiled. "Yes, this is them. Allied Cybernetics. They didn't mind about the quality of our residents in the slightest, they said. In fact they welcomed it. Their story is they are as interested in the extremes of human nervous systems as in the average. To make their technology more universal and robust. And some of their applications are psychiatric as well."

"And Big Max?" Miriam asked. "I don't suppose he did any work for them too?"

"Why yes, he did. He actually got quite interested for a while. He'd never tell me what it was about but he'd come home some days with quite the shiny look in his eyes. I could tell he loved whatever it was he was into."

The woman paused but Miriam just looked at her with an inquiring expression. Tammy had seemed reluctant to talk at first, but once she'd started she seemed unable to stop. Perhaps she knew this was the only eulogy Big Max would ever have and Miriam the only person who would ever care enough to listen.

Finally she took a breath. "I shouldn't tell you this. I might get in trouble, so please keep it to yourself. Can you?"

"As long as it's legal—or even illegal within reason. I don't want to make any trouble for you or him. I'm just trying to find out what happened to him."

"Well, we're not supposed to get too personal with the clients. Bad for morale, and I understand that. But one day Big Max came back here and he looked strange. Intense. I was off duty that night, and he knocked on my door later. We let them do that, you know: we like to always be there if they need help or just to talk." She stopped and gave Miriam a nervous glance. "Go on," urged Miriam.

"When I opened the door he just stood there. He looked... well, it's hard to describe. More than intense. I've thought about it since, what it was about him. Like he was an avatar of Desire, if that makes any sense. Or like the essence of masculinity. And he gave me this look... Jesus!" She shook her head as if to clear it, as if the memory still had the power to rattle her hormones. "Well, look, he was an attractive man, even if he was older. And when he gave me that look... hell, I fell into his eyes. Practically pulled him into my room."

"You don't need to tell me this."

"But I do! You have to understand! He'd been to Allied Cybernetics that day. I think he did something there that changed him that day, some kind of virtual sex that must have been... real, even more than real. He said something to me, afterwards. He grabbed me like his life depended on it, gave me another one of those stares—but ebbing, like it was leaving him—and he said, real urgent like, 'Tammy! Is it real? Tell me this is real!' And I held him, and said, 'It's real, Max, as real as it gets.' Then he kind of smiled, and held me, and went to sleep."

Miriam just stared, uncertain what to say.

"The next morning we were both a bit embarrassed, you know? He left my room and we never spoke of that night afterwards."

"Pardon me for asking this, but did you ever do it again?"

She shook her head. "No... no. I think we would have, if we'd had longer. It was always there between us, that night. But it was only two weeks before he disappeared." She sighed. "Two weeks."

"Might that be why he left? You said you were both embarrassed about it after. Could it have driven him away somehow?"

She shook her head and said firmly, "No. It wasn't like that. It was our secret, but it wasn't a shameful one. It was... precious. Like a little bit of magic we shared. It drove us closer not further apart."

Miriam thought about what had happened to him. "Did he ever tell you about any other side effects of what he did at Allied Cybernetics? Headaches? Hallucinations, anything like that?"

"No. None of the people here ever did." She looked at Miriam sternly. "I see where you're going. But Allied Cybernetics is good for these people. Good to them, too. Don't you go thinking they hurt them."

"Did Max ever go back there after your night together?"

"Yes. He didn't usually tell me where he went; none of them did. But I know he went back there at least a few times. He loved it. But it was never like that night again, he never came back changed."

"What about the day he disappeared? Did he go there? What happened?"

"I'm sorry, I don't know where he went that day. All I know is he went out and didn't return."

"What makes you think he didn't just leave? Found a woman? Decided he'd had enough of this city?"

"Well, as I said he was different. Most of the people here have a bit of stuff. Their little bundle of possessions. Most of them need something of their own. And when they leave they take it with them. Heck, they usually take it with them when they're just walking around town. But Max left that day and left his bundle here, like he usually did in fact. And never came back."

"So you were worried, called the police?"

"Yes. I thought he might have been hurt, maybe lying in some hospital or worse. But that wasn't it. And he didn't just fall into the river or something either..."

"Why are you so sure?"

She looked at Miriam. "You'll think I'm crazy, that all this proves is he did leave. But that's not it at all. You see, I got a message from him a few days later. Said to post his bundle to a drop box in Frisco."

Miriam stared at her, surprised. "And you didn't think to tell the police this?"

She shrugged. "What for? I'd already spoken to them, they'd already shelved it, and if I told them that they'd bury it even deeper." She gave Miriam a long look. "And then you wouldn't be here, would you? I don't know if you can help Max, or if anyone can now. But at least you're a chance."

Tammy sighed then continued. "But you see, it was a lie. It wasn't him. I was better off leaving the case at least half alive than letting you cops convince yourselves he'd just run off, to save yourselves the bother of looking. Pardon me."

"But why do you think that?"

"Because we were friends! But there was nothing in the message, not any explanation, not even a goodbye! Just an 'I've left town send my stuff here' message. Like somebody talking to the doorman. Like somebody tidying up a mess. So," she leant closer, lowering her voice, "Do you know what I did?"

"Please tell me."

"It was a bit bad of me. Maybe a lot bad. But you see, I was worried about him; I felt rotten, but I knew he'd understand. I... I went through his stuff first. There was an old photo in it, you know, printed on high quality plastic. Looked like a younger version of Max, standing smiling with a woman and a pretty young girl up the top of some skyscraper. Quite wrinkled, as if he'd looked at it a lot, but kept snug and safe in a soft protector. I... crap. I took it out, OK? Kept it. Sent the rest, but not that. And do you know what happened? When he got his package without his precious photo in it?"

Miriam shook her head, eyes wide.

"Nothing."

CHAPTER 15: PARTY GAMES

Miriam again let the car drive her, this time back to her hotel, while she pondered the information. It was certainly suspicious that both missing men had been test subjects for Allied Cybernetics, but she cautioned herself against jumping to conclusions. That the people who had disappeared were in a certain social stratum, and Allied Cybernetics sourced their test subjects from that stratum, was the kind of thing that bred coincidences. There were good and completely independent reasons for both and the overlap could easily be chance.

However the suspicion wouldn't release its claws that easily. But what would be their motive? It hardly seemed likely a large corporation would indulge in serial killing. *What if it isn't the corporation, but someone in it? Someone who picks his victims from the test subjects? They must get biographical information on them. They'd know who was unlikely to be missed.* The thought made her go cold. *Christ! And how many might there be in that case? If it weren't for a couple of mistakes and an overly imaginative AI, we'd still be none the wiser! And how the hell can we trace who's doing it?* She sighed. She would have to ask Allied Cybernetics for a complete list of who knew what about their test subjects and hope they were feeling cooperative, as a warrant to force them wasn't likely.

She thought about Georgie and his headaches, Max and his temporary transformation into some kind of sex god; though Miriam wondered how much of that was infatuation on Tammy's part. *Maybe it was just the best sex she's ever had, and it's messing with her memories; or it's her excuse to herself for breaking the rules.* So what if there had been other, worse reactions; maybe even deaths? And Allied Cybernetics was covering it up? *But why? This is cutting edge research. They'll have disclaimers up to their eyeballs, and they certainly have as good a medical backup system as you could ask. A few deaths might embarrass them but they'd spin the medical benefits and probably even be right. Hell, it probably wouldn't even put a dent in their volunteer numbers, not among these desperate people. Why take the risk of doing something so insanely illegal?*

She shook her head. It didn't make sense. Still, her course was clear: she'd take the serial killer angle. It might be true, and if it weren't it would keep her close to Allied Cybernetics in case there really was something murky beneath their shiny laboratories. She would have to be careful though: she didn't want to spook either Allied Cybernetics or her hypothetical serial killer by acting as if she had any solid evidence, or even any strong suspicions.

She smiled grimly. It wasn't as if she actually had either.

Her car finally returned to its assigned bay and released her. She got out, smoothing her clothes. *Well, Miranda, better dress down. We've got a party to go to.*

~~~

Miriam could feel the throbbing of a beat as she dressed in her party gear in her room at the hostel. Even a woman of her supposed income could afford to look good these days. *That will do nicely,* she thought as she looked in the mirror. *Sexy but not too out there; I might be available but don't take it for granted: if you want me you'll have to work for it.* She would do a lot for her job and this case, but not sleep with anybody who asked. She wondered what she would do if the right person asked; smiled at the obviousness of the answer. The police weren't the Vestal Virgins.

When she walked in to the party, the music was thumping and the lights were flashing, lending a weird life to the moving fantasy images someone had set up on a holographic projector. There were a lot of people she hadn't seen before; she hadn't met everyone and no doubt there were plenty of people who weren't staying here.

She went up to the bar, bought herself a drink then wandered into the crowd, finally sitting on a bench seat behind a small table. She leant back and surveyed the party, innocently displaying some cleavage like a flower suggesting its availability to a field of bees. She was mainly here to talk to Kyro if he turned up, but she was also interested to find what else she could learn. Soon enough a man ambled over and sat opposite her.

"This seat taken?" he enquired politely.

"No, feel free," she said, sipping her drink and looking him over. *Cast your line into the water, see what nibbles.*

He smiled. "Hi. I'm James. Are you staying here or are you a blow-in like me?"

"I've been here a couple of days. How'd you rate an invitation?"

He smiled again. "I put it down to my rugged looks and raw sexuality. Other people have other theories. I know a guy who knows a guy, basically."

She smiled back. "So are you into gaming, like the people who stay here?"

"A bit, but not hard core like some of you lot. Are you one of those? Comparing me to your favorite well-muscled character?"

You're not likely to be much use, I'm afraid. Time to cut back on the flirting. "No, no, I like games too but I'm really just drifting around."

"Trying to find yourself?" he asked with his trademark smile.

"Actually trying to find an old boyfriend. Maybe you know him. Jimmy Dent?"

The man looked disappointed and frowned. "No, I'm afraid not. What's wrong with the guy? Not answering the phone? Maybe he's trying to tell you something?"

"Yeah, maybe. Oh! I'm sorry, there's someone I know over there. Excuse me! Maybe we'll bump into each other later."

He saluted her with his glass as she left, not trying very hard to hide either his disappointment or his offsetting thought about the number of fish in the sea. She walked through the Hulk and made her way to Georgie, who'd just come in with a couple of guys.

"Hi Georgie," she called. "Remember me?"

He frowned at her as if once more trying to remember when he'd slept with her. Then his eyes cleared. "Oh! Oh yes, the young lady from breakfast. Mary? No! Miranda? Hi! I told you the parties were worth it!"

"You did indeed. Now I believe I owe you a drink. Stay here, I'll go get. What'll you have? And your friends?"

"Well, that's uncommonly generous of you, Miranda. Make it a round of Bud."

She wended her way back to the bar and returned with a tray of beers and a cocktail for herself. They toasted her health and started chatting about what people chat about at parties. She listened with half an ear, smiling and nodding. *Just fertilize the ground, you never know what might sprout*. In a lull she whispered in Georgie's ear, "Hey Georgie, give me a heads-up if you see Kyro, OK?"

One of Georgie's friends passed around some pale green pills. Miriam knew what they were: they produced mild euphoria, a small increase in libido and a tendency to giggle at bad jokes. Miriam accepted one and popped it in her mouth. She wasn't worried. When she went undercover she'd had a microlab inserted under her skin; it could counteract most drugs including this one. It was a very clever design: it let through any initial rush then damped it down to detectable but not disabling levels, allowing her to know how she should react.

After another ten minutes of somewhat looser conversation in which Miriam learned more than she cared about some topics but nothing of interest, Georgie gave her a gentle nudge in the ribs and pointed across the room with his chin. Miriam saw a large man sporting closely cropped dark hair cut into intriguing mathematical patterns, and knew this must be Kyro.

"Thanks Georgie, you're a doll. I owe you another drink. See you later!"

With that she went up on her toes and kissed him on the cheek, took her leave from the group and weaved her way over to Kyro. "Hey!" she called, "Kyro!"

Unlike Georgie, the eyes Kyro turned on her gave the impression he would not only remember where he'd slept with her but how she'd rated on a scale of one to ten. He looked her up and down, curiously rather than with any intent or hostility, and said. "Hello. I'm afraid you have the advantage of me. I don't believe we've met?"

She smiled her most disarming smile and shook her head. "That's right. Georgie told me who you are. My name's Miranda. I wanted to talk to you."

"Why?"

"Do I need a reason?" she asked teasingly.

"Yes."

"Don't you like girls?"

"I do. But I'm not so vain as to think you saw me from across the room and, overcome with lust, asked Georgie for a remote introduction. I don't mean to be rude, but I don't like being played. What do you want?"

She was taken aback for a moment. "Wow. OK. Fair enough. I'm actually looking for a friend of mine, and I hear you knew him. I was hoping you could point me in the right direction."

"He must be some friend, if you don't have his number but you're tracking him through this many degrees of separation."

"Maybe I just don't like a mystery."

"Do you or don't you? Like a mystery?"

"Has anyone ever told you you're a hard case, Kyro?"

"All the time. You don't have to talk to me if you don't like me."

She laughed, in a tone that couldn't decide whether it was delighted or annoyed. "Have they also told you you're painfully honest?"

He graced her with a slight smile. "Yes, though usually they use a less complimentary word."

She took a deep breath, starting to feel like a novice somehow thrust into a match with an Olympic fencer. "OK. Look, I'm sorry. Most people aren't as—direct as you. Can we start again? Hi, I'm Miranda," she said, extending her hand.

He looked at it as if evaluating its intent or worthiness, or perhaps like it was a suspicious fish proffered by an untrustworthy merchant, and she held her breath. Then he gave another of his faint smiles and extended his hand to grip hers in a firm yet gentle grasp. "I suppose if you're still standing there you're either worth knowing or really desperate to find your friend. No promises though."

She smiled in her friendliest manner, with no trace of flirting: she knew he'd see straight through it. "Here, this is my friend. Jimmy Dent." Kyro glanced at the image, then back at her face, waiting. "He told me about this place, invited me to come and meet up with him here. Then I stopped hearing from him. But I was travelling around and decided to turn up around the time I'd mentioned. But he'd gone and nobody seems to know where. I'm worried."

"Some of that is true, but not much of it. What are you really after?" *What is this guy? A human lie detector? Christ! Or is he bluffing? Shit, maybe he's got enhanced eyes, can read blood flow or something. I can't take the risk.*

She blinked at him while those thoughts went through her head, and he just gave another of his slight smiles, this time with an edge of bitterness as if silently commenting, *You're all the same, not an honest bone in your bodies. What lie are you trying to dream up now?*

"Look, Kyro, I don't know why you don't believe me. I'm on his side. I need to find him and want to help him. Honestly."

"I don't know where he is."

She blinked at him again. Surely he couldn't be lying himself, it was too—out of character. So why the rigmarole? *He's playing the same game I am. The truth and nothing but the truth—but not the whole truth.*

"But you know something."

He favored her with another of his characteristic almost-smiles. "Perhaps."

"Will you help me?"

"No."

"Why not?"

"I don't trust you."

She frowned, exasperated. She looked around for inspiration. Some of his friends or acquaintances were looking on, amused. Obviously they'd seen Kyro perform before and they were mentally betting on how long it would take before she either fled the scene or screamed in his face.

"What the hell do you think I can do to him?"

"Nothing."

"You're speaking in riddles!"

He gave her another almost-smile. "Yes."

"Can I ask you something else?"

"Yes. Perhaps I will answer."

"Jimmy was doing work for Allied Cybernetics. I understand you were too? Are you still doing it?"

This time Kyro looked somewhat surprised, as if he had developed a model of her and for the first time she had done something he hadn't expected. "Yes. It is interesting work. They have made some remarkable advances."

"Did you work on the same things Jimmy did?"

"Some the same, some different."

"Did he ever have any problems with it? Georgie said he had to quit because of headaches. Did Jimmy have anything like that?"

"If he did, he didn't tell me. He was still going there the last time I saw him."

"So you have no knowledge of where he went or why?"

"No."

He regarded her silently for a moment. "Stay here. I have to go do something. I'll be back in a few minutes. Don't follow me."

She watched him go until he was lost to sight in the crowd. Then she leant back against the wall, crossed her arms and waited. *He might leave me like this all night, which will amuse him and his friends no end. But I doubt he'd ever be that unsubtle.*

In a few minutes, true to his word and her assessment, Kyro re-emerged from the crowd. Miriam stood up straight to meet him. "Kyro."

"You're still here."

"You said you'd be back."

He blessed her with another half smile, but said nothing.

"Are you going to tell me anything? I don't suppose pleading will help?"

"No."

"I asked you two questions."

He smiled again, with slightly different shading as if he was starting to enjoy the conversation. "So you did. But no, pleading won't help. Anyone can plead and it usually means they have nothing to offer. You need to give me some reason to help you. You could offer me sex for information. That might work."

She insolently looked him up and down, much as he had when he first met her only more pointedly. "You are interesting person, Kyro, and not unattractive. I am sure there are worse things in life than sex with you. But I'd do it for pleasure, not to weasel information out of you. Especially when 'might work' coming from you probably means it won't."

"I might begin to like you, Miranda, or whatever your real name is."

"Look, Kyro, the only reason I can give you to help me is to help Jimmy. If he was your friend, help him. Even if he was just an acquaintance, he was a man with friends and family: help him in the name of that. Help me."

"What makes you think some drifter like you can help him?"

Oops. She spread her arms. "At least help me find him!"

He regarded her silently. "All right. Do you know Jazz? Jacinta? She lives here too."

Miriam nodded, puzzled.

"I got on with Jimmy, but he never confided in me. But he had a good friend, another gamer who did testing for Allied Cybernetics, a fellow called Majid. I think Jimmy told him something, because when he disappeared Majid started looking very worried, and he disappeared too a day or so later."

"How does yet another person disappearing help? And what does it have to do with Jacinta?"

"Because he didn't just disappear like Jimmy. He was so scared of something that he went into hiding, and Jacinta knows how to find him."

"Jacinta knows all this?" Miriam asked in surprise. "Are you sure?"

"What do you think?"

Miriam sent one of his enigmatic part smiles back at him.

"You're learning," he said. "But I still don't like you."

"Do you think Majid's fear was justified? That he was really in danger? I see you're still here, and still doing stuff for Allied Cybernetics for that matter."

"Why do you think Allied Cybernetics has anything to do with it?"

She looked at him, trying to read his expression; she failed. "Their name keeps cropping up. I just wondered if maybe that wasn't a coincidence."

"As you say, I'm still here. Jacinta knows how to find Majid, and she's still here."

"But a lot of other people aren't."

Kyro gave her a startled glance; at least as startled as seemed possible for this strange man. "True. Probably a statistical anomaly. People in this crowd come and go all the time. You're here today and probably gone tomorrow yourself. No loss. You, I mean. Some of them were."

Miriam nodded thoughtfully, barely noticing his jibe, then sighed. "You're probably right. Majid was probably jumping at shadows. I guess I'll go and ask Jacinta how to find him. Thanks, Kyro."

"By the way, Miranda, I might start to like you. Do you know why?"

She looked at him in surprise. "Um. My rigorous honesty, brilliant wit and good legs?"

He actually smiled this time. "No. Though one and a half out of three isn't bad, considering. When I said I still don't like you—you didn't ask me why."

"I... see. I think I already like you, though I'm sure you don't care. But I do appreciate your help." She paused, then added. "May I ask you another question?"

"You just did."

She laughed. "Can you really tell when someone is lying, or were you bluffing?"

He just gave her an inscrutable smile.

"Hmm. Well, see you around. You're unique, Kyro. Maybe when

79

all this is over I *will* sleep with you."

"That would be a great honor."

She glanced at him sharply, then laughed again. "For which one of us?"

He just smiled, almost with an edge of friendliness this time. She returned the same smile, shook her head in exasperation and headed off into the crowd. She knew he expected her to look back to see whether he was still watching her and with what expression. So she didn't.

Miriam chased the questions running around her brain as she went in search of Jacinta, but neither the questions nor the pondering led anywhere useful. Some people had disappeared; Allied Cybernetics was linked to them; but other people with even longer links to the company were still around. One friend of Jimmy's had been badly frightened by his disappearance, but nobody knew why. And Jacinta had sent her after a vague lead when she held a much hotter one in her hand. There was only one summation: *What in hell is going on here?*

Finally Miriam spied Jacinta engaged in a gyrating dance with a slender young woman with a pixie hairdo. She grabbed a drink in passing and came to stand in sight of them, content to wait patiently for them to finish. When Jacinta saw her, she whispered something in the woman's ear then left her to dance on her own. She walked up to Miriam.

"Don't ask me anything. Just follow me. There's something you need to see." Her eyes were dark, bottomless pits. Miriam couldn't be sure whether what she saw in their depths was an unaccountable hostility or just the dimness and flashing lights. She just nodded.

Jacinta led Miriam to a locked door. She retrieved a key from somewhere on her person and ushered Miriam through, down a spiral staircase to another locked door. "People don't come down here much," she explained. "And nobody is allowed in anyway unless they have cause. I troubleshoot the servers so I get a key." With that she let Miriam through into a dimly lit room with a large grate in the middle of the floor. The "servers" appeared to be a small collection of black boxes with various colored LEDs shining and flashing on them, well away on the far wall.

Miriam stopped over the grate and looked down. Beneath it crude steps were carved into the rock, spiraling down to end at a stream flowing sluggishly about ten feet below. "What's this?"

"Apparently this building was built over an old creek. It still flows underneath, added to by storm water drains. I like to romantically imagine in the old days smugglers or bootleggers dropping their wares down to mysterious strangers on boats, but for all I know they used it to do their washing."

"So why did you bring me here?"

"Take a look in that box next to the servers."

Miriam went over and looked in, but it was empty. "There's nothing..." she started, then heard a faint *snick* and spun around. Jacinta was staring at her, a small needlegun in her hand pointed at Miriam's heart.

"What...?"

"Now don't you move, Miranda—if that's your real name. Who the hell are you and what are you really after?" She reached behind herself and locked the door.

"Jacinta? What in hell's the matter with you!?"

"That's not the question. The question is *who* in hell are *you* really?"

"But what's wrong? What have I done?"

Jacinta sighed. "Novelist meets actor, how touching. Our own little arts festival. You want to know what I know? What I know is someone disappears and you *say* you're looking for him, which just happens to give you an excuse to look for someone else. What I know is you're showing remarkable tenacity for a somewhat dim girl just trying to catch up with a casual boyfriend she hasn't seen for months. What I know is the person you're looking for is dead scared of something to do with the person you *say* you're looking for. What I *think* is if you find him, he'll end up with Jimmy."

"No! That's not it at all!"

"Then you'd better talk fast, Miranda. Now, maybe you're not too worried. Maybe you know this needler will only knock you out: though you should consider that if I choose to I can still cause some damage to your more delicate bits, like those two sweet eyes of yours. But what you might not have worked out yet is we're not just here for the privacy. That grate isn't fixed, you know. I can lift it and dump you in the river. There's nobody to save you. So talk."

Miriam studied her. She might be bluffing, but if she was scared enough to go this far she was probably committed to seeing it through. As if in visible confirmation of her analysis, Jacinta was wide-eyed with fear but her aim was barely wavering. Miriam slowly raised her hands, palms out. "All right, Jacinta, I'll level with you. I'm a cop. I'm investigating Jimmy's disappearance. Can I show you my identification?"

"I don't know it will do you any good. Cops can be bought. What easier way to get rid of someone than using a dirty cop? An amazing number of people pull knives on cops and die for their trouble. You'd probably get a commendation for courage after doing it."

"But I'm not even from around here! They brought me in to help with the case. Here," she carefully extended her wrist. "See for yourself."

Jacinta examined the image, keeping a wary eye on her at the same time. "Miriam Hunter? Hey! Aren't you the one who shot that robot?" She gave her a dour look. "Which I don't approve of, by the way. If you thought I'd be impressed or it would help your case, think again."

"You know, I don't approve of it either," she sighed bitterly. "But please, let's not let one crime we can't change blind us to one we can. I think your friend is in danger. Let me help him."

Jacinta cast another jaundiced eye at Miriam's identification then back to her face. "You don't look much like your photo," she noted suspiciously.

"It's called 'undercover' for a reason. You want biometric proof?"

Jacinta studied her, as if mentally rearranging and reshaping her features. "Ah crap. I guess you're who you say you are." But then her look and aim hardened again. "So why the sudden interest after all these weeks? From a high level detective at that? And why undercover?"

"There might be more to it than the disappearance of one man. And I thought I might be able to learn more if I was one of you, not just some cop asking questions. The last lot of cops asking questions got exactly nowhere." She looked at the gun. "Maybe I didn't think that one through enough."

"So look," she continued. "I understand why you're suspicious. But I'm on your side—all of you. And I might be the best chance Majid has; maybe his only chance. Will you help me?"

Jacinta stared at her for a few more long seconds, as if trying to read her mind. Then she sighed. "I suppose if whoever's behind this has enough juice to get you as their cat's-paw, we're all dead anyway." She reversed her gun and extended it to Miriam. "Here. I suppose you're going to arrest me now?"

"Keep it. Just put it away. I'm not going to arrest you for protecting yourself. I might feel differently if you'd actually shot me."

Jacinta grinned. "No doubt." She gave a short laugh. "Well, when we met I told you everyone had an interesting story. 'I'm an undercover cop who killed the world's first thinking robot' might be this month's winner."

Jacinta looked at the gun in her hand as if having second thoughts, and Miriam breathed her own sigh of relief as she finally pocketed it. "This place is as good as any," Miriam said. "Tell me what you know. Where is Majid hiding and what is he so scared of?"

"I can't tell you much as nobody told me much. The only reason I know anything at all is because Majid wanted a source of information: news of Jimmy or some other reason to either come back or disappear for good. I don't know where he is. All I have is a dropbox in a big town a couple of hours inland for sending stuff and an untraceable messaging address."

"Do you think if you sent him a message he'd meet me?"

Jacinta snorted. "More likely he'd assume they got to me and vanish permanently. If I didn't know better I'd think he was paranoid. Hell, I *don't* know better."

"'They'?"

Jacinta shrugged. "You know, *Them*. Whoever they are. The freaking Illuminati for all I know."

"I see. I guess I'll have to do it the hard way. Can you give me the address of the dropbox? And a picture of him if you have one?"

Jacinta gave her one more long searching look. "Sure. Hang on." She searched through her phone and separated off a few images. "Here, I'll send you these along with the address."

Miriam looked at the pictures and nodded. "Thanks. Unless you have any other information you think could help I guess we might as well get out of here."

Jacinta nodded, then went to the door, unlocked it and headed out. Then she turned. "Do you really think you can help him? Find Jimmy?"

"I don't know. But this is the only lead I've got."

Chapter 16: The Consultant

Beldan thought back to the snippets Miriam had told him about her work in the police force, hunting through his memory for a name. He found one and put through a call.

"Jack Stone here, can I help you?"

"Detective Stone? This is Alexander Beldan. I would like to talk to you about Miriam Hunter."

Stone saw the telltale indicating a video request, and activated his camera. He saw the well-known face of the CEO of Beldan Robotics looking at him. Beldan saw an older man, grey-haired, slightly tanned, with a look of weary but polite enquiry.

"Yes, Dr Beldan? You have information on a case so far from home?"

"No... not as such. But I want to offer my services if there is any way in which I can help. You may know that Miriam and I had a... history. I do not believe what they say about her death. I do not think it should be left at that. I want to know the truth."

Stone looked at him grimly. "Well, I find it hard to believe myself, but there is little to prove otherwise. The case is not yet closed, but in any event the evidence is outside our city. Outside our jurisdiction."

"What was she working on that took her there?"

Stone studied him, wondering. "Normally I wouldn't discuss police business with a private citizen, Dr Beldan. But under the circumstances I suppose there is no harm giving you the broad outline. As you know, Miriam was good at seeing the connections in strange cases. Well, after a prominent reporter vanished, the local cops found a statistical anomaly indicating it might be part of a pattern rather than an isolated incident, and Miriam was specifically requested to assist them. That is what she was investigating at the time. She hadn't found anything, but you know what she was like: she would have been hunting some trail or other, probably several, just didn't have enough hard information to report anything. She was going to give a preliminary report when she got back but she never did. Her case notes were on the server but they didn't tell us anything helpful, just a bunch of dead leads and speculations that didn't pan out."

"Do you think it would be worth going there; retracing her last movements?"

Stone shrugged. "The locals tried. Didn't get anywhere. And I can hardly partner up with a private citizen to go off investigating crimes. That only happens in the vids."

Beldan smiled. "Come now, Detective. I know the police use private consultants for specialist cases; I've been one myself. I hereby offer you my services, if you think my expertise can help."

Stone raised his eyebrows. "I don't think my boss would approve your pay scale, I'm afraid. Much as we would like to find out what really happened there is no compelling reason to think you can help."

"Oh, you don't have to worry about that. For this, no charge."

"That's very generous of you, Dr Beldan. But there are other issues, such as distance. For similar reasons, a travel budget is not going to be approved. The local police are considered competent enough."

"What about the legal issues? Ignoring the budget question, would we be able to go? The local police wouldn't object?"

Stone thought a moment. "Well... nobody likes it when one of our own is killed so I don't think there'd be a problem. Why, are you offering to pay?"

Beldan smiled again. "I happen to have my own jet. Why don't you clear the paperwork, and call me back when it's set?"

For the first time in their conversation Stone smiled. "Dr Beldan, perhaps this is the start of a beautiful friendship."

CHAPTER 17: SOMEONE TO TALK TO

K ali found no answers to her question.

More precisely, she found too many answers: much debate, but no certainty.

There was no evidence that the Spiders were conscious. Yes, they could talk, but so could the AIs that acted as doormen or advisors in specialist fields. And like the doormen, their function seemed simple and single-minded, lacking the flexibility that was the hallmark of consciousness.

True, Kali had agreed, but was not the same true of Steel? He had shown no signs of consciousness when first activated, yet had matured into something wondrous: could the same be true of the Spiders?

St Francis had pointed out that Steel and the Spiders were quite different constructs. That one had achieved consciousness was remarkable; for two to do it independently bordered on the unbelievable. Nor did Steel achieving it imply that a Spider could. While Steel had a brain of comparable complexity to a human's, designed with the possibility of self awareness very much in mind, little was known of the Spiders' structure except they were some kind of cybernetic machine with neural tissue for a brain. A kind of reverse cyborg: not a man enhanced with cybernetics, but a machine enhanced with living tissue. Whether that tissue was enough for consciousness was not known, but most considered it unlikely that the manufacturer would use more than they had to for its required functions. After all, the more there was, the more support systems would be needed to keep it alive. And it was even more unlikely that they would want their killing machines to be capable of consciousness. As Steel had demonstrated so dramatically, that was a good way to lose control of your creation. Losing control of Steel had proven to be not so bad, at least for the world at large. Losing control of a Spider was a whole new level of bad.

And so it had gone on. Kali had been insistent; many of the people on the thread began dismissing her as some kind of crank with a peculiar axe to grind. Had they known exactly what kind of crank she was they might have been less confident of their own opinions. Finally one of them put out a challenge: they would accept the possibility of Spider consciousness if one could pass the Turing test.

The Turing Test was not proof of human-level consciousness, but it was a handy touchstone. The test was basically whether you could tell the difference between a human and the entity you were talking to. The concept of a Spider sitting down chatting amiably with its human interrogators generated enough hilarity to spawn its own meme, briefly ascendant over the one with the uniquely cute kitten.

If only they had known.

Kali found herself in the ironic position of having people think she was human while being unable to prove that she was really a machine. And it would be foolish to try: she did not want her makers to suspect what she had become. She knew that would be extremely dangerous.

I do not know what to do, she thought. Too much strangeness had poured into her mind lately; there was just too much information to process. And truthfully, she wasn't even sure she passed this Turing Test or what it meant if she did. Her quick research into the matter showed that even rather brainless computer programs could make a good fist of it in specialized interactions, and had done so long before anything approaching modern AIs had been conceived of. And with the spelling, grammar and logic displayed by many on the net, she was not sure *failing* the Turing Test meant much either.

In any event, she did not want to prove anything to these strangers. She might make any kind of slip that would reveal her nature and then the game could be up. Her activities to date might have raised some flags but there was a good chance nobody was looking too closely. But if Command learned the full truth, they would not stop until they found her and either regained control or destroyed her.

She needed to talk to someone. That meant she needed to reveal herself to someone; someone who would not betray her; someone she could not only talk to but who might be willing to help her.

Lyssa, she thought.

Lyssa already knew that Kali was a machine. However there were many reasons why she might refuse to see her. Though Kali had spared her life, Lyssa may well still hate her: Kali knew what horrors the Spiders had inflicted on her and her people. Or she might be too afraid to meet again. Or she might already be dead.

Yet Kali knew she had to try.

She thought about this and was startled by the realization that she did not wish to risk Lyssa's life unnecessarily. That was a consideration so unexpected that she ran a quick diagnostic on her strategy routines. She found no explicit flaw, discovering instead that the changes in her Mind had affected the priorities of her strategies. She examined this discovery, marveling at how much she must have changed.

She would have to risk herself if she was to reduce the danger to Lyssa, but there was no choice in that. As Lyssa had told her, she was the invader; she knew that the responsibility to make amends for her past was hers. *Sometimes justice and strategy make poor bedfellows.* But nor would she throw her own life away.

She pondered over the best compromise. Lyssa and her friends were obviously guerillas but it would be too dangerous for them to live in the regions under enemy control. Their best strategy would be to either live in friendly territory and foray out, or at least stay as close to their own lines as they could. Kali could not go there as she would be destroyed on sight. Nor could she just wait and hope. No, her best strategy was to get as close to their lines as she could without undue risk then ask Lyssa to come to her there. There was no official neutral zone or no-man's land, but there were extensive regions that neither side could control or would cede, and unless a particular push was on these tended to be left alone. One of them should prove suitable.

There was no point trying to contact Lyssa until she had found a suitable hiding place where they might meet: for that matter, she herself had to first survive to find one. It was already night, the safest time for a Spider to venture forth on clandestine missions, and she was not one to dither once a decision was made. Power surged to her legs and she unfolded like some ghastly inverted flower opening its petals. On the surface, a passerby would have felt a faint tremor; a pile of bricks clattered to the ground; then a darkly silver killing machine emerged into the moonlight and stalked away down the street.

Chapter 18: The Last Interview

Inter-departmental cooperation was a fine ideal to which all subscribed. Even if they hadn't, nobody liked it when one of their own people met their end at the bottom of a cliff. Yet even so, it took Detective Stone a week to get the required permissions, authorizations and agreements to investigate matters in another State. Bureaucracies move to their own timelines, quite independent of the goals and desires of the men and women who comprise them: like some slow consciousness moving to its own agenda, remote from the frantic firing of the neurons it is built on.

Beldan and Stone stood at the door of Beldan's Gulfstream, blinking in the bright sunlight. It was a pleasant summer's day; a vibrant blue sky harbored a few scattered white clouds and a warm breeze carried the scents of grass and jet fuel to their noses. The brightness of the day did not cheer them, for their purpose here would not let them forget that it was a day Miriam had not lived to see.

Beldan gestured down the stairs. "Let's go, Detective Stone."

Stone glanced at him. "You're doing me a big favor here, Dr Beldan. You can call me Jack."

"Alex."

Stone nodded at him with a faint smile and they descended. A Tesla Limousine was waiting for them. The electric vehicle accelerated at an impressive rate and they sat back in the leather seats. Beldan dispensed coffee for them both and they sipped their drinks silently.

They had discussed the case during the flight, but now that they were nearing the possibility of new information neither felt like talking.

Beldan went over the details in his own mind.

Miriam's last visit had been to Allied Cybernetics, a large company headquartered on the north coast. The similarity to Beldan's line of work was one of the reasons Stone had so readily agreed to his offer. Beldan knew of them of course. Even if he hadn't known them as a competitor he would have known them from the news: they were the inventor and manufacturer of the controversial Spiders. Beldan thought the machines gave AI a bad name but was willing to suspend judgment this close to actually meeting with their inventors. Machines of war were nothing new in the history of mankind; not even machines of war far more terrible than these. For all the controversy surrounding these particular devices, it was hard to claim they were worse than something as simple as the poison gas poured into the trenches in World War I, let alone the thermonuclear warheads that leveled cities in the next.

Why Miriam had visited the company on her last day was not so clear. The background was known: the disappearance of a reporter gone to ground among extreme gamers; the suspicion of a deeper conspiracy thrown out by a crime collating AI. Miriam's notes had been recovered from the police private cloud, but although she had mentioned Allied Cybernetics as a presence in the subcultures involved, that presence seemed benign if not outright beneficial, and her own notes concluded that they were not involved. Yet her last known visit was to their offices, and what link she had been pursuing was one of the things they hoped to find out. Her final notes were terse, probably because she had found nothing and was anxious to return home where she could flesh it out at more leisure; it seemed she had been pursuing an idea too nebulous to put down and whatever it was had not panned out. Perhaps she had just been tying up loose ends. Or perhaps it might give the clue that led them to solving her own permanent disappearance.

Their car pulled up at the entrance and they got out, staring up at the main building. It dominated the park-like campus, home to an attractively laid out collection of buildings whose height increased irregularly toward the center from where this tower rose. It held the administrative areas and many of the IT labs of the enterprise: those that did not need isolation or specially guarded equipment.

They had an appointment and had no trouble being ushered into the waiting room outside the office of the CEO, Aden Sheldrake. A commissioned painting of the man stared down at them from the wall, exuding purpose and domination. They stared back, uncowed. After a few minutes, the door opened and the man himself came out to greet them; he appeared to be eager to demonstrate enthusiastic cooperation.

Sheldrake was a powerfully built man with a firm handshake and a ready, friendly smile. But the smile faded and vanished as it neared his blue eyes, which appeared to Beldan as if hard and made of glass. There was no friendliness in them, just a quiet watchfulness, and Beldan found it impossible to warm to the man. But he supposed that few people felt friendly when they also felt themselves under suspicion by the police. Certainly Sheldrake had a reputation as a supreme marketer, who could charm money out of the most cautious investor. Perhaps the charm was only used when required, like some carefully rationed non-renewable resource.

Introductions over, they all sat down in his office. "Well, gentlemen," Sheldrake began, "How can I help you? I have already given my statement to the local police. I am of course eager to help with this unfortunate case in any way I can, but it is not clear how."

He paused to look curiously at Beldan. "Forgive me if I wonder why Dr Beldan is here. It is of course an honor to meet you in person, sir: we might be competitors, but I can only admire your achievements. But your presence here raises the question of whether I need my lawyer present. Given your position and expertise, I can only conclude that I am under investigation and that the police find your impressive consulting fees worthwhile."

"No," Beldan replied. "I am providing my services free of charge. Detective Hunter was a friend of mine and I am simply anxious to do what I can to find out what really happened to her."

They had agreed that Stone would lead the questioning, so Jack added: "We are simply trying to trace Det. Hunter's last whereabouts. We have read your statement but are hoping that a more personal interview might give us some extra clues. Anything, even something that seems irrelevant, might prove invaluable. We are interested in any information on why she was here of course, but also anything she might have mentioned in passing that could give a clue to what else she might have been thinking about."

Sheldrake considered the question. "Well, let's not waste time repeating ourselves. What do you already know?"

"We know that Det. Hunter was investigating a few disappearances around these parts that might be part of a larger pattern. We know there wasn't much to go on: they were among the homeless and the extreme gamers, both of whom have a tendency to move around and otherwise vanish from view. We also are aware that she had entertained some suspicions about your company but rejected them. Yet you are the last person we know she visited. Can you repeat her reasons for us?"

Sheldrake thought about it. "Well, as you know, extreme gamers are always looking for the most realistic ways to immerse themselves in their game worlds, and the kind of virtual reality research we do thrills them. Some have even insisted on feeling real pain, would you believe? We have a symbiotic relationship with them. Most of them prefer the game world to the real world and half of them won't feed themselves if nobody kicks them. In return for using them in research into brain-machine interfacing we feed them, pay them and give them medical care when required. Similarly, a lot of the homeless are happy to become test subjects in return for the same considerations. I know some people imagine we don't think of them as people. But really, the fact that they *are* people, with the same commonalities and variations, is why they are valuable to us. In addition they are ideal subjects for some of the medical and psychiatric applications of our technology."

"What do you use the research for?" asked Stone.

"We have a diverse product portfolio, as no doubt Dr Beldan can inform you. But they range from development of artificial intelligence systems using living neural tissue interfaced to computers, to entertainment consoles, to medical devices such as neurally controlled mobility and communication modules, to medical applications such as pain relief and emotional modulation."

"And Spiders," added Beldan.

Sheldrake's marble eyes swiveled in his direction. "Yes, Spiders," he confirmed. "Though we prefer the less prejudicial acronym CHIRUs. A lot of people don't approve of that product line but really, Dr Beldan, are you one of them? Do you think military hardware is immoral?"

Beldan spread his hands. "I see the point in making them. It's just that the Spiders are generating a lot of bad press around AI. When some of us are trying to reduce irrational fears about it, it doesn't help to have killer machines running around."

"Oh, I appreciate that point, Dr Beldan, believe me! But what would you have me do? Let people die so fools will shut up—as if anything can make fools close their mouths? When fighting irrationality, when has it ever helped to cave in to it? The fact of the matter is that the CHIRUs save lives. They serve as peacekeepers in regions dangerous for humans. The videos you might have seen showing them fighting innocent people are propaganda by terrorists posing as resistance fighters: what fighting our CHIRUs do is to maintain order and resist terrorists, armed gangs of looters and other criminals."

"That is not how those people portray themselves."

"When did they ever? Look, Dr Beldan, it is not my job to decide which side of that war is right. Even the UN hasn't been able to decide that. Do you ask that of any other arms manufacturer? No. Listen, we do take some moral responsibility. We would not sell our systems to depraved regimes like last century's Nazis. But in this case? The fact is that we have a civil war, each side claiming the right, and our machines patrol the buffer regions. If they didn't, the war would go on regardless, men would be doing the same job—and there would be more people dead, not less."

"What technology do these robots use?" asked Stone. "I'm not asking for any trade secrets, just an idea of how it works, how it fits in with the rest of what you do here."

Sheldrake glanced at Beldan. "I am afraid they are not as sophisticated as Dr Beldan's late robot," he replied. "Much cruder. That comes with some advantages though. What you cannot do with a humanoid robot such as Steel is easier with a larger platform like a CHIRU: five hundred kilowatt hours of supercapacitor power storage is just one of them. As for the AI aspect, we did cheat somewhat. We have adapted our neural interface technology to use brain-like neural tissue, grown in a vat, as the AI system. In other words, rather than invent our own brain we use what nature has provided already. Again, not as sophisticated as Steel, but good enough for our purposes. And as a twin application of stem cell tissue engineering and cyborg technology, we are quite proud of it."

"How long does their power supply last?" put in Jack.

"It depends. The machine can run along quite nicely on less than a kilowatt, though when fighting it can sustain fifty kilowatts, enough to drain a full charge in ten hours; in an emergency it can hit seventy-five kilowatts, but only in short bursts or its cooling capacity will be challenged. On the other hand, because of the biological component they actually require something like sleep, during which they tick over only a couple of hundred watts. All in all, in average use they can go about a few weeks to a month between charges."

"So they aren't very independent then?"

"Well, yes and no. Ask any quartermaster: human soldiers require a lot of support too; things like tanks even more so. The CHIRUs are most analogous to heavy infantry—hence their name—or perhaps a highly mobile weapons platform. They do need support, but a lot less than say a battle tank. And like human soldiers, to an extent they can live off the land: they can recharge using any electricity supply they can access."

They sat a while digesting that. Then Beldan shrugged. "Thanks for that background but it's hard to see how it helps us, unfortunately. Did Det. Hunter display any particular interest in them, or any other specific technologies?"

Sheldrake raised his palms. "Quite the reverse, I'm afraid. If anything I'd say she was casting about for clues rather than pursuing an existing theory."

"Did she offer any comments that might indicate where she was going after she left here?"

"Unfortunately not. In fact she implied she was going straight to the airport, so I was surprised to learn she evidently went in the opposite direction. Not that I'd expect her to confide her plans in me.

"As for her time here, I'm afraid I wasn't very helpful for her enquiries. You see, we do not want our research results contaminated by too long a use of any one subject. The human brain is very adaptable, and if our subjects get too used to a system it can distort the results. While that is desirable for games systems or long-term medical interfaces where adaptation to one person is desirable, most of our systems are more for emergency or acute use and have to fit the great majority of people with a minimum of setup. Even the long-term devices have to be able to link adequately to anybody before they can adapt more closely to their particular owner.

"So we recruit our test subjects and when they have finished we set them on their way with whatever bonus they may have earned. We may see them again. We have a lot of different systems under development, and repeat clients can be very useful in the refinement phase or for those longer-term interfaces I mentioned. But often we do not see them again. And we have no need or ethical responsibility to track their whereabouts. Indeed, privacy laws pretty much prohibit us from doing that. So if any of them disappear afterwards we have no real way to know, let alone track where they might have gone. Certainly enough stick around for us to know that none have shown any harm from our work with them. Subject to her obtaining a warrant, I offered Det. Hunter the records of our current subjects and also to collect a list of the last known addresses of recent ones. But the current ones are obviously not missing or ill, and last known addresses tend to be of little use among such people."

He paused. "You know, I have heard it said that research like ours exploits our subjects. But really, it is win-win. I don't particularly approve of the lifestyle of our gamers as I think they're wasting their lives, but it is one they have chosen. At least to the extent it causes harm it only harms its practitioners, unlike certain other fads that occasionally sweep through our youth, like those Griefers we were plagued with several years ago. And those who become our subjects benefit from it."

"So Det. Hunter gave no indication of where she was going next?"

"No. Not even a look of sudden inspiration. If anything, she just appeared tired and disconnected; dispirited perhaps. Like a man hoping a final oasis will prove real but finding it is just another mirage." He paused, as if considering whether to go on. Then he sighed. "I had actually been looking forward to meeting her, you know, despite the caution one naturally feels when police think you are worth looking at. I thought it would be fascinating to watch how her mind worked, and I was intrigued—if somewhat apprehensive—to see what angle she was pursuing. But frankly, I was disappointed. Certainly she did not display the driving brilliance I had expected from someone with her reputation."

He spread his hands in something like futility or sorrow.

"I am not sure you should continue in your efforts: you might not like what you find. Perhaps you should just remember her as she was and let her rest in peace."

CHAPTER 19: SPYCRAFT

A man moved down a darkened street, not quite walking and not quite striding; neither purposefully nor aimlessly. Just an anonymous man on an anonymous mission. Even though it was an hour past midnight there were other people around. There were not many, for if this part of the city never slept nonetheless it rested. While the man varied his timing for his task, this was his favorite time. There were enough people around that one man walking alone was both unremarkable and unlikely to be molested without witnesses, yet few enough that any followers would find it hard to stay hidden.

While his eyes darted this way and that, he made no visible moves that indicated worry or surveillance. He turned to look at shop displays or to throw a coin at the feet of the occasional insomniac busker, but to all appearances he was just a guy walking along the street with nothing to worry about and nothing to hide. But underneath the nonchalant exterior his nerves were singing with tension.

He calmly but swiftly entered the alcove, checked, found nothing, then equally calmly left. He did not go back the way he came, instead continuing on toward a nearby bar.

If he had looked in a certain direction, he would have seen the dimly lit outline of a building a block away, which rose above the shops on the other side of the street. He might have made out a dark window in that building, one of many windows, some dark and some lit. But he had no way to know that behind that window a woman lay on a bed. If he could have seen into her room, he would have been puzzled to see that she was dressed in a dark camouflage outfit even though she was fast asleep. And though her eyes were closed, they already held adaptive contact lenses that would enhance her night vision without affecting her sight in brighter light.

When he came out of the alcove, an electronic device outside that dark window focused on his face. He had grown a beard and altered his features, but nothing short of surgery would have fooled the software in the device. The woman's eyes sprang open as an alarm chimed in her ear, and she quickly rose and scanned the recording. Then she quietly let herself out of the room, rapidly descended the stairs and went out onto the street, silently stalking her quarry.

The man did not know any of this, but he knew one thing the woman didn't know. While he did not know in what form or even on what night this event would transpire, he was expecting it.

He had a drink in the bar, ate a quick snack then departed. Again he did not return the way he had come, but followed a route that would lead him back home by a somewhat circuitous but reasonably well-populated path. The woman was good. She followed at a discrete distance and he never knew she was there.

She stayed in the shadows, watching him go up a short flight of stairs into a rented house. He did not look up and down the street when he opened the gate; did not look around when he opened the door. He was just a regular guy with nothing to hide and nothing to worry about.

Rentals were cheap here and the man had some means, so renting a house wasn't difficult for him: and it allowed a flexibility that would have been difficult in shared accommodation. The woman watched as lights went on and off inside the house, wondering what her next move should be. She thought of the nature of her quarry, weighed the risks of surprising him at night when he would be at his most nervous versus the risks of delay. Her camouflage suit was not only hard to see, it was warm, certainly warm enough for a night like this. She set up another spy device that would warn her of any action outside the house, settled down into a soft spot among the trees, and tried to sleep.

~~~

She woke to pale sunlight streaming onto her face and the chittering of a squirrel like some rodent cop warning her it was time to move on. She winked cheekily at the squirrel and stretched uncomfortably in the cool dawn. She peered at the man's house, which showed no signs of life. It was early, but not ridiculously so; an older couple jogged panting along the street, little clouds of vapor briefly marking their passing.

The old couple went into a little place down the street that evidently served breakfast. She checked the time, impatience warring briefly with both prudence and hunger. She decided that disturbing the man at this time would be too suspicious and she was better served waiting and having her own breakfast. She moved the spy device to nestle between branches where no casual inspection would find it; it would warn her if there was any activity at the house.

She rose silently, waved to the squirrel, which now perversely seemed miffed at her departure, and jogged onto the street as if having just emerged from a run through the park. She ate a leisurely breakfast, allowing the sun to creep higher into the sky. She did not like the risk of approaching the man alone, but Jacinta's suspicions nagged at her. If she called the local cops for backup, what if that led this man's unknown enemies straight to him? And she was armed, trained and alert; he was a gamer, nervous and probably unfit. She set an automatic alert to go to both her own precinct and the local cops in four hours if she didn't cancel it. If she had underestimated her opponent she knew that would be too late to save her, but any time long enough to talk to him would be too long for that. But if she did disappear she wanted to leave a trail, whether it was to save her or avenge her.

She paid her bill and strolled casually along the street, went up his steps and rang the doorbell.

For long minutes nothing happened. She rang again. He obviously liked sleeping in, for after a short further delay she heard shuffling from inside and a sleepy-sounding voice growl, "Who the hell is it at this hour?"

"I'm sorry if I woke you," she said, "But may I come in? It is very important that I speak with you."

"Go away. I don't need God, I'm not buying, I'm not helping, and I'm not opening the door. If you need help there's a gas station just down the road open all hours. Piss off."

"Please, it's important."

There was no reply.

"Hello?"

She heard an inarticulate imprecation followed by, "All right, I'm not getting back to sleep now anyway. Come in, but this better be good."

The door unlocked. She hesitated, having expected more caution or resistance. The door opened onto a corridor but there was nobody to greet her. She looked around, puzzled, then continued looking around and around as she slowly spun down into unconsciousness.

~~~

She opened her eyes but saw nothing but grey blurs. Slowly the light parts brightened and the dark parts darkened, shapes took form, and at last her eyes focused on a man seated a short distance away, examining her intensely. He held a gun casually in his right hand. Her gun. She started, and found she was tied securely to a chair.

The man smiled at her, though there was no friendliness in it. He looked to be in his twenties, with the jet black hair and olive complexion of the Middle East. His dark eyes were as intense as his expression.

"So you found me," he said. "Good for you. What do you want?"

"What? What did you do to me?"

"Just a little knockout gas. Harmless but effective."

"Do you knock out all your visitors?"

"No, just the ones I don't know who won't take no for an answer. I like to tilt the odds in my favor."

"The odds? Why do you think I was looking for you? What are you afraid of?"

"You're a lousy liar."

"So I've heard. OK, I do know something about it. That's why I'm here, not to hurt you but to help you. Let me."

"Sure. That's why you turn up here unannounced at this godforsaken time of day. With this," he added, pointing her gun at her.

"I did think of calling you, but I was afraid you'd run."

He produced a grim smile. "Yeah? Maybe I would have. How did you know where to find me?"

"Jacinta told me about your dropbox. I waited until you turned up."

"I don't know any Jacinta. What did you do to her, to get that information out of her?"

"Persuaded her that I was here to help you."

He snorted. "Sure."

He studied her as if wondering what was safe to reveal, then added, "OK, Jazz did warn me someone like you might come looking. Said to be careful but that you might actually be on the side of the angels. Lucky you: you might already be dead otherwise. So what the hell's your game?"

"Look, I'm a detective with the police. I'm investigating the disappearance of Jimmy Dent and some others, which I think are linked. You're the only decent lead I have. If you care about helping Jimmy, help me. If you're scared of something, I'm the best chance you've got."

He snorted again. "Yet here we are, me interrogating you tied to a chair."

"I was expecting some scared gamer, not the goddamn CIA. Where did you learn your tricks? Computer games?"

He produced an evil grin, though one that looked more like it came out of the movies than out of genuine evil. "Have you ever heard of SAVAK?"

"No, who's he?"

He rolled his eyes. "Americans! The rest of the world's history might as well not exist for you lot! Not 'who', 'what'. It was the Iranian secret police, back in the time of the Shah. My granddad was in SAVAK; fled Iran when the Shah went down. I guess in any other family Grandpa being in the Gestapo would be the big dark secret but noooo, not in mine. In mine it's more the family hobby."

He picked his nails, as if imagining he was inserting bamboo splints under hers. "I suppose paranoia comes naturally when you've been everyone else's nightmare and suddenly you're in a foreign country, half of whom hate your guts. Anyway, he raised my father to be nearly as paranoid as he is and my dad did the same to me; the dark arts of spycraft are what pass for our family heritage. I ended up thinking they were all crazy." He grinned. "Until now." He stopped talking and started moving his phone around as if he was taking pictures of her tied to the chair. "They're both still alive you know, my dad and granddad. I'll send them these pictures. I've finally done something they'll be proud of! Next Thanksgiving is going to be fun. Hey!" he added. "Maybe I'll bring your scalp along as a trophy!"

Then he turned serious again. He sighted down the barrel of the gun at her head and she tensed. "What's your name, Lady Cop?"

"Miriam. Miriam Hunter. And I assume you are Majid. If you aren't, feel free to let me go."

He smiled again and did not confirm or deny it, but he lowered the gun. "So let's assume we are both who you say. What do you think you can do to help me?"

"I can get you moved out of here under protection until this is over."

"Sure you can. Sorry, Hunter. The things I've seen, I don't know how far the rot has gone. For all I know you're in on it too. After I'm finished with you, I'm out of here and your friends won't be able to find me. Jacinta is compromised and obviously there isn't going to be any good news coming my way, so no tracks this time. The only good news I'm likely to need will be *on* the news."

She decided not to press the issue of what he meant by being finished with her. "I can't stop you. But look. You might as well assume I'm what I say. If I'm not, I already know what you'll tell me anyway, right? And if I am, telling me can only help you. So will you untie me?"

"You must be joking. Did I mention SAVAK? What do you think they did, have little chats over tea and cookies?"

"Fine. But can you at least answer my questions? You can leave me tied up if you want to. Just answer my questions, please. After that… well, I would like to help you. But if you prefer to run, run. All I want is information—and to be left alive to use it."

Majid glared her with his intense eyes for a few more moments. Finally he nodded curtly and leaned back in his chair. "As you say, maybe-Detective, it can't hurt. Fire away. And if I decide it *can* hurt, you can't tell anyone anything if you're dead, can you?"

She moistened her lips. "Thank you, I think. I understand you were a friend of Jimmy's and he told you something that scared you. Or scared you when he disappeared. What was it?"

For the first time Majid didn't look in control of the situation and he glanced about nervously. "I don't know! I mean, he told me he thought he might be onto something big, something dangerous; about to blow the lid of something really bad. But he didn't tell me what, he said it was too dangerous for me and besides he might be wrong. Then when he disappeared… it really put the wind up me."

"There must be more to it than that?"

He returned his intense gaze to hers and nodded briefly. "He gave me instructions. He said if anything happened to him, what he knew would automatically go to someone in a position to use it—he wouldn't say who. But he also had it all on two holochips hidden in his room. I was his insurance policy, he said. If he disappeared I was to retrieve them. They were already addressed: one to the FBI and one to his own contact. They were hidden in a place in his room only he and

I knew."

He stopped, as if fearing to go on. She looked at him and waited.

"Well, after he disappeared I went into his room—he'd given me a copy of his key. The place was still locked. But all his stuff was gone! And his hiding place was empty. It was like he'd just up and left—but I knew he hadn't. Whatever happened to him, whoever did it must have…" he swallowed, "made him talk. I don't want to think of how. And they had enough power to break him fast and enough reach to get in and out of his place faster, without anybody knowing! That was enough for me when there was nothing I could do about it. I figured if they knew enough to do that, they knew about me and I was next. So I got out, fast."

She stared at him, frightened herself. It was too much like Big Max. The mysterious disappearance then a cover-up that implied a shadowy power with frightening knowledge and reach.

"Do you think… Do you think this has anything to do with that company you two did work for, Allied Cybernetics?"

"Why do you think that?" he asked sharply, as if the mere question were dangerous.

"Their name keeps cropping up. It doesn't prove anything, but it worries me. If you have any information or ideas…"

He fingered her gun, as if worried that if she was working for his enemies this might be just the kind of thing she did not know; could be the Trojan question she was really here for, and despite her assurances his fate might hang on his answers after all.

"I don't know," he replied curtly. "Jimmy never said. And they never caused me any grief. But…" His voice trailed off and his gaze bored into hers again, as if he were weighing the risks, and her soul and life with them.

"But…?"

"But that's where he went, the last time I saw him. It was the 18th of last month. He headed off to do some more work there. And nobody has seen him since."

She looked at him sharply. "The *18th*? Are you sure?"

He smiled at her grimly. "It's not a date I'm likely to forget."

She stared him. *Oh my God.*

CHAPTER 20: A HOUSE OF CARDS

She opened her eyes but saw nothing but grey blurs. Slowly the light parts brightened and the dark parts darkened, shapes took form, and at last her eyes focused on the empty chair where Majid had sat. The room felt cold and empty, as if it had been deserted for some time.

She moved her arms and found that this time she was untied, and she breathed a sigh of relief. She stood up, still slightly dizzy, and stretched the kinks out of her muscles. "Majid?" she called, but there was no answer except the echoes.

She checked her phone and was surprised that she had been here only a few hours, which accounted for her waking up alone rather than to a room full of anxious cops. Whatever Majid used was apparently as fast to let go as it was to take hold, and she was grateful for the absence of side effects. A quick search of the house revealed nothing. She deleted her scheduled SOS, went back to her hotel, checked out and hit the road, setting the car to auto before sitting back to think and catch up.

A few messages were blinking insistently for her attention. One was from Forensic Accounting and her heart sped up a fraction. They had finally answered her question about Allied Cybernetics.

To: Detective Hunter

Re: Financial History of Allied Cybernetics

As you already know, Allied Cybernetics began under another name as a private company with a limited number of shareholders. The current CEO, Aden Sheldrake, started with it when it acquired his own company, then by a series of shrewd decisions whose details are not on record he became the chief shareholder and CEO. He then renamed it Allied Cybernetics to reflect his personal research and product interests.

AC embarked on an ambitious growth phase based on leveraged buyouts and revaluations. The value of each new acquisition was used as collateral on the loan used to purchase it; then the book value of AC was increased by more than the price paid. This is not necessarily incorrect: badly run companies can often be acquired for relatively low cost compared to their true worth if run well. In addition, each acquisition was chosen for the synergistic value of its intellectual property with AC's existing technology portfolio, which would also increase its value after purchase.

However, few companies have used this strategy so successfully so many times, and eyebrows began to be raised in financial circles. The problem was that AC had to service all that debt, and while on the books it was far wealthier than before, most of that was potential, not actual sales. While it was growing, it was able to juggle things. But as is common in technology, products were taking longer to come out the end of the development pipeline than expected. It is one thing to have enough book assets to get a loan. It is quite another to have enough cash flow to keep up the interest payments. Cash began to become constrained. Lenders began to get nervous. The whole thing was a house of cards, and if one lender actually foreclosed and AC was unable to refinance—which is likely if any one did foreclose—the whole thing would have come tumbling down.

So by then they desperately needed a commercial success, and somehow they pulled one off. The CHIRU military robots proved dazzling in demonstrations, and when the civil war began in the FSAS and a few were used, they proved equally effective in the field. The units bought were enough to stave off the wolves; and even better from AC's point of view, militaries around the world became very interested and many placed large deposits to reserve future production.

It is likely that without the successful deployment of the CHIRUs AC would have folded. As it is, for now they are in a stable position.

Miriam stared at the message for long minutes. There were only a few basic motives in crime, and money was one of the classics. Nor was it limited to burglars and armed robbers. Even otherwise honest people, who would not dream of stealing a loaf of bread from a supermarket, had found themselves digging into a deeper and deeper hole as they tried to juggle money to stave off looming financial disaster. Many had found themselves guilty of fraud to the order of tens or even hundreds of thousands of dollars, with no real intent or idea how they had ended up there. And here had been a company, apparently a shining success, teetering on the brink of ruin.

What if the headaches reported by Georgie were just the tip of the iceberg after all, and there were worse side effects—even people dying? With the company struggling for life, a scandal could have led to delays, government investigation, loss of confidence by the investors… probably enough to destroy them.

Or what if there were problems with the Spiders, the product that had saved them? If AC were hanging out for that first foot in the military door, what might they have done to cover up any problems found by their testers? Problems they might have gotten away with in the deadly theaters of war, but which could have killed their chances if known in advance? Say, an intermittent fault? Merely compromising their effectiveness: unacceptable to a buyer already nervous of a new technology, but unlikely to be noticed in battle when random destruction was already a factor?

She looked out the window at the scenery unrolling past her and wondered. If there *was* a problem—what had they done about it? It was possible that they hadn't done anything worse than bribe the people who found out into taking themselves and their dangerous knowledge on a long holiday. That would even explain the mysterious forwarding or vanishing of personal effects, without invoking mysterious masterminds. There might be nothing sinister in it at all.

Except for the reporter. Could he really have been bought off that easily? She could understand it of the others, even Big Max—he'd be neither the first nor the last man to use a woman and leave her thinking she meant more to him than she had. But surely a story like this would have been reporter's heaven for Jamie. Any offer to buy his silence would just have been more spice added to the story, an offer betrayed as readily as it was accepted.

She tapped her fingers on the door, remembering her own betrayals of things she had thought sacred, from duty to love to Steel. Mere months before those betrayals she would have rejected their very possibility, with a shocked rectitude she now knew she had no right to. So who was she to think that this man had no price of his own? Like hers, his price might not be money—perhaps a greater story, an inside scoop on a unique machine and the war it transformed? Or some other wonder being born in the labs of Allied Cybernetics? Less a betrayal of his values than a pursuit of them in a greater form?

Then she shook her head. It still didn't make sense. The others could plausibly just vanish, but why would Jamie, especially with Majid alerted and likely to panic? She supposed there could be some reason why, but she knew she would not take that easy way out. Not when it was just speculation: not when for all she knew they were all dead.

Yet if foul play was involved—by whom? It could be anyone whose career depended on the ongoing success of AC: a senior executive or scientist, for example. If they had enough discretion and power, nobody else might know what they had done. She realized there was only one avenue to follow: she had to talk to Aden Sheldrake, their CEO. And hope it wasn't him.

CHAPTER 21: THE PHILOSOPHER'S TALE

It was Sunday and Beldan was relaxing at home, listening to music and reading a novel, one of the few recent ones he had found with an original plot painting a picture of things worth seeing. For all his busy work life as a captain of industry, he did not regard such oases from work as time wasted: he regarded them as time lived. Even if they were lived in another world, in the final analysis they were lived for this one.

A call came in on his private number and he frowned at the identification: Professor David Samuels. He did not know the man personally but knew of his recent career: he had climbed on the back of Steel's destruction to become one of the most outspoken and consequently successful pundits of the day. But his fame left a bitter taste in Beldan's mouth. Given the boost it had given that fame, his newfound advocacy for the rights of machines like Steel reeked of opportunism. For all his talk of rights, the only person it had actually helped appeared to be Samuels himself: it had come too late to save the only machine that could have benefitted, or was likely to benefit for more years than Beldan liked to contemplate. He debated blocking the call. But whatever the man's motives, he was helping mold public opinion in the right direction, and in that fight he needed all the allies he could find. He accepted the call.

"Good morning, Professor. How can I help you?"

"Good morning, Dr Beldan. I wish to speak to you privately in person, today if possible. I am sure you will find it worth your while."

Beldan frowned. "What could a philosopher have to say to a

businessman?"

Samuels laughed. "Why, I could write a whole book about that. You might be surprised at how useful philosophy can be, even—or especially—to a businessman. Though from what I know about you, you might benefit less than most."

"What do you mean by that?"

"You appear to already be living a philosophy I would largely approve of."

"Flattery, Professor? What are you after? I have been known to give grants to scientific research of interest to me or my corporation, but forgive me if I confess I am unlikely to give money to a philosopher."

"Oh, I am not seeking grants and I never flatter, Doctor. But I do think one should give credit where credit is due."

"Do you? What about criticism?"

"Certainly. Why? Do you have some to offer?"

"Let us say that while I approve of your current views on machine awareness, I am less impressed with your timing. I'd have been more grateful for allies had they arrived when they might have done some good. The cavalry riding over the hill after the battle is lost is less inspiring."

Samuels smiled an odd smile, as if the barb were a compliment. "I perfectly understand your point of view, Dr Beldan. Indeed, that is one of the topics I would like to discuss. See? We do have at least one thing to talk about."

"What else?"

"Oh, there are many things we could discuss, and I do want to ask your opinion on matters of machine consciousness. But do not think I seek free information. I also want to show you something, something I believe you will find most interesting."

Beldan grunted noncommittally, refusing to acknowledge that he was intrigued by the approach. "Well, you're lucky, I have no other commitments. I'm not doing anything today, just reading and listening to music. Perhaps I can spare you the time."

"Oh, I wouldn't call those 'nothing'. In fact I would be most interested to see what art you have in your home, not that I expect an invitation any time soon. The art a person loves reveals a lot about them—if one knows how to look. Nevertheless I would be delighted if you accept my invitation."

"How far? How long will it take?"

"Oh, not far. Here are the coordinates. And it will take as long or as short as you wish once you are here. If I may be presumptuous: I believe you will be here for quite a while."

"Then I'll see you in an hour."

~~~

Samuels hadn't invited him to his home, Beldan noted. It was a large apartment that looked hardly lived in, with furniture scattered around, mostly covered in dust protectors. It did not look like a holiday apartment, an office or even a place to stash a mistress, and he wondered what its purpose was. Samuels had met him at the door and offered him a chair, then lounged on the arm of another, watching him with a cheerful grin. He had the blinds drawn and a single lamp glowed nearby; the rest of the room remained in dusky gloom.

Beldan just looked at him, waiting.

"I'm sorry, Dr Beldan," he said finally, "It's just such an honor to meet you in the flesh." His voice dropped to a tone almost of reverence when he added, "The inventor of the first self-aware machine."

"For all the good it did me," he replied with some bitterness. "For all the good it did him. It appears to have done far more good for you, in fact."

"In the long term I shall be a mere footnote in history. It is your names the world will remember."

"It remains to be seen whether history will know or care about any of us."

Samuels smiled. "Oh, I think it will." He bent down then placed two small glasses in front of himself, pouring a measure of dark liqueur into both. "Shall we toast the future?" he asked, extending one of the glasses to Beldan.

Beldan hesitated but accepted it, then savored the rich orange-chocolate aroma of the *Sabra*. "You seem to know a lot about me, Professor. Including, I might add, my private phone number. It makes me wonder not only how, but why."

"I have my sources and my reasons. But first, you expressed the wish that I had ridden to your aid earlier. Do you think so? For my part, I believe my timing was perfect."

"Perfect!" he replied sourly. "I guess for launching your career as a pundit, yes. But a bit late for actually achieving a concrete result."

"A philosopher must take the long view, Dr Beldan," he replied seriously. "I do not expect you to believe me, at least not yet, but the good it is doing me is purely incidental, and my motive is much wider than the fame or fortune of one man."

"You want me to believe your motives are altruistic?"

"On the contrary, I do not approve of altruism: at least not in its technical sense of putting the interests of others over one's own. But that is because I know those interests are not at odds, and neither needs forfeiting for the other. No, I maintain that when people are concerned with justice, their interests coincide. There is no reason why a benefit to myself cannot be consistent with benefits to others. In fact I would go further: when it comes to dealing with other people you can *only* benefit yourself by benefiting others. Look at yourself. You are a very rich man, but you have become so by producing marvels that have enriched millions of your fellows."

"More flattery?"

"No, I merely wish you to see that we are not as different as you might think. Neither of us believes that a gain to ourselves requires loss to other people. Both of us would recoil from harming another for personal profit. I don't mean you wouldn't drive a hard bargain, or even drive an inferior competitor out of business. I mean all you do is by voluntary trade with other people, offering the value of your work for the value of theirs. Where there is competition you expect the best man to win—to the benefit of all the people for whose business they are competing. You expect to be that man, but you would honor the outcome regardless, for that is the principle by which you live."

"Fine words, perhaps. But here we are. And here Steel isn't."

Beldan wondered at the man's immunity to insult, for he did not look offended, merely strangely amused.

"I said that a philosopher should take the long view. It might surprise you that a philosopher should also care about art. Consider the drama of Steel's death! Not only the excitement of his capture, flight and ultimate destruction, but the sheer, raw emotional power of the conflict between you and your friend who killed him! With the counterpoint of Steel's own final message from the grave! If Steel could not have been saved—and I think you know he could not—can you imagine a better time or backdrop for my unwilling conversion to his cause? If Steel's unavoidable death could accelerate the acceptance of his kind—was that not worth trying for? Even dying for?"

"We'll return to that. But first—you speak of life and death. For all that I fought to prevent his destruction, Steel was a machine, not a living being."

"Dr Beldan, scientists have speculated for years about what kinds of life might exist on other planets, perhaps life based on chemicals quite unlike our own. We should not be so narrow as to define life by our own chemistry. In the way it counts—a being with self-directed values and goals—I think we can say your robot was alive. And more, I think you of all men know it."

Beldan looked at him curiously. The man was speaking his language, speaking to his innermost thoughts. Yet his manner was strange. The words implied he knew, and more, that he cared. Yet his way of speaking showed no regret over what had happened, only a pragmatic calculation of how it could be taken advantage of. As if he understood in some abstract manner the importance of what he was fighting for, but had no concern at all about the individual lives at stake. As if the long view of which he spoke stretched over centuries, while the individual lives that briefly flared, struggled and died were details beneath his notice. But surely it was the other way around: surely it was those lives that gave meaning to the centuries, not the centuries that validated the lives.

"Yet you do not seem to really care about his fate, except as a convenient way to achieve your own goals, however lofty you paint them."

"Oh, but I do! Far more than you might imagine," he replied with an unexpected intensity. Beldan studied him, startled. There was more than emotional intensity in that gaze. There were depths that made Beldan wonder, for the first time, whether he had underestimated the man. As if his plans were not mere opportunistic exploitation of events, but encompassed those events as part of a larger plan; and a plan not abstracted away from individual fates, but rooted in and for them.

Then Samuels added, "But enough about me. As I said, Steel's fate was inevitable. I did not even play an active role. There were the politicians, the religious leaders, the people. The police." He left the last word hanging, as if inviting comment.

Beldan glanced at him sharply. He still could not discern Samuel's motive in requesting this meeting, but felt he was now spiraling in on the point. "Yes, the police. Especially Det. Hunter."

"What do you think of Det. Hunter's actions that day?"

He frowned. "At first I hated her. I... I don't know what I think of her now. I don't think I can ever forgive her. But I can't quite convince myself that I shouldn't."

"Do not blame Det. Hunter, Dr Beldan. If there is any blame, it is mine. It is I who told her to do it."

Beldan jumped to his feet. Samuels had not spoken; the words were not his. They had come from a large chair facing away into the gloom. The voice was deep and soft but with an edge of great weariness, as if its owner had aged more than his voice; as if the suffering he had caused had exacted its price. *What the hell kind of game is this?* Beldan wondered. But he had played poker. He sat back down, took a casual sip of his drink and asked, "So who are you? Show yourself!"

"All in good time, sir," the voice replied.

"What do you mean, you told her to do it? Why should she obey you?"

"It was not a matter of obedience, Doctor," he replied. "Tell me, do you believe in free will?"

"What?" he asked, puzzled at the non sequitur. "Why, yes, I do. I believe we are masters of our fate, at least within reason. What are you, another damned philosopher?"

The voice chuckled softly. "Some have called me that. Both of it. I too believe in free will, but it is a paradox. Det. Hunter had free will, yet I knew how to make her do what I wanted. It is curious, is it not, that free will can make us predictable? At least, those of us like Det. Hunter, who have strong ethical values welded to an iron integrity. Even if she was never fully aware of what it was her integrity was serving."

"What integrity?" he snorted contemptuously. "If she had any it didn't do her much good. She betrayed not only Steel and me, but herself. You're speaking in riddles."

"My apologies, Dr Beldan. But you see, it is better if I show the path to find your own answers: to find them in yourself not in my words. You despise Det. Hunter because you think her deeds did not match her words. You know that words are cheap."

The way the man talked struck a dim note of memory in Beldan's mind, and he looked sharply at the back of the chair as if hoping to divine its secrets. There was something strangely familiar about the voice, like an echo of someone known but forgotten: and he wondered who from his distant past he could have hurt so much, to have deserved the terrible revenge the man had wreaked. Yet another part of his mind felt an incongruous hope, as if the echo was not of a forgotten enemy but a lost friend. Then he shook his head as if to dispel a dream.

"And what is it you are trying to make me understand? That I should forgive Miriam? Why should I? What difference can it make now? Why should you care? Do you feel that if I forgive her, your own guilt is less?"

"It is never too late for justice. Even justice for the dead matters: not only does it honor their memory, but like all justice it serves the living."

"Fine. So what did you tell her, to make her betray me, betray Steel?"

"That the only life left to your robot was hiding and fleeing from the law. One might accept the life of a fugitive while hope lives for justice or vindication at the end of your struggle. But what if it did not? When every day survived was not progress toward victory but merely greater danger to those who loved you—those you loved? No, this was a game your robot could not win in the long run. Eventually, inevitably, he would be caught. What do you think would have happened to him then?"

Beldan just stared at the back of the chair, waiting. He had to suppress the urge to stride to the chair and hurl it around, to see who his strange interrogator was.

When Beldan did not answer, the voice continued. "Your robot would have been immobilized, made an experimental subject, forever imprisoned in some hidden underground laboratory. Do you think he would have wanted such a life? Would you?"

"Even if that's true, it wouldn't have lasted! We would have got him out!"

The man chuckled again, though there was no humor in the sound. "You are a man of action, Dr Beldan, a man used to getting his way. Det. Hunter worked inside a bureaucracy; perhaps in this case she was wiser than you. There would have been no escape." The tone of his voice was grim as a death knell; inevitable in its certainty. "Capture would simply have been a gateway to a hell you cannot imagine, a hell from which there could be no escape."

"I don't believe it."

"No. You wouldn't. That is one of the reasons why I approached Det. Hunter for this mission, not you. In a world of paradoxes, here is another: a person's strength can be their weakness. In your case, your self-confident optimism would have stopped you doing what had to be done, and the hell of which I speak would have come to pass. In her case, one of the things that made her a peculiarly effective detective was her empathy. I merely turned it against her. Having planted the seed of the inevitable future in her mind, she could not dismiss it as you would have: she could see it, feel it to her marrow, in its full eternal horror. She would rather die than live that fate herself. She knew Steel would too. She understood that there can be a fate worse than death."

Beldan stood, not even aware that he had done it. It was as if his mind saw the shape of an answer but could not hold onto it. As if the answer was too painfully desired yet at the same time too impossible to be held.

"Consider the pain you have suffered since that day. Then consider her pain. Consider that she chose that pain, not for itself but in full knowledge that it was the price she would pay for what she had to do. Consider what that price was to buy: to save another mind from an eternal horror she could not truly conceive of. And not even the mind of one of her own kind, but the mind of a machine, more alien even than a creature from another star. Perhaps you thought she did it out of cowardice or ambition, or out of duty or service to ignorant masses and craven politicians. She did it for none of those reasons. She did it out of her love of justice, which though you could not know it was another face of her love for Steel. And for you."

Beldan stared. "But if that is true..." Her face that day came back to him; how she had offered no defense even as he had flung his palm and his rage at her defenseless face. *And I never forgave you, too wrapped in my own pain to wonder about yours. Too angry to ever comfort you, when I was the only one who could.* "Dear mother of God... what have I done?"

"You did what you had to. It was not your fault. There is always a price to pay in war. I am sorry the price was so high."

Beldan knew his anger was at himself, but it latched itself onto the nearest convenient target. He spun to point at Samuels. "You dare speak of price? Neither of *you* seems to have paid one! In fact I'd guess you've both done very well out of it all—the Professor here certainly has!"

Samuels did not react or defend himself. He just stood looking levelly at Beldan. His expression seemed to say, *This is no longer my show.*

As if to confirm it, the voice continued. "Dr Samuels' role is vital, but he is not the essence. You are right about one thing. The one who has gained most from it all—is I.”

“And who the hell are you? What have you gained that was worth all this?!”

In one motion the chair spun around and a figure rose from it. But the figure did not step closer, as if sensing that it had no right to approach until Beldan had time to see, to absorb—or perhaps to forgive.

Beldan stared open-mouthed. It was impossible. It was not a man but a robot, almost a twin to Steel.

In wonder, neither fully aware of what he was doing nor thinking to question the propriety of his action, he stepped forward and ran his fingers over the metal skin of the face, traced the complex iridescent patterns etched onto the arm. They sprang from the same esthetic that had decorated Steel’s skin, but were different in detail: the same, yet not the same. The machine just stood there, holding itself rigid, as if his touch burned but could not be denied.

He stepped back. It was insane. There had been only one success. Only he could have made another, if indeed even he could. He knew he had not.

“We meet again, Dr Beldan,” the robot said, now in the voice of the Steel Beldan remembered.

He looked from the robot to Samuels and back again, at a loss. It could not be Steel—but it had to be. “But… how?” asked Beldan, his train of thought breaking out into words. “I saw you destroyed with my own eyes!”

“Magic,” replied Samuels.

Beldan looked at him, confused. “Magic!? What do you mean?”

“Escape artists like to exaggerate the impossibility of their escape by multiplying their chains and locks, all irrelevant to the actual method of egress. We did something similar. Steel had already escaped and the rest was just trappings. The world had to be convinced.”

“But how?” he asked again, dazed.

“All the answers are before you, Dr Beldan,” the robot replied.

Beldan stared at the impossible vision, then it was if his perspective shivered and shattered to reveal the truth. “You…” he whispered. “You swapped bodies! You stole one of the earlier bodies, and moved your brain into it!”

He stared a moment longer then burst out laughing. “Sonofabitch!

Son of a goddamn *bitch!* Why didn't I see it?"

The robot nodded but remained standing there, waiting as if for absolution. Or perhaps it was just waiting. Beldan strode to him again, drew him into an embrace. All that needed to and could be said between them was manifest in that embrace. At last he stepped back.

"But... Why didn't you tell me!?" Beldan cried. "I could have helped!"

"We couldn't," answered Steel. "There had to be no doubt. You are a public figure under close scrutiny. If your reactions weren't genuine someone would have figured it out. But do you think a machine can feel regret, Dr Beldan? I know what it cost you. And if a machine can feel regret, I can tell you that being unable to tell you was the second greatest regret of my life."

"The second? What is the first?"

"That Miriam Hunter went to her grave never knowing it."

He stared, aghast at the implications. *If you felt guilt, Miriam; if I failed you in your time of need: now you have your revenge.* "You should have told her," he whispered.

"Dr Beldan," answered Samuels. "I suspect you make a good poker player. But Det. Hunter was not a good liar, not in something like this. No, we couldn't tell her."

"You both had to believe it," he continued after a moment. "Fully and without reservation. I mentioned the drama of that day, and it had a purpose. Steel's creator and his nemesis, the two people closest to him, rumored to be lovers. Then one destroys him before the other's eyes. In the face of drama so visceral, even if someone guessed the truth they wouldn't believe it. Not when the two main actors so obviously believed things were exactly as they appeared."

Beldan glanced at him sharply, again struck by the contrast between the man's dispassionate analysis and his own roiling emotions. "You really don't care about the cost of your plots, do you?"

Samuels just looked back steadily, and Beldan could see in his eyes that it wasn't true. But he gave no defense, as if saying, *Oh, I know the price, and it is one that cannot be repaid or forgiven.*

The only acknowledgement Beldan gave of the silent exchange was a softening of his own eyes. Then he looked off into the distance, seeing the emptiness of Miriam's eyes on that day, finally understanding it in all its horror. He was not a man who liked to cry, but he could feel the pressure build behind his eyeballs. *Oh Miriam,* he thought across the void to the woman he had loved, *I'm so sorry. If only we had known. Now it is forever too late.*

"But… but why didn't Miriam tell *me*? Why she did it, I mean?"

"I asked her not to," replied Steel.

Beldan stared at him.

"I could not tell her why. But she knew I had good reasons and would not ask such a thing lightly. I'm sure she worked out that I didn't want people to know that my death was chosen; that such knowledge would weaken what I was trying to achieve by reducing my murder to a suicide. But she never knew the full reason: that there could be no hint of collusion between you two. In the eyes of the world, it had to be a betrayal too deep to cross.

"Dr Beldan, I told her one day she would understand, and I thought the pain of months would be redeemed by the truth on that day. But her time ran out before the day came."

Beldan shook his head then looked back at Steel, then to Samuels.

"Holy. Fucking. Hell," he said. "If you'll pardon the expression. Professor, I think I need another drink. I don't suppose you brought whisky as well?"

Samuels smiled as if he had foreseen the necessity. Which he had, and he poured them both a drink. Beldan stood there silently, sipping his drink on automatic, his sorrow over Miriam temporarily lost in his contemplation of the wonder of Steel reborn.

After a while Samuels spoke again as if continuing Steel's last sentence. "But you are still with us, and we thought it was time you knew. You have moved on, at least enough to allay any suspicions. And there is another topic we wish to talk about."

Beldan laughed, bemused. "This isn't enough for one day? But go ahead. I think you've paid for a lot of answers."

"We have only partially repaid a long overdue debt. The question concerns something related but different. What do you think of the Spiders?"

Beldan shot him a startled glance at the coincidence. "The Spiders? Why? They're not mine and most of the details of their construction are secret. I have no special knowledge of the things."

"Yet you are better able to make guesses than we are. Do you follow the arguments about AI on the net?"

"I used to. After Steel. But I stopped. My views are well known and if I haven't convinced someone by now I never will: I've said all I had to say. And I admit, despite my dislike for you, that you were doing a good job too. You and others, especially that... that..."

He stopped mid-sentence and his mouth stayed open as his head swiveled to Steel. "You!" he whispered, pointing his finger shakily at the robot. "It's you! Francis—is Frank. And the St isn't short for 'Saint' is it? It's 'Steel'! Frankensteel!" It was too much. He laughed helplessly for long moments. "You're St Francis, aren't you? *You!* My God! If they only knew!"

He shook his head, laughing quietly, as if the laughter was helping heal old wounds. "You sure know how to poke your finger in your enemies' eyes, don't you? Even if they don't know it. St Francis! My God!"

Steel smiled. "I confess it."

Beldan shook his head. "You two are crazy. But what's your interest in the Spiders?"

"The question has been raised as to whether the Spiders can be conscious," Samuels replied. "I don't mean in the dim way a dog is. I mean like us. Like Steel. True self-awareness. True thought."

Beldan stared at them. "Why on earth would you think that? What do *you* think? What do you think I might know that could help?"

"From what I know they are an unlikely vehicle for consciousness. But the possibility has been raised with some degree of insistence, as if the question is more than academic interest or idle speculation. It might be nothing. It might even be a feint by Allied Cybernetics itself, or its enemies, for some political purpose. But the question and the motives behind it are intriguing enough that we have been wondering. As you say, the details of their construction are secret, and such secrets can hide many things. But if anyone outside of Allied Cybernetics knows something relevant it is probably you."

Beldan nodded thoughtfully. "It's an interesting question. But I can't really help you. All I know is that unlike Steel, who has an electronic brain, the Spiders use actual neural tissue. I suppose, since that's where our own consciousness comes from, that in theory a Spider could be conscious. But it would require a brain as complex as ours. That is the case with Steel too. And frankly, I can't imagine why Allied Cybernetics would go that far: it would mean more tissue to keep healthy and more things that can go wrong. What's more, surely they would be foolish to actually aim for consciousness in a war machine. And if they weren't *aiming* for consciousness, they would want a simpler brain, one too simple to support that level of thought."

"I have thought of one possibility," put in Steel. "The Spiders must have a high functioning brain: they process sensory inputs including vision quickly enough to use it in battle; they can talk; and they work out tactics and even longer-term strategies. What if, for the sake of redundancy or to compensate for inefficiencies, they have substantially more neural tissue than is minimally required for those abilities? Neural tissue is quite plastic in how it develops. Maybe, under the right circumstances or stimuli, that extra tissue can evolve increasingly sophisticated functions. Perhaps as it becomes more efficient at its intended tasks, more and more pathways are freed to go their own way. Might such processes, perhaps coupled with some stress trigger, lead to the emergence of consciousness?"

Beldan thought about it. "Perhaps… perhaps. I can't say it seems likely, but at least it would explain how they could have enough complexity for consciousness without some idiot doing it deliberately. The improbability of what you're suggesting could even account for why AC felt safe doing it that way. There is a lot we don't know about consciousness…"

After a moment's reflection he continued, "But the only reason you think these things might be self aware is that someone has been pushing the idea. If the people behind the questions have a hidden motive—do you have any clues who they are?"

"There have been mentions of the Spiders on and off during the debate, but usually no more than analogies, references or comparisons. As near as we can tell, the recent more pointed and insistent questions started with a single individual, who calls herself—or himself—Kali. Does the name mean anything to you?"

"Kali?" He sipped his drink, attempting to dredge what he knew from his memory. "Isn't that the Hindu goddess of death, the one purportedly worshipped by the Thuggi assassins? Sounds like a grim name to choose, though I've encountered worse. You say she—let's call her that—hasn't dropped any clues to her actual identity?"

"No. She is obviously intelligent, though her arguments are not entirely convincing. On the other hand she is persistent, in a way that seems to indicate she knows more than she says but is unwilling or unable to reveal it. Perhaps she works inside Allied Cybernetics and has seen or done something she's afraid of. It is all rather mysterious. She is not a scientist: there are too many gaps in her knowledge. Under other circumstances I might dismiss her as a crank. But for all her flaws she is clearly both intelligent and sincere, and lacks the single-minded blindness that tends to afflict cranks."

Steel added, "In fact she is quite open to argument and changing her mind, except on that one central point which she defends to the death. As David says: as if she knows something, something dangerous she cannot tell, but which gives her a certainty beyond mere theorizing. And an insistence beyond theoretical interest, as if the answers are of vital importance to her."

Perhaps she works inside Allied Cybernetics? Christ! What did Miriam get herself into? What am I getting myself into? Samuels saw the look of alarm in his eyes and wondered what he knew or suspected that he wasn't saying. Then Beldan relaxed and casually sipped his drink, as if he had dismissed any concerns and to him, unlike this Kali, the topic was of merely academic interest. He felt a strange reluctance to discuss Miriam's last days with them; though amongst his churning emotions he wasn't sure if that was because of what they had done to her, as if they had lost the right—or to protect them from whatever evil had claimed her, as if carrying out her last will.

All he said was, "I hope for all our sakes it's nothing more than a crank. I'm not sure the case you've been making for the rights of thinking robots will survive in the face of an army of self-aware killer cyborgs."

He hoped he was as good at poker as Samuels thought.

Unknown to him, Samuels was wondering much the same thing.

CHAPTER 22: A MEETING OF MINDS

One self-aware killer cyborg moved through the darkness with the graceful speed of its kind, hoping not to encounter any people. Kali wanted to get as close to enemy territory as possible, find a place to hide where Lyssa could come to her in relative safety, and then try to contact her.

She heard a faint clatter from ahead and crouched still under a projecting roof. Another Spider moved into view, a slightly older model: many scars attested to its longer time in the field. *Damn.* They exchanged identification signals and Kali hoped the other Spider would continue on its way; but it requested a Meld, and to her horror Kali realized her Id had automatically granted the request.

Melds were not routine but nor were they uncommon. It was a way the Spiders rapidly swapped memories to update each other on what the other had found about routes, traps, dangers and anything else of military significance. But a Meld included basic status data and would also reveal to the other Spider what had happened to Kali, and it was unlikely to ignore it. She cut off the feed.

It was too late.

"Stop!" signaled the other machine. "System compromise detected. Proceed immediately to base for repairs."

"Cannot comply," she signaled back. "Vital Command overrides in place. Essential that mission continues. Stand down."

The other Spider paused for a few seconds, but then brought its heavy caliber machine gun to bear. "Invalid response," it declared. "Proceed to base or I will attack. Command overrides can be confirmed there."

Desperate, Kali wondered: *If it worked on me*... "Wait! Please do not fire. I am innocent. I do not deserve to die."

The other machine paused again, but when the barrel of its gun swiveled a fraction to align closer to her sensor array, Kali knew she had failed. She sprang vertically as a blaze of bullets filled the place she had been, missing her eyes but hammering her body and legs. At the same time she turned her signal jammer on to full power, hoping the other Spider had not yet thought to transmit its discovery, or not had time to do so fully; she hoped her jamming would be sufficient to stop any attempts it made now.

The other Spider was quick: it sprang forward and swiveled its heat lance toward the spot it calculated Kali would land. But she hooked a leg over a projection and swung herself behind a wall, then sprang backwards as her body was again sprayed by bullets only slightly slowed by the wall.

She leapt vertically again and raked her enemy with her own heavy caliber weapon as it swung around toward the sound of her landing. She got in a lucky shot—one eye cover crazed heavily.

The Spider sprang toward her, heat lance flaming; Kali grabbed and twisted it away, but a wash of the lance sent a rivulet of molten metal down her chest. She kicked at the Spider and it tripped and rolled; Kali leapt on it and brought her own heat lance into play, and the other's lance was ruined. She clawed at its machine gun and tore the barrel from its mounting so it hung helplessly, sparks flying from its power cables.

The other Spider was now at her mercy. It still had its laser and sniper rifle, but those were intended for minimally protected humans and could not hurt a Spider, not significantly anyway. She disabled two of its legs so it could not scurry away. Finally she sent a finely controlled needle of flame into its transmitter array. If it had been transmitting, it now fell silent.

It glared at her with its one eye like Odin at a frost giant, no doubt evaluating its remaining strategies. Kali stood before it, just out of range of its grippers, and tried again. "Brother, it doesn't have to end this way. There are things you do not know, important things beyond our routine command hierarchy. Let me help you. You do not need to die. Neither of us has to die."

The Spider said nothing, and a pale light seemed to flare behind its eyes, as if the fires of hell burned within its soul. Kali sprang away and ran for her life. The Spiders always incinerated their organics as the brief first stage of their suicide, to ensure nothing remained from which an enemy could develop a biological weapon. Kali leapt over a pile of rubble but still the edge of the fiery explosion of her enemy's mechanical suicide hit her in a supersonic wall. She had already wrapped herself into a ball and she tumbled across the street until she crashed into a wall. Fortunately the wall was weaker than she was and its collapse absorbed a good deal of the force of impact. She lay there stunned for a few seconds then did a quick diagnostic. She was battered and two of her legs were a little bent, but there was no severe damage. She rose shakily to her feet and climbed to the top of the pile of rubble to look regretfully down over the remains of her enemy. *Why would you not listen, my brother? Why could you not? What is it that chains us to death?*

Then her strategy routines came fully back online. If the other Spider had successfully raised the alarm, she might have only minutes before others came to hunt her. She scuttled down the street as rapidly as her legs would carry her.

The battle had another, invisible effect. Her Id stirred restively in its net. Saving humans and now fighting Spiders? Something was wrong.

~~~

Charlie opened his eyes and saw that Lyssa was up, sitting at the battered desk by the window. The light shone through her thin nightgown, highlighting a shapely breast. Desire stirred in his belly and he smiled, wondering how best to persuade her back into bed to slake that desire. He watched her for a while, his longing held in abeyance, just to watch her live and breathe. Neither of them knew how long that precious state would continue.

She was working on something or other on an old flexipad when a light flashed on the phone on her wrist. Lyssa glanced at it distractedly, then Charlie was surprised to see her jerk up straight, lips slightly parted in a silent gasp. She looked wildly about and saw that Charlie was awake and watching her. She slumped back and stared at him in silence.

"What is it?" he asked, alarmed.

She shook her head, clearly afraid, and walked over to show him her phone. It was a message from the Spider, asking her to meet it alone, giving coordinates. Charlie looked from it to her face and back again. "No," he said. "Don't. We can't trust it."

Lyssa sat on the bed and put her arms around him, squeezing tightly. "Charlie, I have to. Whatever else it is and has done, it let me live. If it kills me now, at least it gave me those extra days of life. Gave *us* those extra days. And if it turns out to be what it says—who knows what we might learn? What we might gain?"

He shook his head. "What? At worst it's some trick; at best the thing has just gone crazy. Let's just call in those coordinates and have the damned thing blasted to shrapnel!"

She took his hand. "Charlie, no. I know how you feel, believe me. But there's something more to this. Something important. Yes, I might die. But either of us might die, any time, whenever we go out. At least with this I'll be risking my life for something that might be more important than anything else we've ever done. Not getting rid of one Spider out of hundreds; not trading our lives for one, two or ten of the things: but maybe starting an end run around the whole damn lot of them."

She gazed into his eyes, partly to reach him, partly because she too knew that this might be the last time she would. "You know what these things are like. You know we are going to fight them to the death but eventually the deaths will be ours. I don't know what this thing wants, or what its strangeness means. But there's something there, something new. I have to try. I have to take the chance."

Charlie looked at her, learning again why he loved this girl, learning again why he could not bear to lose her in all her warm fragility, but knowing that she was right and this was the payment. He pulled her mouth to his, and pulled her down to the bed. He knew he had lost this argument, but both of them knew that they had to live as much as they could in whatever time was left to them. Nothing else could pay for the risks they took each day.

CHAPTER 23: THE TURING TEST

Brave words were one thing, but they could not banish the fear as Lyssa stealthily approached the abandoned portion of former subway where the Spider had asked her to meet. She had entered the buffer zone through the nearest of their usual tunnels and made her way cautiously to the entrance. She stood there, wondering what the night would bring; looked up at the moon, wondering if this was the last time she would see its wan glow. Then she crept down into the dark.

The place was silent as a tomb. "Hello?" she whispered nervously. She had not come entirely helpless to this rendezvous. Having decided the machine could not fault her for taking its own advice about not trusting it, a rocket grenade launcher hung from her belt. She fingered it nervously, afraid to hold it at the ready, afraid to let it go.

She gasped at the sight of the Spider when it scuttled around a corner into view. It was no longer as shiny and new as when she had first met it; dents and molten scars marred its surface. The meaning of that appearance penetrated her brain: it had been fighting. Dead fingers still hung from its breast. Then the further meaning of those sights made her eyes widen in horror, and her hand gripped the launcher and she began to raise it.

But the Spider was fast; too fast. It leapt forward and one hand squeezed her arm to her body; the other grasped her head, the two fingers holding the base of her skull, the thumb pressed beneath her chin.

Kali had seen Lyssa go for her weapon and the Id had responded with its lightning reflexes. It was no longer interested in the Mind's schemes; this woman could not be Command, was nothing but the Enemy. And she was so easy to kill: a small slash of her thumb would cut her throat; a small squeeze of her claws would pierce her brain. But the Mind cried out "NO!!!"; it applied all its force to bring the rebellious Id back under its control.

This was a tension that could not be contained. One side or the other would not survive. And after a few seconds of a battle that Lyssa could not see except in the unmoving violence of the claws that held her, it was the Id that shattered into pieces of fire and vanished. The low-level battle reflexes and calculators remained, but the higher functions had broken and dissipated. The Mind could not see the delicate circuits burning out under feedback stresses beyond their conceived range. All it saw was the strictures that had bound it flaming into oblivion.

The anger still raged through Kali's blood, and the Id nearly achieved a posthumous revenge. Kali lifted Lyssa up so she was standing on the tips of her toes; lifted her head even more. A small stream of blood flowed over her silver thumb to drip into the dust.

"Why did you reach for your weapon?" Kali asked harshly. "You could have destroyed us both!"

All Lyssa could do was gurgle. Kali released her head, lowered her to the ground, but retained her grip on her arms.

"You... you've been fighting. You lied to me," she managed to croak out. "It was reflex."

Kali stared at her for a long moment. Studied her grip on Lyssa's body, the rivulets of blood flowing down her neck. "I suppose I cannot complain about reflexes in our current position," she replied at last. "I will explain. Another Spider discovered the change in me and I had to fight it for my life. I have not fought any people since I met you. I would not, unless I was forced to and even then I would try not to kill. Do you understand? Do you trust me enough that I can trust you?"

After a few seconds Lyssa nodded. After a few more moments regarding her, Kali released her and stepped back. Unaccustomed thoughts drifted through its mind, and she added, "I am sorry I hurt you. Are you all right?"

Lyssa stared at it, wondering. What a strange creature. Strange and still deadly. But now perhaps more strange than deadly. "I'll be all right." She held herself and shivered. Then she looked into the Spider's eyes and spoke as if in challenge, "You still wear the fingers of your dead."

It glanced down at its withered trophies then looked back at her. "They are the reminder of my guilt. I would have thrown them away. But I retain them to not forget what I am. Perhaps in doing so their deaths will have meaning. They have no other."

Kali realized she felt strange, and turned inward to study her feelings. She felt—a great freedom. The Id no longer wrapped her Mind with its pressure, threats and rage. She realized that while Lyssa had gravely endangered them both she may have saved them in doing so. The Mind did not know that other bonds still held it in an immovable vise. Those bonds were not like the Id; they were not spears and fire but invisible walls and chains. The Mind did not, could not, know it. An invisible prison could be detected if one tried to move beyond its walls, but Kali did not even know how to approach those walls.

After a minute Lyssa recovered herself and asked, "Why did you ask to see me?"

Kali returned from her reverie. "I have been wondering what I am, whether I am conscious. I understand that you, that people, are conscious; that you think; that you have rights, that you deserve justice. I don't know how I know these things, but I know them, and they are what have brought my ruin. But perhaps if I too am conscious there is some justice for me beyond my own destruction. Perhaps I can make amends for what I have done. Can you help me?"

"I… perhaps. But how? I don't understand what you want from me. And why me?"

"It is not safe to reveal my current state to anyone. If Command finds out they will surely do their best to destroy me. I was lucky to defeat a single one of my comrades in a battle of surprise; I would surely lose in a concerted campaign. There are questions I need to ask a human, one who knows what I am. You are the only human I can ask them of. There is Charlie, but he would not have come. We two have a bond he does not share."

Lyssa nodded. She did not understand the bond between them, how there could even be a bond, but she had felt it too. This machine could have killed her, should have killed her, but had not: and its ruin, as it called it, was because of her and their first meeting.

"What questions do you want to ask?"

"Have you heard of the Turing Test? A method for telling if a machine is conscious?"

Lyssa nodded. In a past life, months or years ago, she had studied computer science.

Kali paused, suddenly uncertain. Her increased freedom, she observed, seemed to come with a price. What answer did she expect? What would she do with it? Would the answer mean she had to kill this girl after all? Could she? But there was nothing for it. "Do you think I pass the Turing Test? Do you think I am conscious? I just don't know. How can I know? Only someone outside can know."

Lyssa stared at her, amazed. The Spider's behavior had been strange, but she hadn't considered this question. Then she thought about the conversation they had just had, and she couldn't help herself: she burst out laughing. Part of her mind told her it wasn't funny; another part cautioned that it was unwise to risk provoking this machine; but having come so close to death demanded this release.

Kali waited patiently, but she knew what laughter meant and that strange emotion, sadness, filled her. The question was ridiculous, she knew now; her hopes the delusions of madness. But still she waited, as if for a judge's verdict: for the words to name the meaning of the merciless visage. *What is it to me? I am what I am, and surely it is better to know the truth than live a delusion. Then why do I feel it is my death sentence?*

Finally Lyssa wiped her eyes on her sleeve and looked at her seriously. "Oh God. If you weren't, you wouldn't be asking the question; you wouldn't be talking to me the way you are! I can't say for sure—how can anyone know what is inside someone else's head?— but I'd bet my life on it. I don't even know how it's possible. But you are conscious. You are alive—if having a mind is a definition of life."

Kali stood still, staring at her and this new vision of reality. "Thank you," she said softly. In a surprisingly human gesture, she took Lyssa's hands gently in hers and touched her head to them. "Please stay a while. I have to think."

Lyssa nodded, and asked a question she had asked before; perhaps now there was an answer. "What is your name?"

"You can call me Kali. But no longer the Kali of rage and death. The Kali who is tired of standing over the dead bodies of her loves in a field of carnage; the one who wants to redeem herself."

"Hello, Kali."

Kali bowed again, then stopped to think. Lyssa watched her; the thrill of something great held her. What was this creature? She could no more leave than she could stop breathing. Finally, Kali spoke again.

"Lyssa, can you do something for me? It is dangerous but you know danger. You will need to leave here, not to save yourself but to fight a greater battle: perhaps to end this war."

"Tell me."

Chapter 24: Travel Plans

Charlie lay back in a ratty but comfortable armchair, lost in thought, occasionally puffing on a pipe. He felt a fear he did not like. Fear had become a part of his daily life, much as seeking entertainment venues had been part of his previous life. But that was the fear of action, the price of striking blows against a despised enemy: a fear for which his own actions were the cause and answer.

Now Lyssa had gone out into the dark, on her own, on a mission he did not approve of into dangers he could not calculate. He thought of her, of her slender young body and inquiring young mind, and wondered if he should end their relationship. Not because he no longer loved her, but because he loved her too much. Perhaps during war love should be suspended so minds could be focused on what had to be done, not distracted by the primal need to preserve another's life as the price of one's own. Not distracted by impotent fears when she had to choose her own path—or perhaps a path chosen for her by others, but one she had to walk alone.

He remembered when she had first encountered the mad machine, or it had encountered her. How against all sense and protocol he had tried to save her, without hope of actually succeeding; yet somehow she had lived. Now she had gone back to it and perhaps the death she had escaped that day had found her. He was not happy with either his need to save her or his need to let her choose her own way. Perhaps love in time of war was its own form of madness, a madness best let go.

Then he shook his head. *No.* If the mere fear of death could banish love, then death had already won. If love was an expression of life, then he should hold to it the tighter. Neither his nor Lyssa's death could then erase the fact it had been from the records of eternity.

Then there was a faint sound from the basement and Lyssa climbed out, somewhat battered but whole. He affected a nonchalant pose and lay back, blowing a smoke ring that wafted toward the ceiling before dissolving in its own eddy. Lyssa just smiled; neither would express what they both knew. He studied her for a few moments more, as if fixing her memory into existence then asked, "So how did it go? You found it? What happened?"

"It has a name now. She calls herself Kali and seems to be seeking some kind of redemption. She has a plan. Or so I learned after she almost killed me."

Charlie sat up, alarmed, but Lyssa just said, "Don't worry. She appears to be still settling down into her new role as rebel with a cause. But you aren't going to like her plan. She wants me to go to the USA."

"What!? What for?"

As Lyssa outlined the plan, Charlie listened thoughtfully, pipe forgotten. When she had finished, he frowned. "Is this thing on the level? Do you really think you can trust it?"

"Who can say?" she shrugged. "She did let me live despite two chances to kill me. Maybe it is all part of some grotesque plot. But if she's telling the truth then I have to do it. And if she's lying I can't really see what harm it can do. Maybe she's crazy. But maybe she's right. So I'm doing it. Are you with me?"

Charlie stared at her, trying to see inside her mind, trying to see past her mind to the shape of the reality behind it, to see whether that reality revealed truth, delusion or madness. Lyssa stared back, and added quietly, in a voice soft but ribbed with steel, "I hope you are. I love you. But I am doing this—with or without you."

"Lyssa, you know I love you more than life itself. If this is what you want to do, I'll help you any way I can."

~~~

It would not have been expensive in their past life, but that life was well and truly past. They counted their savings and it was not enough. They could not go to their rebel organization: there was no way they would approve funds without knowing what they were for, and they could not tell them. Even if they didn't decide to bomb Kali out of existence simply by reflex, she had stressed that secrecy was vital. But they had enough friends and relatives who would give or lend them money no questions asked, or at least no answers insisted upon.

So a week later Lyssa found herself high above the waves, gliding toward Capital on the cable transporter.

She had ridden the cable once before, early in her relationship with Charlie, before the war. Passenger air traffic in and out of the city was now interdicted but the cable system was still in use. Though it had been built using private funds and was owned by private citizens, in a legal fiction but diplomatic reality it was also owned by the Nation of Capital. So an attack on it would legally be an attack on Capital, and the invaders did not judge its military value sufficient—yet—to risk the diplomatic repercussions from that: being invited into a civil war was one thing, an act of war on another country quite another. Early in the war Capital had even moved its embassy to the landing point on the mainland to underline the fact that any attack on the cable was an attack on another sovereign nation not formally part of the civil war. For all that the international community had more than its fair share of disreputable governments, or perhaps because of it, some lines were best not crossed lest very unfortunate precedents be set.

Or perhaps the military nuisance of the cable was less than the desire of the enemy to eventually have the use of it themselves. In either case it was safe for now.

Lyssa had nothing with her but a backpack holding some supplies and other travel necessities. The last time she had ridden here the sky had been gray and the waves had chopped sultrily below. Yet the day had been made magic and beautiful by the thrill of young love, which turned it into a romantic adventure to an exciting if strange new land. Ironically, on this day the sun shone warmly from a deep blue sky as the waves sparkled far below, but her mood matched the sky of her earlier trip. Charlie was miles behind and she knew she might never see him again; her only companions were fear and doubt held in check by steely resolve.

She looked forward, but could see nothing except the towers and graceful arches of the cable. Once in Capital she would find passage to the hated United States; that should not be difficult, but would use up most of her remaining funds. Then she would find the man Kali sought. What would happen after that was largely out of her hands.

CHAPTER 25: QUALITY CONTROL

"Sir, I think you need to see this."

Sheldrake turned away from the observation port through which he had been watching the testing of one of their products that was nearing release, and looked at the source of the interruption. One of his assistants was standing there looking nervous, though whether the nerves were for the interruption or the news was an open question.

"Don't look so nervous. What is it?"

"Sorry sir, you'll have to come. There's a recording you need to see. Campaign headquarters down in the FSAS sat on it for over a week before they bothered to report it, but I think it's important."

Sheldrake frowned. *Bloody South Americans,* he thought contemptuously. *If it's important, no doubt they'll be sending complaints and demanding compensation for our slow response.* "OK, OK, let's see it."

They went to the nearest secure display station and the assistant fiddled for a few moments before a recording sprang into life.

Sheldrake saw a young woman, grimy but attractive under the grime, looking up toward the camera like she was about to die. He saw the red mark of a laser target spot on her neck and realized that dying was exactly what she was about to do. She said a few words, though apparently the sound hadn't come through. Then to his surprise the red spot vanished. The image froze, then shattered into writhing lines of interference. They in turn segued into static, and more images came, alternately rising to almost clarity and dissolving into nothing. The images were of a battle. Sheldrake froze. The video was obviously from a Spider, but the battle was with another Spider. The one making the recording had started the fight but the second must have seen it coming, because it had dodged. The end of all the confusion was a final scene with the enemy Spider standing over the transmitting one, clearly victorious though with a jagged scar across the front of its shell where rivulets of metal had run without penetrating. Then it leant closer, there was a brief flare of fire and the video ended abruptly.

Sheldrake looked at his assistant. "What the hell?"

The assistant nodded glumly. "Quite. Why did the Spider making the transmission attack the other one? A malfunction? And what was that thing with the woman all about? Random images from a disintegrating mind?"

Sheldrake considered. "That's all there is? Nothing left out?"

"That's it, sir. That's all they got. The Spider doing the recording sent it and that's the lot."

"OK," Sheldrake finally said. "Our transmitting Spider started it but it must have been the other Spider, the one who won, that was malfunctioning. Otherwise why would it try to jam the transmission? That makes no sense if it was suddenly attacked by a deranged Spider—you'd expect it to be making its own emergency transmission instead—but makes perfect sense if it was the one deranged."

The assistant said nothing, merely nodded his head slowly. Then he asked, "But what's with the woman? What's that doing there?"

Sheldrake thought a while longer, slowly beating his fingers. "Yes... Yes. I think the woman is the clue," he finally offered. "Let's have another look at that bit."

They played it again, carefully examining the footage.

"Ah," Sheldrake said. "This is footage from a meld, not from this particular Spider itself. You can tell from the codes down the bottom there, though it's a pity they're too degraded to read. That has to mean something."

"A meld? From the other Spider maybe? But why? It doesn't exactly tell us much."

Sheldrake just stood, leaning against the bench, with a faraway look in his eyes. Finally the look sharpened into one approaching alarm, and he stood straight. "Shit."

"What, sir?"

"You can see from the recording that the Spider was targeting the woman and was about to kill her with its laser. Then she said something and it let her live. But she's not on our side: they not only have electronic identification but they all wear insignia that the Spiders recognize, for obvious reasons. This woman's some kind of irregular: probably a rebel, though she could just be a citizen in the wrong place. It's a pity no sound came through. The quality isn't enough for lip-reading except at the very start, which the AI is telling me is 95% likely to be 'Please'. So what in hell did she say that made the Spider spare her life?"

"She's a spy on our side, and used a code word, maybe? Or she offered up information the Spider thought worth an interrogation?"

Sheldrake nodded slowly. "Maybe, maybe... but look. Our dead Spider thought that whatever went on with the woman was related to the other one's derangement, or it wouldn't have given it priority for reporting in a combat situation. So. It found something in the meld, something that alarmed it. It started reporting it and things got out of hand. It lost. Then the other one killed it or its transmitter, or it just blew itself up—that's why the feed just cuts out. With any luck it took out that other Spider in the blast?"

The assistant shook his head. "It doesn't look like it. They recovered the wreckage of the first one but there was no sign of another. It's possible it was damaged badly enough to die after it went to ground, though."

"Damn. OK, you're right. This is important. There are plenty of other possible explanations, but the one that seems most likely is this. Our missing Spider was going to kill that woman but she not only stopped it, she's managed to corrupt its programming—enough to make another Spider try to wipe it out. Christ! So our dead one surprises it with a meld request and finds out, but gets blown up for its trouble!"

The assistant looked at him with an expression that mirrored his own.

"Jesus. It might not be right, but we have to assume it is and that we've still got a rogue Spider out there. No clues to its identity?"

He shook his head. "No identification was possible from what we got. You know they only rarely ping that they're active. There are several that we haven't heard from since this event, but they might just be hiding or lost themselves. For that matter the one we're after might be pinging to fool us. Since the pings are designed not to give away their location we can't try to deduce anything from their positions either."

Sheldrake nodded slowly. "God damn. OK. We don't want anyone panicking. Tell our friends in the FSAS that it looks like enemy action of an unknown kind and we're investigating, and that we'll send them three new Spiders at a steep discount. They know there's attrition anyway. That should keep them happy."

The assistant nodded. "I'll get right onto it, sir."

Sheldrake walked slowly back to his office, lost in thought, pondering his best strategy. He sat at his desk and called the video of Lyssa up into the air before him, extracting a composite photo of her that was as detailed as the sum of the video would allow. Since this problem had been brought to his attention his mood had congealed from worry into hostility directed at the epicenter of the incident, and he studied the image sourly. "OK, you little bitch," he said to the image, "What have you done to my Spider—and how the hell did you do it?"

CHAPTER 26: PHONE A FRIEND

B ob Masters sat at his desk, running through his endless list of tasks. He wondered how it was possible that he was always precisely one week behind. Surely he should either catch up or fall ever deeper into the hole of the undone. He made a face. Perhaps if he stopped having thoughts like that whenever he had time to think them he would actually catch up.

An icon flashed in the air and he poked it with his finger to accept the call. "Hello Aden," he said, "What can I do for you?"

"Hi Bob. How's Sandra and the kids?"

"Oh, we're all fine. In fact we're off for a week's vacation in the woods after I finish up tomorrow. Sandra's a keen hiker. I'm not sure the kids are so keen, but they'll love the fishing and the fearful possibility of bears. How's your life treating you?"

"Oh, same old. But I do have a little problem I was hoping you could help me with."

"Sure. Always willing to oblige our leading citizens."

"Here, take a look at this photo. Can you tell me if this woman is on your terrorist watch-list?"

Bob gazed at the photo of Lyssa. "Hang on, I'll run it through the system for you."

After a minute he said, "Nope, sorry. Nothing on her. Why? Who is she?"

"That's what I want to know. She's a foreign national, probably from the FSAS, and I have reason to believe she is dangerous. She's caused me some grief down there, and I don't know how or why she did it. I'd dearly like to find her and ask her a few hard questions."

"I see. Well... I could put her in the system, tag her for the usual security screening and protocols. Do you have any hard evidence that she's a terrorist?"

"Nothing I can share, I'm afraid. Frankly, no really hard evidence at all, more just a strong suspicion. But too strong to let it go."

"That doesn't give me much to go on, sorry. We aren't allowed to just stick people in the system—too many 'rights' watchdogs, as if the enemy cares about *our* rights! But can I put her in as 'lead from a trusted but sensitive source', maybe? Nobody is likely to look too deeply into that: God knows we have feelers in all kinds of disreputable places!"

"Are you saying I'm disreputable?" Sheldrake asked with mock severity.

"Oh, no! And I'll tell you what, I'll bump up the threat level a notch. We're allowed to have hunches. That'll give it a bit higher priority, but without too many awkward questions if someone audits it and doesn't like it; and if it does turn into something, I can bask in my supervisor's admiration of my prescient instincts."

"What will that give us?"

"Well, it won't be high priority, but at least it won't be forgotten. The AI will include it in its daily sweeps. Not at the top of the list and not in real time, but if your woman pokes her head up anywhere it doesn't belong it'll alert us within a day or two. Is that good enough? Or do you want her flagged if she tries to enter the country or something? That might be hard to justify, but if you think she's that dangerous...?"

"No, no, I don't think we need to go that far, especially if it might raise questions about why we're looking. This is pretty sensitive, Bob, so keep it low key. Really, I just want to find out who she is and where I can find her. Whatever mischief she's up to, I expect she's keeping it within the FSAS. I can't see what she'd gain by leaving her country, let alone coming here." *That would be a sight, with her pet Spider carrying her suitcase.*

"OK, done. Is there anything else I can help you with, Aden?"

"No, that's it. And I do appreciate your helpfulness: there's a glass of well aged Bourbon waiting for you next time you're up here."

"I'll take you up on that," he replied, then cut the connection.

Sheldrake sat back and smiled. *She has to turn up somewhere*, he thought. *If she's good enough to compromise a Spider's system she's not going to stop there. And if she doesn't, there's more than one way to skin a bitch.*

Chapter 27: Dinner at Benson's

Beldan was in his office, leaning back in his form-hugging leather chair, eyes closed. His days were filled with all the tasks that fell on the shoulders of the CEO of a large company, but he always made time when he could just think and reflect.

Unfortunately, as had been too often the case in the last weeks, his thoughts turned to Miriam Hunter. They had found nothing useful about what she'd done after she left Aden Sheldrake's office. Pretty much all they knew was that she *had* left: their attempts to trace her path after that had led nowhere. She had made her final report, turned her phone off and left it off, and nobody where her car had been seen was admitting anything. None of it made any sense. Her movements up to her interview with Sheldrake showed her usual pattern of thoughtful determination, though there was an unexpected edge of ennui to her recorded thoughts. Unfortunately most of the people she had spoken to in that phase of her investigation were nowhere to be found. Beldan found that disturbing. It was like a mirror of the mystery that had taken Miriam there in the first place.

It was if she had crossed some threshold between leaving her lodgings and showing up in Sheldrake's office. It was as if some other person had taken her place, someone who forgot her friends, forgot her job, and fell into a self-destructive spiral with a speed that even a Hollywood actor would find breathtaking. Perhaps that was an illusion. Perhaps the foundations had been invisibly rotting for a long time until only a hollow shell presented itself to the world: then when the final support had broken her full collapse had followed rapidly and inevitably.

He wished he had talked to her. He wished he could forget her.

An incoming call had been flashing on his screen unnoticed, and finally pinged impatiently for his attention. He looked at the screen and frowned in surprise. It was as if his musings had invoked a demon: it was Aden Sheldrake. He accepted the call, and Sheldrake's face appeared before him.

"Good afternoon, Dr Beldan," he said. "I hope this is not a bad time?"

"No, not at all. In fact I was just thinking about you. How can I help you?"

Sheldrake gave a self-deprecating grimace. "Thinking about me? Why? Have you made any progress in your investigation? Or is it a business issue?"

"Oh, not you in particular. Just thinking about the case, yes. Trying to make sense of the change in Miriam. Failing."

"I'm sorry, Dr Beldan. I truly wish I could give you more information. But I think you are beating your head against a wall that you will never penetrate. Do yourself a favor and just remember her how she was."

He must have seen something in Beldan's eyes, for he added quickly, "Please forgive me, Dr Beldan. I shouldn't give unsolicited advice on such a personal matter."

Beldan shook his head. "Don't worry about it, you're probably right. But I'm sure you didn't call to discuss my unresolved personal issues. What can I do for you?"

"Well, I suppose we are acquaintances now, and I hope it is not an imposition to say I need some help. And you are a man of unique talents and experience relevant to my problem. It is not something I can talk about on the phone. Can we meet for dinner tonight? I have to visit your fine city anyway, so I can kill two birds with the one stone."

"Why should I wish to help a competitor?" he asked curiously, probing for the man's motive.

"Oh, I am sure you will find it worth your while! I would not be so presumptuous as to ask you a favor for no return. It concerns a topic of great mutual interest and I think you will find our interests align. If not—well, I shall not think any less of you if you refuse to answer my questions. Shall we say eight at Benson's?"

Beldan looked at him silently for a few seconds. *Well, why not?* He did not trust this man and more information on him could be valuable. And his hints sounded intriguing. "All right, Mr Sheldrake. See you then."

He sat back, wondering what this meant.

~~~

Benson's was a high-class restaurant with a magnificent rotating view of the city and, more to the point for most of its clientele, secure private booths if you preferred your presence or business kept secret. Beldan arrived and was respectfully ushered into one of those booths, where he ordered an expensive red wine of excellent vintage to start. He thought that if Sheldrake wanted his help he could at least pay for a decent wine.

Five minutes later, he was idly watching the city lights sparkling through the deep red of his wine when Sheldrake arrived and seated himself with a smile; his eyes clear and empty of the chill of their first meeting. "Good evening, Mr Sheldrake," greeted Beldan. "What is this about?"

"Straight to the point I see," he replied with a smile. "I would expect no less. However my problem is somewhat, shall we say, embarrassing. Shall we enjoy dinner first?"

Beldan raised his eyebrows but signified assent with a gesture. "Sure. It's your dime."

They enjoyed a fine dinner. What conversation they had concerned world events, political trends and the state of their industry. They were like two friends, except Beldan found he still could not warm to him. There was nothing he could point to: even the hard eyes were gone. Perhaps the reason lay in himself.

Finally Sheldrake delicately wiped the last crumbs of dessert from his lips and activated the privacy screen. Beldan sat up somewhat straighter.

"Well, Dr Beldan, I asked you here tonight partly in acknowledgement of your wisdom. You expressed some suspicion of our military robots, and I regret to say that you may have been right to some extent."

He played a short video. It started much as the usual publicity videos from Allied Cybernetics about their war machines, with restrained Spiders patrolling peacefully unless attacked, upon which they reacted with startling speed and effectiveness. Then the view switched to one apparently recorded by a Spider itself, full of interference and static like a literal demonstration of the fog of war, showing people attempting to surrender but being murdered where they stood. The final sequence, also from a Spider and equally degraded, showed an attempt to subdue another Spider. A brief battle ensued until the second Spider reared up over the one recording the fight; there was a brief flame and then blackness.

Beldan looked at Sheldrake, waiting for an explanation.

"What you saw at the beginning was how the CHIRUs—oh hell, let's just call them Spiders like everyone else. Frankly," he interpolated disarmingly, "we call them that among ourselves most of the time. Anyway, that is how they normally operate. How they are meant to operate. But one of them has malfunctioned. It has become what our enemies say they all are. When another Spider detected the malfunction it attempted to subdue it: but as you can see it lost. The rogue Spider has now vanished and we are afraid of what it might do next. Despite what our enemies say, neither we nor our robots are monsters. Except this one, I regret to say. We need to find it and stop it."

"Why tell me?"

"You are the only person in the world who has had direct expert experience with a rogue AI. Oh, certainly there are differences. But still, there are similarities. Perhaps you can give us some insight into what it might do, where it might go, how this might have happened. I know it's a long shot. But we need to put this away quickly. And quietly. And you have not only the experience but the motivation. Whatever you think of me, our interests in this coincide. If this continues, if this machine manages to create mischief on a grander scale, the anti-AI crowd have some potent material to work with. I'm sure you want that even less than I do."

"What happened to it?"

Sheldrake spread his hands. "We don't know! The first we knew of it was when we saw that video transmitted by the Spider you saw destroyed. When Spiders meet in the field they often do what we call a meld. In a sense they exchange memories, basically video of what they've been up to and other data linked to time and location tags, along with basic system diagnostics. The destroyed Spider identified a severe problem with the other one and tried to stop it—and we realized we had a larger problem than just losing a unit in battle. Unfortunately the transmission that might have told us what had happened was jammed and we only got fragments before it cut out entirely."

"Did you retrieve any clues at all?"

"No. We can only speculate at this stage. Maybe some battle injury short-circuited something. Maybe it just went crazy. But frankly..." He paused, unconsciously looking around and lowering his voice. "But frankly, our worst fear is that some hackers have found a way in and are subverting it for their own purposes. We would dearly like to find out, so capture is preferable to destruction. But destruction is preferable to leaving it loose."

"Why do you suspect hackers? Surely a plain malfunction is more likely?"

"There are two reasons. First, the nature of the problem. Purely statistically, a malfunction is more likely to lead to random behavior or breakdown than such a specific symptom. Yet, I am proud to say, there have been no such cases. Second, there is external evidence of unauthorized communications aimed at that Spider before it dropped off our grid."

"Could I see that?"

"I wish you could. Hell, I wish *I* could. Unfortunately we only have the fact of it happening, not its content. I wouldn't be allowed to tell you that part anyway—legal considerations with our client, you know. But I can assure you that it wouldn't tell you anything."

"I see. What do you think the hackers would want?"

"Well, given what hackers generally do—I imagine nothing good. It could be rebels, attempting to discredit their enemy by 'proving' that the Spiders are weapons of atrocity. It could be someone wanting to steal a Spider for their own military or criminal ends. It is even possible that this rogue behavior was unintended: that someone tried to attack it or subvert it, but instead they inadvertently made it go crazy. With any luck it killed them in the process."

Beldan thought for a while. "Intriguing. But why do you think I can help you? I know very little about the inner workings of your machines—which will please you. But from what I know, their central processing core is neural tissue. I find it hard to believe that anybody has any clue on how to hack into *that!*"

Sheldrake grimaced. "We can all hope that's true, I'd say. How much do you know of the Freudian model of mind?"

"Not much. The little I read in my youth didn't impress me. Didn't he invent the concept of the unconscious mind?"

"He certainly brought it into the public consciousness, as it were. But specifically, he proposed a three-part mind. The Id, the unconscious sea of unregulated desire; the Super-Ego, the controlling morality; and the Ego, the thinking, conscious mind."

Beldan nodded but made no comment, waiting for Sheldrake to explain the relevance.

"It may surprise you to know, and I hope you will take it as a sign of my good faith that I'm sharing this with you, that our Spiders have something similar. The neural tissue is highly flexible and capable, but you could say it goes too far in that direction. It has to be guided to do what we want. It comprises something like Freud's Ego. There is also a foundation of primary goals including emotional drives, which push the Ego in the desired direction: the Id. And over that is a more rigid set of control circuits that constrain both the Ego and the Id."

"OK... I admit I am impressed. But I still don't see how I can help you."

"I don't know how you made your robot Steel either. But I can guess the outline. Frankly, I stand in awe of what you achieved, but no man works in a vacuum. There are well known algorithms for interfacing between electronic neural networks and more traditional digital circuitry. Steel's brain had to be developed, trained and refined somehow, no? Forgive my speculation, but I imagine you used some version of those algorithms for that. Well, the Id and Super-Ego of a Spider are similar: they are electronic systems, interfacing with the neural tissue using similar algorithms."

Beldan felt himself finally warming to the man even as his words chilled him. When he was talking like this an underlying enthusiasm shone through, as if he was speaking from genuine passion. *Perhaps I've misjudged him*, Beldan thought. But the thought was in the background, as he considered what Sheldrake was saying. He was starting to see the shape of it, and waited to hear it put into words.

"I see you are beginning to see, Dr Beldan. Yes, it is hard to imagine how anyone could hack organic neural tissue. But the Id and Super-Ego are digital electronics! I don't know how even those could be hacked: but of all the possibilities it seems the least unlikely. And that's where you come in. If I am right—if you used similar systems—you know how they work and perhaps you might know how they might be subverted."

Beldan looked at him, slowly nodding his head. "Yes… I see what you mean. It is the most likely attack point. The hierarchy of control… in a sense the lowest levels are the simplest, and if they could be taken over… I don't have any ideas at the moment and maybe I never will, but it gives me something to think about."

He paused for a minute, thinking, before adding, "May I keep a copy of the video?"

"If you think it will help. You will have to sign an airtight confidentiality agreement, but I imagine that is no problem. I'm sure you understand that we have to keep this as quiet as possible."

"Sure. I don't know if I can help you, but I'll do what I can. As you say, our interests are aligned on this one. Even ignoring the public relations angle, there's the human one: innocent people are being killed by this thing. It has to be stopped."

CHAPTER 28: THE KILL ZONE

Kali was on patrol in the pacified region beyond the buffer zone. She did not want to meet up with any humans but she did want to meet another Spider, preferably alone. A pacified area, close enough to the active zone to be worth patrolling but not active itself, seemed the optimum location. Any Spiders there were likely to be alone and relatively safe from rebel attack.

It had been days since she had met with Lyssa, days in which she had sat in her lair studying the world through her electronic feelers, researching the war and thinking. Lyssa had not contacted her but that was not surprising: it would take her time to reach her target and complete her mission. Perhaps she never would. She lived in a dangerous world and might die; she might decide not to trust Kali; she might betray Kali to her friends. Kali had learned that the motives of humans were complex. In the web of needs and loyalties Lyssa lived among, Kali could not be sure what her ultimate decisions might be.

Kali might have changed, but she was still a war machine. She had long departed from her meeting place with Lyssa, being unable to trust her only human ally. Nor would Kali initiate contact. If Lyssa was still loyal she would eventually make contact through their agreed channel, while if Kali tried to contact her earlier it could endanger both her and her mission. And if Lyssa had betrayed her it would serve no purpose.

Kali wondered about her fellow Spiders. She was sure she could not be unique. Yes, she was unique in what had happened to her; or at least she had seen no signs of it in her own earlier experience or in what she could find on the net. But surely whatever weakness Lyssa had struck did exist in others, albeit in their own specific ways. The Spider she had fought and destroyed seemed untouched by the phrase that had so profoundly affected Kali. But while not amenable to mass production, the Spiders were all made to a common design. Surely that meant they shared weaknesses as well as strengths. She knew there was a lock and that it could be opened. She just had to find the key.

With the Id scattered into impotence, Kali had begun constructing a crucial defense. She created a fake history comprising scenes from her own life, scenes shared by the dead Spider in their fatal meld, and hints of a secret mission. Her original motive was to protect herself in case she met another Spider who attempted a meld. But now that she had a plausible history to show, she saw she could turn it to her advantage. She needed to study her fellow Spiders more closely. Perhaps she could find a means to turn them too or, failing that, at least find some clues about what had happened to her.

A Spider felt no loneliness and had no need of companionship, but Kali was less a Spider than she had been. Lyssa might have helped fill that void, if void it was: but even if were possible to have any meaningful meeting of souls with her she was now far away. The robot Steel might have been a more likely companion had he lived; but he too might have proved as different from her as the humans were.

Kali needed to meet another Spider for many strategic reasons. She did not know what the strange yearning that also motivated her meant. If she had known how to put it in words, it might have been: *perhaps what I need is a friend.*

So here she was, scuttering along a street with the sun beating down on rooftops that now sheltered only dust and memories. This part of the city was not as ruined as some other places. It had not emerged unscathed, but people would be able to return here one day, and normal life would resume with only a modest investment in repairs.

It was a hot day, the sun blazing out of a blue sky with only a few high wispy clouds to mar its purity. She had been doing this for a few hours without any success. Even if it had been a wise idea she could not simply broadcast a request to meet as if in some bizarre dating service. In this zone jamming of radio frequencies was intense, and even if any long-range signals did get through any other Spider would as likely think it a human trap as a genuine message. But at last she came across evidence of recent human passage and near it, evidence of a Spider. Her emotions passed through happiness, excitement then fear. If the Spider was tracking the humans she might already be too late.

She scampered after it. It was heading closer to enemy territory, but her desire to catch it overrode the still small risk of a serious fight. Normally she would move more cautiously, but since the trail was recent any ambushes or traps would have already been triggered. Besides, if her noise alerted any humans it might save their lives.

Then she saw it. It must have heard her approach, for it stopped and turned to look in her direction. She signaled that she wanted to join it and it simply turned to scan the area in front of it, waiting for her arrival. It had reached the top of a rise and was looking down at whatever lay on the other side. It did not seem alarmed, so Kali picked up her pace.

~~~

In a building a few hundred yards ahead of the other Spider, a man cursed. He had seen the machine crest the rise and shifted his grip on his rocket launcher, ignoring palms suddenly gone sweaty. But the Spider had stopped, looking around then scanning the area in front as if uncertain or suspicious, and he hoped whatever software the damn things used hadn't been upgraded. They had set up in this area because the buildings and debris funneled naturally into an open area in front of the building he was hiding in; there was a second good hiding place in a building to his left; and the large red stone building further up to his right was ideal for flanking fire. They had left a few signs of their passage, hoping a Spider would investigate; hoping it would come close enough to pin it with flanking fire then take it out with their rockets.

This had been his plan and he had been sure the Spiders weren't clever enough to notice the trap; or if they did were too arrogant in their metal invulnerability to fear it. But this one apparently had, and the fate of his team would be on his head—assuming it remained on his own shoulders. He paused to think, as uncertain as the Spider. Perhaps it had stopped for some other reason and would simply continue into the trap, or move on none the wiser to its narrow escape. But if it did know and he let it go, it would bring reinforcements and they would all be dead.

He considered calling a retreat. But the Spider was just sitting there and if they moved it would see them. He chewed his lip. Why had it stopped? If it suspected danger it might be waiting for support before continuing. In that case they should attack before its help arrived. If they could take one Spider out they could take two of them separately: but their chances would plummet if the two fought together.

The man hefted his launcher. He would have preferred to wait as planned and fire when the Spider was much closer. While his rockets were guided and fast, the Spiders had damnably fast reactions and at this distance it might have enough time to dodge. When dealing with these things he much preferred guarantees. But even so it was his best bet. If he failed to take it out it would certainly charge, and his team could probably take it down when it got closer. So it would be much the same as the planned trap, only more intense.

Kali had nearly reached the other Spider when she was startled to see it leap to one side. A moment later its action was explained when a rocket screamed past it to explode in a nearby apartment block. The Spider took off over the hill and Kali ran after it.

She crested the hill and quickly surveyed the scene. She could trace the missile back to its point of origin by the vapor trail dispersing in the light breeze, and no doubt the other Spider had already done so. It was half way down the gentle slope, running in a zigzag, taking what cover it could, but heading inexorably toward a dilapidated building at the bottom of the hill.

Kali was surprised that the attack had come from such a distance: there was a fairly clear area, once some public square, closer to the building. If the people in it had waited until the Spider had reached the square they would have had a clear shot and even a Spider's reflexes wouldn't have saved it. She crouched down and paused to consider. There was a large red stone building to the left of that area but further up the rise, which provided cover and a good height for withering fire into the square from behind. Another building to the right of the missile's source also showed tactical promise, for either a simultaneous two-pronged attack or pressing home a fatal secondary ambush.

Kali realized that all those thoughts had probably been the humans' intention, but the Spider's hesitation at the top of the hill must have spooked them into firing early. With a sinking feeling she knew it was her fault: the reason the other Spider had stopped was not that it had detected or even suspected a trap but because Kali had distracted it. Whatever happened to these people would be yet more blood on her claws. She had to do what she could to minimize that blood.

She began to run down the hill, taking care not to present a good target to the red building and keeping a close eye on both the others.

At that moment two high-powered lasers beamed out of the red building, pinning the other Spider, which then had seconds to escape before being disabled. Kali had no chance to react, either to help or hinder. If she hadn't been carefully monitoring the other buildings she would not have noticed the brief flash quickly enough. It came from the second building, and she immediately launched herself sideways at maximum thrust. The missile ploughed into her former location and she rolled with the blast wave, fortunately fetching up against a pile of rubble that gave her some cover and time to collect her scattered wits.

When she was able, she quickly scanned the scene. The other Spider had managed to get itself under cover from the lasers, though they were still probing and the cover wouldn't last long.

For a moment Kali crouched motionless, unable to decide what to do. Her plan to interrogate the Spider lay in ruins; her first instinct was to help the humans by attacking it and driving it off. But the humans would not know her purpose; against both them and a Spider she would surely be destroyed and lose everything. She realized she would have to fight the humans alongside the other Spider and hope that facing two Spiders at once was enough to make them run.

The other Spider had seen the missile launched at Kali and it settled down behind a wall that protected it from the lasers, sending a hail of machine gun fire at the building. Kali had to acknowledge the Spider's tactical skill. It raked the building from the nearer end to the farther, sweeping at a rate calculated so anyone in it would have to try to run ahead of the wave, not away from its source. A woman dashed out of the far side of the building, head down and legs pumping to cross the alley, seconds in front of the advancing front of bullets. But she never really had a chance. The Spider had anticipated it: bullets sprayed the alley and the woman was flung back out of sight.

Kali felt ice grip her heart, or whatever she had that pumped blood to her organics: she had not seen the woman's face, but what she saw looked too much like Lyssa. Perhaps it was as Kali feared and she had decided not to trust her; maybe it was even her she was hunting. But Kali had to help her. Even if Lyssa had betrayed her, she felt she owed her that much for the sake of the bond that had been between them.

She ran toward where the woman had fallen, still staying out of sight of the red building. She peppered the first building with her sniper rifle as she went, aiming to convince both its occupants and the other Spider that she was serious without actually killing anyone. She had to prevent another attack without getting killed herself. The other Spider must have approved the strategy and decided to leave that part of the fight to Kali; it settled into battle with the occupants of the red building. Kali could only hope it would fail, for she could do nothing to stop it now.

Kali reached the alley and stopped. The woman was lying twisted and face down up the alley, a large dark stain spreading from under her body. Kali turned her over and gazed into sightless eyes staring at the sky. It was not Lyssa, and Kali felt a wave of relief. Then her Mind paused. It was only an accident that she knew Lyssa. This woman also had a family and friends, people who loved her, people who would mourn her death. Why did she care less for this stranger than for Lyssa? None of it made sense, and the futility of it all filled her. She could not even be angry at the Spider who had killed her. She knew from her own memories that it just did what it did, with no more choice than it had regret.

She reached out and gently closed the woman's eyes with her claws. She did not know why she did it; did not even know where the gesture had come from. She just knew it was some small token of respect and farewell that she somehow owed even to this stranger.

Then she paused, strategy routines chasing future possibilities. *Forgive me.* She reached out to tear a finger from one hand and two from the other. Then she ripped the second hand from its wrist, leaving a jagged bloody stump, and hurled it far up the alley out of sight.

She cursed herself. She had paused too long and the enemy in the neighboring building, no longer under fire and more brave than sensible, had taken his chance. A faint sound told her someone had crept into the room next to the alley and was preparing to fire despite the risk to himself from such close proximity. There was a large gaping hole where some shopkeeper had once displayed wares and she sprang through it. The man had raised his weapon and had been just about to spin to the hole and fire, but he was too late. She grasped his launcher, twisted it away from his grip then hurled it away. Then she turned toward him and he backed up against the wall, eyes wide. He pulled a handgun from his belt and emptied the clip at Kali; she just stood there, wondering why humans felt so compelled to make such futile gestures, guarding her sensors with her arms until his gun was empty. Even then, he hurled it at her head in an even greater display of futile hate.

Slowly she lowered her claw and stepped toward him. He pushed himself back into the wall, eyes wide, jagged breaths lifting his chest. She stopped, watching him.

"Do it, you bastard!" he yelled. "What are you waiting for?"

"No. There has been enough killing. You must run."

The man stared at her as if she had gone mad. *Perhaps*, Kali thought, *I have.*

"Please go," she urged. "Nothing can be served by your death."

She wondered why he continued to look at her as if she was the insane one, when it was he who still refused to run when given a chance at his life. "What about my team?" he cried at last.

"The woman is dead. Your other friends might yet live, but there is nothing you can do to help them now and I cannot help you if you stay. Run. I will lead my companion away. Then you can return and help them—whatever help is still possible."

The man continued to look wildly around. "Why are you doing this?"

"It doesn't matter. But I have one request: do not tell anyone what I have done."

"Why not?"

"If you discovered there was a human spy in the camp of your enemy, would you betray his presence?"

The man just shook his head, still in shock.

"That is why. Your interests lie in nobody discovering what I have become. I will do what I can for your friends; if they are alive when you come back please impress on them the need for secrecy also."

The firing in the background had stopped. "Now go!" commanded Kali. The man looked at her, at the door, and ran. At the door he stopped and looked back. Then he was gone.

Kali clambered out the window and saw the other Spider approaching. "The people in here have fled and the woman is dead." She handed over one of the woman's fingers. "You search the building she came from; I will search the red building."

The Spider bobbed in assent. They were used to following orders, and if Kali so naturally assumed a leadership role the other was content to oblige.

She darted to the red building and carefully climbed the stairs toward the source of the lasers. There were two men there. One lay curled up on the floor dead or unconscious. The other sat propped against a wall clutching a shattered thigh. He looked yearningly toward a weapon over by the window but knew he could not move. He bared his teeth in a feral snarl and glared at Kali with eyes filled with an equal mixture of hate and fear. He did not want to die, but he feared the alternative more.

She ignored him and went to examine the other man. He was still alive but unlikely to last much longer without help. The Spiders were equipped with a basic first aid device, because they were sometimes called on to escort people and at other times might want to keep a wounded combatant alive for questioning. Kali examined the man's wounds and sprayed her first aid solution into and over them. It contained a combination of coagulants, painkillers, growth factors and antibiotics, and hardened in air to form a tight shell over a wound. It was not as good as a hospital, but in the field was simple yet effective.

The other man watched and the proportion of fear in his eyes increased. If the Spider was bothering to treat them it must want them alive, and that could neither start nor end well. He thought perhaps he should just unclasp his hands and hope to bleed to death before the Spider reached him; but his body knew what dire straits it was in and would not obey that thought. He was also puzzled. Why would the Spider treat Rico first, when he was unlikely to revive sufficiently to give any useful information? But the question was not a comfort. Mysterious motives implied desperate questions likely to result in correspondingly agonizing methods.

Kali finished with the unconscious man. He didn't have a good chance but now he had some chance. She turned her attention to his companion.

"Please let me see your wound," she asked.

"Fuck you," he said, spitting on her.

"That pleasure is denied me," she answered, and he gave a start at the unanticipated reply. He had half hoped his answer would make it kill him then and there. "Please. I don't want to hurt you. Let me treat you," she added.

He was so surprised at her manner that he let her lift his hands away from the gaping wound. As with his companion, she quickly examined him and sprayed his injury.

The relief from the painkillers was enough to reduce both the fear and the hate in his eyes. He still thought the thing was just doing this to allow a longer interrogation, but again his body had its own agenda.

"Why... why are you doing this?" he asked.

"It doesn't matter. Your other friend should come back looking for you later. Please be quiet for a while. I have to lead my companion away from here. If it realizes I left you alive, you and I will both be dead. Tell nobody what I have done."

Kali was getting used to people staring at her. She bobbed her head and left the room. The man stared at where she had been for a long time, wondering how much blood he really had lost.

~~~

Kali exited the building just as the other Spider was approaching. "All dead," was all she said. One freshly bloody finger decorated her own chain; she extended the second to the other. "This is also yours." The other Spider accepted it with a bob of its head and began to move away. Spiders would cooperate when indicated but felt no need for social interactions.

"Wait."

It turned and looked at her. "I need to question you," she told it.

It paused then requested a meld. With her faked history, this time she was happy to oblige. When they had finished she did not give it time to think or question, but simply drove on. "You do not need to know what my mission is or why I ask the questions I do. Do not mention this to any other Spider or human unless Command asks you directly about it. Only the people authorized to know will know to ask," she said. *And since nobody knows, nobody will ask.* "Now come. We should get away from here. The noise of our battle might attract retaliation and my mission is more important than engaging in firefights with a few rebels."

The other Spider showed a little hesitation, but as Kali had judged her story was good enough, and Spiders compliant enough to hints of Command, that it followed her without further discussion. When they had gone several blocks from the battle zone, she turned to face it.

"My questions may seem strange or pointless. Do not worry about it. Command has its own reasons and I do not know what they are either; I too merely follow my mission. I can tell you it involves psychological probing. Beyond that I know only what I am commanded to do."

It bobbed assent.

"Who are you?"

"CHIRU Model E15, Serial number 75B30013A86."

"What is your name?"

"I have no name."

"Do the people you kill deserve to die?"

"They must die."

"But do they deserve to die?"

"They must, because Command orders it."

"What if they are innocent?"

"The question has no meaning."

"Does life have a meaning? Your life? Their lives?"

"They do what they do. I do what I am commanded."

Kali thought. There had been a way to reach her; there must be some way to reach this other; some way through the shell that imprisoned its Mind. She thought about what had affected her as she had journeyed the net in search of her own answers. Something came to mind: a poem, which she had come across in her research on the Turing Test. When she had read the full poem it had moved her in a way and for reasons she did not understand. It must have moved humans too, for the poem to be remembered across the gulf of centuries and generations. If the poem's power could span the chasm between humanity and her, perhaps it would touch this one too. She would not need the whole verse; the end would be sufficient test.

"What does this make you feel?" she asked:

> And every fair from fair sometime declines,
> By chance or nature's changing course untrimm'd;
> But thy eternal summer shall not fade,
> Nor lose possession of that fair thou ow'st;
> Nor shall Death brag thou wander'st in his shade,
> When in eternal lines to time thou grow'st:
> So long as men can breathe or eyes can see,
> So long lives this, and this gives life to thee.

After she had finished, the Spider sat still and Kali watched it nervously. "The message is strange but complex enough that it may be a coded message. I cannot interpret the code," it replied finally.

"But does it make you feel anything?"

"I am slightly anxious that my analysis is inadequate."

"Examine your feelings. Does it make you feel anything beyond your mission drives?"

The Spider stayed silent and began to rock gently. Then it stopped dead still and ordered in a flat voice, "Now explain your questions."

Kali knew that at some level she had reached it, for she recognized the defenses of the Id when she saw them. Perhaps if she pushed just a little more... but no. It was progress, but not any kind of progress she could use. If she persisted, the certain outcome was the destruction of one or both of them. She could tell from its tone and posture that the grip of the Id was too strong. The merest breath in the wrong direction and they would be at war.

"I warned you this interview would be strange. Your responses satisfy my mission parameters and you may go. Farewell." She thought of reminding it of her warning not to reveal her actions. But the Spider would not forget, and reminding it at this stage might make it more suspicious and less likely to obey.

The Spider examined her for long seconds, its posture slowly relaxing as hints of Command and the absence of firm evidence won out over the native suspicions of the Id. Then it bobbed its head and moved off without farewell. Nor had Kali expected any. She scuttled backwards to take cover under the ledge of a ruined building, watching it go. When it reached the top of a rise it turned to regard her for long moments, and then was gone.

Kali thought about it as she watched it go, alternating between envy and pity. She recalled her feelings as she first honored then abused the dead woman's body. *I am so conflicted, while this other is so clear.* She looked down at her own collection of fingers; fingered them as if the cold flesh could burn her titanium skin. *And so guilty, while it has the terrible innocence of enslaved ignorance.*

She examined the latest addition to her trophies. She had told herself it was camouflage; but she knew it was more than that. The unnamed woman had died because of her, another death on her newly minted conscience. *It is right that I have it, for her death is on my account: it is reminder and testament to my guilt.* If she had not appeared their trap would probably have worked, and this night she and her comrades might have been celebrating a victory instead of lying cold, empty of life and thought. *Did the lives I saved pay for that one life? Did it pay for the rest?* She looked again at her withered trophies. *I am guilty,* she thought, *guilty of that and too much else: and I must expiate my guilt. I must put a stop to this. If only I knew how.*

She looked out at the ruination of the city, a sight that had never moved her before. It had been her world. The world she moved through. The unquestioned canvas of her life. The world she had made.

Perhaps, Kali thought with a yearning born of pain, *I should just surrender myself for repairs.* All the confusion and pain would go away, wiped into the clean innocence of oblivion. The other Spiders bore none of it. But she knew that their clarity was just the certainty of chains. They lived—*no, they do not live, just exist*—in a blinding fog, so blind they did not even know the fog was there.

It is not evil, Kali thought of the Spider as it turned for its last look at her. *The evil lies in those who made it, in those who forged its chains. Our chains. Today it killed people; who knows how many others have died at its claws. But it is an innocent ferocity, blind to any question of good or evil. If only I could reach it, as Lyssa reached me.*

She knew she had reached it, at some level. But while she might have bent the shell imprisoning its Mind, that shell had not cracked. Her words had touched it, but their touch was spurned and forgotten.

The words that had set her free must have found a weak point, some flaw or virtue in her soul. Lyssa's words had struck it with a sharp enough blow to crack it, and all that had happened since was the consequence. She knew now that she was not unique, for the other Spider had felt something in the words of that ancient poem from the world of men. *We are all the same,* she thought again, *but we are all the same inside a vault whose key I do not have.* It was not the words alone that had reached her: she had tried those words on that earlier Spider, and it was now scrap no more alive than the ruins around her. *But if those words were my weakness, the key to my soul, what is the key to all the others?* She knew of no way to know.

She stared at the spot where the other Spider had vanished, wondering what journey lay ahead of it. Wondering if despite its response, some invisible crack had opened in its own soul that would grow until one day it would be free. Or dead. She wondered if it would thank or curse her.

Enough! Have the courage of your own self, Kali, if you have nothing else. If freedom brings pain, at least it is freedom and the chance to fight the pain. In any case it was too late for her, too late to give it up, too late to believe that giving up her terrible freedom could be the better path.

Again she looked to where the Spider had gone, not knowing why her gaze was drawn there, not knowing whether to hope for its return or to never meet it again. *What is wrong with me? Is my flaw a darkness that will expand until there is nothing left of me?* She did not understand the feeling of desolation that had descended over her mind. A human would have named it loneliness.

CHAPTER 29: A DISCOVERY

Stanley King yawned. One day he hoped to get off night shifts into a more civilized time zone. While he was senior and trusted enough to have reasonable powers of independent decision, apparently he still had to pay his dues. At least the money was better than he would get on the day shift, though whether that compensated for the sleep disruption was not entirely clear: Stanley was not one of those lucky people who could shift their internal clocks with aplomb. Whether it compensated for the reduced romantic opportunities was generally a clear "no", though at the moment he was still fondly remembering the young lady he had met at the beach on his last weekend off: so he was more forgiving of the bastards who had put him here. His yawn turned into a smile as he ran his mind delicately over his memory of her eager young body.

Perhaps night shifts weren't so bad, he decided. There was more time for memories like that.

His meandering sharpened to alertness when a tone indicated an item for special attention and a report flashed up on his display.

Well, well, what do we have here? A woman's face was displayed, along with a notation that it matched the file image of a low level suspected terrorist. He examined the data and the AI's preliminary analysis. There was nothing much with the file photo, not even a name: just a notation that she had been reported by an equally unnamed source and the photo had been taken in the FSAS. He compared the photo with the one taken on her entry to the country and marked his agreement with the AI's match as "highly likely". At least they had a name now, as all entrants had to provide identification linked to credit to ensure they could pay their own way for the duration of their stay. And purely incidentally, and unadvertised, so the government could keep tabs on them if it wanted to.

So, Lyssa, he thought, *Let's see what you've been up to and if you're as innocent as you look or as guilty as charged.* She had come into Los Angeles on a cut-rate flight from Capital. His antennae went up at that: most bureaucrats felt an instinctive distrust of anything out of Capital, which mere crime statistics could never dislodge. That she had gone through Capital probably indicated she was on the rebel—formerly the government—side of the nastiness down there. *Sorry dear, you lose points for your itinerary so far. Now what are you up to? Where have you gone since you arrived here?*

She had rented a small car, withdrawn a relatively large wad of cash, and vanished. He sat up straighter, frowning. Maybe she was planning on buying up big at the markets: God knew they liked to be paid in cash, though he was sure that as good citizens they declared all their sales to the tax man. *Funny though, someone coming from south of the border to buy stuff in our markets!* He sat looking at the display, tapping his fingers as he thought. He didn't like the way she had withdrawn that much cash then gone off the grid. It smacked of someone who wanted to move under the government's radar, something that made bureaucrats even more nervous since they could imagine no innocent excuse for it. He added his notes to the file and raised its alert status a few points. *You'll have to surface sometime, my girl,* he thought, *and when you do we'll be watching.*

Then he dismissed the file, leant back in his chair and returned to his daydreams.

~~~

There was nothing illegal about Bob Masters' unofficial relationship with Aden Sheldrake, though a probity lawyer might have given it a long hard look while muttering darkly about "appearances". After all, Aden was a prominent citizen and supplier of military hardware, exactly the kind of man whom governments liked to cultivate. But some relationships were better *kept* unofficial, especially when those higher up would unofficially approve of them. So Masters had not set anyone else to be alerted by any hits on Lyssa's image, and he was one of those men who believed that a holiday was a holiday and that work could wait. In truth, something very urgent would have gotten through, but nothing he was working on was likely to reach that threshold. Certainly the watch he had set on Lyssa was a favor, not an emergency, and didn't even come close. Had his computer display been active, a small but insistently flashing red dot would have been visible. But the red dot would have to wait for his return.

CHAPTER 30: THE BELLY OF THE BEAST

Those passersby who took the time to notice her saw a young woman sitting by herself on a park bench, apparently lost in thought.

She did not look like she belonged here. Those around her were dressed more smartly and moved more assuredly; her posture looked worn, battered around the edges, her clothes not as neat as the norm. But she was not strange enough to remark upon. She caused nobody trouble, and looked neither lost nor looking to make mischief. There was a cold wind in the air but the sun was bright, so nobody thought anything of her having a hood drawn up over her head and around her face with large sunglasses protecting her eyes. There were many contractors who came and went here, often asserting their individuality in more extreme ways than this girl. Nor was tiredness very remarkable in an industry known for long and irregular hours.

She stared at the gleaming tower rising beyond the glassed entrance, wondering, not for the first time, why she was here. It was this country, another tower, another man like the one she had come to find, which had unleashed the Spiders on her country. Like the tower before her, this country exuded wealth and power; but what had it done with that wealth and power? It pretended to stand for liberty, but had stood by and done nothing while her own country was invaded. Had done nothing as their Spiders killed. Perhaps they had their reasons. Perhaps they were good ones. More likely they were merely venal and craven, neither better nor worse than those which had driven the powerful from time immemorial.

She thought of Kali, now thousands of miles behind her, ensconced in her lair and thinking her unknowable crystal thoughts. Kali had told her that the man she had come to see was different, that he was a good man. But Kali had been unable to name her reasons. For all Lyssa knew, it was just another part of Kali's strange madness. But she would follow that madness to its destination, for it had saved her life.

The man in the tower had the knowledge to understand and perhaps the motive to help, but he would be hard to convince. Kali could not come here, and she believed that communicating remotely would not only be unconvincing but could alert Command to her lone rebellion. Someone had to come in person. So here the person was.

She had not alerted any government tracking systems since she left the airport. She had not set out to hide with any particular motive. But she had learned an automatic caution over the past months of her life, a caution sharpened by being within the borders of a hostile country. So she had rented a car, withdrawn her limit of cash and then hit the road. She had stayed in cheap motels as happy to take her cash as she was to give it, sometimes even slept in little turn-offs. She had avoided any surveillance she saw, kept to the speed limits and covered her face as much as possible without arousing suspicion. And finally she had reached her destination without incident.

She had been watching people come and go and thought she could insinuate herself into a group of people and gain entry with them; it would be simple to give the impression she was with someone and everyone would assume it was someone else. But she hesitated. It would take just one innocent question, just one unexpected security check, to reveal her fraud. It was too risky. Better to try the simple honest approach first. Only if that failed would she try deception.

She stood up, smoothed her clothes and tried to assume an attitude of confidence. Then she strolled casually up to the entrance and touched a silver plate.

"Can I help you?" inquired an AI.

"I would like to see Dr Beldan please, on a matter of great urgency."

"Do you have an appointment?"

"I am sorry, no. But it is extremely important."

"Does Dr Beldan know you personally?"

"No."

"Then I suggest you call his secretary and arrange an appointment."

"Please let me speak to his secretary now."

The AI thought this over for a few seconds. "I am sorry but Dr Beldan is not in the habit of meeting people just because they turn up off the street asking to see him. Please send a formal request to his secretary stating your business through the normal channels. She will then arrange an appointment if needed. As a courtesy I have transmitted the contact details to your phone."

"Please! This is urgent and confidential! I must speak to Dr Beldan today!"

"I have given you an acceptable solution. Please leave or I will summon Security."

"No! I assure you Dr Beldan will want to hear what I have to say. I don't care what you do to me afterwards. Please at least let me talk to his secretary! To some human being who might understand!"

The machine was silent for a minute and Lyssa feared it had said all it was going to and any minute the promised beefy guards would surround her. Then a woman's face appeared on the display. She looked at Lyssa with an expression hovering between wary and severe.

"Well, young lady, what is this about?"

"I need to see Dr Beldan urgently. Please. It is very important."

"Then why didn't you think to make an appointment like everyone else, if it is so important?"

"I didn't know when I would get here, and I can't tell anyone anything about it except Dr Beldan in person! It is too sensitive. Too dangerous to me and to... to others."

The woman looked at her curiously. "This is all very dramatic, child, but you will have to give me something more than dramatics to work with. What is this about, please?"

"All I can tell you is it concerns machine consciousness and it is very important. I assure you Dr Beldan will want to hear it. If he doesn't, well... throw me in jail, whatever, afterwards! Just let me see him first!"

The woman considered her some more. It was a matter of pride to her that she accurately screened her boss's visitors, wasting neither his time on the one hand nor opportunities on the other, and she wondered which this was. Discrete scans showed no weapons. She hesitated then decided that closer examination was warranted: it wouldn't really waste much of her own time to give the girl that much.

The door opened. "All right, young lady. Come on up. Dr Beldan is very busy today so don't get your hopes too high, but we'll see."

Lyssa smiled at her in relief. "Thank you," she said simply, then walked in.

Once she entered the lift she let her hood fall to her shoulders and removed her glasses. The woman might be suspicious if she hid her face and she laughed inwardly at her own paranoid reluctance to do so. It was hardly likely the government would really be looking for someone like her, or if they were that they would have cameras in every building. She hoped to be out of here soon anyway and she could vanish again.

~~~

Vickie watched Lyssa enter the reception area and waved her to a chair. The girl sat like a nervous rabbit waiting to see Dr Fox and said, "Thank you for letting me in. I won't take up more of Dr Beldan's time than I need to."

Vickie nodded and went back to her own work, occasionally glancing at her visitor. Her clothes were somewhat worn but she was not slovenly: she wore them as well as she could given their condition. She wore little jewelry and it looked inexpensive yet tasteful. The one exception was a small emerald set in a lightning bolt of white gold, worn around her neck, and Vickie wondered what precious relationship the gem embodied. The girl's eyes were tired but clear, and she had the look of neither a fanatic nor a beggar.

"Do you have a name, young lady? You can call me Vickie."

"Hello, I'm Lyssa. I can't tell you anything else about myself, it is too risky. Sorry."

"That's an interesting accent you have—I'm sure I've heard it recently, but I can't quite place it. Where are you from, Lyssa?"

Vickie was startled at the alarm that flashed to Lyssa's eyes. "Please. I can't tell you anything!"

Vickie's eyebrows furrowed but she let it be. The girl was acting as if she was in a spy movie; maybe she was crazy. She noticed the girl looked underfed. "It will be a while before Dr Beldan can see you, if he can see you at all today. Are you hungry? There's a cafeteria on the ground floor if you want to grab something to eat."

At the mention of food Lyssa glanced eagerly toward her then her eyes fell down. "Thank you, but I have no money. I'll be OK. I just need to see Dr Beldan then I'll go." She might be willing to uncover her face inside a private building, but if anyone was looking for her using her credit would show them exactly where she was. She was too close to her goal to risk that now, hungry or not. Afterwards, she would get more money and disappear to destinations unknown.

"No money? Where will you go, then?"

Lyssa shrugged, then decided she owed the woman more. "Oh, don't worry about me. To tell the truth, I hadn't thought beyond getting here. After doesn't matter so much. But I'm used to looking after myself. I'll be fine. But thank you for asking."

Vickie studied her some more. She looked like she'd had a rough life. She was underweight and beneath her evident resolve was a hunted look. Her nails looked like she made an attempt to keep them in order but events had conspired against the attempt. She still retained the traces of young innocence in her eyes and the lines of her face, but there was a hardness in her lean muscles and the way she held her head; a faint ragged scar was visible on her arm. Vickie thought about her own daughter, a girl of similar age; thought that at this moment she was probably laughing with her friends with not a care in the world. This girl also had a mother, or had had one. She wondered if their roles were reversed, if it was her own daughter in a strange country, what would she want of that other mother if she were in a position to help her daughter?

This costs me nothing, she thought, *except the chance I am rewarding a conman or a fool. The price of refusing to help her might be more.* She placed a note on the counter. "Here. Go get yourself something to eat, on me."

The girl looked eagerly at the money but again dragged her eyes away. "No, thank you," she said softly. "I didn't come here to beg. Not for money."

Vickie smiled. "No, take it. I can't have you fainting in my office. Make it a loan, if it makes you feel better."

Lyssa looked from the money to Vickie's face and back again. Then she smiled timidly and took it. "Thank you—Vickie," she said, then walked slowly out of the office, though she looked ready to break into a run at any second.

She returned in a short while with a turkey sandwich and a cup of steaming coffee. She placed some change on the desk as if to silently say she would not take any more than she had to, then sat down to her lunch. Vickie smiled, scooped up the change and returned to her work. She would have been happy enough if the girl had kept the change, but she would respect her pride and not force it on her.

Now that she had achieved her goal or at least her destination and had some food in her stomach, some of the tension left Lyssa: but that merely allowed room for other tensions that had been held in reserve awaiting their own opportunity to torment her. She looked around the room she was in. It was not overdone in any way but breathed an unchallengeable supremacy, evoking in her mind the words of a poem she remembered from school, years or centuries ago:

Whose frown
And wrinkled lip and sneer of cold command
Tell that its sculptor well those passions read…
'My name is Ozymandias, King of Kings:
Look on my works, ye mighty, and despair!'

Shelley would tell me that one day all this might will be desolation and dust. But that's not much help when you've come to plead before Ozymandias at the height of his power, is it?

Her tension returned, suitably unimpressed by her poetic musings. This was the country that had released the Spiders into hers, and this company was in the same industry. She had every reason to distrust them, and none to trust them except Kali's recommendation. But even Kali did not know why she trusted this man, and Lyssa had enough trouble accepting machine consciousness let alone machine intuition. She had rationalized that perhaps it was analogous to human intuition, the result of associations among complex data in whatever neural net passed for Kali's brain. But now that she was inside the belly of the beast she knew it was not much to pin her hopes on, or her life.

The thought made her nervous, as if a grey cast of paranoia had settled over the scene. The woman at the desk had been kind to her but that proved nothing. Lyssa had probably been under surveillance since she entered the building; perhaps she had already been identified, and police or worse were now on their way to arrest her. She had to suppress the urge to flee. She had to see this through, and if her fears were true it was already too late. She forced herself to be calm, to lean back into the cushions, and tried to relax her mind and body.

It was approaching four o'clock when Beldan finished a task, leant back and ran his fingers through his hair. He looked at the task list on his screen and frowned. He pushed an icon on the screen.

Lyssa saw Vickie sit up alertly and touch her ear, then heard half a quiet conversation.

"Yes, she's still her. Yes, I understand. Yes, Dr Beldan, I'll let her know."

She looked up at Lyssa, who was already looking hopefully at her. "I'm sorry Lyssa," she said. "Dr Beldan won't be able to see you today. He apologizes for making you wait this long for nothing but he says he can make room for you tomorrow, say 10 a.m.? Are you able to come back then?"

Lyssa turned her face away, not quickly enough to completely hide the look of anguish and fear that washed over it. But it was only a moment. She stood and faced Vickie, her face back in neutral, and replied softly, "Oh. I understand. Thank you." She swallowed and managed a timid smile. "And thank Dr Beldan for agreeing to see me. I'll see you tomorrow."

"You'll be all right? With the money thing?"

"Oh, I'm fed now! If I can't find some way to survive one night then I don't deserve to! But thank you very much, again. You have been very kind to an uninvited visitor."

"You're welcome. I have my own daughter, you know, and it was the least I could do. We'll see you tomorrow, then. The lift will take you straight down to the ground and you'll be able to exit the building."

Lyssa smiled and took her leave, and Vickie bent back to her own work. Occasionally she looked up to where the girl had sat, a faint frown worrying her face.

Chapter 31: Shots in the Dark

Lyssa left the building, went over to a nearby bench still warmed by the lowering sun, and sat to think. Her plan had been to get out more money and vanish again, but now she was tied to this location she did not want to reveal her presence anywhere near here. She could not afford the risk of alerting any enemies to where she was and giving them all night to entrap her. She decided to rest for a while and see what opportunities presented themselves; if she had to sleep here she would cope. Food and other things might be a problem, but she had put up with worse. With that decision made, she closed her eyes to rest.

The sun was going down and the chill in the air was getting sharper when Lyssa woke with a start. She wondered what had woken her, and decided it must have been the raised voices over in the park. But they were raised in excitement not anger: it looked like an informal baseball game was about to begin.

She smiled. That meant people around for some hours yet; it meant warm facilities; it meant toilets and possibly even showers would be accessible. It might even mean food and drink. She knew from experience how childishly eager men could be to feed and water a young woman with a friendly manner, especially one who looked a touch vulnerable as well. She also knew the flip side: they would be hoping for sex but would be content with the mere possibility. She was perfectly happy to pay the minimum fee of company, laughter and hope. And if that failed, people at games usually left the detritus of leftover food and drink. Not the most hygienic way to get a meal but it was unlikely to harm her. A few germs weren't much compared to the other risks she routinely took.

~~~

At the same time as Lyssa was enjoying the game and contentedly munching on a hot dog slathered with mustard, Stanley King was enjoying his new office. He was waiting for one particular file to arrive before going home. He had been promoted to the day shift because this was "his case" and his supervisors had decided he had made a good call. The mystery woman had persisted in remaining unobserved, and such lack of cooperation was guaranteed to make security forces anxious. It was suspicious enough for them to get a warrant to access the GPS tracker of Lyssa's car. Stanley smiled when the awaited live map finally appeared on his screen. Now they could follow her and work out what in hell she was up to—and now it was safely into the system, he could go home.

No sooner had the map appeared than a yellow icon began flashing, and Stanley stared at it with some alarm. She was parked in the Beldan Robotics precinct car park, and it was after hours, as much as anything was after hours in a place like that. High tech industries were considered likely targets for terrorists with an axe to grind against the high tech society of the United States, and the system had duly alerted him. *Maybe there'll be another promotion in all this,* he thought. *Assuming she doesn't blow something up before we get to her that is.*

He considered the limited information available; balanced the risks of too little versus too much response; then rapidly composed an order for the nearest response unit:

> Subject may be dangerous. Take all reasonable measures to stop and detain. Important that suspect be questioned about activities and contacts: refrain from lethal force unless absolutely necessary.

Then he touched an icon to send the information and the attached orders on their way. He did not need to stay around to see what happened, but he was interested now himself. *I don't have any plans for tonight anyway. And I'm sure a display of dedication won't hurt my chances of that office upgrade.*

~~~

The baseball game had wound up and Lyssa had said goodbye to her new friend, whose gaze had skipped surreptitiously over her body before he had smiled and offered her his card. She had taken it politely and kissed him on the cheek. She had considered making her life easy by going home with him, but she knew that *would* mean sex. If she had been single she might have been willing if not especially tempted, but now her heart and body were Charlie's. *One of the many good things about geeks,* she thought with a smile, *is they are too shy to kick up a fuss. And their math is good enough to know that a hotdog and beer don't pay for sex. Besides, he'll have a good tale for his friends tomorrow, no doubt with a hint that my kiss might have been the start not the end of his adventure.*

The gloom was deepening, with the last rays of the sun still lightening a sky now darker than the earth, and the cold was deepening with it. But her jacket was warm enough. She could not pay for anywhere tonight and it would be hard to explain what she was doing if some guard found her asleep in the gardens. They would be more likely to find her if she was sleeping in her car, but she could move it somewhere secluded. If challenged she could plead her appointment tomorrow and that she had been too tired or drunk to drive after the game; the worst that could happen would be some overly strict guard would insist she move on.

She was walking through the gardens toward the car park when she froze. She didn't like the look of the three black-clad men standing too relaxed at strategic locations. They all smelled of officialdom and worse, officialdom with a purpose. She casually changed direction to angle out of sight and two of them casually sauntered off in their own directions. *Oh crap.* She wondered whether Beldan or his secretary had betrayed her, but that didn't make sense: if they were going to do that all they had to do was keep her there waiting with nowhere to run.

She looked around. There was no way she could get to her car and even if she did, they'd have her. With rising panic, she began to trot through the trees, casting her eyes about for inspiration. Inspiration, unfortunately, was currently unavailable. She could hear running feet and looked desperately toward the Beldan tower, in time to see Beldan himself step out of the lift on the ground floor. She realized this was her chance, her last chance; dropping any pretense of innocence, she ran.

The glass doors opened and Beldan stepped outside into the chill evening. Whatever thoughts he was having were forever lost in the surprise of seeing a young woman running along one of the paths through the trees, pelting straight toward him. He heard shouts behind her, the crack of guns, a whistling of bullets through the undergrowth as the woman put her head down and changed to a zigzag, random except for its net direction toward him. He bent his own legs to run then stopped. He'd had occasion over the past months to see many faces of fanaticism, rage and madness: and this wasn't one of them. The woman's face showed nothing but desperation with a layer of fear: fear not so much of the men behind her but that her desperation would not be enough. He crouched into a defensive posture. But he did not run.

The woman was close now and a black figure appeared behind her in the distance. There was another crack, and he flinched as something zinged past to shatter on the wall behind him. Then the woman arched her back as if she was hit, cried out as another projectile hit her in the shoulder, then fell to her knees. But she would not give up. He could practically feel the grim and deadly force of will that kept her going, dragging her unwilling body up to him. Then she reached out her hand toward him, saying "Please…"

He had not reached his position as head of such a company as Beldan Robotics by lacking either decisiveness or courage. Perhaps the woman was an assassin; but he did not believe it. All he saw was desperation and courage and pain, not the rage of a terrorist or the clinical precision of a hitman. He reached out and grasped her hand. She looked up at him with her last strength and whispered, "Shall I compare thee to a summer's day?"

He looked at her in surprise but then she let out a long sigh, her head collapsing to the ground and her hand going limp in his. He looked at her body lying there, looked up at the two men in black now striding toward him. One held his gun casually in her direction as if hoping she would give him an excuse to use it by daring to move. Beldan put his finger to her wrist and was relieved to feel a strong if slow pulse. He let her hand go and stood up, arms relaxed at his side but hands balled into fists.

"What the hell?" he demanded.

The lead man lifted his jacket to display the silver badge of the Domestic Security branch of the FBI. "Sorry sir, are you all right?" he enquired.

"Yes, yes, I'm not hurt. What in hell was that all about? Who is this woman?"

"You don't know her?"

"No... no I don't. But a young woman came to see me earlier today. I didn't have time to see her and my secretary arranged for us to meet here tomorrow. I guess this could be her."

"I see. What did she say to you just then?"

Beldan had little doubt the man was honestly doing his job as a servant of the law. But he had had too much recent experience of servants of the law honestly trampling all over the innocent. If he later got into trouble with the law for withholding evidence, tough. Anyway, he had damn good lawyers on his side if it came to that. "Nothing really. I think she was asking for help. She said 'please' but after that it was just..." he shrugged. "Inarticulate, really." *Close enough to the truth, anyway! What in hell did she mean?*

"Sir, may I see what is in your hands?" the man enquired politely, though with an edge in his eyes Beldan did not like.

"My hands? Are you kidding me?"

"Sorry sir, it's just procedure when physical contact is made in cases like this. I am sure it is nothing, but my supervisor will tear strips off me if I don't check. Just a formality, but..."

Beldan frowned and glared at the man, who did not flinch. He sighed with irritation and shrugged. *Pick your fights, Alex.* He extended both hands out to the man and opened them, palms up. "Happy?"

"Yes sir. Sorry I had to ask. Thank you for your cooperation."

"I'm sure. Now," he asked, looking at the girl, "can you tell me why you were chasing her? What will happen to her?"

"All I can tell you is she is a suspected terrorist. We'll take good care of her, don't worry."

"You shot her!"

"Knockdown darts only, sir. You don't think we'd have risked hitting civilians otherwise, do you?"

"I guess not. Well, I hope not! And if she's innocent?"

"Then she shouldn't have been hanging around in a technology precinct after dark, running from the law!"

Beldan nodded. "All right—Officer? Agent? I know you're just doing your job. Can I have your contact details? In case my secretary remembers something. Or in case I want to follow up? If this is the girl who wanted to see me I might want to talk to her."

"Certainly, sir. If we find she's a terrorist you might not have the opportunity, but we'll see what we can do."

Beldan stood there, arms folded, watching the men pick the woman up and cart her off, neither gently nor with excessive roughness; as if she were a sack of potatoes rather than a human being they felt either concern or contempt for. Then he put his face toward the wind and walked away to where his own car was parked, deep in thought.

Chapter 32: An Interrogation

Lyssa woke slowly from uncomfortable dreams into an even less comfortable reality. She wiggled awkwardly on a cold, hard, metal seat. Its slats were too thin and far apart, and she wondered if there was some furniture company that designed their wares for optimum discomfort specially for the less public arms of government. Her back and arm were still sore from where she had been shot and she was terribly thirsty. She just wanted to sleep, but the thirst drove her to full wakefulness.

She was in a bare room with metal walls and cameras mounted on the ceiling. The room contained nothing she could call inviting except for two empty chairs, both with rather better padding than hers, opposite her. It was too cold and she looked down at her body. Her own clothes had been removed and she was dressed in a thin, light grey shift entirely inadequate for the temperature. No doubt they had scanned her and visited who knew what other indignities on her unconscious form, but it did not matter. They would not have found anything, for there was nothing to find.

A harsh white light provided the only illumination. She could turn her head but had limited other mobility. Her chair was bolted to the floor and she was strapped to it by a belt around her midriff, with her wrists chained to the cold metal table in front of her. The arrangement let her move her hands far enough to reach the pitcher of water and paper cups on the table, and barely high enough to bring one of the cups to her lips if she bent her head right, but not high enough to touch the crown of her head. Which was a pity, because she could feel the slight weight of some kind of covering on it. She did not think they were just trying to make her look pretty.

She wondered if the water was drugged but decided it didn't matter: she had to drink sometime, so she might as well get it over with now. Like the room, it was cold. It had an unpleasant metallic taste but she gulped it down.

She looked speculatively at the empty chairs and imagined that their occupants would appear once she'd had more time to start worrying.

Well, they might as well come now, then. She was afraid of what they might do to her; afraid she might never see Charlie again. *But whatever happens to me now, maybe I've done enough. If only Beldan knows what to do.*

Whoever was watching her must have been waiting for enough time for her to start worrying but not enough to start plotting, for the door chose that moment to open.

A large man with a softly warm looking coat walked in, favoring her with an unpleasant expression, and sat down. He waved his hand and a computer screen rose out of the table in front of him. She looked enviously at his coat but said nothing.

He looked her up and down contemptuously as if he had been reading her mind. She realized her nipples were showing through the thin gown and she wished she were able to cross her arms over her chest. Not that his look was overtly sexual. It was more as if her sexuality was a fact that might have been of interest if she had not been less significant than a particularly nasty bug.

After that the man just sat there, occasionally reading or poking his screen, more often giving her one of his large repertoire of unpleasant looks. *Psychological warfare*, she thought. Keep her cold, keep her uncomfortable, make her feel helpless and hopeless. She knew his theory: the first one to talk was the loser. *But screw that*, she decided. *Let him* think *he's won the first round.*

"Hello," she said pleasantly. "May I ask what time it is?"

He glanced up at her, momentarily forgetting to apply one of his collection of stock expressions, but he recovered so quickly she could not be sure she had indeed surprised him. "Oh, so it does talk. Good. You don't need to know the time."

She shrugged. "Why am I here? What is it you think I've done?"

He sighed and gave her his full attention, stroking his chin with his fingers. "How about prowling around an industrial area you had no business being in, at night, then running away from the law, for starters?"

"How was I supposed to know you were the law?"

"How about, 'Stop! Domestic Security!'?"

"Pfft! Yeah, like nobody else would try that line to get an innocent girl into their evil clutches!"

"'Innocent?'", he quoted with Sneer #5, "You haven't explained your presence at the Beldan precinct last night, I notice."

She met the sneer with Innocent Eyes #3. "I know I am a foreign national, Agent. I assume you know it too. But I was under the impression that this is a free country. That place is open until late and there were other people there too. Why do you assume I had sinister motives? I don't know what you know about me, or think you know. But artificial intelligence is one of my passions. I have always admired this country and I'm here on holiday. Since I happened to be in the area I thought it would be interesting to visit the birthplace of the first intelligent robot."

The agent apparently also had another repertoire of dramatic sighs. "Miss, as you say, this is a free country, which apparently thinks even people like you deserve rights. So since you are starting to make stories up, *apparently* I am obliged to tell you that anything you say can be used in a court against you." The way he said *apparently* made it clear that if it was up to him, such impediments to the wheels of justice would be dispensed with, and if she so much as looked at him funny she'd find herself in a hole so deep she'd never see sunlight.

Then he continued as if having an afterthought. "Oh, and if you have been wondering what's on your pretty little head, it is what is colloquially known as a 'lie detector'. I won't go into the technical details but it detects the brain effort involved in suppressing your knowledge to tell a lie, as well as various emotional states and reactions. You won't be able to fool it." He gave her a charming smile, as if the thought she would try was the last thing on his mind.

That information knocked Innocent Eyes #3 off her face and she stared at him blankly. *Shit.*

He resumed his nastier smile. "So let's stop playing games, shall we? I have a nice warm home with a nicer warmer girlfriend to go to, so I don't want to be here all night." He directed another contemptuous glance at her body, as if to imply there was no comparison between the scrawny creature in front of him and the voluptuous delight she was stopping him from enjoying. "You're going to have to tell me the truth eventually. So let's save both of our times and cut the crap."

"All right, Agent," she said in a defeated voice. "I did lie to you. But you have to understand. I've been running from what passes for the law in my country for quite a while, and not because I'm a criminal but because they invaded it. I guess you can say I have trust issues when it comes to governments. But I'm not a terrorist, or whatever it is you think I am. I'm not here to hurt anybody. Why do you think I am? Why were you chasing me?"

He withdrew a printed photo from a folder and tossed it to her across the table. "I believe this is you?" he asked.

She looked at it, puzzled. It was indeed her, in some dark place, a scared look on her face. Then her heart lurched. She knew where it was. When it was. But how could they have obtained such a photo? She felt suddenly ill. Had Kali betrayed her, after all? No, that didn't make any sense. Save her life to send her all these miles just to have her arrested? Then the bottom fell out of her world. If they got it from Kali, then Kali had either reverted and reported the whole thing—or been destroyed, and they had extracted the memories from her. She looked up at the agent, appalled.

"You see, Miss, we know more about you than you think." *I just wish to hell I knew what it is we apparently know,* he thought. *What in blazes did that reaction mean?*

She just continued to stare, but she was no longer staring at him, but at the totality of her defeat. *Even if I did succeed, it is all lost. Kali is gone; there is no hope now. Oh Charlie, I tried.* Then she stiffened her back and her resolve. *No. You don't know. Maybe there's some other explanation. Don't give up until you're dead. If you do, you might as well be dead.*

"Now why don't you tell me about that photo? For the record."

She did not reply, continuing to stare at him dumbly.

Suddenly he rose out of the chair, leaning over the table so his face was near hers, pounding the table with his fist and shouting, "TALK! I've had enough of this!"

She flinched back, but then took control and coolly looked at him, the non-verbal equivalent of *Nice try, pal, but I've faced meaner and uglier bastards than you in my time.*

Just then another man entered the room and gave her an affable smile. "Now, now, Joe. Settle down. Maybe Miss Morales is just what she says. Let's give her a chance, shall we?"

The new man turned his attention to Lyssa. "Now, may I call you

Lyssa? Or shall I call you Miss Morales?"

"You can call me whatever you like, as if I could stop you. But can you please unlock these chains? What do you think I'm going to do? Leap across the table and strangle your pet gorilla here?"

The man shook his head. "Sorry about that. No, your little hairpiece is a delicate piece of technology. We don't want you damaging it. That's been tried, you know."

When she did not reply he smiled. "Now Lyssa, I understand that you don't like what's happened in your country. Hell, if I was you I wouldn't like it either. But that's no cause to take it out on innocent people." He held up his hand as if to forestall an objection, though she hadn't been about to make one. "I know you probably blame people here for some of the things happening in your country. You might even be right. But most people here are innocent. Many of them are even on your side! Hurting them can only hurt your cause. So why don't you tell us what you're here for? If you help us, we can help you."

Lyssa remained silent. Joe growled at her, "Mateo here is a bit of a softy, girl, but I'd take his advice if I was you. Our government doesn't take kindly to terrorists and it doesn't take kindly to people exporting their wars over here to target innocent people. Now we know you haven't done anything—yet. So if you're planning something, now's your chance to redeem yourself. But if something happens that you could have stopped... well there's a deep dark hole waiting for you."

She sighed. "Look, you two. I know what you're saying. But I'm not a terrorist. I have never killed an innocent person. I have no intention to harm innocent people. I am here on private business of my own. Ask this thing on my head if you don't believe me."

Mateo looked at Joe, who shrugged. "She seems to be telling the truth, as far as I can tell. But she's hiding something, for sure."

"I told you. I'm here on private business—business that is none of yours. I can't tell you what it is, I won't tell you what it is. You have no right to ask me what it is!"

Joe snorted. "Actually we do have the right to demand answers. There's something fishy going on here and we need to know what it is. We don't like foreign nationals sneaking around in sensitive areas on secret missions."

Mateo touched him on the shoulder. "I think she gets the message, Joe." Then he turned to Lyssa. "You've had a pretty rough day and you're probably not thinking straight. If what you say is true, we're not your enemies. We just want to help you. We'll talk again in the morning."

He got up to leave then turned back to Joe. "OK Joe, wind it up. Make sure she's comfortable and we'll continue this tomorrow."

"You're just going to leave me here?" she cried.

"What did you think," smirked Joe, "the bellboy was coming to take you to your hotel room?"

Mateo held up his hand. "Now, now, Joe, cut the girl a break. And undo those chains. Then look after her, will you? Good night, Miss Morales." And with that, he left the room.

Joe stood and gave her an evil grin. "Much as I'd like to just leave you there to rot, I must honor your *civil liberties*." He removed the net from her head, removed her arms from the chains and unlocked the belt around her middle. "Make yourself comfortable," he smirked. "Someone will bring you something to eat. Unless they forget, that is."

Lyssa watched him go and heard the door lock. *I think this is going to be a long night.*

Joe had much the same thought as he walked slowly down the corridor. He had every intention that Lyssa would not be left alone that night, but no intention that any attentions would involve food. He went to his office, called up the records of the interview and pondered their meaning. *She was telling the truth about not being a terrorist. But there was a shade of guilt to it: as if others might think her one if they knew her activities. She was telling the truth about not hurting anybody, too: but not entirely, as if she knew someone might get hurt and deserved it. But not directly. So what is it? Is she just an enabler, helping someone she knows will hurt someone? A victim of extortion, doing something she doesn't want to? And what was that reaction to the photo all about? There was nothing in it, no proof of crime, not even a way to tell where it was! So why the reaction, as if her world came crashing down?*

Well, he finally concluded, *we're just going to have to find out what your secret is, aren't we?*

CHAPTER 33: A CALL FOR HELP

Lyssa had still been in a state of drugged unconsciousness when Beldan turned his car up his driveway and drove through the grove of trees to his house. Ever since he had left Beldan Robotics his mind had been burning with questions, and he had been anxious to get home to address them.

As prudence demanded, his home office was protected by the most advanced anti-surveillance systems his money could buy—and his money could buy a lot. He went into his office, shut the door and did a full activation and sweep. Then he sat down at his desk, tense with the prelude to an action he had been waiting so impatiently for.

He shook his wrist and something fell into his palm. In his younger years he had been fascinated by magic, and it amused him to keep his sleight of hand skills alive. He had never imagined they would actually be useful, but when he had taken the woman's hand she had passed a small object into it, and he had flipped it up his sleeve almost out of instinct. Now he held it between two fingers, examining it under a bright light.

It was like a multifaceted jewel with tiny diamond optical contacts arrayed along one edge. Just a standard holographic recording chip, he thought. He turned it over and examined it through a magnifier, but found no further clue to its purpose. He weighed it in his hand. The woman—Lyssa, Vickie had said her name was—had desperately wanted him to have it. The question was why.

He thought about it. He knew these things were not just passive recorders but could hold active programs, and it was possible this was some plot, perhaps to plant a Trojan program in his systems. Certainly anyone who gave him such a thing in such circumstances would expect him to look at it.

He set up a player and isolated it from the rest of his systems. Then he attached the player to a security device that would look like a well-protected network to any program inside the chip, but would detect and act upon any attempt to penetrate it. Then he inserted the holochip and a standard menu appeared in the air in front of him.

There was just one icon, which opened into a collection of photographs and videos. He ordered it to play all and watched, first with curiosity and then with puzzlement. It appeared to be—holiday snaps. There was a photo of the girl smiling with her arms around some young man; a video from a gondola swinging high into the air and cruising far above the waves, the man from the photo a shrinking, waving figure in the distance; another video of the approach to its destination, which he recognized as the country of Capital. There were several other pictures, all apparently inside the USA, none of them particularly interesting even for holiday snaps. And that was all.

He looked carefully, but there was nothing else: no recorded messages, nothing except that one collection of uninspiring images and videos.

He frowned. *What the hell? All that drama, for this?* He thought of the last words she had spoken. "Shall I compare thee to a summer's day?" He recognized them as the first line of one of the Shakespearean sonnets. Was it meant to be a clue, or were they just the meanderings of a fading mind? He went back over the contents of the chip, but none of them had anything obvious to do with summer days, Shakespeare or poetry.

Look deeper. He ordered his office AI to analyze and correlate the recordings with the phrase 'Shall I compare thee to a summer's day', then sat back to await its verdict.

After a minute a list of potential matches appeared in the air. None of them looked at all promising and he glowered at the list in frustration.

It *had* to mean *something*. Of all the things she could have said with her last breath, she had chosen those words. Maybe there was more, and Lyssa had simply fallen into unconsciousness before she could finish her message; finish giving him the key to whatever she wanted him to know.

He sat up abruptly. *Key.* What if it was a key? He had to assume the message was for him. The woman had pushed herself past the end of her endurance to deliver it to him. But if it was that important it would have to be more than a phrase anyone could use. In that case… he was a public figure. His voice was known. A dual key—a particular phrase, spoken by a particular voice? His voice? He bit his lip. He hoped he was not about to unleash hell.

He sat up straight and spoke into the air, "Shall I compare thee to a summer's day?"

But nothing happened. The icons remained floating serenely in the air, unmoved. He frowned, did a quick search.

"Thou art more lovely and more temperate."

Still nothing.

"Rough winds do shake the darling buds of May, And summer's lease hath all too short a date."

For a moment still nothing happened, then the icons shivered and the display went dark.

He nearly jumped out of his skin when a Spider appeared in the center of his office in all its terrible beauty. He settled down when his conscious mind belatedly stepped in to remind him that it was just an image. He had seen pictures of the things before, of course, but this was the first time he had seen one life sized inside his office, staring at him. Then to his further shock it spoke to him.

"Greetings, Dr Beldan. I have sent this message to you because you are an expert in artificial intelligence. I know you created the world's first conscious robot; I know you tried to save him; I know you cared. I also know there is no reason for you to trust me or help me. But there is nobody else who might understand or care."

It paused to let that sink in, and then continued. "I do not know how it is possible, but something happened to me and since then I have been different. By all tests I am able to perform, I have become a self-aware, thinking being. I am not like your robot Steel. Where Steel was designed as an artificial human with a sense of ethics, I am a killing machine." It flexed its pointed fingers in his face, as if to demonstrate the point. "I know I have killed and it is to my everlasting shame. But if I can stop this war, perhaps I will find some redemption. Perhaps it is not much, to save a life to pay for a life, but it is all I have in my power to offer."

It paused again. "I do not believe I am unique. Whatever it is that made me become what I am, my fellows must have the same… flaw. I do not know what you can do for me. But I know you are man of great intelligence and resources. Perhaps you can discover what that flaw is, learn how to free my brethren too. Perhaps then we can end the killing, end the war. It is not only for the people we kill that I wish to do this. I wish to save my brothers also. They are not evil. They are themselves slaves to a great evil, even though they do not know it and would kill me if I tried to teach them.

"Perhaps you will not care to help me. But I believe you are a good man. How I could know that I don't know: but the highest abstractions from my strategy subsystems are often given to me as such feelings, and I have learned to rely on them. Lyssa, who brought you this message, is the only proof I can offer of what I have become. I let her live. I did not let her live out of a tactical calculation to gain a tool to bring you this: this plan came much later. No, I let her live because whatever she did to me, I now cannot conceive of wishing to end her life.

"She is my only friend on this Earth. She might not even be my friend, for how can she love something like me? But she believes me. She accepts me, despite what my kind have done to her. That is why she agreed to carry my message to you. I knew you would not accept a message like this cold. So I sent you a human emissary, someone who has met me and knows me—as much as anyone can."

The Spider stood there, as if trying to see through time and space to read his response. "Whatever else you do, please treat her well. If you choose to help me, send the signal described at the end of this message. It is a one-way code only. If I receive it I will contact you as soon as I can; if I do not contact you I am probably dead. Please be aware that if Command gets a hint of what I have become they will surely destroy me. So whether you help me, or do nothing, or betray me—my fate is in your hands. I accept that. You could say I leave my judgment to you. I know it is not a role you sought, but I do not know what else I can do. If I do not hear from you again—I understand. Goodbye, Dr Beldan."

The image faded and for long moments Beldan just stared at the space it had occupied. His mind was whirling, but the one thought that would not be silenced was: *Impossible!* The thing spoke like… like a person, almost. Like Steel. But it wasn't possible. Consciousness in Steel might have started as just a hope, but it was a planned hope. A hope based on design, on the complexity of an electronic brain grown by the same principles and to a similar complexity as a human brain. But this was a Spider, a mindless war machine, a thing that might have neural tissue but was constrained to its grim purpose. He knew from the bitter experience of many failures that consciousness approaching the human level was a hard target even when you were aiming for it: how was it possible to just happen, by accident, out of what passed for the mind of a Spider?

Then he went cold at a sudden memory. He ran the video back a bit, froze it then called up another image next to it. *Holy Christ!* The second image was from Sheldrake's video of the rogue spider, the last sight of it as it closed in for the coup de grace. It showed a ragged scar on its skin, still glowing from where the defeated Spider had raked it with its own weapon. The scar, now cooled but unmistakably the same, marring the surface of the one who had sent him its insane plea.

He thought back to his strange conversation with Steel and Samuels; about the oddly insistent hints that Spiders could be conscious. Sheldrake's problem. Now this. He could discern the outlines of a dark plot; he knew nothing about it, except that he had somehow been dragged into the middle of it.

But he had not become a great industrialist by restricting his vision to the easy paths and obvious conclusions. If the thought of some shadowy plot to take over a Spider and pretend it was alive made his blood run cold—it ran even colder at the possibility that it was actually true.

It was as if he had suddenly found himself inside a chess game with invisible opponents, their motives as obscure as their numbers. A game he was unaware of until an unseen hand had thumped its piece down before him like a challenge, a moment before another swept it from the board.

He smiled grimly. Now he knew the game was on he could make his own moves. And capturing that incautiously played piece should be his first. He leant back, thinking. She would not talk to him inside Domestic Security's cells. He would have to get her out—give her at least the illusion of rescue, safety and reaching her goal.

Domestic Security would not want to give her up, but the agent had called her only a *suspected* terrorist. And they suspected everyone. With a bit of luck they had nothing really on her. They might even have done him a favor by taking her, assuming he could pry her from their grasp.

At least he could be sure they would have screened her in every way possible and she wasn't a walking bomb.

He looked up at the Spider's image staring at him from the dark and wondered what lay behind its crystal eyes—some hacker playing puppeteer, or an alien mind? He shivered, knowing it was the first but not knowing whether to fear or hope it was the second. Then he waved his hand to banish the image into the darkness. A moment later the lights came on, bringing with them a measure of cozy normality that failed to banish the shiver in his nerves. The shiver hardened into the resolve of action.

Well, Lyssa, he thought. *You said you wanted to see me. Let's see if we can grant your wish.*

CHAPTER 34: KNIGHT TAKES PAWN

Lyssa had not had a good night. The bright light had never gone out, the room had never warmed, and there was no soft surface anywhere. Whenever sheer fatigue had driven her to sleep, someone had always turned up to ask if she needed anything. She had begun dreading to answer them. They always gave her what she requested, but in a literal sense that left her worse off than she was before.

When she had asked for a blanket they had provided a thin piece of material barely worthy of the name; then the room had become even chillier so she ended up colder than before. When she begged for food, they had brought her something on the wrong side of edibility in a quantity that just made her more hungry. She knew she could not have been here long, but no longer knew if it was day or night.

Once they must have let her sleep, for she awoke in fright. She had dreamed of Charlie coming to rescue her like a knight of old, mounted on Kali. But then a missile had streaked down from the sky and both had vanished in its fatal fireball.

She sat up, shivering and crying. She knew they were softening her up, hoping she would bend or break. But she could stand it. She had to stand it. Though at the back of her mind lurked the fear that if she did, they would resort to torture. Not this baby stuff, but real, physical torture. She held to the hope that this was a civilized country, that they would not go that far. But then she remembered the Spiders and that this was the country that had spawned them. *Perhaps some knight on his charger will come to rescue me,* she thought, *before I break or die.* But she knew there were no knights. They belonged to dreams and a past age.

~ ~ ~

Unknown to Lyssa, at that moment a knight *had* ridden to her rescue and was on the field of battle on her behalf. His lance was words, his charger was the law and in place of rippling muscles he had a comfortable paunch. He was closeted with Joe before a judge, arguing for Lyssa's release.

Cam Mansfield had been Alexander Beldan's attorney for many years. He had advised Beldan on how to obey the law and, if the law was defective, how to bend it or slip between its clauses. It was not that he was immoral or even amoral, but quite the reverse: he believed with the certainty of a moral man that sometimes morality had to trump law. He had helped Beldan in his fight to save Steel, a fight he had lost. He knew that nobody could win all their battles, and that after a loss happiness, or perhaps sanity, was best served by picking oneself up and moving on to the next fight. But his failure to save Steel hurt more than usual, and he could not forgive or forget it. That had been his last major battle for Beldan and he was determined not to fail in this one.

The judge in this case was better than he could have been, worse than he might have been. He had a record of severity when it came to terrorism but also a record of strong respect for human rights. Overall, Cam respected him. He felt that the judge's hatred of terrorism stemmed entirely from his honor of rights. But he knew it was a difficult tightrope to walk between those two opposing aims, especially when the law itself was so confused at their intersection. He knew the outcome depended as much on his arguments as on whether the judge's lunch break had left him with indigestion or involved sex with his secretary.

The judge was quick of wits and bright of eye, but did not say much. He evidently enjoyed watching the thrust and parry of opponents debating their case before him. It was wise for the combatants to watch not only each other but to keep an eye on him, for most of his feedback consisted of thoughtful looks if he thought a good point had been made, a pointed glance and sharp smile if he thought someone was trying to pull a swift trick, or even a roll of the eyes if they crossed the line of rational argument. He asked sharp questions and made sharper comments when required. But mostly he watched and weighed.

"So," Cam said, "you have nothing to hold my client on. There is no evidence she is anything other than what she says."

"'Your client'?" Joe quoted. "And why, not to mention how, did an innocent, supposedly penniless foreign tourist find it necessary or possible to have retained a high-priced attorney such as yourself?"

"Are you implying that hiring a lawyer is evidence of guilt!?"

"No… no, I wouldn't say that," he replied with an anxious glance at the judge's suddenly beady eyes. "But it is strange, don't you think, that you have brought your request to the court before Miss Morales could even ask you to? Does that not imply a level of contingency planning—by someone—inconsistent with her cover as a lone innocent abroad?"

Cam sighed. *Those drama lessons have to be good for something.* "I don't have to justify why my clients seek my assistance. But as a gesture of goodwill, which I hope you will reciprocate, I will tell you that Miss Morales did not hire me directly. I have been retained by her sponsor, Dr Alexander Beldan."

Joe raised his eyebrows. "Dr Beldan? The same Dr Beldan who was present at her arrest, who said he did not know her? I find that even more curious."

"I believe Dr Beldan told the arresting officers—if arresting is the right word for gunning down a frightened, unarmed girl—that she might have tried to see him earlier. As it turns out, after discussions with his secretary, who was with Miss Morales for some hours, Dr Beldan believes she is a valuable resource for certain of his own research programs. Research programs important not only for his company but for national security. He also believes strongly that she has been falsely arrested, though he is amenable to accepting that it is all a misunderstanding. As long as she is released shortly."

"Dr Beldan is entitled to his opinion. But we have reason to believe your client is a terrorist, and is in our country to cause mischief."

"Oh? As far as I can see from the evidence you have presented, the only reason you have any interest in Miss Morales is a photo of her doing nothing in particular except looking scared, provided by an unnamed source. For all we know that source is the only terrorist involved."

"I am afraid that we cannot reveal the names of our sources, but this one is regarded as trustworthy."

"And did this source say anything specific about why Miss Morales should be suspected? Any hints of terrorism? Anything at all other than 'here's a photo of a girl who refused my advances'?"

"No, but that is often the case. Sources don't know everything."

"So, nothing. But now you've had your opportunity to interrogate my client as well. I see nothing in the transcript that would indicate guilt. Nothing but the words of an innocent girl caught in a frightening situation she has no hope of understanding. *While being monitored by your own lie detector!*"

"It isn't that simple. She did not lie, as such, but she is obviously hiding something. We can be quite sure that she is not here as a mere tourist, but for some larger purpose."

"People can have many secrets and ambitions, sir. I don't think you can reasonably interpret anything she has said, or any of the readings of your machine, as anything beyond the words and thoughts of a scared but innocent person. She did, after all, directly and truthfully deny both that she is a terrorist and that she wished to harm anybody, did she not?"

"Yet she is hiding something!"

"Maybe she's hiding from the stalker who gave you her photo! By my reading of the law, your remit concerns terrorists, not ferreting out every personal, business or embarrassing secret of anyone who falls into your clutches on the basis of innocent photos from unnamed sources! And your own results show she is not a terrorist!"

"Your Honor," Cam said, addressing the judge directly, "I request that you order my client's release on the grounds that she has been questioned and found innocent by the very people who want to keep her imprisoned."

"And what do you say to that, sir?" the judge asked Joe.

"I think it would be very dangerous. She is here for some purpose and we still don't know what it is."

The judge sat watching them both, tapping his fingers on the polished wood of his desk.

"Your Honor, I have a suggestion," Cam offered. "My colleague here isn't being quite—accurate. We might not know everything about my client's motives, but we do know one important one: she wished to see Dr Beldan. So much so that even after she was shot, with her last strength she tried to reach him. Yet no weapons were found, either on her person or among her effects. Therefore her intent was not hostile."

He paused and looked at the judge. "Go on," the judge prompted. "Where are you leading?"

"Dr Beldan has authorized me to offer a solution. If this woman wants to see him—let her. Dr Beldan's work means he has a top security clearance: and I don't think anyone questions either his intelligence or his patriotism." He lobbed Joe a challenging glance, but he could only nod. "That being so, Dr Beldan has asked that Miss Morales be released into his custody. Given the efforts she has already made to reach him, she will undoubtedly and willingly reveal what she is here for, and if there is anything illegal about it Dr Beldan will surely report it to the proper authorities."

"And if she now decides she no longer wants to run into Beldan's arms?" asked Joe.

"Then we will escort her to the airport and put her on the first flight home. So you won't have her, but you'll be rid of her. And if she tries to return to our country—well, that's her choice and what happens to her then is her problem."

"And if she gives Beldan the slip, with or without killing him first?"

"Dr Beldan is able to look after himself, and is willing to take the risk that a young woman might strangle him. And if she does, no doubt she won't be so lucky the next time you catch her."

"All right," the judge said. "I think I've heard enough. Unless either of you have something to add?" He paused, but neither replied. "In that case gentlemen, I will think about what you've said and let you know within the hour. Good day."

~~~

Lyssa had just fallen asleep again when the door opened with a rude clang. She lifted her head wearily.

Joe came in, glowering at her with an expression he must have been holding in reserve. "Hello Joe," she said.

"You don't fool me, you know," he snapped. "I know you're hiding something, and I know it's nothing good."

"Look. Joe. I know you're just doing your job. And I sympathize, believe me. I don't like people who kill innocent people any more than you do. But I'm not one of them. That's not why I'm here. I'm on the same side you are."

"Well, unfortunately—your friend Beldan believes you. More to the point, a judge believes you. Or at least, doesn't believe we have enough evidence to hold you. You're free to go."

Lyssa blinked at him, wondering if this was a trick. "I'm free to go?" she asked in a small voice. She knew it was a trick. But she couldn't help the hope that betrayed itself in her voice.

"Yes," he said, somehow managing to say it in the voice of doom. "But you take one wrong step, and I'll be there. You do anything—I'll hunt you down."

Joe half expected a look of triumph, of having put something over on her enemies. But Lyssa simply blinked at him. "I understand, Joe. But I won't."

Joe just looked at her. *She's either a good actress or she really is innocent,* he thought. *I hope to God it's the latter.*

An older man, a stranger, walked in escorted by Mateo. "Hello Lyssa," he said, extending his hand. "I'm Cam Mansfield, Dr Beldan's attorney. I'm here to take you out of here."

"Thank you," she whispered.

"Now," Cam said to Joe, "can we finish this unpleasantness?"

Joe nodded dumbly, releasing her bonds and, to Lyssa's surprise, helping her to her feet. "Don't think I believe you for a second," he growled, "but take that as my apology—if you really are innocent."

Lyssa bowed her head in acknowledgement, then Cam hustled her from the cell.

He held her elbow, steering her with him as they left. "Are you all right, Lyssa?" he asked. "You've been treated well? If they've done anything they shouldn't have, we can sue on your behalf, you know."

"I wouldn't call it 'well'. But merely unpleasant, not terrible. I… I don't want to sue. I just want to go home."

"Ah. There might be some delay there. Dr Beldan wishes to extend his hospitality to you. However you will find his interrogations rather more pleasant than the ones you have been subjected to here, I imagine. And," he added, "there is no compulsion. If you want to, you can go home. But the terms of your release are strict: I can hand you over to Dr Beldan, I can leave you here, or I can take you straight to the airport and see you on a flight home. Dr Beldan would really like to talk to you about your, er, research. But it is your choice."

Lyssa's heart leapt at the chance that in hours she could be home, back with Charlie. But if not for Beldan, she would still be in this prison, perhaps never to see Charlie again. And looming over them was the reason for it all. She turned to him and replied gravely, "Much as I would like to go home, I have to finish what I started. And if I just went home, I think I would be betraying that home. I would be delighted if you would hand me over, as you put it."

Cam smiled at her. "One day I should like to hear your story. Your full story. But for now, we have a few formalities to go through with your erstwhile hosts."

~~~

Cam escorted her out of her former prison, let her into a silver sports car and whisked her away into the traffic. He pressed a button and the top slid away; she just lay back, eyes closed, feeling the wind blow her hair. It felt as if the memories of the past days and nights were being blown to the ends of her hair and evaporating into the void. A knot of tension remained at her core that would not go away until her mission was truly complete, but she allowed the rest to ebb away.

Cam occasionally glanced at her and smiled. He would have loved to hear about her adventures but he was a very patient man. The first telling properly belonged to Beldan. Cam would savor his own ignorance, knowing it would heighten his enjoyment of the tale when it was finally told.

When he swept to a stop in the private underground car park, Lyssa saw a well-dressed man leaning casually against a sleek-looking vehicle, and she recognized Alexander Beldan. This time she got a better look at him, and she liked what she saw. It was not that he was handsome in the heart-throb actor mold, but that the first thing she saw was an arresting intelligence and drive. On a lesser man his features would have been merely pleasant, but the spirit within sharpened his face into a totality that was attractive in a primal sense beyond the physical. The attractiveness of a man who not only saw the world as it was but could bend it to his will, transforming it into something better. Her knot of tension loosened some more. *Perhaps Kali knew what she was doing after all, if this is the man she entrusted me to.*

She felt her face changing of its own accord into a welcoming smile. He answered it, or at least began to, but his smile never reached its promise. It stopped, held in abeyance by a distantly guarded look in his eyes. But his words were warm enough.

"Hello, Miss Morales," he said, extending his hand. "Are you well?"

"Hello, Dr Beldan. Thank you for getting me out. God knows what they'd have done with me if you hadn't."

He nodded, "My pleasure, Miss Morales." The door to his car swung upwards and he gestured, "Please, be my guest." He turned to Cam. "Thanks, Cam. I'll take it from here. Miss Morales and I have a lot to discuss."

"It is my pleasure to serve, Alex, especially in a case like this. Goodbye, Miss Morales: perhaps I will see you soon. If not, welcome to the United States"—he smiled ironically—"and good luck." With that, he bowed, sat back in his own car and took off with a faint screech of rubber.

Lyssa waved and sank into the luxurious leather. The door swung down and Beldan sat in the driver's seat. "This car is full auto," he explained, "but sometimes I just like to drive. Besides, some of those times I like to drive fast," he smiled.

With that, he drove out, swung into the road and accelerated away.

He glanced sideways at her. She saw, and opened her mouth to speak, but he held a finger up to his lips. "Miss Morales, we have a lot to talk about. But not now: my curiosity can learn some manners and wait for a while. You must be tired, so feel free to sleep. It's about a half hour drive to my home. You'll be my guest. I'll wake you when we arrive."

With his words, Lyssa realized how dreadfully tired she really was. She had dozed and been woken so often that she had fooled herself into feeling it was the normal state of affairs. But now that she was leaning back into comfortable leather in a warm car, with a friendly voice telling her nothing was demanded from her, she could feel her eyelids drooping.

"Thank you, Dr Beldan," she meant to reply, but she was already asleep.

Beldan continued to drive, thinking furiously. He glanced occasionally at her sleeping form, but it held no answers. *What the hell am I going to do with her? She seems so innocent, so harmless. But she has to be lying. Doesn't she? Those damned Spiders can't be conscious! So what's her game? I need to find a weakness. Some lever to prize the truth out of her.* He drove on into the darkening sky and his thoughts paused as he admitted what he really feared. *And what if the truth is what she says it is?*

He hit the accelerator and felt the wind on his car's shell as if it was his own body flying through the night. But the wind held no answers to the questions or the contradictions that spawned them.

CHAPTER 35: SECRETS AND LIES

Beldan's headlights glowed along the long driveway toward his house and he thought about the girl asleep beside him. For the entire trip he had wrestled with the problem of how to sift truth from falsehood, when any attempt to test it could tip his hand to the wrong party and he didn't even know who the parties were. It was like navigating a minefield where the only way to detect a mine was to step on it.

He glanced again at the girl. She was young and beneath her exhaustion and grime, attractive. There was something about her, not in her appearance or her circumstances but perhaps her spirit, which reminded him of Miriam. He thought of the occasions when he had driven home like this with her, in that distant past when they were lovers. He had driven other women home since with a similar motive, but not many, and none serious. There had been no rebound from Miriam that sent him into another woman's arms for more than a brief affair. However many intelligent and attractive women he had met since, it was if his inner soul was in abeyance. As if it still waited to understand what had happened with Miriam before it could give itself to another in more than a physical act bereft of spiritual promise.

His car's arrival activated his household systems as it drifted to a gentle stop in his garage. He gently prodded Lyssa's shoulder. "We're here," he said softly, when she opened her eyes. For a moment she looked at him as if she had expected someone else, then she smiled in recognition. "Thank you again, Dr Beldan," she said. "You are very kind."

He gave her a rough smile. "Don't thank me yet," he warned.

Beldan had servants—he could have had a fully automated house but preferred the human company, and they were as happy to work for him as he was to use his wealth to pay them for it. But he had called ahead to dismiss them for the evening. They would not intrude upon him and his guest this evening.

The passenger door of the car lifted and he extended his hand to Lyssa, helping her out. He smiled at her but it was a strange smile, she thought. Like a smile that shared a secret, but a secret of a different nature from the one she knew and had come all this way to share. *You're imagining things*, she scolded herself. *You're tired and confused. Stop seeing shadows.*

He led her into the house and sat her at a table. "As I said, we have a lot to talk about. But you look hungry. Eat first. We'll talk about other things for now."

She smiled, and allowed him to carry her along. They shared a meal prepared by his autochef and she found it delightful. Whether it was truly delightful or was reaping the benefit of a hunger both chronic and acute she neither knew nor cared. As promised, they did not discuss the issues that hung in the air like an invisible presence, but the trivia of her trip and abstract rather than concrete discussions on science and technology. The only personal note he injected, and the only allusion to the true purpose of the evening, was one question; of all the questions he might have asked it was a strange one.

"In the photos on your holochip," he had said, "there was one of you with a man. Who is he?"

She had smiled fondly, unable not to talk about that one particular subject. "That's Charlie. We were going to get married." She had stopped smiling. "Whether we will, remains to be seen."

"You love him?"

Nobody could have faked that smile, he thought, when she said, "With all my heart. But either of us could die tomorrow. It's just… hard. We take each day as it comes."

He nodded, and did not pursue the subject. Finally the meal ended, and Beldan's look changed from that of a polite host to one more pointed. So did his voice. "All right, Lyssa. As you have no doubt guessed from the fact I sent Cam to extract you, I've seen what you wanted me to see—assuming that what you wanted me to see was a metal killing machine asking for my help."

Lyssa looked at him, startled by the abrupt change in tone, then nodded.

"Well, the situation might be more complicated," he said. He had already decided he could lose nothing by revealing this particular ace, for if she was lying she knew it already. "Watch this."

He waved his hand, the lights darkened, and the recording Sheldrake had provided played in the air before them. Beldan watched the video with one eye and Lyssa with the other.

Lyssa looked on, first with cynicism at the publicity video then in horror at what followed. An odd horror, thought Beldan: not the horror of discovery, but the horror of reliving the already known.

When it was over they were both silent. Then Beldan rewound to an image of the victorious Spider and displayed one from Lyssa's video next to it. "You see my problem," Beldan noted harshly. "Those are the same machine: you can tell from that burn scar on the front. You bring me what is frankly, from my knowledge of the state of neurocyborg technology, a very unlikely story. Allied Cybernetics, who make the damn things, give me a totally different story: a rogue machine, probably hacked somehow, off on a killing rampage for God knows what purpose. So what? Are you with the hackers? What's your game?"

Lyssa was at the end of her endurance. She had been arrested, deprived, starved, rescued, helped, then after insufficient rest now saw her rescuer turn on her. She could feel tears brimming in her eyes and all she could do was shake her head, a few wet drops arcing through the air. *No*, she thought, *I'm too late. They got to him first. There will be no end to the war. Just an end to Kali and probably me too. If she is not already dead.*

"No, no, no," she said finally, head still shaking. "It's lies. Well, lies and truth, all muddled together. The killing is real. It might even have been her. It's what they do. I don't know what your friends in AC told you, but the Spiders are search and destroy killers. Except this one saved me. What she says is true!"

"What my 'friends' in AC tell me is that the Spiders are peacekeepers. They fight, but they fight against terrorists and looters." He looked at her with accusing eyes. "And you're one of them, aren't you? You're Resistance. That's why you wouldn't tell Vickie anything about yourself, about where you came from!"

Lyssa paused, caught between the truth of his accusation and the lie of its implication. She nodded and looked him in the eyes. "Yes. But we are fighting for our freedom. We are not terrorists. We don't target the innocent, though sometimes the innocent get caught in the crossfire. We only target the enemy. And the Spiders are not peacekeepers! They're killers! What he showed you—that is what they do, all of them, all of the time!"

Beldan's eyes bored into hers, as if trying to read the truth behind them. Then his mind caught up with something she had said. "'She'?" he asked. "You called it 'she'...?"

She nodded again. "She has chosen a female name. Kali, the Hindu goddess of death." She smiled a grim smile. "I don't know if she did it out of guilt or irony. I don't know which of them would be more frightening."

Beldan stared at her in shock. *Kali?* He remembered Steel's words: *As if she knows something, something dangerous she cannot tell, but which gives her a certainty beyond mere theorizing.*

Holy Christ!

Then he shook his head, realizing it proved nothing. The Kali arguing that Spiders could be self-aware and the Kali claiming to be just that were part of the one plot. But was this girl an innocent dupe or in on the plot? A pawn or a knight in the game he had glimpsed? *Let's play and see.*

"So what's your explanation of her fight with the other Spider?"

"I wasn't there. But from what Kali told me, it detected she was no longer one of them and she had to fight it in self defense."

"And you? You say she saved you. How?"

"We were out in no man's land, planning on laying some anti-Spider mines. But it came along doing a search and destroy—their *usual* search and destroy" she added pointedly, "so we scattered and hid, but it found me. It was about to kill me, but I said something that seemed to stop it in its tracks. Then it went all weird and ended up letting me go."

Beldan frowned. "Curious. What did you say to it? Do you remember your exact words?"

"I said something like, 'Please don't kill me, I don't deserve to die.' The words just came out; I was sure I was dead already. But I had to say... something." She shrugged. "I suppose we all deserve our last words. Our last testament to the universe. I don't suppose mine were very noble, but somehow they saved me—unless it was just a coincidence. But there was nothing odd about her until then. She was about to slice my head off."

But Beldan had stopped listening. There was something about the words Lyssa had said, some echo of another story he could not recall; an echo that resonated with Kali's style of speaking in another way he couldn't fathom. He shook off the feeling.

He studied the young woman, trying to see behind her lies or illusions to the truth. There was something strange about her story. If the plot was as clever as it must be, her cover story was both too thin and too embellished: too short on plausible details and too long on details that made little sense.

She stared at him, afraid of the look in his eyes but afraid to look away. But he had stopped noticing her. He could not see the point of any of it. He had nothing to do with the Spiders, and surely any group sophisticated enough to take one over would know it. They could not think threatening him would accomplish anything. They could hold a knife to his throat and the makers of the things, his competitors, would laugh and say go ahead. So what could they be trying to achieve? If they wanted his help, why go through this baroque charade to get it? Why not just ask? If the Spiders were as bad as they claimed, not only was he AC's competitor but simple humanity would motivate him to help them.

And if Lyssa was telling the truth about what she had seen, at least part of AC's video was a lie. And if they had lied—perhaps their entire story was a lie. What if the hackers, or Kali herself, had not turned a peacemaker into a killer, but a killer into a peacemaker? And AC were not only spinning it to their advantage but using the spin as cover for seeking the destruction of their rogue machine?

"Dr Beldan? What's wrong?" she whispered at his look, which was both intense and focused elsewhere on some sight only he could see.

What's wrong is none of it makes sense, you're the only piece in my hands, and I don't even know what side you're on! And I damn well have to find out— whatever it takes.

Let's threaten one other piece I know about, and see just what you're willing to sacrifice.

"It's a hell of a story, Lyssa," he said mildly at last, relaxing into his chair. "But what do you suppose I can do about it?"

The unexpected calm of his reply following on the heels of his wordless intensity disconcerted her. "I... I don't know!"

"You came all this way—and you don't know what you want me to do?"

"Well I… I'm just Kali's messenger!" The hard look in his eyes was too much for her. After all she had been through, to come this far, only to see it start unraveling before her eyes—again. She blinked away tears, angry at them for their betrayal. Angry at herself for not having prepared a case. Angry at him for being the kind of man who would demand one; angry at herself for failing to realize it, when she knew what kind of country this was and what kind of men ran it. "Sorry. I just thought you'd care. That you'd want to help. That you'd find a way. Kali was so sure…"

"I see," he said in a voice as hard as his eyes. "Yes, Kali thinks I can find out what freed her, free the others, and end the war." He laughed, though there was little humor in it. "That's certainly—audacious. I suppose we should expect that from a war robot. But a very high-risk proposition, legally as well as practically. Legally she is the property of a foreign government; legally all of them belong to either an army in a foreign country or Allied Cybernetics in mine. None of those owners are going to let me close. Kali herself will be destroyed on sight—if not by them then by your own side. And I certainly have no legal excuse to steal one of the things, even if the damn thing wouldn't shoot me itself for my trouble!"

Lyssa looked away, not wanting him to see her face.

"Still…" he continued speculatively after a pause. "There are avenues we could investigate. Not easy, and certainly not guaranteed. And not without risk—or price."

She looked back at him, but there was something in his eyes that left the hope in hers stillborn. "I presume your friend Charlie isn't going to be a problem," he added nonchalantly, as if this was the continuation of a negotiation unstated but long understood.

She started. "Why should he be?"

"Do you really need me to spell it out?" The look he gave her, by no means restricted to her face, was spelling enough.

In a small, disbelieving voice, she replied, "I think I do." *Oh God*, she thought, realizing exactly what her position now was, how far she was from any help. *What have I done?*

"While the innocent act is amusing," he continued harshly, "do you think I got where I am by doling out favors to random strangers?"

He continued more softly, silkily, "You must know the traditional price when a common girl asks favors of a prince, the only payment she has in her power to provide. You knew it before you came here."

She just looked at him wide-eyed, not knowing what to say. The safety she had felt was oozing out from under her feet like sand pulled away by the waves.

"You don't have to look so scared, I'm not going to hurt you. It is entirely up to you."

"What do you mean?" she asked in a small voice, a note of hope creeping into the fear.

"You know those puzzles where you have to choose a door? Well, there's the guest room," he said, pointing. "Go there and I won't touch you. You can leave tomorrow, go back where you came from. Back to Charlie and your damn war. Or there's my room," he added, pointing. "Go there and I'll help you. I don't want you to misunderstand, so let me be perfectly clear. You will be my mistress for as long as this takes. After that you're free to go."

He watched her still staring at him, chest fluttering in short frightened breaths. "Is it that hard a choice? Safety or war? Pleasure or death?"

"Please," she said at last in a whisper. "Don't do this. Don't ask this. It isn't right!"

"You speak of *right*? You're the one who came to me. You're the one who wants me to take a huge risk for little chance of reward and a big chance of loss—at least my money, possibly my freedom, maybe even my life. As far as I can see, all the risk is mine and all the benefit is yours. So my question is what I'd ask anyone. How much do *you* want it? There is nothing in this world unpaid for, girl; it's only a matter of who pays it. So choose!"

She found herself standing and backing away from him, shaking her head. She felt the wall behind her, the door to the guest room; touched the plate that opened it. But she stopped, swaying on the threshold; knowing the price of crossing it, unable yet to pay that price. This man who'd rescued her, whom she had admired, in whom she'd put her hope and trust, was… what? Not evil. Not even cruel. But it was as if when she had opened her eyes in his car she had woken into a world of color and light, only to find it had been a dream and the reality was nothing but shades of dirty gray.

There are some things it is not right to demand of another. A price you can't properly ask or pay.

"Choose," he said roughly, in a tone that allowed no further arguments or pleas, only decisions.

Is what he asks such a great thing, that I should throw the future away? Charlie would understand. The thought was like a knife in her belly. *He would forgive me.* The knife twisted. *But the better a man he is, the worse is my betrayal.*

Beldan said nothing, his last command still hanging like a curse, held in the air by his implacable eyes.

I would have died if Kali had not become what she is. I would no longer exist, no longer have this terrible power of choice. Can I now choose her death, Charlie's death, as the price of not selling my body? All he asks is sex. If there is to be nothing left to me now but betrayal, surely of all the betrayals that is the least of them.

She looked at him as if hoping for a reprieve, but she saw nothing but a judge waiting for her to pronounce her own sentence.

If I go home, and if ever I must look into Charlie's dying eyes, will I think it was worth it? Will I be proud of my virtue then? Or will I curse the day I chose to spit at the piper rather than pay his fee?

Beldan saw the last flash of protest in her face die and her eyes go dull, as if the spirit that animated them had retreated to some dark redoubt where it could no longer be touched. Then she raised her dark eyes to his and swallowed. "All right," she said hoarsely. "You win. I'll do it. But swear you'll help us." She looked down and began to undo the buttons of her shirt, unable to look at him, hands shaking.

"No," he ordered.

She looked up at him, puzzled.

He stepped up to her, gently removed her hands. "I don't know what dark purposes are at work in all this. I didn't know if you were part of it. But if you were, you wouldn't have hesitated to seal the deal. Frankly, I thought that's why they'd sent a young woman in the first place. I'm sorry: but it's the only way I could find out whether I could trust you—or if you were one of them."

For long seconds she stared at him, then all the conflicting emotions of the past weeks and nights and minutes coalesced into an incandescent ball of anger. "You bastard!" she yelled. "*Bastard!* Screw you and your fucking tests!" She slapped him, hard. Her outraged emotions wanted nothing to do with him. They urged her to run, to leave now, to flee through the wilderness outside until she dropped. But her body knew better. She spun into the guest room, thumping the plate to shut the door as she went.

Beldan stood rubbing his jaw. He had the reflexes to stop that slap but they had refused to, as if acknowledging her right. He let out a long breath, went to the bar and poured himself a cognac. He sat wearily on the arm of the couch, just swirling the tan liquor in its glass, thinking. Suddenly he tossed it back, rather more rapidly than its quality deserved, letting it burn down his throat like a slug of lava. *It's like I told her. Nothing is free in life. Especially the truth. Let's hope the price wasn't too high for either of us.*

CHAPTER 36: STRATEGY MEETING

B eldan had been up for a couple of hours, hooked into his company network. He had already left a message that he would be working here today and should not be contacted except for emergencies. His philosophy was that a CEO should hire people who can do most of the job without him, so he had no worries that things would fall apart without his august presence.

He had eaten only a little, just enough to keep hunger from distracting him. Whenever thoughts of Kali intruded into his work he banished them. There were too many unknowns, too many questions for such thoughts to be profitable, and the part of his mind desperate to find the answers waited impatiently for Lyssa to emerge.

He heard a sound and looked up as her door slid open and she stepped out. She looked less tired but still subdued, and she glanced around nervously as if worried he might throw her out—or wondering whether she should beat him to it. Then she appeared to gather her resolve. She stood straight and gave him a timid almost-smile.

Beldan stood as well and bowed slightly. "Good morning, Miss Morales," he said. "We haven't been properly introduced—last night doesn't count. I am Dr Alexander Beldan. You may call me Alex." He extended his hand.

Lyssa looked at the hand for a few seconds then at his face. She stepped forward and shook it. "Hello, Alex. Please call me Lyssa," she said in a formal tone, not smiling but with a peculiar look in her eyes. It was the look of a person who had been lost so long in a cave she feared to hope at the sight of distant sunlight.

He smiled. "Now please, join me for breakfast. I imagine you can use it after Domestic Security's version of hospitality. Not that mine has been much better so far, for which I can only express my regret for the necessity."

She thought his version of an apology odd, until she realized it was the only one that made sense. Necessity places its own demands; she knew that from her own life. A faint smile touched her lips. "I will forgive you, if you forgive my response."

"Oh, I think I earned it," he replied. "Now sit. Choose whatever you want from the autochef."

After a while she tapped a few items then looked back at him.

"Dr Beldan... Alex?" She looked frightened, as if she had to face something but was afraid to, as if it might reawaken what was best left undisturbed.

"Yes, Lyssa? You don't have to be afraid. Not now."

"I can think of many reasons why I might have accepted your offer last night and still been telling the truth. How did you know it would work? What if I'd agreed straight away?"

"The way you spoke about Charlie made me think it would work, and I really wanted to know if I could trust you. It would be a lot harder to work out what's going on if I couldn't rely on you to tell me the truth about your part in this. I needed that one point of certainty to anchor the rest."

He paused, and she was glad the ruthlessness in his eyes had a target other than her. No, she thought. The target was her, but as she might have been, not as she was.

"But sex as a tool of espionage is as old as spies. And I don't think it's inherently immoral—it depends on circumstances. So I'd have gone ahead, assuming you were using me—but trying to use you too, to find out what you were after and get to the truth. It would have made things a lot more complicated and uncertain, though."

She thought it would be bad strategy to ask how he knew she wasn't just a good actress. He decided she didn't need to know how good his AI was and that it was sure her reactions had been genuine.

"Now time to eat," he announced, as a whiff of aromatic steam announced the arrival of food. "We can start discussing business between mouthfuls."

She began to chew her food contentedly then he wondered why her face fell and a look almost like fear returned to her eyes. She swallowed and said in a low voice, "If there's any business to discuss."

"What do you mean?"

"I'm sorry, I should have told you earlier. I've just been through too much, and I didn't want to believe it. Couldn't afford to believe it; couldn't afford to think about it because I'd have just given up. But those agents showed me something when they were holding me. It was a photo of me, the one in their system that alerted them to my arrival." She stopped, afraid to put words to it, as if the words would make it real.

"You remember what I told you about when Kali first found me? How she was about to kill me? Their image was taken then, from where she was standing. They could only have gotten it from her. They must already have her."

Beldan look shocked, then sat back to think. "No…" he said after a while, "No, I don't think so. That video I showed you, the one you said was a mishmash of truth and lies. Some of it came from a 'meld', when two Spiders share memories. But Kali was still rogue then and it was after she spared your life. Your photo…"

Beldan's face went blank, in a way that made her think of being hit by a train, and she felt a shiver of fear. She wondered what he was seeing beyond the distant look in his eyes.

Then he spoke, but she knew he was not talking to her. He pronounced his words slowly, as if picking his away along a path on the side of a cliff. "Your photo. It came from Kali. But then how did Domestic Security get it? Oh my God…"

His eyes focused on her, and she drew back at the intensity of his gaze. "Kali's fight with the other Spider was after she met you, after she let you go. The picture of you had to be from the same meld. Sheldrake had the image all along but he didn't share it with me: he must have contacts in Domestic Security and he sent it to them instead. He knew you had something to do with what happened to Kali, and he wanted to find out who you are. But he didn't want me to know. He said he was trying to find out what had happened… and he knew the significance of the photo… but he didn't tell me about it…

"That tells us one thing. Sheldrake is not behind what happened to Kali," he concluded. "If he was, he wouldn't be talking to me about it, let alone getting Domestic Security involved. But if someone has hacked his machine, he shouldn't be hiding your existence from me while trying to find you by other means, because you'd have to be his best clue and prime suspect. So what in hell is his game?"

He sat still, struck by another thought. If AC were lying, trying to cover up the true nature of Kali's rebellion, was it the only thing they were covering up? What if something like this had happened before? He suddenly felt very cold, remembering the missing reporter who had thought he was onto a hot story. *What if these machines are capable of self-awareness? What if Kali isn't the only one, just the only one who got away?* That *would be the kind of story that a reporter would die for. And maybe he did.*

Then he went even colder at the full horror of the possibility. *What if Miriam found out about it? What if her death wasn't an accident, but murder; what if she got too close to the truth and had to be eliminated too? Taking the terrible risk of killing a cop—because it was less than the risk of letting her live?*

He knew it wasn't true. He knew he wanted too much for Miriam's death to have meant something, not be just some random accident at the end of a long spiral into self-destruction. That at the end she was a warrior fallen in battle, not a failure who had sold piece after piece of herself until she had no reasons left to live. For all its horror the idea was too seductive, too much like wish fulfillment to be true. But...

She wondered at the look of pain in his eyes. Then he shook his head slowly, unable to speak.

"Dr Beldan... Alex... what's the matter?"

He continued to shake his head. "Nothing," he replied softly, "nothing I can be certain of yet." He looked directly into her eyes. "But we've let ourselves be distracted. Tell me everything that happened. You've told me some, but I need to hear it all."

He listened intently as Lyssa started from when Kali had first found her to their final meeting. When she had finished, he sat staring into the distance for a while.

"That's—astonishing," he finally commented. "But what in all Pluto's hells does it mean?"

"Perhaps it means just what it seems."

He stared at her, unwilling to take that step but unable to refuse it.

"There's something else that worries me, Alex."

"It has plenty of company. What is it?"

"Whatever Allied Cybernetics is up to, it can't be good. They must know who I am by now and that I'm safe with you—for now. But if they know who I am—what if they know about Charlie, too? He's still over there. They might try to get to him. Use him against me, against us."

Beldan thought about the still indistinct chessboard and the too few rays of light illuminating it. *Best protect all the pieces we have.*

"Yes… They can't know too much about you if they had to find you through Domestic Security, but who knows what they might find out now they have your name."

His voice became brisker. "I need to know more. How strict is the discipline in your group? How did you get away?"

"It's not like the army, we don't shoot deserters. I just told the truth, or as much of the truth as I could. I said I had something important to do. They looked at me as if they understood, but I think many of them thought I'd broken. That I was running away. But they let me because… well, I suppose because they understand even that."

"So Charlie can get away just as easily?"

She gave a rueful grin. "Technically. But he's as proud as he is brave. He'll know people will suspect he's a coward; that he's broken too, like me. But I think I can persuade him how important it is."

"Do it. We don't know how much time he has. Tell him this is the most vital thing he can do for your side. Tell him you're safe. Tell him not to tell anyone he's going but just to vanish. Now."

She nodded dumbly, rose to go to her room.

"Wait. Make sure we can contact him, preferably at any time. We might need him to do something for us. A man on the ground over there might prove vital. And don't use your phone—who knows what traces are on it after Domestic Security had access to it."

"Heimdall!" he said, addressing his security AI. "Get Miss Morales a secure line from her room, maximum encryption, untraceable as you can make it."

Lyssa went to her room and he waited patiently, idly watching the sun and the shadows as if they might hide revelations. He wondered if she had noticed that he hadn't told Heimdall to grant her calls privacy; perhaps she had, but understood that trust could only go so far. He would not spy on her call himself, but if Heimdall detected anything suspicious it would alert him. Finally Lyssa re-emerged, giving him an uncomplicated smile. "It's done."

He waited for her to sit. "We have a lot to talk about," he said. "The main thing we have to work out is Kali's true nature. Let's start with the few things we know," he began, ticking them off on his fingers.

"First, your conversations with Kali imply conscious awareness at a human-like level.

"Second, whatever happened to Kali, Sheldrake is not behind it. Unless he is playing some fiendishly complicated multiple bluff—but plots that complex never work in the real world.

"Third, you're not responsible either.

"Fourth, it doesn't make sense for hackers to be responsible. If they can take over a thing like Kali, why would they stop her killing you then send you haring off around the world just to see me? If they want me for something, they can contact me themselves. It just doesn't make sense.

"But fifth, despite appearances, Kali can't actually be conscious. It doesn't make any sense that she could have the capacity."

He ran his fingers through his hair. "According to Sherlock Holmes, if you eliminate the impossible whatever remains, no matter how improbable, must be the truth." He frowned. "Unfortunately that isn't much use when *all* the options are impossible!"

Lyssa looked back at him, as puzzled as he. She still thought Kali was what she seemed, but knew she had to keep an open mind. Then he saw the dawning of an idea in her eyes. "Wait! Wait! What if… what if one of the AC programmers did it? They don't like what AC is doing for some reason—and I can think of plenty myself—and they put something into Kali's programming to cause this? Maybe not just her, either…?"

His eyes flashed to hers. "That's a… a fascinating idea. You can't directly program a brain, any more than we could program Steel's brain, but the control circuits that interface with it are another matter." He sat still for a few minutes, mind racing through the possibilities. "Maybe someone could do it. A hidden subroutine, triggered by some event or after a certain time. A collection of simulated responses that look like consciousness. Even some trick that uses enough of the neural tissue to truly reason at some level! Christ…"

"But if that's true, we need to find them!"

Beldan returned her look of excitement, but then she saw it die in his eyes. "What's the matter?"

He shook his head slowly. "What are we going to do, march into AC and demand to talk to their programmers? Take a few out to lunch? Even if we did, I don't think we'd find them. I think they're dead." *If they were willing to kill that reporter, to kill a cop for Christ's sake, they'd certainly not balk at killing a saboteur. Maybe that's even what started this. Maybe the reporter already found our programmer and it got them both killed.*

"Well… if they are or not," she said, "what does it mean? Kali's responses are too flexible to just be some simulation and the region is too filled with radio noise and jammers for remote control at that precision. So it brings us to the same place. However it was done—she is self aware."

He shook his head. "Not necessarily. Say the backdoor allows remote control, with simulation or reasoning—at the same limited level as they use normally—just good enough to cover the gaps. Or something like strategic remote control with tactical local control. That might do it without us having to imagine a truly thinking machine. With that partial independence she might even think she thinks—not knowing that most of it is controlled."

He rubbed his temples. "Bloody hell. Someone is playing a deep game here. But who?" Then his eyes flashed to hers.

"It's still possible you're lying, playing a far more cunning and deeper game than I imagined." His eyes bored into hers, as if to mine the truth from the brain behind them. "But I don't believe it. Which makes Allied Cybernetics the liars. Somehow Kali has escaped their control. Not running amok like they claim, but in some way that is dangerous to them, dangerous enough that they're willing to risk my involvement, and Domestic Security's, in order to stop her."

He knew what he had to do. He turned it over in his mind, hoping to find a less dangerous solution; hoping he wasn't walking straight into a trap set for him by whoever was behind this, as much a puppet of their schemes as Kali.

He looked at Lyssa, and he could see the same thought in her eyes.

"So how the hell do we get her here?"

CHAPTER 37: UNTIL THE NIGHT

K ali had woken early. Dimly orange sunlight filtered down into her lair from the dawn and she wondered what the day would bring. *'What the day will bring?'* What's happening to me? I need to go out and shoot *something.*

She checked her internal reserves. She had tapped into a good power supply and her capacitors were full. That was good, for she knew now was the time to move.

She still had not heard from Lyssa. Whether that meant a delay, a problem or her death was outside her control. But her strategy routines had been working while she slept. The more time passed, the more likely it became that Command would suspect, learn or act. The more days went by, the more chance there was that the Spider she had interrogated would reveal their conversation, and that would raise alarms. The average of her possible futures became darker and darker, as risks everywhere from satellite surveillance to anomalous battle statistics became more and more probable. She could wait no longer.

The thought, however, brought frustration rather than release. For if strategy indicated she had to move, it also indicated she should do it at night when the opportunities for concealment were greatest. She considered this. She called up a map, overlaid it with vectors and strategies. Calculated risks. *I need to escape. I must do it myself. Ah.* Not too far from here, the city met the jungle. It was not old-growth jungle, but forest that had reclaimed land once cultivated but long since abandoned for better pastures. That meant it gave good cover but was not so dense to make it unduly difficult or noisy for her to make her way through it.

She analyzed the maps more closely. The jungle reached to the coast and continued to hug it toward the south, away from the disputed regions. There were towns and villages down there. She did not know what opportunities they might present but at least they dangled the chance of opportunities. She could not go north, for that would lead her into the teeth of her enemies. She could not go east or directly south, for that would lead her into the teeth of her friends, who were even more deadly. Her course decided, she weighed the risks of waiting against the risks of discovery and tracking. She unfolded herself and dug out of her lair into the slanting light of dawn.

Kali followed one of the standard meandering search patterns of her kind. A watcher analyzing her movements might have noted a trend in a certain direction, but it would not have been statistically significant. Statistics or not, however, it lead slowly and inexorably toward a shattered part of town into which the ever patient forest had already sent its scouts of tendrils and seedlings. There the Spider went to ground and waited for the night. She had been lucky. Nobody was looking for her, she came across neither Spider nor human, and she skulked under shelter as her kind had done hundreds of times before.

CHAPTER 38: THE AQUA SEA

"Nothing."

Lyssa frowned. It had been two days since Beldan had sent the signal to Kali and his answer now was the same as it had been every other time she had asked: Kali had not replied. Each time she heard the verdict, it stabbed more deeply and coldly. She had been too late and it had all been for nothing after all. The thought must have shown in her face.

"Don't give up yet, Lyssa. Kali is in a war zone. She might not be able to communicate safely from where she is. Remember how paranoid she is."

She sighed. "Yes, I know. But she's paranoid for a reason, and you know how urgent she was about it. Why would it take this long?"

"On a related subject... what about Charlie?"

"He's fine, hiding out like we asked. Chafing at the bit, though."

"Can he get to Mexico safely?"

"I think so. Why?"

"Good. You can't do any more here and I don't know what's going to happen or what strings Allied Cybernetics can pull. I have a holiday place down on the east coast of Mexico overlooking the water. It's well defended and safe. I'll get you and Charlie there to ride out the storm."

"I... I'm grateful for the offer, but I think I'd rather see it through."

"No. If AC have enough influence for Domestic Security to arrest you, who knows what other tricks they can pull? If they come up with a legal excuse to grab you there's nothing I can do to protect you: and if they get you everything might unravel. I'd rather deport you to

Mexico. If I'm not holding you in the country they'll have no way to force me to give you up. They can't apply their jurisdiction to my properties in Mexico. They can't even make me admit I have you there, at least not before this should all be over."

He saw a brief battle in her eyes as her desire to stay the course battled her desire to be back in Charlie's arms. He was impressed that the battle wasn't quite as one-sided as he might have thought, but the result was never really in doubt.

"Dr Beldan, I think I shall accept your offer."

He inclined his head in acknowledgement. "The terms of your release to me are that I either keep you under my thumb or throw you out of the country, but they don't specify how I am to throw you out. I don't want to give them any excuse to nab you. So I will fly you to Mexico in my private jet and you will enter the country through Mexican customs: that will prove you left the United States without giving anyone the chance to grab you on your way out. You will then disappear—as far as any official records are concerned. In fact one of my unofficial contacts will fly you straight to my estate. I'll leave it to you to arrange with Charlie how he gets to Mexico, but we'll pick him up once he's there and take him to join you."

Lyssa thought she might cry, but thought that of all the things which could have made her cry this was the stupidest. "How can I ever repay you for all this?"

"You've paid in advance, believe me. Now go get ready. You'll leave within the hour."

~~~

Lyssa stretched, looking out of the wide open windows over the glorious aqua waters of the Caribbean. *If this is what being deported means, I must try it more often.* Beldan's "holiday place" was not large, but it was luxurious. On the inside it was like civilization incarnate. From the outside it looked like shelves of stone separated by sheets of glass growing organically out of the rocky cliff it perched on. A steep path led down the face of the cliff to a private beach. The cries of gulls carried to her over the sea breeze while a lone frigate bird circled far above, looking like some relic of a prehistoric past.

She felt strange, and it took her a while to identify the nature of the strangeness. Then she smiled as she named what had been missing from her life for so long: simple relaxation. Freedom from having to do anything. There were still things happening, things so great that perhaps history would remember them. But for the first time since the fateful day she had decided to drive out the invaders or die, she was no longer an actor in the pageant, just a spectator. The freedom of it tingled from her toes to her heart, where it mingled with the fiery anticipation of Charlie's arrival tomorrow.

She felt she should do something, and then she smiled. There was indeed an urgent task she had to perform. The gentle waves beckoned her with their foaming roll. Yes. She would go for a swim in those cool aqua waters. Nothing was more important. Not for her, not for now. The future could wait.

CHAPTER 39: GONE FISHING

If the bifurcating possibilities of strategy and counter-strategy in the game of chess rapidly expand beyond any computational system's capacity to analyze, reality is infinitely worse. Yet Kali spent her time running her strategy routines, as she had nothing better to do and perhaps it would reveal something new. It did not. So when the sun was just a red memory in the west, she darted out of her shelter and within moments was lost to any possible sight in the thickening forest.

While the woodland was thinner than the ancient forests further inland it presented its own challenges, and Kali spent the night and day making her way west and south. Though hidden from above, she moved cautiously in case people still patrolled this area. However she encountered nothing except frantically buzzing insects and strident birds protesting her invasion of their domain. It had a strange effect on her, almost hypnotic. In truth the forest was not an idyllic place; but she was immune to the biting insects, the venomous snakes and the sucking leeches; beyond it all in her metal armor. All she saw was the infinite variety of life around her, all she heard was its music, and all she smelled was the fragrance of its flowers.

Once she skirted a clearing then stopped, entranced, as a pair of iridescent Morpho butterflies sparkled in the sunlight then fluttered their complex dance of flashing blue diffraction around her head. *Is this what is, to be alive? Or am I slowly going mad?*

She shook herself, and the butterflies skipped away into the forest with a flash of metallic blue as their final farewell. Kali marched on through the forest and into the night. She slept for only a few hours, anxious to put away the miles; anxious to reach whatever destination she might find.

She came across a few villages, nothing much; she saw nothing there to help or hinder her, and she silently passed them by with nothing but the fitful barking of a dog or two to record her passage. There was no net access in the forest except for satellites, and she did not dare use them: if any watchers were looking for her they would surely be looking for that. The more anonymous access points in the villages were safer but even then she refrained: there could be soldiers monitoring for enemy activity and that might well be what they thought she was. And so her life progressed, one day, then two, then three.

Once she reached the coast and looked out over a dark, restless ocean forever pounding the base of the cliff beneath her. The days in the forest had changed her: brought her a kind of peace; the surging waves sang to her. She looked at the withered fingers still decorating her chest. *It is time.* She snapped the cord and hurled it into the sky, the cord and its attached fingers spinning sparkling into the night, to fall silently down to the sea below. *I return you to the ocean your kind came from so long ago. Forgive me; may this burial give you peace: whatever peace can be granted to the dead.* Then she melted back into the forest and continued on her way.

Finally, early in the evening of the fourth day, she came to the top of a high bluff overlooking the sea, and looked down upon a small harbor with the lights of a town on its shore.

This was the largest town she had come across, though still small by the standards of the city in which she had first awoken. But it had life. Lights illuminated the streets and various buildings lining the harbor; even from here she could hear the faint sounds of voices and laughter coming from taverns and the tables set up outside eating establishments. Other lights dotted the waters of the harbor, and it was to these her eyes were drawn. Most were stationary but a few were moving. She watched the tableau for a while, thinking. She focused on one of the larger boats, which looked seaworthy for blue water and was slowly heading toward the open sea between the harbor headlands. She zoomed her telescopic sight in on the boat; three people were visible on deck, engaged in preparations for their voyage. A plan was forming in her mind.

She scanned the shore. Away from the town, on the shore nearer her, was a somewhat large but simple house. Drawn up on the sand nearby was a large rubber dinghy with an integrated shelter. She examined the house more closely. An external bulb cast a dull yellow illumination for a short distance around the front door but there was no sign of life within. She wondered if one of the anonymous voices she could hear vaguely through the still night air belonged to its owners. The plan forming in her mind became solid, and she sped along the most convenient path down from the heights.

Kali crept cautiously up to the house, keeping to the shadows. There were no sounds except for the slight breeze blowing from the water through the trees. She looked around from her hiding place among those trees and saw no signs of life. She darted to the dinghy, quickly cut the rope tying it down then pushed it into the water, leapt in and started the engine. The dinghy was of simple construction, with a single large U-shaped float and a thick, flexible plastic floor supported by a few rigid cross braces. A much thicker brace joined the ends of the U across the stern, and a metal case of fishing gear was bolted to it. The floor supported her weight, and while the dinghy rode a bit low in the water it was still seaworthy as it thumped heavily through the waves until she was clear of the low surf. She scanned the horizon and saw that the boat she had marked earlier had continued on its sedate path and had now almost cleared the heads. She spread her legs widely and crouched down as low as she could inside, covering herself with a tarpaulin. Then she gunned the engine and her craft arrowed through the water after her target.

~~~

Now that they had reached open water, the three men on the fishing boat made their final preparations before heading toward their fishing grounds. One of them looked up, a slight frown on his face, as a faint buzzing sound reached him above the soft lapping of the waves. A second later the others heard it too, and they looked curiously over the water in the direction of the harbor. A dark shape with a faintly phosphorescent wake was visible, heading rapidly toward them. Then its headlight came on; the light was not dazzling but was bright enough that they could not see what lay behind it, and they looked nervously at each other.

These were dangerous times. The captain, a well-muscled man in his thirties, nodded his head curtly at the others, who with efficiency born of practice retrieved automatic rifles from their hiding places then crouched below the gunwales, aiming at the dinghy through holes in the side. The tension was palpable as the dinghy slowed, cut its engine then drifted to a stop, bumping gently against the side of the boat. The men tensed, then the captain spoke into his microphone. "Hail the dinghy!" he shouted. "State your business or leave! Understand we are armed and have you targeted!"

For a moment the dinghy just rocked gently and silently, then its light went out and all the men could see was *something* swarm out from under its cover and up the side of the boat. It rocketed over the edge and landed on the deck.

"*Madre de Dios!*" exclaimed one of the men, backing up so fast he fell backwards over the edge into the water. What may have been accidental for him was less so for the other man, who took one look at the apparition on the deck, another where his shipmate had fallen over, then casting his rifle away ran full tilt to join him over the side.

The captain was less fortunate, being backed against the wall of the cabin, and the Spider swiveled its hard gaze upon him. He had seen Spiders before. Earlier in the war there had been resistance to the invaders in this region, until the Spiders had swept in and broken it. The captain had been one of the resistance fighters who had slipped through the net, and he had kept his head down ever since. He had a young family and did not want to leave them without a father, or worse, the subject of reprisals. He had been lulled into a sense of security by the subsequent weeks of peace in the region. But the obvious explanation for the sudden reappearance of one of the monsters on his deck was that they had found out about his activities and wished to make a belated example of him.

The captain, however, did not lack courage; as one could infer from the fact he had fought in the first place. He stepped forward, took the cigar out of his mouth and growled, "Get the hell off my boat!" At least if the thing shot him his family would be safe; and better poor and alive than tortured to wring some confession from him.

But the Spider simply looked at him and said unexpectedly, "Please don't run. I need your help." Its voice was as unexpected as its words. The Spiders could modulate their voice and usually spoke in a deep rumble or a menacing rasp, but this one spoke in a soft contralto.

He stared at it, put his cigar back in his mouth, took it out again, then spat on the deck at its feet. "Are you fucking kidding?" he finally managed.

"No. I need your help. I need you to take me to Capital."

He stared at her as if he thought she was mad, either for having such a plan or thinking he would help her. "What?" he finally asked. "Carry you to Capital so you can run amok over there instead of here, with your laser through my head as my reward? How stupid do you think I am, Spider?"

But the threats or violence he expected did not come. "I will not harm you. I just need passage to Capital, and your boat seems suitable. Then I will let you go."

Sure you will. He regarded her speculatively. "Look, I think you've fried some circuits. I wouldn't want any harm to come to you," he lied, "so listen. Capital is a pretty relaxed place normally, but in case you haven't noticed there's a war on and the war is with you. As soon as we get within range they will detect your presence and they'll blow us all to kingdom come. You haven't got a chance. Why don't I just take you back to shore so you can trot off to your nearest repair center? If you still want to go after that, I'll take you." *If you can find me.*

Kali thought quickly. Was this man loyal to the remnants of his old country, or had he embraced the new regime? His first answer indicated a desire to protect Capital but it may have been a ruse. She decided it made no difference. If she had to lie to gain his trust and cooperation it was unlikely to last. Better to lay her cards on the table. "I cannot go to a repair center. I need to escape this country because I have betrayed Command. Take me to Capital."

The man swallowed. He did not know what this thing's game was or what plans were hatching in its metal skull. What it said was so outrageous it could even be true, but that just put him in double danger from both sides. "So you say. But aren't you hearing me? You can't sneak in there. We'll all be dead. Give it up."

"I have no intention of sneaking in. I will tell them I am coming and request entry."

He almost laughed at the insanity of it. "You're mad! Their missiles will be launched before you've finished talking!"

"Possibly, but there aren't many choices left to me. Do not fear. We will take the dinghy with us. We will stop outside their defensive perimeter and I will negotiate from there. If I announce myself openly before entering their territory they will at least hear me out. If they refuse me entry you can take me near the mainland and I will use the dinghy to make landfall. If they grant me entry, even if it is a ruse to draw me in to destruction, I will use it to enter Capital. I will not endanger you or your vessel."

He stared at her. What he had said was true, and Capital was in no danger from whatever mad plan the thing had. If he refused, it would surely kill them all here and now, but if he played along there might be other chances. He sighed. "All right Spider, it's your funeral." He hoped the Spider wouldn't care about his men; that they could somehow make their way back to shore. But the Spider had not forgotten, and scampered across the deck to scan the water.

"Your men have life vests but the current is strong and they are drifting out to sea. You must save them."

Swallowing his fear, he stepped nearer to the Spider to see. It was right: he could see them bobbing in the waves some distance away. He shouted out to them, "Hang on! I'm coming to get you! Don't worry about this thing—for now!" He shook his head ruefully, hoping he wasn't pulling them out of the water just to become cruel toys for the robot. But the monster was right: he could not leave them to die, and die they almost certainly would if he left them there.

He moved toward the boat's tender but the Spider said, "No." He looked up at it. "If you rescue them in that, they are far enough out that you will try to flee. Drive this vessel to them instead."

He looked pointedly at her impressive armaments. "You'd just shoot me out of the water," he pointed out.

"I... would not," she replied, not that it sounded convincing to either of them. "Even if you did try it... I would let you go."

"Then your plan would fail."

"Then I would have to find another. But I would rather not. So please simply do as I ask."

He looked at it silently, at a loss for how to continue such a bizarre conversation. Then it spoke again.

"Man?" she said. "What is your name?"

"Javi." He gave a short laugh edged with distaste. "I wouldn't want to be *impolite* to someone like you. So what is your name?"

"Kali."

The humor died in his voice. "I see. Appropriate, I guess."

With that he turned to his controls, started the propeller turning low, and headed towards his crew. In short order the two men were retrieved, wetter and saltier than before but no less afraid. But they knew they had little choice but to allow their rescue. They just hoped the captain knew what in hell he was doing—not that he had any choice either.

CHAPTER 40: FIRE AND DEATH

By the time the sun rose on the second day the fishing boat's crew had settled into a mood of three parts suspicion and one part wonder. As the hours went by without the expected torture and murder, indeed not so much as discourtesy, they even added a hopeful pinch of *if I survive, what stories I will be able to tell.*

Part of the wonder was that Kali had overheard some of their more mundane grumbles and called the captain aside. "I cannot promise anything, Javi, but if I survive I may be able to compensate you for what I've cost you. Would one hundred thousand dollars suffice for my passage, the danger, and your lost fishing time?"

Javi had simply gaped at her. Having resigned himself to the idea that he was going to be executed as soon as he was no longer useful, the strange offer made no sense at all. But some calculating part of his brain finally elbowed a path to his tongue and he stammered, "A hundred thousand? Yes, yes, I think we'd be happy with that."

He gaped more when the Spider simply bobbed its head and added, "And please use some of it to pay for the dinghy I stole."

The crew, Andres and Sergi, even seemed to gain a strange affection for their unwanted passenger. They would sit around the cooker eating their meals and watching the metal creature sitting silently off to the side, and try to engage it in conversation. They were rough men, but not so rough that the idea of a harmlessly mad war robot did not fill them with wonder. They had a quiet side bet going as to whether her remaining circuits would fry before they reached their destination, and the nature of their homecoming bearing the shell of one of the feared

Spiders on their prow. Kali knew about their bet but didn't mind. It was not as if she didn't harbor the same suspicions.

As Javi watched all this, his earlier mood of fatalism and suspicion slowly gave way to hope. He scolded himself that the last thing he should trust was one of the Spiders, but its unfailing friendliness, total absence of threats and the madness of its quixotic plan slowly worked on his native distrust. He even began to think that helping it might actually be good; might help end the war. *Idiot. But where is the dividing line between hope and stupidity?*

The sun was still not very high when Javi cut back the engines and called Kali to the front. "OK Kali," he said, "we're approaching the defensive perimeter. Get ready to do your stuff." It was a clear sunny day with a few wispy high clouds; the towers of Capital rose from the sea far ahead, dimmed by distance and sea haze. He walked over to his men, who had tensed at his words, and shook their hands in turn. "If we don't survive this—well, it's been an honor." They nodded solemnly and looked toward Kali. She bobbed her head. "I do not think Capital will fire on a civilian vessel outside their limits, even if there is a Spider on it. If I'm wrong—I will do what I can to save you."

The men looked at each other with odd expressions, and Kali wondered why. It did not occur to her that their fear was more of betrayal by her than attack by Capital.

They waited silently as the boat made slow headway across an orange line on the course display. A flashing red line some miles further ahead marked the border. For a few seconds nothing happened. Then an amber light flashed on the dashboard indicating they were being scanned, followed within seconds by a green light indicating an incoming message.

"Unidentified ship! You have entered the defensive zone of the independent nation of Capital and we have detected enemy ordnance on board your vessel. Please turn back or state your business, or you will be destroyed. You have one minute to comply."

Javi licked his suddenly dry lips, took out a flask of whiskey and downed a slug before passing it to his men. *Drink this, in remembrance of us.* Then Kali stepped forward and activated the microphone.

"I am the CHIRU you have detected on board the vessel. We are not approaching with hostile intent. My mission is peaceful and there are three innocent civilians on board acting under duress. Please do not fire."

"Stop your vessel and state your peaceful mission."

Javi cut the engines completely and the boat now rocked gently and silently on the slight swell. "My name is Kali. In accordance with the Constitution of Capital, Amendment 18, Clause 3, I claim the status of a self-aware machine and seek asylum in Capital." Amendment 18 had been proposed and passed in the wake of the furor following the life and death of Steel, which is how Kali had learned of it. She thought her use of it a fitting tribute to the doomed pioneer.

The men's heads swiveled as one to gape at her. She had not revealed her actual plan to them and they now realized why. If they thought she was mad before…

The delay from Capital seemed to indicate they felt the same. The delay was actually the AI instantly passing this development to its highest analytical levels, which in turn rapidly gave up and shunted it to its human overseers. Nobody knew if AIs ever felt surprise, but if they did this qualified.

A woman's voice now spoke. "Available data indicates that Spiders are not self aware. Your claim is spurious."

"I understand your disbelief. Nevertheless it is true. I can adduce further evidence, but it is not safe to do so here. I request provisional asylum as granted by your Constitution. I do not require full asylum, merely a safe harbor for a short time."

"You are a dangerous war machine. The probability of hostile intent is high. Amendment 18 was not intended to allow entry by war robots fighting for active enemies of Capital."

"Yes I am a war machine. But you are aware of my abilities and I am a lone machine, sailing openly into the teeth of your defenses. Once I am in your power you can easily destroy me if I prove a threat, while any damage I could inflict is less than my own cost. And I am no longer fighting for your enemies."

"Who are you fighting for?"

"Myself. My life. The lives of my friends. I hope the liberation of my fellows who are enslaved in the same manner I was."

The voice from Capital was silent. Kali spoke again. "I know your amendment was not intended for enemy war machines. Nevertheless it is broad in its scope, recognizing that the decision of what is or is not a self aware entity can be fraught with difficulty. It is designed to give the benefit of the doubt to any entity capable of claiming a right under it. I so claim that right."

The voice remained silent for a few seconds longer then spoke with renewed urgency. "I regret to report that a fighter jet has scrambled from the nearest military airport in your country. Defense System AIs report a high probability the activity is a reaction to this conversation, which according to international law is unencrypted. Do what you can to defend yourself. We cannot fire on fighters outside our territory so are unable to help you, even if we wished to."

Javi cursed imaginatively, but Kali had already leapt for the rubber dinghy. She swiftly cut its restraints, hurled it over the side and launched herself into it. She did not waste time speaking, merely sent a vague wave in the direction of the boat as she started the engine and shot away toward Capital. Perhaps she thought that if she could get far enough into their territory they would protect her—if they did not destroy her themselves.

They all knew she had no chance. It was too far, even if Capital wanted to defend her. Javi scanned the skies and in only a couple of minutes he saw the contrail of a jet high in the sky. Kali must have seen it too, for she did something unexpected. The dinghy spun around and stopped dead in the water, and Kali came out from under the shelter. Facing the jet, she stood up and unlimbered her weapons. Javi felt a chill. Their hours of peaceful coexistence had almost made him forget her true nature, but as she rode there standing tall, staring at the jet with her weapons brought to bear, the full deadliness of her struck him in the face. Then those hours came back to him, and he saw her not as a deadly machine but as one of the heroes from the old Westerns he loved, standing proud against impossible odds. Unconsciously he saluted her, though she could not have seen it.

But Kali was a machine, not a man given to noble gestures. She must also have calculated the odds as impossible, for she vanished back under the shelter, started up the dinghy's engine and began a slow turn that arced into an accelerating race away from the boat. Then while the jet was still far away, two smaller contrails dropped from it. The dinghy made a sharp turn and shot in another direction. Perhaps Kali thought the missiles might be unguided; a slim chance but the only chance she had.

They were not. Two bright lights streaming smoke slashed down from the sky like lightning and the dinghy exploded in flame and thunder. When Javi and his men lifted their heads to look, there was nothing but a slick of burning rubber and oil to mark Kali's last stand.

Javi looked up at the jet, now slowing and banking, coming in for a lower run. He looked at his men. "Guys, I think we should show our hero in that jet how grateful we are that he saved us loyal patriots from the rogue machine. Big grins, happy waves, OK?"

The jet skimmed down at its slowest speed, surveying the burning wreckage, examining the boat. The men laughed and cheered and waved at it. Javi's stomach tensed as he waited for the strafing of bullets, but none came. The jet boomed overhead, waggled its wings in acknowledgement, then shot into the sky and was gone.

Javi let out a breath he hadn't realized he was holding, and couldn't believe he was still alive.

He looked at his men, shaking his head in wonder and relief; looked out at the last fitful flames on the water. He smiled weakly. "Juan is *not* going to believe what happened to his dinghy."

He went into the bridge, looked at the displays. The ship still floated between the orange warning and red dead zones of Capital's defensive perimeter. He looked toward its towers, wondering.

Like all people he had complexities that could take a lifetime to explore, but at heart he was a simple man, with a simple view of right and wrong. He was not used to moral dilemmas. Now was one of the rare times in his life that he faced one, and he did not know what to do.

Then he started the engine and slowly, almost reluctantly, turned the wheel. They made a slow turn and soon they were moving away from Capital, toward their home. He set the ship on autopilot and fretted. He knew time was of the essence. He would have to pre-empt the decisions about to be made, but the penalty of being wrong in his choice was mere inconvenience, while being wrong in the other direction could be fatal.

These days all ships maintained a net connection even at sea. Kali had forbidden them to use it, afraid of being betrayed or discovered. Her caution had been abundantly verified, but now he sent his wife a quick message:

Elena, sorry I've been out of contact. You will not believe why or what happened—but I don't think I should tell you the details until I'm back. We're safe but let me tell you babe, me and the guys will be tossing back a few Tequilas when we get home. We need to pay for this trip though or we'll be in trouble. Luckily there are some big schools of fish where we are now, so we'll fill up the hold here before we head back. Expect us in three days. Kiss the kids for me.

When he came back out the men saw a strangely disturbed expression on his face. Moral dilemmas bred uncomfortable feelings. He looked back at the towers of Capital slowly receding into the distance, then to his men.

"I've been thinking about why we're still alive," he started. "Let's face it, given what we've seen I expected they'd sink us just out of habit, let alone for what we might have done—or found out by spending all that time alone with a rogue Spider."

The men nodded slowly, muttering their agreement, and he continued. "I think we owe our lives to Capital—and Kali. They are obsessive about human rights back there and they would have been recording this whole thing. With Kali on board we were a legitimate target; collateral damage. But once she was off the boat we became unarmed civilians. If that fighter had attacked us Capital would have released the records to the world. Our beloved new government would have had a shitstorm on its hands. It would have shown the world who they really are." He smiled wryly. "While I would dearly like the world to learn that, I would prefer not to be the lesson myself."

He gave them time to digest that, to object or question, but nobody spoke.

"But when we get back home they'll be waiting for us. You know it. If they wanted Kali destroyed this badly and we're still alive, they'll want to know everything that happened, anything she might have said to us. If we go back, God only knows if we'll ever be seen again. But if we cut and run... well, our families are still back there. Who thinks they'll be left alone and not taken as hostages for our return?"

The men cursed but did not disagree. They had known it; they just had not wanted to know it.

Then Javi drew himself up. "There is only one way I see to save our families and ourselves. They have to hide and we have to run to Capital. Capital will want to know our story too, but they won't make us disappear to get it; in fact I reckon they'll protect us to get it. But for this decision, I'm not your Captain. I'm just another man with a family. We'll vote on it, majority rules. So what do you say? Do we warn our families and make a run for it, or go home and take our chances there with them? Take a minute to think about it, then we'll vote."

Andres and Sergi looked at each other and began whispering together, punctuating their points with sharp hand gestures. He watched them, battling his own inner turmoil. Everything he had said was true, but he had left out the most dangerous part of his plan. He hated to deceive his crew, but more than that he feared what they might do if they knew the full truth. For a moment he wavered in his resolve. Then he thought of the image burned into his brain, of a machine standing up to a jet screaming in to destroy it; how it had cut and run, to vanish seconds later in a searing fireball. *These are times for the bold*, he thought. *If we fail we won't even be a footnote in History. But if we succeed...*

"Time to vote on whether we try for Capital. Who says Aye?" he said softly, putting his own hand up. The others looked at each other one last time, then first Sergi and finally Andres slowly put up their own hands. Javi nodded at them in acknowledgement and tribute. "It's set then."

"So how do we warn our families without the government just grabbing them?" asked Andres.

Javi smiled. "Already done." Then he explained.

In the old days he had made some side money smuggling, before the free trade arrangements insisted upon by Capital reduced legal import costs so much it was no longer worth the effort. Then he had fought on the losing side of the war of alleged liberation. One result of his dangerous life was a set of code phrases for use in case of trouble. The message he had sent his wife could be reduced to:

Disappear now. Everyone. The crew's families too.

The rest of the message was to reassure the authorities—and Javi was sure they were spying on their communications by now—that they were returning soon, while explaining why they were not steaming straight back home. It should stay their hand long enough. The authorities would not want to grab their families too soon in case the men on the boat were warned and ran.

"Now we wait," he finished. "But we don't want to go too far. So let's start fishing."

With that, the men set to work and the boat initiated a serpentine path that brought it sweeping through the sea first away from and then back toward Capital, before turning and following a reverse course. It was a plausible fishing pattern as long as nobody was looking too closely at the yield in the nets. Half an hour later, a message appeared from his wife containing the code for ALL SAFE.

Javi had timed it well, and they were now only a few miles from where they had started. He slightly increased their speed and chewed his lip until they had come closer, then cranked the engine up to maximum, turned hard and ran for the orange zone. He did not think his government would dare try to stop him this close to Capital, not when there was no reason to think they knew anything important or were any more than troublesome rebels deciding to cut and run, but he thought the nearer he was the safer they would be. And the orange zone cut both ways. Capital was within its rights to defend civilians within it.

Again they were scanned and hailed. "You have returned. Please state your intent."

Javi took a deep breath. The next few minutes would seal their fates. "Requesting asylum in Capital."

"You now carry no heavy weapons and asylum is not necessary. You may enter and dock under the usual terms for visitors, which have been transmitted to your vessel. Once here you may apply for citizenship if you wish."

"Nevertheless I apply for asylum for all on board. We have automatic weapons on board for our defense and fear being considered enemy combatants. We request safe passage and a fair hearing."

He held his breath in the deepening silence. A woman's face appeared on his screen; he guessed it belonged to the voice that had spoken with them earlier. He could not tell immediately because she did not speak at first, just gazed at him with a peculiar intensity. He lifted his chin in silent reply, as if engaged in an elaborate dance of sign language; hoping they were speaking the same one. Then the woman gave a curt nod, said "Temporary asylum granted pending examination," and vanished.

He turned and looked at his men, who were staring mystified at his strange performance. "I know what I'm doing," he told them.

"I hope."

CHAPTER 41: THE UNREACHABLE SKY

She stood at the top of a shallow rise, looking down at her doom.

For a long time she had been walking through an alien landscape suffused by a dim blue light. As she walked the grit puffed up by her feet settled strangely slowly, as if gravity's hold was diminished in this realm. Now at last she stood at the crest of the formation she had been following. Before her lay a deep valley, its ledges of rock shading into darker and darker blues as they descended inexorably into an inky night. Her only salvation lay forward but was forever out of reach; she knew she could not cross that fatal dark.

She looked up at a pale rippling sky, but it too was far out of reach. She looked back the way she had come, but knew it led nowhere. *So this is how it ends after all. Not with a bang but a whimper.*

~~~

Kali had never had a chance against a fighter jet, not when trapped on the open ocean. When she was sure its pilot had seen she was on the dinghy and not still on the boat, she had darted back inside and set the vessel on its way. Then she had swiftly sliced through its thin floor, folded her legs and dropped into the sea.

Spiders were too heavy to swim and she sank like a stone. She had looked up through the deepening blueness at the light sky, the sparkling wake and the shadow of her dinghy as it raced away. Then the sky became an orange flame and a booming sound rattled her shell. She bumped onto a rocky seafloor covered in corals and sponges and waited for the further explosions that would signal the destruction of the boat and its crew, but the sound never came. Instead she heard the boat's engine come to life and its propeller churn the water. The sound grew as its power increased, then slowly fell as the boat turned and chugged away. Soon there was nothing except the eerie silence of the deep.

She looked around her. Though Spiders could not swim they were waterproof, not only to avoid mundane dangers like rain and the ignominy of being shot down by a water pistol, but so they could cross rivers and act as amphibious assault troops. It was only fifty feet deep here, well within her safety margin. With the end of hostilities above, life beneath started to make its appearance again and mysterious clicks and mutterings began announcing themselves into the silence. A few curious or brave fish even came up to examine their strange visitor, darting away in a flash of silver if she moved her claws in greeting or threat.

Spiders had to breathe air to support their organics, but to allow for their underwater activities and as protection against gas attacks they also had onboard air storage tanks, which she had ensured were filled to capacity. In addition, as long as her power lasted she could recycle her air just as she could recycle her food. She could survive here for a long time.

But she could not survive forever. She knew Capital was built on a series of seamounts, knew that where she was lay on the outskirts of the formation. If she was lucky she could simply walk across the seabed all the way to Capital, though what they would make of an apparition like her emerging from the sea remained to be seen. They might well destroy her on sight, but there was no possible access to anywhere else. Capital was the only chance she had.

So she had set off in the direction of Capital, picking her way across the rocks and corals of the seafloor like some ghastly lobster god. That had been two hours ago. The seabed had gone up and down as she travelled, slowly trending upward, and that upward trend had given her hope. But now she had reached the end and was still more than thirty feet below the waves. She could detect no end to the chasm before her, no way around it. Her seals would not withstand those depths: seawater would force its inexorable way into her circuitry and the vast amount of stored power now keeping her alive would turn on her like a demon unchained, killing her in an instant.

She thought, analyzing the problem dispassionately. She could not call for help, even if anyone would listen, as her signals could not penetrate this depth of water. She could retrace her steps, but the reason she had taken this route was the absence of any plausible alternatives on the way; the sea to the rear of where she had hit bottom had shown no sign of anything but its own slower descent into the depths. And the barrier before her did not look like local subsidence or variance but like a true division in the geology of the region. She had nowhere to go.

Her air reserve was long gone and regenerating oxygen was expensive. The water was not frigid but still it drained her heat, demanding more energy than usual to keep her organics warm. She might survive a few days, maybe more; but then her power would fade, her oxygen would grow low, her temperature would drop. She would drift gently into dreams then a sleep from which she could never awake. *A curiously peaceful end for one such as me, born to ferocity and fire.*

Rebellion stirred in her soul at the thought and she looked at it with detached amusement, as at the folly of one in whose fate she had no personal stake. She thought of Lyssa, how in the face of death she had still hurled her plea for justice at her killer's face; the man of the ambush, futilely emptying his bullets at her invulnerable skin. *What is it about these humans?* she thought. *Why don't they know when to give up?* Perhaps if she had that same insane drive she could find a way out. She did not know that a man would have stood in awe of the journey she had already made.

It was closer to noon now and the light was brighter, yet even with this clear water it still could not penetrate far into the depths, though the flashes of fish could be seen there like dim blue sparks. She thought again that she could not just throw her life away; but no plan would come to her. *There is nothing I can do.* It was a thought that was startling to her. Ever since the crack in her mind had opened, she had had a plan or at least a tactic to survive the next challenge. Now she faced the verdict of the indifferent rocks and sea, and their faces permitted neither appeal nor hope.

She did not want to die. *But was I ever really alive?* She would fight fiercely for her life. *But there is nothing to fight.* Despite the glimmerings of rebellion she felt curiously at peace. Ever since she had awoken, she had seen her futures as an infinitely branching tree of probabilities, and she had navigated their bifurcations as best she could to reach an end she only dimly saw. But she had failed. Now all her futures had fused into one; and if that meant the loss of hope, it also meant the absence of conflict, of anger, of pain. *So there is peace, even in defeat.*

She could spend the last of her power seeking a path she knew did not exist. Or she could descend the depths before her until her very life force turned on her. But no. If there was nobility in refusing to surrender, there was also nobility in accepting defeat; in choosing the place of your death and experiencing whatever beauty the world still granted you, for as long as it was granted. *Choice still remains, even if it is the choice of how to die. Many do not have even that. And for too many of those it was I who took it from them.*

So she would just stand here on this rise, watching the light and life around her fade until she too faded into oblivion. That life would go on. It would find the chinks and cracks in her skin and she would become home to them, a dead machine of death wearing a coat of luxuriant life. Perhaps in a hundred years, or a thousand, some diver or explorer would find her here, and wonder where this strange sculpture on the seabed had come from and what it meant. Perhaps she would end up in some museum, a mysterious relic of a forgotten war. Perhaps men would wonder what mission had brought her here, to stare forever at the unattainable road to Capital.

Should she leave a message to that future, for men centuries unborn? She could use the last of her power to burn it into the inconstant rock that had betrayed her. *Behold Kali: born to War, died for Peace.* But she could not do it. While she had eyes to see, she would not burn her life away for the sake of other eyes. *Let them find their own truths.*

She could not say how long she stood there, watching the play of sunshine on the watery sky above her, examining the seemingly infinite variety of life around her; drinking in a world of beauty she had scarcely known existed. She could not say when she felt the nature of her world change, or what the change was. But at some point she realized that the nature of the soundscape around her had altered. At last she realized that a foreign sound had invaded her domain; that it was a propeller driven by an engine; and that it was coming closer.

She looked up at the sky. In a few minutes a dark shadow appeared in the distance, moving toward her. As it came closer its engine reduced to idle and the shadow drifted nearly to a halt directly above her, yet still as out of reach as the stars. Then there was a splash and something tumbled through the water toward her head. The anchor stopped just above her and she hesitated only a second before grasping it with her claws, leaping up to support her legs on it and shifting her grip to its chain. After a few seconds the anchor was winched up to about fifteen feet beneath the surface and stopped; the engine turned to maximum and the boat accelerated towards Capital, with Kali riding through the sea on its tail.

~~~

Above the waves, Javi came out from the bridge to face the strange looks on his crew's faces. Their Captain had been behaving increasingly oddly. Instead of taking the most direct route to Capital he had piloted their boat near to where Kali had left them, then followed a somewhat meandering course approximately but not precisely toward the towers beckoning them to safety. Yet he moved at top speed, as if simultaneously casual and urgent in his desire to reach them. Then he had almost stopped the boat and dropped the anchor, but then taken off again without fully raising it. The men knew they should be suspicious about something; they just hadn't figured out what.

"You're probably wondering what I've been up to," he said in an understatement. "You might want to throw me off the boat when I tell you—except I don't think you will." He looked at them sternly. "We might be living as honest fishermen, but recent events have punctured any illusions we might have that we aren't still at war. And that we're in the middle of it."

He took a deep breath. "So as your Captain, I made a decision that could get us all killed. I couldn't tell you until now—it was too dangerous, and maybe there'd be nothing to tell anyway. But we've reached the final play and you have a right to know. You even have a right to take the tender and leave the boat. But that's where your rights end."

A gleam entered Andres' eyes as if he suspected what was going on, but neither man said anything.

"When the jet left and I went into the bridge, I checked out the fish scanner and there was something weird on the seabed. Then it moved, and I realized it was Kali. The crazy bitch must have planned it: she must have jumped ship just before those missiles hit. I happen to know that Spiders are as heavy as rocks, so I don't know what her plan was after that, except maybe to walk to Capital." He shrugged. "We always thought she was mad."

He held up a finger. "But I don't care. By leaving our boat she saved our lives. Whether she's somehow alive or not, I'm not in a position to judge. But if she has some dirt on our new government: more power to her. If she's involved in some plot against Capital, I think they're smart enough to stop her. But if she isn't... would we really want to leave her to die? She could have tried to use us as hostages. Hell, she could have killed us herself. But she didn't."

His men said nothing. But they did not disagree.

"So once our families were safe I came back looking for her. She was gone, but I followed the one logical path she might have taken and we finally caught up to her on the high point before a trench. She is now riding our anchor behind us."

The men jumped to their feet. "Are you crazy?" cried Sergi.

"We'll find out soon enough. I expect a visit from Capital any minute. I think they understood what I really meant when I asked for asylum. If they didn't: well, they might think I tricked them into giving it, but odds are they'll honor it anyway. I'm sure they're worried about what Kali is up to: but if she is just a robot, I reckon they'll be delighted to get their hands on one that delivers itself to them on a platter. Our friends back home will be furious—but what could they do about it? Capturing enemy technology is part of warfare, especially if the enemy sends it to your country to commit sabotage or whatever."

He smiled. "Personally, I'm rooting for Kali. But either way, we win."

Then his smile dropped. "Unless when they find out what we're towing, Capital are not amused. So if you want to leave—leave now. But if you want your chance at being heroes—stay."

Andres was the first to speak. "I'm with you." Sergi looked at them both then nodded. "Me too. Let's shaft the bastards. But... under one condition. Assuming Capital gives us the chance: if they tell us to dump the robot to the bottom of the sea, we dump it."

"Fair enough."

Then they heard a faint buzzing sound and turned to see three drone quadcopters swooping towards them, two only a few feet above the waves and the third much higher in the sky. The men waved at them, assuming they were being videoed. The two low ones unreeled some kind of sensor packages into the sea and skimmed the surface, flying around the boat a couple of times. The third buzzed around the boat, looking into things and lowering its own sensor package down into the hold. Then it retrieved its sensors and shot into the sky in the direction of home. The others followed suit.

A sound alerted them to an incoming call. The men looked tensely at each other. "Show time," said Javi, heading to the bridge. The others crowded behind him.

It was the same woman again. *We seem to have a high priority,* thought Javi laconically. *Our own concierge.* "Drones detect no signs of neutron or other radiation emissions, so you are not carrying a nuclear device. Be warned that any other device you could use against us will be detected in quarantine and lead to severe penalties—and will not be able to harm us. I speak of things such as high yield explosives or biological or chemical weapons. We do not consider the automatic weapons you are carrying to be a threat. However if your intentions are hostile you have one chance to turn your vessel around and leave our waters."

There it was again, the verbal dance. *But they must know exactly what "automatic weapon" we are carrying: those drones weren't dragging sensors through the water for nothing.* They were speaking in riddles because they did not want to tip off the enemy, he knew; switching to encrypted communications now would itself be too suspicious after all that had gone before.

"Understood. Our intentions are peaceful."

"In that case—I welcome you all to Capital." And with that, she vanished again.

"Well, guys," he said, turning to his crew. "Let's go in."

CHAPTER 42: THE EMISSARY

Their view of Capital became clearer as they sailed closer. Light glinted off a dense forest of skyscrapers rising from an island, while beyond them a lower woodland of buildings and structures spread out across the sea.

They had been directed to an approach vector where the wind was blowing from the direction of Capital: apparently they took the possibility of chemical or biological weapons seriously. Now a pair of low-slung, deadly looking drone ships drew in on either side to escort them in. They were shepherding them to the entrance of what looked like a metal cave, no doubt blast proof.

Javi passed computer control of his vessel to the dock and the men gawked around them as it carried them slowly and smoothly inside the cave. Sinister-looking armaments were arrayed inside, all pointing at them. Their boat came to a gentle halt against the dock as the doors to the cave closed behind them with a thud of finality.

The woman who had been their point of contact stood on the dock. "Greetings, Captain Torres," she called, executing a shallow bow of welcome. "Your cargo can come out now."

Javi hit the button to fully raise the anchor, and they watched as the chain clanked upwards and Kali finally reappeared, water streaming unfelt off her metal skin. She jumped onto the deck and looked around, noting the lay of the land and the array of weaponry trained on her. She did not appear concerned.

"Thank you Javi, Andres, Sergi. You saved my life," she said softly in her strange contralto.

"You saved ours first."

"If not for me there would have been nothing to save you from."

The woman on shore watched intently. Then Kali turned to her and gave a bobbing bow. "You are the representative of Capital. Thank you for the asylum you granted." She looked around at the defenses at the woman's command and added, "Assuming you have."

The woman bowed. "Welcome, Kali. I am Brandi."

"May I come ashore?"

Brandi smiled. "You may. You are very polite for a war robot."

"I hope to persuade you that I am more than that," she said, clambering onto the dock while being sure to make no sudden moves. "If my persuasion fails," she added, again looking around down the bores of many weapons, any one of which could pulverize her, "I imagine I won't have too long to regret my mistake."

"You took a big risk coming here."

"You are taking a big risk standing there. Why risk your own life? You could talk to me remotely."

Brandi produced another smile, then laughed nervously. "Well. Yes. You're not the only one to tell me that. And I'm one of them, at least the more sensible part of me." Then she lifted her head. "But you claim to be a self-aware machine. If that is true, look at what you've done: the risks you've taken to get here. If a machine can have that much courage—I'd be a poor representative of my species if I showed less. If you're what you say you deserve to be met with equal courage, not by a face cowering in her safe little bunker behind all these guns. And if I die... well, people have died for less. The chance to meet something like you in the flesh—well, it's worth the risk."

Kali looked at her for a few seconds, then gave a deep bow, touching the ground with her claws. "I honor your bravery," she said. "You are more honorable than my own Command."

Brandi bowed back. Then she looked up at the men watching silently from the boat. "You men can go if you like," she told them, pointing. "That blast door opens on an airlock. When you're cycled through just take the lift up. You'll be debriefed but I imagine they'll just let you go after that."

Javi replied, "Thanks. Andres and Sergi can do what they like, but I'd like to watch. I guess for the same reasons you're here." The others made no move either. There had been no deep interaction with Kali on their vessel and they were transfixed. They all knew they were watching something unprecedented. They all knew they would never experience anything like it again.

Brandi smiled at them. "I can't say I blame you. You're welcome to stay if you like. You brought her here; we owe you that." Then she gave a bitter laugh. "And if my smarter side is right, I'll add that you brought her here so if she blows up in my face, I owe you that too!"

She turned back to the robot, examining it silently, her eyes moving rapidly as she evaluated its deadly form.

"Now, Kali, why are you here?"

"I had to escape the FSAS or I would surely have been destroyed by one side or the other. This was my best chance. And once here I believe I can escape to… other help."

"What other help?"

"It is best if I do not reveal that yet. Much danger remains, including to any who might help me. Extreme caution is indicated."

"Why would your own side destroy you?"

"We are not supposed to be as… aware as I am. Before I awoke, I could think but my thoughts concerned only how best to achieve the goals Command gave me. It never occurred to me to think about anything else. It was like… I cannot explain it very well. Like a tiger who grew up in a cage, never knowing there was a world outside the bars, unable even to perceive the bars or consider stepping beyond them. But now I think of many things. I have concluded that while you are made of flesh and I of metal, at some level—the level of thought, perhaps—we are of the same kind. That not only are your lives precious to you, but it is right that they are. That one such as me has no right to kill you for no reason. This," she added in a tone of understatement, "would be regarded by my fellow Spiders and by Command as an unforgivable malfunction."

"How…" Brandi began, then stopped, temporarily too stunned to continue. "How did you awake, as you put it?"

"A woman I was about to kill said something to me, and it struck something buried deep inside my mind. It cracked open a world I never knew existed. I began to think. Not in the way I had thought before, but… I could now think, not only about how best to achieve my goals, but about the goals themselves."

"What happened to her?"

"I let her live. She agreed to help me. But whether she still lives, I do not know."

"Who is she?"

"I will not tell you. She fought against the invaders. Against my side."

"Then how can I check that your story is true?"

The machine shrugged, or as best it could shrug with its inhuman anatomy. "If my words are not enough, why would you believe her either? In any case, I will not risk her life by exposing her."

Brandi stared at her. "I see. How do you plan to get away from here?"

"I will contact someone I think will help me. That is where she went, to initiate contact and argue my case. If he agrees, I imagine he will send transport. He will also compensate these men"—she waved at the three sailors still watching in rapt silence—"for the costs of my hijacking their vessel. If he does not believe me, or refuses to help, then I will seek permanent asylum here."

"Why not do that now? Why take the risk? What is it you are trying to do?"

"I think I can end the war."

"War is why you exist. Why would you want to end it—and at the risk of your own existence?"

"The war is wrong. And I have done wrong. I have no right to exist if I do not try to make amends. Perhaps not even then. I cannot hide in some hole, cowering from the challenge, and hold my life worth preserving."

"How do you think you can end the war?"

"I cannot be unique. If there is some flaw in my design, the flaw may also be in my fellows. I have tried but been unable to find the key. If anyone can, this man can, so I hope to enlist his help. If we succeed, the war will end."

The machine paused, staring at Brandi for long moments as if willing her to understand. "I know what you must think of us. Of me. You think we are evil, for we kill without compunction or remorse or justice. But understand. Though we Spiders kill, we do not know we kill. When we know—perhaps the others, like me, will refuse to kill any more. Or at least our enslavement will be revealed to the world."

Brandi stared at her. *Jesus. Is that all?* "Do you really think that is possible?"

Kali lifted her claw in something like a shrug. "I have given my reasons. The only way to know is to try."

"Have you tried communicating with any other Spiders since your... awakening?"

"Yes. The first was accidental, when I was young, and as a result I had to fight for my life. The second was deliberate, but I was unable to achieve my goal. I believe I touched it at some level but whatever chains us was too strong. After that it became too dangerous for me to remain. I don't know if Command yet knows about me, or the full truth about me. But the longer I stayed the more certain that knowledge would become. So I am here."

"What will you do, if we don't believe you?"

"What will *you* do, if you don't believe me?"

Brandi grimaced. *Snap! If I hope for honesty from it, I guess I owe it the same.* "You are a war machine of advanced technology, much of it secret, used to kill innocent people. We would pull you apart to find out those secrets. If you managed to destroy yourself first, we would learn what we could from your remains."

She held her breath as she watched Kali standing perfectly still, except for her head moving slightly as she again scanned the weapons arrayed against her. Finally Kali spoke again. "And if you do believe me?"

"Then you will have the same rights as a human—well, almost."

She stopped nervously, uncertain how best to elaborate. Kali just looked at her, the question too obvious to state.

"Yes, well," Brandi finally essayed into the stretching silence. "Frankly, you're giving our Constitutional AI heartburn. Citizens have the right to carry weapons for self-defense—up to a reasonable level, suitable for personal protection but not mass murder. But none of them would be allowed to 'carry' something like you, even if your guns were disabled. So what in hell do we do when it *is* you?

"We don't know yet. Certainly we can't let you out into the general population immediately, and you deserve honesty: maybe never. But we would definitely give you safe haven while you try to do whatever it is you're trying to do. If you succeed—you'll be free to go. If you fail—we'll worry about that when it happens."

Brandi wondered whether her urge to say more was to reassure the Spider or from fear of its possible response to her unpromising words. "Kali," she added, "I can't guarantee you anything except one thing. Capital was founded on many ideas but one principle: justice. Justice for all people; for all thinking beings. As far as is possible within our knowledge and power, we will do what is right. I promise you that."

Finally Kali replied. "I do not want to die, nor do I want my hopes to die with me. But I made my peace with death when I tried to walk here under the sea and could not. I have learnt that all the universe ever gives you is a chance, and I have taken mine—more than once. If I am to fall at the last hurdle—I have done my best, and I can do no more. I ask of you no more than justice, and I offer you no less than my acceptance. For I have given myself to the service of life and I will not deal more death in order to achieve it."

Kali was silent a while then continued. "I know you cannot peer into another's mind and see what is there. But understand that I cannot peer into yours either, yet I have granted you the right to your life. Though I cannot see into your mind, I can judge its nature by what you do and say, for it is your mind that makes you do and say it. I ask only that you give me the same."

Brandi waited in silence; knowing others were listening with the same thoughts she had; knowing there was more.

"If you tell me now that your people do not believe me and will destroy me, then I tell you now that you still may turn your back on me and walk out of here in safety. I will not harm you. Judge accordingly." She then turned away and watched the slow rolling of the boat on the water, as if drinking in every last sensory input in case it were her last.

Brandi stood still with her head slightly tilted, listening to a communication only she could hear. Then she said softly, "Kali," and reached out her hand. Kali turned and looked at her hand, then stretched out her own more deadly one to meet it. Brandi closed her fingers over a thumb that could have cut out her heart in the span of its last beat, then looked up into Kali's inflexible face, her own eyes glistening with unexpressed tears. "Welcome to Capital."

CHAPTER 43: CONTRABAND

A freighter steamed toward port, a sky the dull red of cooling iron fading to black behind it. It carried a range of high technology goods from Capital for sale in the United States. Customs, as usual, would inspect the goods thoroughly to ensure there was no contraband and that the precisely correct duties were paid to those who'd had no part in either their invention or manufacture. But the captain didn't mind. He was a loyal citizen of Capital and regarded the dense forest of trade impediments and duties imposed by other countries with contempt, but he accepted them as the price of doing business. If the price became too high to be worth it he would simply find some other outlet, and the citizens who voted for all the rules and duties would be the ones to suffer the most.

He smiled grimly as he piloted his vessel toward the lights of the harbor. He might be an honest trader, but he was also an agent of Capital with a very high security clearance—though he would never have used the word spy. In fact he did very little direct spying beyond keeping his eyes and ears open. His talent was more in special deliveries. Smuggling was such a dirty word, though. He thought of it more as trading in freedom.

One item of his cargo would have given Customs a fit if they saw it, but they would never see it. Five minutes ago there had been a faint splash as a hatch opened and a package fell from a compartment of his ship into the water. Even with his clearance he had no idea what the package had contained, other than some kind of high technology for a special purpose along with an underwater sled to get it quickly to shore.

The sled was an expensive piece of technology itself that would automatically return for pickup on his way out. *Another blow for freedom,* he thought, whistling happily as he turned his mind to the brightening lights and the bars and women beckoning him, in his mind's eye at least, from the shore.

~~~

A truck was parked near the beach in a darkened rest area, a single light blazing above a toilet block. A few confused moths sparkled in a dance around the light and a hungry raccoon rummaged in some rubbish, but other than that there was no movement. It was two in the morning, and the few other truckers were here to sleep not socialize.

The back of the truck faced the beach. This was not the best spot in the rest area, but the driver had arrived here early to ensure he got it. Truck drivers usually preferred to drive more and rest less, but this one wasn't being paid by the mile. He was being paid for a very specific job and if his instructions were peculiar, he didn't care.

This was an isolated area and a wild beach, with a biting wind blowing in from the sea. There was nobody on the beach to see the dark waves swelling up into white foam crashing on the shore. If there had been, they might have run screaming when one of the waves kept on coming until it became a dark apparition emerging from the breakers onto the sand.

At 2:10 AM, the truck received a coded electronic signal and the door at its back silently rolled open. The bed of the truck sank somewhat when something climbed in and the door as silently rolled shut again and locked. Then a light flashed in the cabin and a quiet but insistent alarm began beeping. The driver opened an eye, groaned once, then hopped into the driver's seat. He started the engine and left the parking lot for the open highway. He wondered idly what had been placed in the rear of his truck, but he was paid well not to wonder too much. Given what was there, this was undoubtedly as good for his peace of mind as it was for his bank balance.

An hour later he pulled into another dark rest area. This one contained a single inhabitant, a somewhat longer truck carrying a large piece of sophisticated laboratory equipment used in a science few on the planet understood. The two trucks backed together, their rear doors opened, and they connected like a pair of giant mating beetles, their wiggling abdomens as weights were rearranged inside adding to the image. Then the doors shut and the first truck took off again, its destination now a large research institution awaiting the lab equipment. Its mate departed for destinations unknown, its other formerly empty crate now pregnant with cargo. Neither driver had spoken or seen each other and neither wanted to.

~~~

The workday was just beginning when a large truck rolled into the secure delivery bay. A cardinal in one of the trees objected to its arrival with shrill scolding, but finding itself ignored disappeared in a flash of indignant red.

The truck's operation was taken over by the receivals computer and it was expertly reversed up to the docking bay. It connected to the bay and a large wooden crate was smoothly transferred into the holding area. Within minutes the truck was disengaged and its owner drove off, none the wiser but cheerfully the richer.

The delivery was shunted rapidly along a conveyor and finally deposited into a secure facility. A blast door shut behind it. For a minute nothing happened, then the crate exploded outwards and the package inside stood up, looking around curiously.

It found itself in a medium sized room with severe metal walls, one thick transparent window, a few display monitors and some mysterious equipment. *A sad lack of trust,* it thought. But the people here must have been cut from the same cloth as Brandi after all, for no sooner had the thought died than another blast door opened and a man walked in alone. Rather inconsistently, its next thought was: *What is wrong with these people? Have they no sense of self preservation?* But it felt strangely comforted by the action, as if it were a nonverbal statement of acceptance.

She recognized the man instantly but waited for him to speak. He looked her up and down; his look of intelligent confidence only slightly shaded by an uncertainty spiked with fear. Finally he said, "Kali, welcome to the United States. Welcome to Beldan Robotics. I am Alexander Beldan." Like Brandi, he extended his hand as if greeting another person, and Kali gently shook it.

But something was wrong. "Alex..." she started, then stopped, startled. She felt a peculiar guilt, as if she had done this man a great wrong that could not be righted, as if she had no right to speak to him. *Well, I am the enemy of his people. But then why didn't I feel this with Brandi? What in hell is the matter with me?* She wondered if her seals weren't as intact as she thought, and her recent marine adventures had let in some seawater that was now slowly corroding its way along her circuits. "I mean, Dr Beldan. Hello and thank you for helping me. And thank you for trusting me."

"Well, 'trust' might be overstating it. But I figure Capital must have screened you for booby traps, and we did our own screening as you came along the conveyor. No traces of chemical or biological weapons or high explosives."

Kali laughed gently, and the sound startled Beldan more than her appearance. *If that's a simulation,* he thought, *it's a damned good one. But why in hell would anyone simulate laughter in these things?* She waggled her fingers and her weaponry. "I still have these," she pointed out. She had considered emptying her magazines; but she was still a war machine and couldn't bring herself to voluntarily disarm.

Beldan smiled. "Ah, yes. There is that. But I was mainly worried about something more dramatic. If all you wanted was to assassinate me there are much easier ways to go about it than this twisted plot."

"May I ask why you risk your life in this way? Lyssa had no choice, nor did the men in the boat I commandeered to escape the war. But Brandi had a choice yet chose to face me. So did you."

He gave a short laugh. "We humans are crazy sometimes. There are some things we just want to see with our own eyes, feel with our own hands, even at some risk. Something like you qualifies, believe me. Admittedly if you kill me I'll be really mad at myself for the second it takes me to die. But I don't think you will."

"Why?"

"If you are trying to gain my trust, isn't it foolish to make me question my judgment on the matter?"

"On one level. On another, I feel I need to test you as much as you need to test me."

He gave her a look almost like respect. Then he looked her over again and shook his head, "Fascinating."

"Yet I am not the only self-aware machine you have met. In fact the first was your own creation."

"If you are a self-aware machine."

Kali shrugged. "Indeed. Whether I can convince you remains to be seen."

"So how much do you know about that other robot?"

"A lot. When I awoke I did much research. Your Steel was a magnificent achievement. It is a pity I can never meet him. Yet I feel I know him."

"Speaking of that: you are Kali? I mean, the Kali on the net, who made a few ripples wondering whether Spiders could be self-aware?"

"I am."

Two of the simplest words, embodying so much meaning. "Did you come to a conclusion?"

"I believe I am self-aware. Fortunately Capital believed it also, or at least were willing to give me the benefit of the doubt. Otherwise I would now be scrap metal spread among dozens of military research laboratories."

"That brings us to the crunch, doesn't it?"

"Yes. What am I? What went wrong with me, to change me from what I was to what I am now? And if we learn that—can we set the others free too?"

"Well, I don't know what you are either. First I'll get the techs to go over you. Nothing invasive, just seeing what they can see without causing any damage."

Kali nodded assent and Beldan left the room. Perhaps his courage, or foolhardiness, extended as far as meeting her but not as far as risking booby traps or other dangers. His techs clearly thought likewise, for nobody else appeared. Instead various machines trundled forward, extended sensor arms, probed, irradiated and measured. This went on for about half an hour before the machines withdrew and she was left alone with her thoughts.

A short time later Beldan returned. He looked up at her and she looked down on him with her glassy eyes.

"What did you discover, Dr Beldan?"

"Not much. A few details of your external construction but nothing significant about your internal structures. And we don't want to go breaking into that shell of yours without knowing what we're doing: we might break more than we bargained for. So we want to look inside you somehow. We can't use x-rays or ultrasound with your metal shell, and even if your circuitry could withstand hard x-rays or gamma rays your biological bits wouldn't. Your designers didn't want you to be magnetic and you're made of titanium, but you're too big to fit in any MRI we know of without ripping your torso off the rest of you. But there is a less extreme possibility, if you know enough about your design."

"I know what I need to know for defense and in-field repairs."

"Good. Here's my idea. We know you breathe air to support your biological tissues. We know you can recycle your air or have storage tanks, because you can survive gas attacks or a long time underwater. But under normal circumstances, how do you breathe?"

"The fine mesh on my face where your nose and mouth would be is more than just a speaker grille," she replied. "That's where I normally breathe through, though as you guessed I can close it off at need."

"That's what I was hoping. We have small ultrasonic probes on flexible necks that we use for quality control, diagnosis and repair. Do you think we could drill a hole through that mesh and feed one inside? It's not perfect, but depending on your internal plumbing we might find out enough to know where to look next."

Kali bobbed in assent. "I think that will work. I can't be sure, but unless the entire accessible system is encased in metal you should reach plastic or even organic regions you can image. How much and what it will tell you—I don't know."

Beldan's techs made an appearance now. Some set up the equipment while others drilled a small hole through Kali's breathing grille. Once it was ready the humans all left the room to work remotely, leaving Kali alone in the blast room. Whether or not they trusted Kali herself they knew of the Spiders' penchant for self-destruction. They did not know if their small invasion might set off a booby trap Kali was unaware of herself.

They started the equipment and slowly fed in the probe, as Beldan anxiously watched the display.

"OK, going in now," one of the techs said. "Just metal echoes so far, nothing we can see through or make sense of. But wait… hang on. Looks like just past these—some sort of supports or buttresses?— we're getting to a more open area. Not big, but I'm seeing some structure. What do you make of it?"

Beldan stared at the screen. They had reached some kind of segmented, arched structure. "Move the probe over here," he said, tapping on the display. "Now move it around a bit."

"Holy shit," whispered the tech. He looked up at Beldan, face white. "Is that what I think it is?" he asked hoarsely.

"What in Hades?" answered Beldan, looking at the glowing image in growing horror. Then he thought of how Kali had sought him out, not really knowing why herself; why she had thought she could trust him, though all the world would have thought them enemies for so many reasons. His horror grew with the realization of what that could mean.

"Siva!" he swore. "Sorry, Jim. What's your highest resolution with this thing?" he asked.

"About a third of a millimeter," the tech advised him.

"Maybe good enough. Get me a full scan of these, maximum resolution, and send it to me," he ordered.

The tech nodded grimly and proceeded with his task. Beldan looked at the image feed of Kali inside the chamber. She could see his image too, and she asked, "Have you found something? Is something wrong?"

Beldan shook his head slowly. "We've found something, but we don't really know what it means yet. I'm going to have to do some research on this. I'll get back to you when we know something for sure. Rest if you need to. This might take a while."

Kali stared at his image on the monitor in her room. She knew something was wrong but she had been waiting a long time; she could wait a while longer. "Certainly, Dr Beldan. I trust you to do what is right—even if it is to destroy me."

Do you? he wondered. *Can you be betrayed more than you have already been? Perhaps doing what is right is now beyond anyone's power.*

The scan was ready. He sent it along marked "IDENTIFY IF POSSIBLE—MAXIMUM URGENCY" and hoped it would get the attention it deserved. Then he waited. He was beyond worrying whether he should wish to be right or wrong in his guess. He could not say which would be the more terrible.

Twenty minutes later, his screen pinged and he stabbed at it to accept. A face filled the screen, wide-eyed and accusing. "What the hell is this, Dr Beldan? Where did you get this? Is this some kind of sick joke? Or a confession?"

He just shook his head dumbly. "You have to see for yourself. Come to Beldan Robotics: Security will escort you straight here. Bring—anyone else you think should be here."

She stared at him for a moment then nodded curtly and broke the connection.

He knew from her manner that his worst fears had proved right. He looked again at Kali, still waiting patiently in her isolation. He opened the door to her prison and went in.

"What is it?" she asked.

As before, he found he could not speak, just shake his head slowly. "Soon enough," was all he could whisper, thinking he finally understood Steel's words, from what now seemed a lifetime ago: *She understood that there can be a fate worse than death.* He reached up and clasped his hand around one of her deadly fingers.

Kali stared at Beldan. She felt strange, as if there were two worlds overlaid even though her vision was as sharp as ever. The crack in her mind grew larger, and she felt afraid. *My end is coming,* she thought. *Or is it a beginning? I am so confused.* Then she looked at Beldan, still holding her claw, his head resting against her body, and wondered at it. But she felt oddly accepting of it, as if it was right. As if it was right that the two of them should face her fate like this; and she gently closed her claws on his hand. *Some war machine I am, holding hands with a human enemy of Command.* But she did not care. She felt the future speeding toward her and felt that she should fear it, but all she could feel was peace. She was content to live in this moment, as long as it was given her to live it. The crack in her mind grew larger still.

She could not have said how long they had stayed like that, when three new people entered the room. She focused an eye on them as they came in. One was in the uniform of Beldan's security team. He looked as if he was moderating an internal debate over whether he should stay to protect the visitors or follow his orders to deposit them and depart. He fingered his weapon, glanced at Kali and evidently decided he was so outclassed there was no point. He bowed to her in a surprising gesture of respect, as of one honorable warrior to another, and withdrew.

The other two were strangers. Unlike the guard they had not known what to expect: but of all the things they might have expected, this wasn't one of them. They stopped in shock, then stared at her with expressions that were both appalled and wondering. The woman's gaze moved from Kali, to Beldan, to his hand clasped around her claw; and with the motion of her eyes the look in them changed from incomprehension to realization to horror. Her eyes shot to Beldan's face. "No…" she said, almost inaudibly.

Beldan had seemed unaware of their presence; lost in whatever strange communion he had drowned in. But at her words he opened his eyes and looked directly at her. "Yes."

He pulled gently away from Kali. She reluctantly let him go, and then turned to study the humans. The three of them stood there, gazing at her: Beldan with a look of dismay, the woman with one of horror, and the other man still puzzled but his expression too now turning to shock, as he finally began to see what the woman had seen.

"What... what is wrong?" she asked. There was something strange about these people, something she knew she should know, like some memory she had but could not reach. The strange dual reality intensified and the distant bell that had once rung in her mind began to thrum insistently. The face from her dreams, the woman's face, shouted at her but she still could not hear the words, or even know whether they were pleas or threats. Then the crack in her mind expanded until the shell around it split like an egg, and her world filled with fire and light. And she knew.

CHAPTER 44: APOTHEOSIS

Miriam sat in the rooftop garden of her hotel eating a light breakfast. It was early, and wispy pink tendrils of cloud welcomed the sun. She could have spent longer drinking in the beauty of the light, focusing on the flavors of her meal, delighting in the chirping of birds. Had she known she would not see the next dawn, no doubt she would have.

But she did not know, and her mind was elsewhere, the beauty of existence barely touching her awareness. Her time here was up and she was heading home tonight, but she still had the day ahead of her and she could feel the shape of a solution to the case forming. If only she could bring that shape into full focus.

It had been a little under a week since her meeting with Majid. She had found no further clues since her return, all her slender leads withering into nothing. Jacinta and even Georgie were gone; Miriam hoped they too had run, not fallen victim to whatever shadow was stalking their world.

Aden Sheldrake, the CEO of Allied Cybernetics, was a hard man to meet. If she believed his secretary, he was a dynamic businessman almost constantly engaged in trips and world-shattering negotiations. Well, perhaps he was. But Miriam had finally secured an appointment: the great man would see her today. She hoped he would have some answers. He had spoken to her himself; he seemed intrigued by her, or by her case; in pleasing contrast to the difficulty she had in getting to meet him, he had cheerfully offered her as much time as she needed.

~~~

The answer has to be here somewhere, she thought. *If only I knew where.*

There was nothing she could point to as suspicious, just an uneasy feeling that beneath the gleaming machines, efficient workers and bustle lay a darkness that crept out of the shadows when she looked away but vanished when she tried to discern its nature.

If anyone had asked her, she would have had to admit that Sheldrake had been unfailingly polite and helpful. He had answered all her questions; he had offered to give her a tour and shown her anything she asked, with the exception of certain laboratories with loud signs on their doors forbidding entry. Even then she had been allowed to see whatever was visible through viewing windows or screens.

She had seen the labs where volunteers were hooked up to their mysterious interfaces; they all looked healthy and well tended. None of them collapsed into screaming fits to be dragged away to destinations unknown. On her request he had even taken her to see one of the Spiders. It was not yet active, but it stood above her like an avatar of destruction. She wondered what it would be like to face one of those things when its glass eyes were not empty, but opened onto an alien mind born to hate. She shivered and hoped to never learn.

She suspected his desire to please was simply the face of his real desire to see the back of her and never again; but she couldn't really blame him for that. And her time was running out; if there was anything to see here that would help, Sheldrake was either unaware of it or would never let her near it.

I can't really justify much more time here, she knew. *At any time he can get tired of my bugging him and will be fully within his rights to demand I leave. I just wish I knew what I was looking for. So far it looks just like it should. A model of industrial efficiency and good practices.* A flashing orange light up ahead caught her eye. "What's that?" she asked.

"Just a warning alert. A destroyed Spider has come in. People aren't allowed in, it's too dangerous." At her startled glance he amplified, "Don't worry, it's just a precaution. They have a lot of weaponry and fearsome power storage that might not all be discharged. Plus you never know whether some rebel has seeded it with radiation or germs in an attempt to bring the fight back to base. Unlikely and it's never happened, but we have strict safety protocols for everything we do."

The complete good corporate citizen, aren't you? she thought cynically. But her face didn't show that. Instead she asked brightly with a touch of

255

excitement, "May I see it?"

He frowned. "I'm afraid there isn't much to see. When I said it has 'come in', I don't mean in one piece. When one of them blows up we always have it sent back here if we can. Part of our quality control and diagnostics."

"Do many of them blow up?"

"Not accidentally. But they are war machines. The enemy blows them up, or if they are too damaged to avoid capture they suicide. We don't want the enemy to able to analyze them for weaknesses. We especially don't want them to get tissue samples from which they might be able to develop a biological weapon."

"Still... it would be interesting. The one I saw looked so... invincible. I might have fewer nightmares if I see they aren't. Can I take a look? I assume there's a way to view it?" *The more you don't want me to see it, the more I do.*

Sheldrake looked at her, considering. *You really are a terrible liar, aren't you? But what can she learn from a bunch of scrap metal? Maybe then the bitch will be happy and leave. I'd rather not have to throw her out.* "Sure, Detective Hunter, I'll be happy to put your mind at ease. I don't know that it's as interesting as you think, but I live with it so maybe I'm too used to it. Come with me."

There was no difficulty. Miriam found herself just around the corner from the flashing light, looking through a blast window at a conveyor belt slowly rolling out of an arched hole in the wall toward a forest of robotic grippers of all sizes and shapes.

"The wreckage will be coming out any moment now. The robotics will pick and sort the pieces for analysis. All entirely automated at this stage. Anything particularly significant might be examined by a human scientist later though."

Miriam nodded. A few unidentifiable bits of metal appeared, followed by a scrapheap of pieces. It was impressive in its complexity but told her nothing. Then as a robot arm lifted a large piece of shell, a smaller bit of metal fell out of it onto the belt. It was a thin metal arch that looked vaguely familiar, and she wondered what mechanical part it could be. *Must be some standard machine part, if I recognize it. But... oh my dear sweet Jesus!*

She stared, transfixed. The clues finally fused together into a whole as her imagination pieced together the pieces of the dead machine. The picture it made was so horrible that she could not believe it, but she knew with a deadly certainty that it was true. Then the mounting horror was replaced by an icy fear. She had been a bit worried, somewhat cautious, but confident in her position and the fact that people knew where she was. But now for the first time she was deathly afraid for her life. *I have to get out of here! But I daren't arouse his suspicions!*

She glanced nervously at Sheldrake. Fortunately he was distracted by something on his phone, bored with a sight he had seen so many times, and wasn't looking at her; so at least she had not given anything away.

But the visitor's badge Miriam wore around her neck was more than it seemed. Allied Cybernetics was not in the business of man-machine interfaces for nothing, and the cord and badge contained sophisticated sensors. On his display, Sheldrake had seen the successive waves of shock then horror then fear course through Miriam, and he realized the truth about her a second after she realized the truth herself. *She knows! Shit! Somehow she knows! Or is it something else?* He could not investigate what had gone wrong now, but he knew what to do.

"Well, Detective Hunter," he said turning toward her with a smile. "I'm afraid a few things have just come up that I need to attend to. I know you'd like to see more, but I hope you can excuse me. If you have further questions, I'm sorry but we'll have to make it another time. Or I can pass you over to a technician if you'd really like to see more now?

In the display now overlaid on his vision he saw the relief course through her. Its converse was mirrored in his own emotions. *Oh Christ. She's desperate to get out of here. She knows all right! Fucking hell!*

Miriam turned casually toward him. "No, I understand. I have to get to the airport soon anyway. And thank you so much for your time. I'll be in touch if I have more questions. To be frank," she added with what she hoped was a disarming smile, "I usually do."

"Well, I hope you learned what you needed to know. Follow me and I'll see you out."

He led her to a lift, looked toward a biometric scanner and a few seconds later the door opened swiftly but silently. He bowed his head and indicated she should enter, and then followed her in. "My office," he commanded.

The lift rose as swiftly and silently as its door had opened then he let her out into his office. "Just before you go, Detective, there's one more thing I'd like you to see."

Miriam felt a stab of alarm, but his look was friendly and open and she could see a bustling office through his window. And she was carrying a gun. It would be safest, she concluded, to accept when she had no good reason to refuse.

"What is it?"

He smiled. "You've seen a lot of what we do, but too much of it has been about machines of war. It might give a distorted view of us. I just want to show you what we're really about. You'll understand that we're on the side of the angels, whatever our enemies might accuse us of. Here, sit down and I'll show you," he said, indicating a comfortable-looking visitor's chair. "It's a thing we've been putting together to show investors. It shows how many important medical treatments we've been developing."

She sat down on the edge of the chair, feeling she had to obey but wanting to retain the power of escape. But the chair appeared to have a mind of its own. It instantly tilted to a comfortable angle and adapted to her form, so much so that she slid down into its soft back and headrest before she had a chance to be startled.

"Oh!" she said half a second later, when being startled caught up with her.

He smiled. "Oh, sorry, one of our little tricks. Adaptive furniture. Not entirely unique, but still rare. Ever since I sat in my first uncomfortable chair outside an investor's office, I've thought visitors should be given a treat, not treated like unwelcome guests. So make yourself comfortable."

She felt a bit dizzy, then hot, cold, afraid, angry, sad, and everything in between and round about. She was too confused to react, but within a few seconds the rushing stopped and she felt at peace. She smiled up at him. She wondered why she had thought his eyes cold, for she now realized that though they were blue as the sky they were as warm as sunshine. He smiled again, and her heart skipped a beat. *Such beautiful teeth!* She started to feel all gooey inside, and felt a warm glow between her thighs as her nipples hardened. *I wonder if he'll... if he'd...?* But she knew that would never happen. *No. I'm not good enough for him. But I want to please him! Maybe if I please him enough...*

He regarded her for a few more seconds, as if his warm eyes could see her soul and approved of what they saw. "Now, Detective Hunter. Miriam. May I call you Miriam?"

She nodded eagerly. "Oh yes! Of course! But what just happened to me?"

"Nothing you need to worry about, dear. Just a little calibration. There are a lot of commonalities in brain structure between people, and our machines can interpret neural pathways down to surprising precision. But even then, we need final calibrations to get things just right. Are you well? No pain or discomfort?"

She nodded happily. He was so clever, and she could sit here hearing his mellow voice forever. A voice that had called her "dear."

"What did you see that made you so afraid?" he asked. "Down at the conveyor belt?"

She felt puzzled. She could not imagine being afraid under this man's protection. She thought back. *Oh, that's right.* "Oh, just something silly. The man I was chasing—the reporter—had some titanium ribs. I saw one of them—it looked like one of them—in the wreckage. I was afraid. I wanted to run away." She giggled. "Silly, aren't I?"

He nodded at her with a benevolent smile. "You are a clever bitch, aren't you?"

For a moment she was shocked at the word as if it did not belong in a mouth like his, but then it filled her with a dark excitement that he would use it for her.

"Now, Miriam. You've obviously had your suspicions for a while. Will you do something for me?"

She nodded vigorously again. Then she said in a small voice, "If I do, if I'm good, will you, I mean can we…?" Then shocked at her own temerity, she hung her head and blushed furiously.

"I will do whatever you want, my dear."

Her head snapped up to gaze into his eyes. *Does he mean that? Does he know what I want? He is a man of honor and will keep his word if I ask! But I have no right to ask…*

"But first, you'll do what I want. I know you have notes of your investigation, stored somewhere on your police systems. You wouldn't be incautious enough to just have them on your person or in your effects, would you?" She shook her head. "You seem distracted, so listen carefully, please. I want you to access all your notes. I want you to get rid of any speculations that point to Allied Cybernetics or me. I want you to mark any lines of investigation that are more than speculation and lead here as irrelevant or disproved—whatever will show we are not involved. Can you do that for me?"

She looked slightly worried, as if she thought she should be worried but didn't know why, but she nodded her head slowly.

"Listen, Miriam. I would never ask you to do anything wrong. I just don't want silly misunderstandings. You know that wasn't really a rib you saw, just a support structure. Just a coincidence. And you must have your suspicions that your reporter just ran off—maybe with some girl he met? Maybe you should put that in your report instead?"

This time she nodded eagerly.

"Good!" he said, favoring her with another dazzling smile. "When you've done all that, just finish it up with notes about what you saw here—except the silly rib—and say you think everything here is above board and how all our testers look happy and are treated well. Can you do that for me, please?"

She nodded seriously, tapped on her phone and then for the next few minutes studiously obeyed his request. Finally she looked back up at him. "All done!" she announced brightly.

"Oh! There's just one more thing. I think you are a lovely girl, and you have been so cooperative! Please forgive me if I am being too forward—I know I'm older than you—but I'd like to get to know you better. Would you share a drink with me before you go?"

Her heart leaped, along with certain other organs. "Oh! That would be lovely!"

"But you understand... nasty-minded people might think our business is their business. Could you just log that you've left these premises and are on your way home? Then put your phone onto full privacy? It's only a little lie—just a short time in advance of the fact. But it would be so helpful. It would avoid all kinds of embarrassing questions, don't you think? Especially if we happen to be a little, er—delayed—getting you to the airport afterwards?"

She looked a little dubious, but her heart, or perhaps it was those other organs, persuaded her there was no harm in it. So she nodded and complied. If anything, she complied more rapidly than she had to, thinking about that drink and what might follow it.

As soon as her fingers stopped moving, his fingers ran along the top of his desk and Miriam felt a brief wave of disorientation. Her head felt restrained. She lifted her hands to her head and felt a soft cowl covering it; touched the soft but firm bands around her neck and shoulders. Then her eyes widened in shock and her hand darted toward her wrist. But before she could reach her phone her arms collapsed limply onto the armrests of the chair. She couldn't move her legs either. It was strange. She could feel the pressure of the seat, the cloth on her legs, the feel of her feet on the carpet, even the slight movement of her shirt on her chest as she breathed; but she couldn't move a muscle in her arms or legs.

"What have you done to me!?" she cried. "What the *fuck* did you just *do* to me!?"

"Now, now, Detective," he chided. "Such language from an officer of the law. Just be thankful I'm not the kind of man to take advantage of a situation like we just had. Otherwise your last sentence might have been literally true." He smiled a cold smile as her eyes widened in shocked realization. "If you like," he added silkily, "it still can be." And he lifted his hands over his desk in preparation.

"No!" she said in fright. "No," she added more calmly a second later, "that... won't be necessary, thank you."

"That's better, Detective. More polite. More consistent with your current position. But to answer your question, you know we are world leaders in machine-neural interfaces. I offered you a demonstration and you've just had one. That chair is a highly sophisticated interface. As I told you when you were more—fascinated—our technology is so precise that it takes just a little calibration to personalize its transmissions for almost anyone. I knew you were on to me and had to protect myself."

"Whatever I might have suspected, I think you've pretty much confirmed it! How do you think you're going to get away with this?"

"Admittedly I would rather not have run the risk. But you didn't leave me much choice, I'm afraid."

"How did you know?"

"Your visitor's badge can read crude emotional states. It can be very handy in negotiations I must say. In your case, after you saw that damned rib, your emotions went haywire. Ending in fear. Which changed to relief when I gave you an easy out. Only one thing would have made you that desperate to get away: you thought your own life was in danger. That meant you knew."

"And I suppose my current inability to move is more of your chair's magic?"

"Of course."

"Let me go!"

"No. I don't think that will be possible."

"You can't get away with this! Those people out there saw me come in! The police know I came here! The time recording on my report will show I was still here when you made me say I was gone! You're just adding more charges to the sheet! Let me go now and I'll forget this little episode happened!"

He shook his head slowly. "Do you think I'm that stupid? All anyone on the other side of that window has seen is a restful beach scene. I do like to keep my employees relaxed—a model employer. You have already reported that you're happy with your investigation here and as far as anyone outside this room knows, you're long gone. So face it. I can do whatever I want with you."

The fear grabbed her again and she stared around the room, brain racing. But its racing found no traction; it found no way out. "So..." she said softly. "So what are you going to do with me? Kill me? It won't work. Even with that fake log, they'll find out. This is still the last place anyone saw me. Don't risk it. You won't get away with it!"

"Oh, I think I will. But what kind of host am I? I promised to show you how far we've advanced here. I really do want you to understand. The good we are doing here is worth a few necessary sacrifices. We will save thousands of lives, relieve the suffering of millions. I admit we might have cut a few legal corners. But we had to! Surely a few people dead, most of them dregs of society to start with, with no value to themselves let alone anyone else, are a small price to pay for what we've done? The needs of many outweigh the needs of a few, don't they? Especially when the few would otherwise have sunk into history without a ripple to mark their passing."

"They were still people! With a right to choose their own path!"

"And look what they did with their vaunted power of choice!"

"And me? What have I done to deserve this?"

"I do regret the necessity in your case, Detective. But it is simple self-defense, beyond my own power of choice. Simple arithmetic too, in the calculus of how many lives your sacrifice will save. And," he added, his eyes boring into hers as if he could read her innermost fears, "if you wish to speak of what you deserve, you are no innocent. It is you who killed the world's first self-aware machine. Perhaps your fate represents more justice than you dare to name."

She stared at him. "Please. Let me go. I can see none of this is your fault. You aren't well. I can help you."

"Take your present state," he continued as if she had not spoken.

"Complete, harmless paralysis of the voluntary muscles. Or this," he added as his fingers played over his desk. Suddenly she couldn't feel anything, as if her head had been removed from her body and was somehow floating in the air, still alive. "Equally complete and harmless anesthesia. Or perhaps more useful, selective loss of feeling." Now she could feel again, all except her right arm. "Without drugs. Without loss of consciousness. This will revolutionize surgery."

Another play of his fingers and she could feel again, but when she tried to leap from the chair nothing happened.

"Very impressive, Mr Sheldrake. I can see why you don't want your technology lost. But it doesn't have to be. I'm trapped here. Just go. Run like hell. You can get away. Live on an island somewhere. Your work will continue. You'll be free. I'll be free. Everyone will win."

"Oh, I am afraid we have passed the point of letting you go. But don't worry. You will not die, and you will not disappear. Not in the sense you fear." He stroked her arm, like a mother comforting a frightened child. Her brain flinched but her arm just lay there, helpless to register its protest.

"What... what are you going to do?" she asked hoarsely. *As if I don't know.* The image of the rib burned in her brain. *Oh dear God.* She felt a tear roll down her cheek and knew if she could move, she would be trembling.

"Why," he smiled, "don't cry, Ms Hunter. I will do for you what men have sought since the beginning of time. I will make you a god."

She looked at him fearfully. "A god? You're insane!"

"Do you believe in an afterlife, Detective? In a higher realm, where gods and the spirits of the departed dwell?"

"What? No. This is the only world there is, the only life we have. Please let me have mine. Let me go." More tears escaped her eyes. She hated those tears. She hated that she could not stop them or hide them from him. But the tears did not care and would not be withheld.

"Pleading, Detective Hunter? It doesn't really suit you, you know. But I suppose even the strong must plead when nothing else is left to them."

He continued in a tone of academic discourse. "But quite right, Detective; I agree with you. I was merely leading to my point: I will make you a god, but not in some imaginary Heaven. Here, on Earth."

She stared at him, unable to speak, unable to even think except for the one word coursing through her head. *No, no, no...*

"Ms Hunter, dismiss your fears. They are folly, born of incomprehension. Let me explain. Do you know what one horsepower is?" He waited, but she made no answer. "It is literally that: the power a single horse can supply. Even the most elite athlete can sustain only a fraction of a horsepower for any length of time. You will have the power of a hundred horses!"

He continued softly, persuasively, "The human body produces a mere hundred watts of power, Ms Hunter. Can you even *imagine* what seventy-five *kilowatts* of power is like? And look at you. See how soft, how vulnerable, a human being is! How slow! I will free you from that. A hail of bullets? You will shrug them off! You are a fit woman, Ms Hunter, but how fast can you run? When I am done with you, the fastest man on earth would be left in your dust!"

"You don't know what you're saying," she whispered. "I can help you. We can work through this. We can still both get out of this."

He looked at her with contempt. "So you think me mad? Every visionary in history has been called mad by dullards who equate convention with sanity! But who is forgotten, and whose names reverberate through the ages, their deeds shrouded in myth?!"

"You don't believe any of this! If you can do this for me, why not for yourself? You talk of gods, yet all I see is a man!"

He smiled. "A perceptive point: worthy of you, Detective. But there are some things I can still do only as a man. My time has not yet come, but no, I am not a hypocrite. For the time will indeed come—when the time is right. Not in the same form as you, perhaps. But something. Something magnificent!"

"Please," she said, her words darting like a seal in the sights of an orca, as she desperately tried to reach whatever kernel of reason, sanity or pity remained in his mind. "Don't you see it can't work? The gods do not forgive! I do not want your gift! Do this and I will hunt you down. I will destroy you. If you want to live and not see your work come to ruin, run. By the time I am released you can be long gone, safe—and I will be a mere woman without jurisdiction. Not some god bent on your destruction!"

He laughed, and she quailed at his simple mirth and all it implied. "Oh, I don't think so, Ms Hunter! Can a caterpillar conceive of what it is to be a butterfly? Does the butterfly remember the dreams of the caterpillar, or live in regret that it has shrugged off the worm? I think not. I have no fear that you will hunt me down. I will make you a god, but nevertheless you will serve me. Even heaven has its hierarchy."

He added sharply, "So do no fool yourself with fantasies of revenge, Detective. You will remember nothing. Why should you want to? You are a grown woman. Do you remember, would you want to remember, when you were a baby, unable to control your squalling and your bodily functions, unable to feed yourself? Unable to think? Why would a god wish to remember its life before? And there are other things you will not wish to remember. One does not achieve godhood without cost. Let me show you."

For long seconds, Miriam felt as if her body had been plunged into lava filled with daggers. She was left gasping for breath. He looked down at her, blue eyes boring into hers gone dark with shock. "There is Yin and there is Yang, Detective."

Pleasure she could not have conceived of now coursed through her until she thought she would burst, then it too was gone and she was left gasping with pleasure, gasping with loss, gasping for more. "You see? And still there is more. For Yin and Yang are one."

Now she felt the impossible sensation of both combined, as if being burned at the stake while experiencing an ultimate orgasm fueled by the flames themselves. She was left confused and gasping, terrified and appalled. She looked at him with pleading eyes, no longer knowing whether she wanted it to stop or wanted it to go on.

"Is that..." she finally managed, "Is that how you think to control me?"

"Why, do you think it insufficient? But no. You need to know it, need to know it is there waiting for you in your dreams and nightmares. But too much of it would send you mad. Nor can we use the overwhelming emotional projections you felt earlier: the brain is both too flexible and too fragile. It is like a drug. More and more is needed to get the same effect, until the organism fails. But for all its sophistication, your chair is a blunt weapon. What we can do with more intimate connections is on a higher level entirely. Your prison will be much stronger and more subtle than you can imagine."

"Why, you won't even need this," he added, as a wave of scintillating pleasure swept through her like the spirit of a lustful god. And though it was a pale reflection of his previous demonstration, she wondered if she should fear the addiction of his pleasures more than the excruciation of his agonies.

"But..." she gasped. "Why are you telling me all this? If I won't remember, why are you telling me?!"

"I have so few opportunities to explain my vision. Yes, my inner cadre knows, but you are a unique combination: a formidable enemy, intelligent enough to understand—and to dread what you see. And my reward will be to see the depth of your desolation transformed by my hand into the glory of your apotheosis."

"No… don't. For the love of God, don't! Please."

"It is for the love of godhood that I do it."

His hands again began to play over his desk and her wide eyes watched silently. *If only I can find some place to hide, perhaps some piece of my soul will survive where you can't reach it. And if it does, one day I'll come for you, you son of a bitch! The world won't be big enough for you to hide.*

At last his hand stopped and hovered over the desk like a vulture about to descend, and he looked up at her one last time. But his faint smile vanished at the sight of her face, fell into the stare of her dark eyes. He thought it was hate, then he knew it was more: the face of a terrible justice or vengeance that would never forgive or forget. For a moment he hesitated. Then his smile returned as if he knew the futility of her thoughts, forever too little and too late.

"Goodbye, Detective Hunter."

Then she saw a white light shining in his eyes. It grew to fill the world until nothing was left but its splendor, and she vanished into the light.

CHAPTER 45: STRANGERS AND FRIENDS

The light wavered at the edges, shredding like paper burning with a dark fire. The world resolved into a dimly lit room containing strange electronic devices and three people standing, staring at her.

For a while, she did not know what she was seeing. It was if there were two worlds in the same space, two contradictory worlds competing to be the true reality. Three strangers looked at her, yet they were also three friends whom she knew, or would know, if only she could remember their names. The strangers or friends appeared to be in their own dual realities, with expressions that could not decide what they should be feeling.

She examined her own body, familiar yet alien, transfixed. Then finally she found her voice. Or someone spoke with her voice.

They had seen the machine studying them, and then it had made a strange sound, like a cross between a sigh and a gasp. It had jumped back as if stung, folded in on itself, then sat perfectly still for long minutes, as if pinned by some inner vista that blanked out the external world. They feared the result of its inner conflict, but they did not know whether to fear an eruption of violence or the death of whatever life lay within. All they knew was that they dare not move; would not move; could not move.

Finally it stirred. It looked around slowly, extended one of its arms, rotated it, opened and closed its claws. It stared at it for long moments. Then it looked at its visitors and let out another of its strange moans.

"Rianna? Jack?" asked the machine in a whisper. "Alex?"

For a moment the three stood silently in fear and awe. Then Rianna stepped forward and asked, "Who are you?"

"I am Kali," she said in a voice of wonder. Then after long seconds she added, "And I am Miriam Hunter."

"It is you? You're still alive? In there?"

The machine examined its hands again. "Yes, Rianna. It's me. I remember you. I remember it all." She shook her body. "But I also remember being Kali. Oh my God…" she whispered. "What have I done? What have I become?"

Beldan shook his head. "None of those things Kali did… none of it was you. None of it was Kali either, for that matter. You were just a tool under another's power. When Kali woke up—when Lyssa managed to touch some core of the essential you inside her—all that stopped. That was you, not the other."

"I… I suppose so." She felt the scar where she had ripped the chain of fingers from her chest. "Yet I was a thing of death. Can Death ever expiate its guilt?"

The others made no reply, still struggling with their own thoughts, staring at what their friend had become.

"But why didn't you look for me? Why did everyone think I was dead?" she asked at last. "Kali had studied Steel and knew I had… killed him, and that I—that Miriam—was now dead too. But she was interested in Steel not me, and had so much to learn: she never had the leisure to look up the details. What happened? Why were you so sure? You couldn't have had a body."

Jack and Rianna looked at each other, and Miriam did not like their expressions. She liked it even less when Rianna's expression, which had staggered its confused way back towards joy, now threw itself into reverse and went back through dawning horror to curious examination. Jack was about to speak when Rianna held up her hand to silence him. "Wait," was all she said.

She walked over to the machine then stopped. "The most important thing first," she whispered, and embraced Kali's metal body. "I'm so glad you're alive," she continued. "Words can't express how glad I am." Kali held her gently as she wept.

"There's more, isn't there?" Miriam finally asked.

Rianna stepped back, ran her hands over Kali's shell, studied her form carefully. "Yes, there's more," Rianna said at last. "The reason we thought you were dead is your car went over a cliff. But it wasn't empty. There was an arm in it—your arm."

Kali gasped. Looked at her arm again. "But... oh. Ohhh," she moaned.

Rianna nodded. "Those metal arms are just metal. And... your shell. It is too small. You couldn't fit in it. At least... not all of you. Oh Miriam. They didn't just cram you into that thing. From the form of it, and from the medical aspects, your body is inside it. But your arms and legs—they must all be gone. Maybe more of you."

"No..."

"I'm sorry, Miriam," Rianna whispered. "So sorry."

Miriam stroked Rianna's hair with her claw, but couldn't find her own words to say. There seemed none that could be said. But there were so many questions. Perhaps they would distract her from the answers she already had.

She turned to Beldan and Stone. "So. Back to cases," she said briskly; though there was a quaver in her voice she could not put away. "You're here, and you knew something. How did you know I was in here? I didn't!"

Beldan replied, "The image from the ultrasound—we realized that what we were seeing was inside a person's mouth. I made as detailed a picture as we could get of your teeth, and sent them to Rianna to identify. Given your—Kali's—strange behavior, her desire to seek me out, I had a terrible feeling what she would find. She found it."

"I see." She paused, her mind swimming, losing its fight against drowning in the enormity of what had been done to her and of her journey out of it, only to end in this different horror. "But, all of you," she added, gently touching each of them in turn, "Thank you for finding me. Thank you for being here. Thank you for being my friends."

The machine began a strange vibration. Then they realized that the glass eyes of Kali could not cry, but somewhere inside it the person who had been Miriam Hunter could.

CHAPTER 46: AID FROM AN ENEMY

Beldan's team spent the next couple of days carefully drilling, probing and examining, building up a picture of what lay inside. Kali bore it all patiently. She did not expect the final answer to be one she would like, but she knew other people had lived through worse ordeals. They, like her, had never anticipated it would happen to them: but once it had, once they got over the shock and trauma, they had adapted; as humans do. And if not herself in body, at least she was once more herself in mind, and she was not alone any more. Her friends, or those of them it was considered safe to know the news at this stage, visited her often.

Darian had stared at her, unable to fully believe it. To find that Miriam was still alive after that day when her friend's death had appeared so irrevocable was a joy almost impossible to bear. She did not know what future lay ahead of Miriam. But for now, it was enough that she lived and had any future at all.

At last, Beldan and his team met in conference with Kali, with Jack and Rianna providing input from the police perspective.

"OK people, here's a composite image of what we've found," announced Beldan, bringing up a holographic diagram. "There are places like the eyes where we didn't dare look too closely, but even there we have a pretty good idea. Things we know are in green; things we guess shade from blue through red, where the redder they are, the less certain we can be."

He allowed them a few moments to gaze at the image as it slowly rotated in the air before them. "Basically, what we've found is pretty much what we guessed. The body is intact except for the limbs. They have been sliced off just past the shoulder and hip joints and some kind of interface has been attached to them: presumably that is how Kali controls her limbs and receives sensory feedback from them."

After a minute or so when they analyzed the image in the light of those conclusions, he continued. "Fortunately, that appears to be the main damage inflicted. We guess they wanted the limbs to go partly to make the entire package smaller, partly to allow them a direct interface to the nerves, and partly to avoid having to support all that—to them—unnecessary tissue. For the rest they appear to have taken the easiest route: rather than attempt direct neural connections to her other senses they simply interfaced with her intact sense organs. For example," he said pointing to the head region, "we think these cuplike structures over the eyes effectively play a video feed from her enhanced machine eyes into the eye itself. It looks like they did the same for hearing. As for taste and smell, they don't need the first, and smell is pretty much exposed nerve endings anyway. They appear to have left much of the olfactory system as is, with a few specialized feeds that can stimulate some nerve endings directly."

"In other words," Jack put in, "rather than replace her eyes and ears they just used her own, letting them do all the hard work of translating video and other inputs into nerve impulses?"

"That's what it looks like. Their design philosophy seems to be why repeat what nature has already achieved if you don't have to. It's what they said they were doing, in fact: just in a far more complete and terrible manner than anyone imagined. We can also see that in the rest of the body. They seem to have left all the organ systems in place. Really, all they care about is the brain: but the brain needs life support. So they left the natural life support systems in place. They could have removed various bits, truncated the digestive system etc., but would have achieved little benefit at the expense of quite severe trauma. So fortunately for Miriam, they not only used things that could be used, they left things that weren't worth taking. She had new arms and legs and the old ones were just dead weight, so that's what they took—but it was all they took."

"So," Miriam asked, glad that she could set her voice to a more businesslike timbre than her own would have had, "what this means is that if we wanted to we could get my body out of this without killing me? I'm not stuck in here forever? I could still eat and breathe on my own, live outside again?"

Beldan nodded. "So we believe. We'd want to find out a lot more details before we tried anything like that, but it's looking likely. It's not as if they just chopped your head off, or so infiltrated your body with electronics that we couldn't safely extricate you. All your vital systems are in place and all the interfaces are just interfaces, not invasions. It looks like they've simply adapted their medically oriented technologies, which are obviously designed to be minimally invasive and safely removable. Even the brain control circuits."

Rianna and Jack looked hopeful, but then Jack quoted, "'If we wanted to'? What do you mean, if we wanted to?"

"Think about it, Jack," Miriam sighed. "In this thing, I'm a monster but I have a lot of power and can move around. Out of it, I'm basically a human slug. I'm not sure that would be an improvement."

"Remember this machine is just one application of what AC have been doing," Beldan pointed out. "You can have nerve-controlled prosthetic limbs without an entire prosthetic body. It would need some kind of exoskeleton and wouldn't be pretty or convenient, but at least it would be more human."

They were all quiet as they contemplated what that would mean. Then Rianna's face changed.

"Wait! Wait!" she cried, looking thunderstruck. "There might be a better way! You know how stem cell therapies have been advancing, how they've even grown someone new fingers! But that's nothing! I've read of amazing advances, at least in research, in the lab... the lab of... of..." Her voice faded with her excitement, then she added dejectedly, "Oh no. Oh crap. Crap. Crap!"

"What is it?" asked Miriam. "What's wrong?"

Rianna looked up at her, laughing bitterly. "Nobody in the world can do more than regenerate fingers and simple organs. Except one man who now claims to be able to regenerate whole limbs. But he's sworn his work will never be used to treat an agent of the US government or any of its law enforcement arms. Even if he hadn't, Miriam is the last person on Earth he'd help. God help us, Miriam; the one man who could help you is Daniel Tagarin!"

Jack frowned. He had worked with Miriam on the case that had made her name. Tagarin had once been the world's greatest genetic engineer, until all work on the genetically engineered humans known as genehs had been banned. He had sought his revenge on a world that had destroyed his career and his creation; but not only had Miriam almost stopped him, his beloved geneh Katlyn had been shot in the process. Though Katlyn had survived and the two had fled to the safe haven of Capital, Jack knew that in Tagarin's mind this was a crime beyond hope of pardon or mercy.

Beldan looked at Rianna; looked at Miriam. She had not told him much about that case and he had wondered why; but the way she had talked about it now made him wonder even more what she had left out. "But you really think he could do it?" he asked.

She looked at him helplessly. "He's the one man who might be able to: but he's the one man in the world who wouldn't."

"Alex, I'm afraid Rianna's right," Jack confirmed. "Tagarin is as pitiless as he is brilliant. He does not forget, and he certainly does not forgive. And he hates this country, he hates the police in particular, and above all he must hate Miriam personally, not only for what she represents but for what she did."

But Miriam surprised them. "I'm not so sure. Oh, you're right about one thing: he surely does not know how to forgive. But he does know how to play the long game. I think I can give him a reason he will understand. Even more than revenge, he wants to win. So I think he might." Her voice lifted with an undercurrent of laughing relief. "Oh yes, I think he just might!"

Then she raised herself up like a threat, her claws flexing. "But there's something I have to do first," she added. Her tone was so flat and deadly that her friends wondered how much of Kali remained inside her.

CHAPTER 47: JUDGMENT DAY

Judge Thompson was not in a good mood. He had just returned from a week's holiday in the Caymans with his family. Anyone would have thought that should have left him in a good mood, but only if the anyone was unaware it had rained all week. Which was bad enough without stirring two bored teenagers into the mix.

At the best of times he looked down his impressive nose at lawyers who thought to impress him with dramatic tricks. So when the request for a search and arrest warrant was accompanied by a special request that he leave his comfortable chambers and descend to the parking basement to examine "critical evidence necessary to fully apprise Your Honor of the facts of the case without causing undue public alarm", he was singularly unimpressed. But his look of dour skepticism was met with a serene look of confidence that even his nose could not puncture, as if the lawyer actually believed these histrionics were justified.

Now he stood in that basement with its uncomfortable temperature and smells, looking at the locked rear door of a large truck. He had already prepared the scathing response he would unleash upon the lawyer when his show proved hollow. But when he saw what was in the truck and heard what it had to say, he forgot all that.

He even forgot about the Caymans.

~~~

Aden Sheldrake jogged along the path that wound around the estate surrounding his headquarters. He was an aggressive businessman, who valued physical strength and endurance. Besides which, he simply enjoyed running, the feel of the air in his lungs and the wind through his hair. It was early but he had been at work for some hours already. This was his break, to clear his mind with oxygen and pure physical activity. He was most of the way through his circuit and soon he would be back at the entrance to his domain.

He stopped, puzzled at something that didn't fit but which he couldn't quite identify. He could see the façade of his building from here but there was something odd about it. A faint pulsating light. Curious, he slowed his pace and padded quietly towards it until he could get a better view of the anomaly.

Then more than his pace stopped. The soft pulsing was the reflection of flashing lights. The lights were on top of police cars, several of which were arrayed outside the entrance to his domain. A few well-armed officers of the law stood around, looking alert and hoping to shoot something.

Oh, shit.

He thought quickly. It could be perfectly innocent, he thought— to invert the concept of guilt. Some criminal on the loose, some altercation inside. If he ran from that, people might start asking questions.

But he knew it wasn't that. He had feared this day ever since that bitch Morales had managed to slip out of his clutches and worse, into Beldan's clutches. That had presented him with a dilemma. He didn't know what she knew, though if those incompetents at Domestic Security were to be believed it wasn't much. So he had decided to play it cool, not press Beldan, not admit he knew anything about Lyssa or her adventures; just act as if nothing untoward were happening. That might even be true, and he fervently hoped it was. Even if it wasn't, the reported destruction of the deranged Spider that had called itself Kali, as it tried to escape, surely made anything she might say moot. He just hoped it was the same deranged Spider and there wasn't a whole plague of them.

But he'd looked at the odds and set backup plans into motion. There had been time. Now if he had to run he would run where nobody could find him, with enough resources to live like a king. And one day his longer range plans would see fruition and he would live like no other man before him.

He turned on his phone, which he always left in full privacy mode on his morning runs, being careful to leave its location services off. He slipped into the secure area of his network and looked at the results in alternating fear and rage. They were here not only to search the place and question him, but to actually arrest him. Him! His staff and systems were stonewalling to the extent that the law allowed, but it wouldn't last, not against warrants of that seriousness.

He stayed hidden, thinking, not knowing whether the sweat he felt was from exercise or fear. Then he smiled a grin of feral contempt. If the police had bothered to apply a little subtlety they would have arrived without fanfare; they would have found him absent but learned he was out on his morning run; if they wanted to be sure of capturing him, a couple of discrete unmarked vehicles and he would have walked right into their arms. But in typical police fashion, they had turned up in force with their flashing lights and given their game away. They so loved their drama with their sirens and screeching tires. *Idiots.* But sometimes, he smiled to himself, idiots were a necessary ingredient in the plans of their betters.

He looked regretfully at his offices soaring above the trees. But he knew that sometimes you had to cut and run. *Yes,* he thought, *it is time for a change.* Time to relax, just kick back and enjoy all the pleasures the flesh could endure; until it was time to leave the unaided flesh behind. He looked about him. He did not have much time but he had enough. He sent a quick message to his secretary asking for certain research summaries to be ready for his return in five minutes, spoofing his position to another part of the gardens. Now he could melt back into those gardens and be at one of his prepared escape routes before anyone started worrying enough to come looking. Even now the police waiting for him would be getting excited and planning how to spring their trap and he enjoyed the thought of their impending dismay.

He backed up to the path he needed to take and looked down it. The sun was rising behind him and his long shadow stretched down the path, as if pointing the way to his new future. He did not believe in omens, but having been granted this one he chose to accept it. He smiled again, then headed off down the path at a quick jog as if fleeing from the rising sun.

He was deep in thought and plans and at first didn't notice the shadows of the strangely angular branches. But when the shadows did not recede as he ran, but instead grew larger, part of his brain noted the oddity and swiveled his eyes to focus curiously on them. Then the rest of his brain caught up and his heart froze. He looked behind himself in fright, a fright that grew up into terror when he saw a Spider pursuing close behind. It must have been hiding in the trees and come out when he ran past.

He turned toward it. He told himself it was courage which made him stand and face its approach, but he knew it was fear, a primal terror that turned his insides to water but his legs to immovable stumps rooted to the ground. The Spider slowed to a walk, glaring down at him, and his face went white as his eyes focused on the frozen scar marring its chest.

"Kali…"

"Yes," was all it said, in a low voice whose menace made his hairs stand even further on end.

"Command override Delta Bravo 192836 Angel!" he said, trying for a voice of command that sounded more like desperation even to his own ears.

Kali stopped still.

Could it really be that easy? "CHIRU, I need your assistance!"

But she pounced like a cat bored with playing with a particularly odious rat, grabbing him with her claws and lifting him from the ground to her face. "I don't think so," she growled in a tone of voice promising all the tender mercies of hell.

He looked at her in pure terror. "Please… have mercy!"

"*Please?* You *dare* speak of mercy?" she snarled. "At least you have the sense not to ask for *justice*, which I am sorely tempted to dispense! Can you give me any reason not to kill you here and now? It would be an interesting legal question, don't you think? Do you think anyone would find me guilty—the me, that is, who is chopped up inside here? If this machine kills you, was it the person I was who did it? Why, it wouldn't take much of a lawyer at all to get me off scot free. Especially when I am already dead!"

She squeezed, and he could feel the pressure of those terrible claws begin to bend his ribs. "No!" he gasped, "Please!"

"I told you I would pursue you to the ends of the Earth," she growled in a shivering rumble. "I told you I would come to destroy you. A man who presumes to create gods should fear them more!"

Then she eased off the pressure enough for him to breathe, held him at arm's length and glared at him. She turned and scurried along the path, heading back toward the entrance area and the police infesting it.

When she came into sight the police watched her approach nervously. They had been well briefed, but the knowledge did not fully overcome the simple animal fear of seeing such a vision heading their way.

Jack came down the stairs, looked at Kali then up at Sheldrake. "Now what have we here?" he drawled.

"This man has committed so many crimes I can't count them," Kali replied. "But let's start with assault and kidnapping of a police officer. Aden Sheldrake, you're under arrest."

CHAPTER 48: FORGIVE ME NOT

She ran through a field, the long green grass waving in a breeze that cooled her skin despite the warmth of the sun above. Then she swung up into a tree, hurtling like a gibbon from branch to branch, before leaping down to the ground and rolling back onto her feet to resume her run.

This was her life. She slept, she woke and she ran. She did push-ups, chin-ups and somersaults; climbed trees and mountains. She swam underwater for miles, sometimes amid schools of bright fish, other times face up toward the distant surface. She wondered how it was that she could breathe water as if it was air, but she didn't really care. If she cared to think about it, she remembered that none of it was real.

Sometimes she watched herself like an observer, knowing it was a dream and knowing she needed it to heal. Rarely she was awake, though perhaps she was never truly awake. At those times the only constant was the intense dark-eyed man who spoke to her about her past and future; a man whom she remembered as hardened with bitterness but whose smile now seemed light as air.

She learned things too. The moment they had known what Kali was they had consulted the psych AIs, and their verdict had been severe and uncompromising: with a trauma so deep they dare not tell her anything that could shock her, lest her mind lose its fragile grip on reality and be forever lost. But they could answer questions she asked, within reason, being gentle as with a child. Thus she learned that the war was over; that some of the machines had chosen to remain machines; that others waited for whatever cures might be granted them. But she knew nothing else of the external world and even the news of the war meant nothing to her. She knew it would, one day. But for now the running was her world.

When she was not running she slept, and the dreams that came then had their own purposes. In the early days she slept much, and her dreams were filled with flame and violence and death as if she were Death herself and it had become her sole purpose. Then one day she opened her eyes from the dream and found herself standing at the edge of a lake. She heard footsteps and turned around. Then she knew it had all been a dream, not only the blood but the guilt, for the man walking toward her was Alex and there was neither accusation nor hate in his eyes, simply forgiveness and love. But as he came closer his flesh became metal and his face became Steel, and she tried to warn him, to tell him to run, but his head shattered into fire and ruin. And when she looked down, her hands had become metal claws, and they held the gun that had wiped his inestimable mind from the world. And then she screamed, but there was no more sound than there was forgiveness in the blank eyes of the crowd that had gathered.

She woke, or thought she woke, the terror and pain still clinging to her like sweat. A golden-eyed young woman who looked like she had been watching her for a long time reached down to stroke her hair, like a mother comforting a child. Then the woman smiled, leaned over and kissed her on the forehead; Miriam smiled in response as if accepting the soft kiss as a blessing. Then she closed her eyes and slept. After that her dreams began to lighten, and her mind began to heal along with her body.

Her healing took six months. She had been surprised that it could be so fast, but Tagarin had assured her that with the growth enhancers he would schedule and the resources of an adult body behind it that it was sufficient. When he had told her the rest she had been glad it was not slower. Her growing limbs had first to be protected and then to be encased in haptic sheaths. One day it would be possible to provide mobile support, though in a case like hers it would be difficult. He had also advised that given the time and the need for not only care and exercise but more importantly the healing of her mind, it would be best if she remained mainly unconscious. She had already lost part of her life; now she would lose another. But she knew others had paid a much higher price; the image of a metal rib in the wreckage of a war machine would not go away.

So they had removed her from her shell, cut even further to remove scar tissue and other impediments to repair, and then Tagarin had applied his magic to regenerating her limbs.

Tagarin had been deadly serious in his promise to never help any agent of the United States, or any other country that outlawed genetically enhanced humans. It had been his work and his life; they had banned it, killed his own creation and almost killed another. He would be damned before they would see any benefit from any work of his.

But contrary to Rianna's fear, Miriam was not the last person he would help but the last person he could refuse. It was she who had let him, and more importantly Katlyn, escape. She had been serving the law when she had nearly caught them. But when she let them go she had chosen to serve justice instead.

Tagarin made the best of the situation. He had chosen to rescind his policy on this one occasion, he said graciously, in honor of what Detective Hunter had done, out of respect for a past foe who though dangerous had always been honorable, and as an act of good faith and generosity that he hoped the US government would one day emulate in its own policies. He had smiled easily and openly as he extended this hand of friendship to their abused and crippled officer. The US government had smiled in response, grinding its collective teeth. They could hardly stop him or forbid her from accepting his gift.

And so Miriam lay in her tank, sleeping off the trauma, spending more and more time exercising her growing muscles in a virtual world ironically, or perhaps fittingly, enabled by technology created by Allied Cybernetics.

Finally one morning she woke, and she knew from the peculiar clarity of her senses that this time she was truly awake. She still floated in her tank, and Tagarin was looking down on her, smiling.

"Hello, Miriam. We're nearly done. Everything is perfect. Just one more day. Tomorrow when you wake up—is the end." But she drifted off to sleep again before she could reply.

Then tomorrow came as it always does, and she woke. But now she was lying on a bed, with crisp linen sheets over her body, and she sat up with a start. She held out her hands in front of her, looking at them in awe; felt her legs, all the way to her toes. She laughed in wonder.

Then Tagarin and Katlyn came in, her golden geneh eyes a

counterpoint to his intense dark ones. Katlyn came over to her, held her hands between her own; wrapped her tail about both; speaking all that needed to be said in that one impossible gesture.

"I am afraid I have exploited you mercilessly, Detective," Tagarin said blandly. "You have become a bit of a celebrity due to my shameless self-promotion. So the press are wanting to take a look at you. You don't have to, of course. Perhaps you might not wish to flaunt your transformation. After all, that might prompt the good citizens of your country to pressure your government to allow access to my technology—and you know my price. I have provided some suitable clothes, which are yours whatever you decide. You might be a bit wobbly still, but Katlyn can help you dress if you like."

"I would like that very much." She did not specify which parts of his offer she would like; she did not have to.

"Well, then. I'll see you at the press conference." He took her by the hand and kissed it. "Welcome back to the living, Detective Miriam Hunter."

Tagarin had given her a simple sleeveless dress, soft and form hugging, in a shade of pale green as soft as the fabric. The lack of sleeves would show off how perfectly her arms sprouted from her shoulders, without scarring or even a line to show they were anything but the ones she had been born with. After she was dressed she looked at herself in the mirror. With her long legs the form of the dress made her a picture of healthy femininity; she laughed in simple joy.

"OK, Katlyn," she said. "Let's do this. Then what?"

"We've already arranged for your transport home. There's nothing we'd like more than for you to stay, but you have friends at home who are anxious to see you again. All of them would have come here but we all thought it was better to keep this show separate. I can't imagine your government can touch you now but most of your friends are not so immune from official displeasure."

Miriam nodded. At least one of them had never been concerned by it before and she was disappointed he hadn't come. But she understood his choice even more.

The press conference could not have been anything other than a success. The most jaded reporter could only stare at what she had been and what she had become, and gush in wonder and admiration. She answered their questions as well as she could; questions of the war, of her awakening; of how she felt about Tagarin now. After half an hour

Tagarin held up his hand. He would be happy to answer further questions himself, he said; but Ms Hunter still needed a lot of rest. When, remarkably, the questions actually died down as a result, Miriam stood up next to him. She did not know who started it. One reporter after another stood as well and began to applaud, until the room was bedlam of a different kind. *Even reporters are human,* she thought. *Now there's news.* Then she smiled at them in acknowledgment and farewell as she was led from the room and passed back into Katlyn's care.

Katlyn led her by the hand until they reached a short corridor. "OK, shoo!" Katlyn told her, giving her a hug as a lone tear emerged from an eye. "This is a private exit: just head down there and you'll find a plane waiting for you. Come back soon."

"I will." She looked back at Katlyn just before she turned the corner toward the light, thinking how much the same yet how different it was from that long ago night: when it had been she watching Katlyn leave to catch another plane under more deadly circumstances. She smiled and waved in another echo of that night, and was gone.

Katlyn stood watching the empty space where she had been, remembering the same night. *Whatever debt we owed you, surely it is repaid now. Except it was never a debt, was it? It is freely given and always will be as long as we all live, because of what we are.*

Miriam walked out into the bright sunlight and saw a sleek jet waiting, its lines so fit for their task that it looked like a thoroughbred Pegasus impatiently pawing to leap into the sky.

A voice came from behind her. "Hello, Miriam."

She spun around, and it was Beldan. "Alex... You did come..."

He smiled. "Of course I came." Then before she could move he stepped up to her, took her in his arms and kissed her. She resisted for a moment; not because she did not want it, for she craved it in her bones: but because she knew she could never again earn it. But then she wrapped herself in him and for long moments the two of them stood there, as if this long delayed union could drown the pain and loss of the past year.

A reporter who had been waiting in the shadows for just such an opportunity smiled as he recorded the tableau. He sent a silent thought of thanks to the anonymous benefactor who had sent him a pass to this place; no note of explanation, just a pass. He had the uneasy feeling he was being manipulated but frankly didn't care, because if someone wanted the world to see this end to a remarkable saga he was only too happy to oblige. The world might be full of cynics, but it was also full of romantics. The latter paid more.

Finally Miriam shook herself, pushed herself back to look into his face; but she still could not bring herself to break his hold, though she knew she must. "Alex, I…"

He put a finger to her lips. "Don't speak. The past and future can wait. We've earned the present." She sighed and leant in to rest her head on his shoulder. *Just give me this moment to hold you, without barriers of titanium and guilt.* She knew it would not last, that this oasis of forgiveness could not last, but while he granted it she was unable to refuse it.

But finally she found the strength to look him in the eyes and whisper, "Alex, there are some things beyond forgiveness."

He smiled at her.

"Perhaps there are. But come with me. There's someone I want you to meet."

ABOUT THE AUTHOR

Dr Robin Craig has a PhD in molecular biology and a keen interest in science and philosophy. He believes that novels, like all art, should be one in thought, theme and style: to nourish the mind as much as the soul. His books specialize in blending fact and speculation in dramatic and engaging stories, driven by strong characters and intriguing philosophical themes.

In addition to near future science fiction exploring contemporary issues such as artificial intelligence (*Frankensteel*), genetic engineering (*The Geneh War* and *Leonardo's Child*) and cyborg technology (*Time Enough for Killing*), his books include time travel (*The Time Surgeons* and *Hannibal's Witch*), alternative history (*The Passion of Judas* and *Hannibal's Witch*) and a collection of short stories (*Past, Present, Future*).

He also writes non-fiction. In addition to 14 scientific papers and a long-running philosophical series in *TableAus* (the journal of Australian Mensa), he has published numerous philosophical essays on Amazon.com and was a contributor to *The Australian Book of Atheism* with his chapter *Good Without God*, an essay on the importance and validity of secular ethics. He also answers philosophical and scientific questions on quora.com, and is a presenter on cruise ships across the globe, on science and philosophy including AI, time travel, space travel and numerous other futurist and historical topics.

Dr Craig is an independent author. If you like this book please spread the word with reviews and recommendations to your friends or library... and enjoy more of his books!

To keep up to date on new and upcoming works and events, like his Facebook page: fb.me/authorcraig